The Waters Fall-A Journeyer – Rob Mylo Vazquez

The Waters Fall

A Journeyer

Rob Mylo Vazquez

The Waters Fall-A Journeyer – Rob Mylo Vazquez

Contents

Copyright

Foreword

The Waters Fall: A Journeyer shows how combining fiction with reality can take a story beyond our wildest imagination. Intense research, including a trip to Europe, was done in order to capture the essence of a moment in European history, which this story covers to an extent. Visiting so many historical sites allows you to take your imagination to the point in time where all these extraordinary events took place. As research progressed, you can see the vast number of people and events that contributed to that time in history yet never accredited. Rob felt it was important to make that inclusive and as accurate as he could. History, whether good or bad, served a purpose. We must preserve it for future generations so they too can learn from it.

My name is Madeline, and I am Rob's older sister. There are no words to express how proud I am of my brother Rob for striving to become a first-time author. Of the four of us, he has always been the creative one. Was I surprised that he wrote this book? Not at all. He just needed a nudge, which he found and went for it. I am grateful he made our family inclusive on his journey as a writer. I traveled to Europe with him and learned so much through his research. This trip also helped us begin the healing process from the loss of our older brother, Randy, who had passed several months before. It was supposed to be a sibling trip, just the three of us. I almost opted out of the trip; however, at the last minute, I decided to go, and I am so glad that I did.

With this book, Rob's imagination allowed us to dare to dream and took us to places we only saw in movies or read in books. It is a story that shows his love for family and people as a whole. This is only the beginning for him. He has always been an inspirational writer, something he only shared with us, and now he is sharing it with the world. Rob is making his mark in history, and he will also pass it on.

With love, your older sister.

Prologue

Born a Pisces, I have always felt spiritually connected to water.

I cannot recall ever having taken swimming lessons, so I assumed I was just a natural-born swimmer.

A pool is a safe but limited place to swim, while finding the ocean to be my vast and open freedom.

As I float on my back, I allow the waves to toss me about, affixing myself to the liquid universe that is entwined within our planet.

Water, being the giver of life, can also bring about the death of breath.

It cleanses the body as well as quenches the thirst.

In passing time, water can evaporate within minutes, in some instances, after lifetimes.

While swimming, one can perceive a transcendent experience of another world.

Sometimes literally!

Acknowledgement

This book is dedicated to my mother, Aida Luz Febles; my dad, Isaiah "Jay" Lozada; my angel, Luis Motta; and my brother, Randy Michael Vazquez. Your spirits have given me my light.

Thank you to my family and friends for tolerating my constant requests for feedback, especially to Omayra, LaLiz, Junior, Kevin, and my siblings, Madeline, Dennis, Jessica, Jose, Carmen, and Arantsa. Thank you, Dido, for being my mentor for 37 years, and my lifelong friends, Jeff, Omayra, and Fabian. Thank you to Charles Rice-Gonzalez, Orlando Ferrand, and Alexi Maisonet. Your suggestions inspired me and kept me going.

Lastly, thank you to my creative nephew, Wil Del Valle, for imagining such a beautiful book cover!

The Waters Fall-A Journeyer – Rob Mylo Vazquez

Introduction

The water wasn't nearly so cold as I'd expected for late May, maybe sixty-five degrees at a guess, and it felt a perfect balm against my skin. It was still a bit chilly, yes, but not so cold as to stop me from plunging in. This time of year, the Georgia coast waters were usually only just beginning to warm, but I'd found myself in the ocean for a good hour already, basking with the little fishes in the stillness of Stafford Beach. After a long, boisterous school year spent wrangling teenagers, the rhythmic sounds of the waves had become an anchor for my frayed nerves. I'd come to the secluded Wave Shores Resort to recuperate and gather what little stamina I had left before the final week of school—a little appetizer before the main course of my upcoming holiday in Ireland.

The resort had been a refuge, but the outside world was calling. Early Sunday morning, I'd called the front desk, asking for a late checkout so I could visit a local museum. The place had a new exhibit on loan from the Irish Historical Preservation Museum in Dublin: a collection of Renaissance-era implements of war, including military uniforms from the Siege of Drogheda. The local historical society, primarily composed of Irish men and women and descendants of families who fought in battles dating as far back as the fifteenth century, had arranged the loan in remembrance of the Cromwellian invasion of Ireland in 1649.

Reymond, an FBI agent and my best friend, was an immense admirer of military history. He couldn't get the weekend off to attend the exhibit, which was only on display for one day. He had threatened to have me pulled over and arrested if I didn't bring him back pictures and souvenirs. His wicked sense of humor was a perfect foil for his serious profession.

The items on display were immaculately preserved, with one specific piece catching my attention: a sixteenth-century Saxon wheellock, rumored to have killed Sir Henry Bagenal during the Battle of the Yellow Ford in 1598. It had a brass plate on the handle just above the pommel with the initials "A.T." carved in. My knowledge of Irish history was vast, but for the life of me, I could not recall anyone significant with those initials.

Chapter 1 – Complicated Simplicity

The rhythmic patter of rain on the roof was a steady, lulling companion to the slow drip of the coffee machine. Having arrived late the night before from Stafford Beach, I'd missed the weather report, though the sky had been a bruised gray, promising a dreary morning. I didn't mind, though. I rather enjoyed rainy weekends—the only time I had to myself to binge-watch a show or lose myself in a movie with a tub of buttered popcorn and a cold beer. But this was Monday, and with a sigh, "Sucks that it's Monday," I whispered.

A hot shower and a freshly brewed cup of what I called "toxica"—extra-strong espresso—were all that was needed to shake the sleep from my eyes. I hoped to make the start of this last week of the school year less chaotic and more enjoyable than the last. I'd already graded the exams and prepared the week's final lessons a few days prior, leaving only one task: completing the questions for the surprise quiz I'd planned for this morning. My students wouldn't be happy about a quiz so close to the end of the year, but the questions would be focused entirely on a topic we'd recently covered, so the answers would still be fresh in their minds.

As I drafted the quiz questions, my gaze drifted to the window, and I found myself daydreaming, a habit as old as I was. I often wondered what life might have been like in centuries past. I imagined it as a simpler, safer time, though I knew it must have been equally complicated and dangerous. Even in the seventeenth century, there were guns of a sort, but no AK-47s, no machine guns, no automatic rifles, no nuclear bombs. The world now, I often thought, was one of complicated simplicity—full of computers, smartphones, and electric self-driving cars. In past centuries, one's daily tasks would have been hunting a stag, rabbits, turkeys or pheasants, or simply milking the cows and grinding wheat or corn before sunrise.

I came back to myself, surprised to find I'd been continuously fixated on the thought of a life I might have lived long ago, in some distant place. This feeling was ever more present after watching historical television shows. I would experience such peculiar, overwhelming notions—almost hallucinatory—as if I had lived through the very scenes I was watching. Perhaps I should just start watching cartoons instead.

I gathered my thoughts and refocused on the quiz, but just then, I glanced at the clock. "Shit, I'm going to be late!" I swore. I dashed into the bathroom, then raced into the bedroom to dress. I packed my laptop, filled my to-go cup, and tossed my backpack and briefcase onto the backseat of the car. I saw the umbrella sitting on the bench by the door, but absentmindedly got into the car, fastened my seatbelt, clicked the "close garage door" button on the remote, and drove away.

As I drove, an email notification popped up on my phone from the Cottages of Caisleán Dhún na nGall in Donegal, Ireland. I pulled over to confirm my reservation. The email described the cottage as small and quaint, with a stunning view of the castle, only a thirty-five-minute drive from Eas Gorm i Bhfolach. *I remember reading about that waterfall*, I thought to myself. *Could be an adventure.*

A sudden surge of sadness constricted my chest. This vacation was bittersweet. Two years prior, my oldest brother, Randy, and I had planned this European trip together, but he had passed away unexpectedly. Randy had seemed more eager for the trip than I was, which I found odd, as he had been to Europe many times before. During our last phone conversation, he'd asked if I had finished the itinerary. I told him I needed to add one or two more places. As I detailed the tourist destinations I'd found, he'd quickly cut me off, babbling in an excited voice, like a child about to visit Disney for the first time. "Well, first we can fly into London and spend two days there, then hop over to Paris for a day or two. Later, we can fly into Denmark," he'd expressed enthusiastically. "From Denmark, we can take another flight over to Scotland, spend three or four days, then shoot into Ireland and finally fly back home from Dublin."

I'd laughed at his rambling, repeating in my head, 'I can't wait, I can't wait,' before teasing him mercilessly. "Why are you so damned excited? Haven't you been to Europe like a billion times?" The memory of his excitement made the sadness a little easier to bear.

His tone snapped, reverting to its familiar growl. "Why are you an idiot? It's because it'll be your first time going there, stupid, so I want you to have a good time. I want us to have a blast!"

I chuckled, a soft, breathless sound. "Aw," I managed, the word catching in my throat.

The memory settled, and I felt the stark, raw emotions of that last conversation with my brother resurface. I fought them, forcing the sentiment down, whispering fiercely to myself, "Nope, not going to cry, not going to cry, not going to cry!"

My thumb moved, tapping the phone screen, pulling me back to the present task. I scrolled down the email to the "Confirm Reservation" button. A reply appeared almost instantly, displaying the confirmation number with bright clarity.

"Groovy," I breathed, a spark of excitement igniting in my stomach. The day of my long-awaited trip was, at last, quickly approaching.

A blare of a car horn, sharp and insistent, ripped through the silence. I jolted, my eyes darting to the rearview and side mirrors. I hadn't realized I'd parked squarely in front of someone's driveway, blocking them. I shoved my phone into my bag. Before pulling away, I rolled down the window, offering a hasty wave and shouted, "Sorry!" as I sped off.

***

Having left the house in a genuine flurry, I arrived at the school to find myself an hour early. The teacher's parking area, usually packed, was surprisingly abundant with open spaces. I turned off the engine and retrieved my keys, but as I reached for my coffee, my hand went instinctively to where my umbrella should have been—only to remember I'd left it at home.

"Damn it!" I muttered under my breath.

Fortunately, my parking spot was close enough to the entrance to allow for a quick dash, minimizing the drenching. Yet, in my hurried sprint, with backpack and briefcase adjusted, and coffee clutched in my hand, I failed to notice my keys had slipped from my fingers.

"Mr. Roberts, you dropped your keys," a voice called out from behind me. I turned to find Kaylani, one of my history students, extending my keys from beneath her umbrella.

"Here you go, Mr. Roberts. Can I help you carry anything?" she offered kindly.

"No, Kaylani, thank you. I've got it. Come, get inside," I replied, gesturing toward the building.

Once safely inside, I noticed Kaylani was still lingering, with a slight apprehension in her posture. She tapped me lightly on the shoulder, her brow furrowed with a worried frown. "Mr. Roberts," she began, pleading, "are you going to overload us with work during this last week?"

"Since when have you known me to make anything easy for you guys, young lady?" I countered with a raised eyebrow, trying to suppress the laugh that threatened to escape at her continued frown.

"Come on, Mr. Roberts," she whined. "It's the last week of school. Cut us some slack."

"If I were lenient," I mused in a didactic tone, "and allowed you to do as you please, especially during the last week of school, your grades would suffer significantly, wouldn't they?"

She pouted, clearly defeated. "Yes, I guess you're right, Mr. Roberts."

"Indeed," I replied sarcastically. "Now, head to class. I'll be there shortly."

With a resigned shrug, she offered a respectful, "Yes, sir," and turned, heading down the hall.

I entered the teachers' lounge to reheat my coffee and stow my belongings in my locker. An orange flyer tacked to the announcement board snagged my attention. After securing my backpack, I pulled the flyer free.

"The announcement for this year's Renaissance fair," I murmured to myself, a bit of disappointment echoing in my chest. I had attended the fair every summer since high school, but this year, the festivities unfortunately conflicted with my vacation. *I'll ask one of the staff members to purchase a dated souvenir for my collection,* I thought, re-pinning the flyer. I retrieved my now-hot coffee from the microwave and headed to class.

***

The voices of my students echoed boisterously down the hallway. To catch them by surprise, I crouched low beneath the small peekaboo window on the classroom door, swung it open with a flourish, and jumped inside, shouting, "Aha!" But they were ready for me. All of them sat with expectant grins, their expressions showing they had anticipated my antics.

"Well, so much for that." I sighed ruefully. "Good morning, class!"

"Good morning, Mr. Roberts," they responded, a unified groan of a sound, as if they'd been robbed of their puppies just moments before.

"Seriously, people, let's try this again!" I said, turning and repeating the greeting with more volume. "**GOOD MORNING, CLASS!**"

Being the smart asses they sometimes were, they roared back in the loudest voices they could muster. "**GOOD MORNING, MR. ROBERTS!**" The sound rattled the room, and then they all broke out into laughter.

"Well, that's better," I said, unable to suppress a smile. "Now, we're going to have a little fun today."

"Woo-hoo!" they yelled excitedly, some thrusting their arms into the air.

"Yes, I'm glad you're all so excited about this," I replied.

"What you got planned for us, Mr. Roberts?" Christopher hollered from the back of the room. "A field trip?"

"Sure, you could say that," I answered, a theatrical pause stretching the moment. "Today, we are heading to ... drumroll, please." The students complied, drumming on their desks in unison. I waited until the sound reached a fever pitch, then held up a hand. "A trip to ..." The silence that followed was palpable. "The past!" I hollered, barely containing a laugh. "I have prepared a quiz for today, which will count towards your final grade—a win-win." The cheer died, replaced by groans and looks of utter betrayal. In my mind, I cackled, a tiny, silent, and entirely gleeful villain's laugh.

"Man, that's not fair, Mr. Roberts," EJ complained, as he always did, the words a low rumble of discontent.

Giving him the side-eye, I held out the test sheets. "Take one and pass the rest around, please." In a small show of defiance, EJ stood and let out an audible sucking of his teeth. My eyebrow arched—a warning sign they all knew meant *not-today-kiddo*. The subtle movement was all it took. EJ's demeanor shifted instantly, and he began handing out the test sheets with the focused efficiency of a well-trained soldier.

The quiz comprised only forty questions, all multiple-choice. To ease their collective misery and, more importantly, to give them the best chance for a decent grade, I didn't set a time limit. The questions were basic, leaning entirely on Irish history, a subject we had been focused on for the past few weeks.

I often found my mind drifting back to college and my friend, Cian, an exchange student from Our Lady and St. Patrick's College in Knock, Ireland. We would sit together in history class whenever we could, and he was a natural storyteller. He recounted countless tales of Irish history, but his passion for the 1649 Siege of Drogheda was infectious. He insisted that his own ancestors had perished in that battle, and his fervor led me to take a profound interest in the subject. It became the focus of my thesis on the events leading to the Cromwellian invasion, a profound and rarely heard part of history that had stayed with me. To share that same passion, I incorporated the narrative into the curriculum, hoping my students would find it as interesting as I had.

Twins Isaiah and Bella could be heard muttering the questions to themselves, their brows furrowed in matching looks of intense concentration. They were always competitive, but in a quietly supportive way. "Hush. Silence, please, and keep your eyes on your test sheets, not on each other." They both looked up at the exact same instant, fully aware the reprimand was aimed squarely at them.

Halfway through the period, the silence was shattered by Gabby's triumphant shout from the back of the room. "All done!" He waved his completed test sheet like a victory flag.

"That was a little too quick, but bring it up here, please."

The room settled into silence once again, save for the quiet rasp of pencils circling answers and the occasional soft rub of an eraser. As the bell neared, I announced sternly, "Okay, guys, time's up, pencils down." A chorus of groans and sighs followed.

"I gave you all plenty of time to complete the quiz," I said over the noise. "So I shouldn't have to hear any complaints." The bell rang, and I shouted my final instruction above the clang. "Please put the papers face down on my desk as you're walking out."

***

Following my last class of the day, Basics in Science, I entered the teachers' lounge to retrieve my backpack from the locker. There, I found Mrs. Winters hunched over a stack of papers, furiously pounding her coffee mug on the table.

"Dammit!" she snarled, a scowl etched across her face.

"Everything alright there, Mrs. Winters?" I asked, baffled by her aggressive treatment of a piece of ceramic. "Looks like a bit of a day."

"Yes, yes, I'm fine, Myles," she replied grumpily. "I simply spilled coffee on some test papers I was grading."

I reached for a couple of napkins from the counter and handed them to her. "If you put them over by the fan, they'll dry faster," I suggested.

She looked up, raising her recently trimmed eyebrows, her eyes peering at me over the top of her yellow reading glasses. "I scanned them earlier, Myles, and backed them up to a flash drive. I'll just trash these."

With a grunt, she rose and tossed the stained papers away, placing the few that remained dry into her milk crate. I'd never understood her attachment to that thing—a white plastic filing cabinet with tabbed hanging folders she lugged around all day from class to class. It never failed to make me smile whenever I saw her with it.

***

A hum of excitement and anticipation filled the hallways on the last day of the school year. The schedules were shortened for the intended half-day, and I had a surprise waiting for my history class. I'd brought in snacks inspired by the 1600s, including sweet round breads I'd purchased from a local bakery, bannocks baked by my best friend, Myra, who took the time to research the recipe, along with jars of honey, bags of grapes, and assorted containers of juices.

I led them first to the gymnasium for a bit of competitive fun. I set up a line of orange cones leading to a basketball hoop, each one placed farther back than the last. "Alright, guys, I want you all to line up behind the cones, boys on the left and girls on the right." I unlocked the storage closet at the back of the gym, brought out two basketballs, and handed one to the students at the head of each line. "What we're going to do is stand between the first two cones. The girls will go first." Using my 6'2" height advantage, I positioned myself behind the furthest cone from the hoop and shot the ball, watching it *swish* effortlessly through the basket. A chorus of cheers and yells erupted. I loved my students, and in that moment, I felt they loved me back. At only twenty-five, just a decade older than them, my appearance didn't put a huge gap between us, being light-skinned from my Puerto Rican/Spanish roots, with green eyes and light brown hair. Having grown up in a similar neighborhood, we shared a close bond; they saw me as more of a big brother than a teacher.

"You'll begin at the first cone and work your way back to the last one. Whoever sinks a shot from every cone will get a twenty-five dollar gift card." The kids cheered excitedly.

"Yo, that gift card is mine," EJ declared, puffing out his chest.

"Forget him, Mr. Roberts," Yaritza shot back confidently. "You might as well give the card to me now since I'm going to get them all in."

One by one, they each took their turns. Not everyone managed to sink the ball, but Christopher came closest, only missing the second-to-last shot. "Well, it looks like the person who will receive the gift card is Chris."

"Whatever," Gabby grumbled, kicking at the floor.

"Hey," I said reproachfully. "Don't be disrespectful. Let's all head back to the class. I left the gift card inside my desk." I walked ahead of them, opening the classroom door and instructing them, "Wait out here for just a moment."

I slipped inside and shut the door behind me, scrambling to set up the food. I had only twenty-five minutes left before the end of the class period. Using a beat-up wooden table I'd gotten at a garage sale, I had earlier taken the time to adorn it with plastic hay and small wooden trays for the snacks. Plastic goblets I'd bought during last year's Renaissance fair completed the look, making it as authentic as possible.

The students waited impatiently, tapping endlessly on the peekaboo window of the door. Yaritza stuck her lips through the opening between the door and the frame, her voice muffled but clear. "Can we come in yet, Mr. Roberts?"

I kept them intentionally detained, replying in a stern voice. "Just one more minute, please. Let us practice the art of patience."

Once everything was in place, I drew open the curtain covering the tiny window and quipped, "Are you guys ready, or would you prefer waiting in the hallway a little longer?" Huffing in frustration, they jiggled the doorknob, yelling, "Open the door!" I taunted them back. "What's the magic word?"

Humming rhythmically, they finally yelled in unison, "Pleeeeease!"

I surrendered to their plea and swung the door open. They all swarmed inside, beelining to the back of the classroom and surrounding the table. They respectfully looked over the treats, their eyes wide with anticipation, without touching anything until I gave the signal. Christopher was the first to speak. "Whoa, this looks cool! I'm starving from all the waiting!" Seeing the sheer delight on their faces, I instructed them to dig in.

The contentment on their faces warmed my heart. After filling their plates, they each made their way to their desks, instantly devouring the snacks. I stood at the front of the room, leaning against the edge of my desk with my legs crossed, picking at sweet bread and grapes from my own plate. As they ate, they joked and exchanged stories about their summer plans. Stuffing his mouth with a handful of grapes, EJ blurted out, "I got a job working at the Family Fun Amusement Park as a tour guide in the history exhibit!" His news brought a genuine smile to my face. In that moment, I felt a deep sense of joy and pride, knowing that my teachings had reached not only EJ but hopefully the rest of the students as well.

As the last bell of the school year rang, the kids rapidly popped out of their seats. In a disciplined manner, they made their way to the waste bins and discarded their trash. Kaylani and Bella both approached me and, to my surprise, offered me a goodbye hug. "You two be safe and have a fun summer," I said, my voice adopting a dad-like tone.

Isaiah and Gabby were the first to reach the door, but before they could leave, I asked them to wait. "What I forgot to tell you is that you were all winners at the basketball competition," I said excitedly, bringing a stack of gift cards out of my pocket.

They shouted appreciatively, "Thank you, Mr. Roberts!"

They collected their gifts as they headed out. Just as the last student walked out the door, they turned in unison and shouted, "Have fun on your trip, Mr. Roberts! We'll miss you!" They gave me the thumbs-up and walked away.

"Thank you, guys; I'll miss you too!"

Once the room was cleared, I began to clean up. I folded the table, stacked the plates, stored the goblets in a crate, and packed the leftover food into aluminum trays. I made sure to discard any garbage left on their desks and straightened out the chairs, pushing them in. With the cleaning completed, I went to the drawer of my desk to collect my laptop and briefcase, packed them up, and headed straight to the door. Before switching off the lights, I took a long look around the room and smiled, completely unaware it would be the last time I would see them and this place ever again.

Chapter 2 – Impromptu Date

Three weeks had passed since the last bell of the school year, and with only one day left before my trip, I ransacked my closet, suddenly realizing that my current wardrobe simply wouldn't do. I had a specific intention: to meet an exotic European woman, preferably a redhead. For that, I needed a serious sartorial upgrade.

I arrived at the mall, circling the parking garage like a hawk, hunting for an open spot. The fluorescent lights hummed as I drove endlessly. Just as I was about to give up, I spotted a car pulling out. I sped up, put the car in reverse, and snatched the spot with a satisfying screech of tires. Pressed for time, I rushed across the parking deck, dashed past the pedestrian bridge, and, to avoid the perpetual wait for the always-crowded elevator, hopped over a gate enclosure and bolted for the stairs.

I was practically running, a fast-paced walk born of being a bred New Yorker, and a habit I could never quite shake. "You need to slow down, man, before you knock someone down," a familiar voice called out behind me. I turned, a grin already on my face, to find it was Devon, with his cousin Alexander beside him.

Alexander Jose Garcia and Devon Vega were cousins, twice-removed, but had been raised together. I later found out that Devon's mother had been a coworker of my mom's. I'd come to think of them affectionately as the ball and chain. We'd met in high school and bonded instantly over *sancocho*, of all things—a rich Puerto Rican stew made primarily of root vegetables. We'd spent an entire afternoon arguing over which protein went best with it: pork or beef, with pork being my firm choice.

"You're a jerk," I said, reaching out to shake Devon's hand. Alex mischievously intercepted my hand, balled his own into a fist, and tried to take me in a headlock. I was well acquainted with his high jinks, though. I managed to seize his wrist and bend his arm behind his back, teasing him sarcastically in a deep voice. "Ha-ha, sucka."

"What are you guys doing here?" I asked, releasing him with a playful shove.

Devon walked ahead, gesturing for Alex and me to follow. "I'm buying a gift for Tina."

"What's the occasion?" I asked curiously.

"It's for—"

Alex quickly cut in, blurting out the words as if a dam had broken. "He's buying an engagement ring for her, *papi*! She finally made an honest man outta him!" he exclaimed, laughing hysterically.

"You're an asshole," Devon remarked with a laugh. "I wanted to tell him myself."

I lunged at him, pulling him into a hard, congratulatory hug. "No way, that's amazing, bro! When are you popping the question?"

Alex, unable to stay out of the conversation, answered for him. "He's having a party next Saturday—"

"Seriously, Alex?!" Devon snapped, backhanding him playfully on the arm.

"—but you know I won't be around that day. I leave tomorrow," I said, genuinely disappointed.

"I know, man. Bad timing. I'll send you pictures," Devon quipped.

"Dude, that sucks," I replied in the tone of a disappointed kid. "I guess I'll see her when I get back from my trip and congratulate her in person."

"When's your big day, Myles?" Alex asked, his eyes gleaming with another tease. "I'm not getting married!" I shot back.

"I know, dumbass, I meant your trip."

"Ha, I know what you meant, *idiota*. Didn't I just finish telling Devon that I won't be here for the engagement party? You're a dingbat. I leave tomorrow morning!"

"That's right, you did just say tomorrow morning!" Alex replied, a clueless look on his face.

"We're going to have to go out tonight and celebrate," Devon expressed enthusiastically.

"Sounds good to me. Let's meet up at 8:30 at the Pub on Peachtree."

"Excellent. We'll be there."

"I'll see you ladies later."

***

After spending a frantic two hours at the clothing store, I rushed out of the mall and headed home to finish packing my suitcase. I laid my new white running shoes—with their gray lightning bolt motif—alongside the gray shirt I planned to wear on the flight, a perfect match. With the remaining essentials placed inside, I zipped the case closed, completing my vacation-related chores.

Time seemed to melt away as I cleaned and secured the house. I considered making dinner but decided to leave early and grab a bite at a restaurant near the pub before meeting the guys. That way, I would have a full stomach and not feel impaired from the get-go.

Damn, it's already 6:00.

I dug through my closet, found an old pair of jeans and a button-down shirt, laid them out on the bed, and hopped into the shower.

Singing like a madman was my daily ritual. Using the showerhead, I belted out the iconic song by Minnie Riperton: *Loving you.* I held onto the shower wall, a wave of dizziness enveloping me from my futile attempt to hit that last high note.

Stepping out of the shower, I dried myself with a towel, then wiped the fogged mirror with it. I froze, suddenly taken aback by what appeared to be a semblance of an ocean wave manifesting from within the glass. I quickly shut my eyes, shook my head, and blinked repeatedly, daring to look at the mirror again. Now all I saw were the streaks left by the damp towel.

"What the hell was that?" I muttered. "I know I'm hungry, but not so much as to cause me to hallucinate!" I shrugged off the thought and continued to dry myself. Taking notice of the time, I dashed into the bedroom to finish dressing. As I sat on my bed, securing the laces of my new running shoes, I took a moment to reflect. *If this is a taste of things to come,* I thought with a wry smile, *tonight should be exciting.*

Seven minutes until the car arrives. Perfect. Just enough time to brush, floss, and rinse. I checked my reflection in the mirror, making sure my nose was clear of any debris, then sprayed my favorite cologne and grabbed my keys, ready to head out.

Before locking the door, I waved to the driver to give me a moment. I'd forgotten my wallet. As I strolled back inside, I heard what sounded like faint Celtic music coming from my bedroom. I walked to the door to investigate, but the music stopped just before I passed the threshold. I inspected the radio on my nightstand, checking the power button. It was set to the off position. *Of course, it would be if nothing was playing,* I thought. I dismissed it as the neighbors watching a movie, so I locked the door, and headed to the car.

***

I sat in a pizza shop drinking a soda, waiting for my order to be ready. I was about to reply to a text from Devon when the entrance door swung open, and my attention was immediately captured. A breathtakingly beautiful, petite, long-haired redhead entered, her hair flowing like a peacock's feathers, billowing as the doors closed behind her. Her full pink lips and smooth, milky-white, freckled skin were mesmerizing, but it was the small, crescent moon-shaped birthmark on the left side of her neck that drew my eye and held it.

My eyes met hers, and for a long moment, we were locked in a frozen gaze. I offered a slow, charismatic smile and a nod of my head in greeting. She reciprocated with a smile of her own, a hesitant, lovely curve of her lips.

"Wow," I whispered.

She walked straight to my table, her voice a soft bell. "Myles?"

My eyes widened in bewilderment. "How do you know my name?" I blurted out.

She laughed, a delightful, lighthearted sound. "The guy at the counter is calling ye. Yer pizza is ready."

"Now that's embarrassing," I mumbled, a hot flush rising to my face. I glanced around, half-expecting to see someone she might be meeting. Seeing no one, I dared myself to ask, "Would you care to sit and join me?" I gestured to the empty stool beside me.

"Sure," she replied, accepting the offer with a simple, decisive nod.

As I stood to pull the stool back for her, a smug grin crept onto my face. *Well, now I know she's alone,* I thought.

"What a gentleman," she said, stepping onto the stool and struggling to push herself in. I noticed her struggle and, from the back, used my foot to gently shove the stool forward, giving her an assist.

Her hand accidentally brushed against my arm, and a smile spread across my face. Whether or not it was intentional, I couldn't be sure.

"Excuse me for a moment," I said. "Let me go grab the food. Can I order something for you?"

"I did come here for a pizza," she replied with another lighthearted laugh. I walked to the counter, grabbed my plate of two slices, and then ordered two more.

"Would you like a drink, um ..." I paused, my face flushing again. "Sorry, I didn't get your name."

She smiled bashfully, a faint blush of her own rising on her freckled cheeks. "Lisa, me name is Lisa."

"Lisa. Such a beautiful name," I said, a little too earnestly. "My name is Myles ... but you already knew that."

18

"What can I get you to drink, Lisa?" She wrinkled her nose in the most adorable way, debating what she wanted. "A Diet Coke would be grand."

I placed the drinks and plates on the table, then sat, positioning my stool just a bit closer to hers. We ate and talked for over an hour, the time simply vanishing. It wasn't until I glanced up at the clock above the door that I realized my friends were waiting for me. "Oh, man," I said, the words a sigh of regret.

"Anything wrong?" She asked with concern.

"No, there's absolutely nothing wrong," I said hastily. "Everything is perfect. I'm just supposed to meet with friends over at the Pub on Peachtree and completely lost track of time."

She placed her hand on mine; her touch warm and light. "I'm sorry," she said apologetically. "It's me fault. I didn't mean to keep ye."

"You didn't keep me from doing anything I didn't want to do; I tend to lose track of time when I'm enjoying myself." I placed my hand over hers, a small gesture to reassure her. "Under any other circumstance, I would cancel, but one of my friends is getting engaged next weekend, and I won't be in town for his engagement party, so we're celebrating this evening." I raised my eyebrows with a suggestive grin, politely offering, "Would you like to come and join us?"

"I wish I could, but I'm meeting with someone too—a coworker, at the Dockside Bar. She resigned this week and is moving overseas."

"Overseas? Where to?"

"She's moving to Barcelona, Spain."

"That's exciting," I replied. "I just so happen to be flying overseas tomorrow morning to Ireland for two weeks on a well-needed vacation."

"Ireland, ye say? Ye will love it. I am originally from Kilkenny."

"I thought I detected an accent. What a coincidence," I expressed zealously. "Maybe we can exchange phone numbers. I'd like to take you out on a proper dinner date once I return, that is, if you'd like to."

"Sure, of course, I'd like that," she replied graciously.

"Great," I said, reacting a bit too fervently.

***

Lisa and I walked for several blocks, allowing me to learn more about her life, and the time, once again, seemed to slip away. When we reached the Dockside Bar, I realized our time was all but done. We soaked in the last details of each other's lives in the limited moments we had, then exchanged phone numbers and final pleasantries. "It was a pleasure to meet you, Lisa," I said earnestly, already feeling the ache of her departure. "I'm looking forward to seeing you again, in person, not in a dream."

Her eyes, bright and direct, met mine. "I found it so comfortable talking with ye and getting to know ye, Myles," she replied in her soft voice. "It's as if I have known ye forever. I hope I didn't creep ye out!"

"Even if you tried, I would never be creeped out by you!" I countered, and then, as if by some strange instinct, I bowed. "Always at your service."

Why in God's name did I do that? I muttered to myself. She giggled, finding amusement in my sudden awkwardness.

"Enjoy yer trip, Myles. Can't wait to speak with ye again."

"Enjoy your night and be safe," I said before turning to walk toward the pub, the echoes of her laughter still warm in my ears.

***

Crossing the street, just a few blocks away from the pub, I checked my phone. Several missed calls and text messages from both Devon and Alex flashed on the screen. I tapped out a quick reply to Alex's last text: "On my way," followed by

20

a tongue-sticking-out emoji. It took me fifteen minutes to reach the pub, the sounds of conversation and music growing louder with every step. I hurried inside, scanning the room until I caught sight of Devon, standing by a booth and waving me down like a madman.

Pushing past the Friday night crowd, I made my way to the table and slid onto the bench next to Alex, swinging my arm over his shoulder in a familiar hug. Alex, however, was in no mood for pleasantries. He intercepted my arm midway, his eyes narrowed. "Here, we got you a frosted mug. Now pour it yourself, *cabrón*," he snarled. Without hesitation, I took hold of the pitcher, filling the mug to the brim and sipping on the froth to keep it from spilling onto the table.

"Hey, man, before you both get your panties in a bunch," I began, raising a hand in placation, "I stopped at a pizza shop to grab a bite and met a girl there. We were talking, getting to know each other, which is why I'm late. Sorry," then I curled my lips into a grin, "not sorry."

"A girl? Nice!" Devon exclaimed, his eyes widening. "Was she hot?"

As I launched into a vivid description of Lisa, Alex suddenly lurched out of the booth, almost losing his footing, his arms flailing. "Myles is getting married! Myles is getting married!" he chanted, humming tunelessly and spinning clumsily in a circle.

"Shut up, *borrachón*. Sit down before you hurt yourself," I said, pulling him back down onto the bench with a laugh.

We continued drinking, laughing, and joking the night away until the bartender's voice boomed over the noise: "Last call!" I checked the time, then got up, grabbed my half-full beer mug, and chugged it down.

"Guys, it's time for me to go. My flight leaves at eleven in the morning, and I need to be awake, ready, and out of my house by seven." I opened the Uber app and reserved a ride back home. Meanwhile, Alex poured the leftover beer into

21

the mugs, then proposed a toast to Devon and Tina. We emptied our glasses with a final gulp.

"I hope you guys are taking an Uber home!" I admonished firmly.

Sipping on the last drops of his beer, Devon replied, his words slurred, "Ye ... yes, sir," while attempting a sloppy salute.

"Great! Call me as soon as you get in!"

We walked outside together and headed over to the curb just as my Uber pulled up. "Have a safe flight and enjoy your va ... cation, bruh," Devon said, pulling Alex and me into a triple-hug. We held still for a brief moment, then he pushed us away, becoming emotional as he usually did after downing a few too many drinks. I laughed, then hopped into the waiting car. As we drove away, I looked back to wave goodbye to my buddies, suddenly overcome by an eerie, unsettling feeling.

***

When the Uber turned the corner, two blocks away from the Dockside Bar, I peered out the window, and there she was: Lisa, crossing the street. "Stop, stop, stop!" I yelled abruptly to the driver, causing him to slam his foot on the brakes with a jolt. I threw open the window, stuck my head out, and hollered, "Lisa!"

She turned, startled, then spotted me. A wide smile lit her face, and she waved, crying out, "Hey, Myles!"

"Are you okay?" I asked, concerned. The thought of her walking the streets alone in the middle of the night worried me.

"Me Uber driver must've gotten lost," she explained, her tone a touch exasperated. "So, I'm heading to the main avenue to catch a metered cab."

Chivalry, a notion I rarely gave much thought to, asserted itself. "Would you like a ride?" I offered, then turned to the driver. "You mind making the extra stop?"

The driver gazed at me through the rearview mirror, his eyes crinkling at the corners. "Not a problem, buddy," he replied kindly.

Lisa hesitated for a moment, observing the empty main avenue before she shrugged. Then, with a decisive pull, she opened the car door and hopped inside.

"Where do you live?" I asked.

"In Peachtree City," she replied, settling onto the seat.

I instructed the driver to head to her side of town first, feeling a warmth spread through me as she settled beside me. We talked as if we had never stopped, picking up exactly where we had left off on the walk. It was a peculiar, potent feeling, just as she had described—as if we had known each other forever.

We came to a stop at a red light. Without a word, she moved her arm, her fingers brushing my face, gently redirecting my gaze toward her. Our lips met, an intimate, passionate joining, locking together as if by ancient design. In the midst of the embrace, with her lips still pressed firmly against mine, she mumbled something unintelligible. I pulled back slightly, my breath mingling with hers. "What did you say?" I asked in a husky murmur.

"Ye can go straight to where he's going," she ordered the driver, her eyes still holding mine, a silent challenge in their depths.

"You got it," he replied with an amused *ah, yeah* grin I could practically see in the rearview mirror.

We arrived at my house, and I exited first, stepping out to offer her my hand, the gentleman in me asserting itself again. I peeked back inside before closing the door and whispered to the driver, "Expect an extra hefty tip on the app for you." I discerned his laughter by the movement of his silhouette as he drove away.

It was close to four in the morning when we walked through the door. *I'm not getting any sleep tonight,* I thought, a strange mix of weariness and exhilaration swirling inside me.

"Beautiful house," Lisa complimented softly in the quiet space.

"Thanks. Would you like something to drink?" I offered, gesturing toward the kitchen.

"No, thank ye," she said, her voice dropping to a low, flirtatious purr, "but I would like to continue where we left off in the car!" For such a dainty woman, she was unexpectedly bold, a delightful surprise. I certainly wasn't complaining.

We fumbled toward the sofa, our mouths finding each other again. Kisses were exchanged, passionate and probing, our bodies pressing closer. *Dang, this girl can kiss,* I thought, even as my hands found purchase, caressing the soft curve of her breasts, then charting a course downward to the sweet valley of her cleavage.

With a dominant shove, she pressed me onto the sofa, then knelt, straddling me, her hands working quickly to wrench off my shirt. Our kisses held a fiery intensity now, her tongue tracing a scorching path down my neck, causing *El Gallo* to stir and awaken. Blood surged through my veins like a streaming river, causing it to become stiff and elongated, more so than usual. In response, my fingers worked at the buttons of her blouse, loosening them with surprising speed, then unfastened her bra in near-record time. Our naked bodies shivered from the searing impact of our skin pressing against one another.

Her descent was slow, deliberate, her tongue a warm, wet line tracing the firm contours of my abs. A low groan of pleasure rumbled from my chest, an ache I hadn't felt in a while. I felt myself losing my senses, a swirling feeling taking hold. Her tongue traced figure eights on the swollen veins with a delicate, maddening grace. I leaned back into the cushions, absorbing the moment, a startling thought cutting through the haze: *for a man who always takes charge, I'm being tamed into submission.* A perverse grin touched the corners of my mouth. *There's a first time for everything,* I thought to myself.

The warmth she gave off was overwhelming in the most satisfying way, an intoxicating sensation that drove me to the very edge of my control. "Hot dayum," I whispered. "That feels… so fucking good."

She doubled back, tracing a path past my navel, outlining the lines of my abs once more. Her mouth returned to my chest, circling my nipples until she reached my neck, and my head spun from the dizzying sensation of her touch.

She was on her feet in a flash, her knees finding their place beside my thighs. I reached for her hips as she mounted me, her soft moans a low hum. I tangled my fingers in her beautiful, long red hair, my hands then moving to cup her breasts. I slowed our pace, thrusting in long, wavelike motions, savoring every moment inside her, a delicious friction of hot and cool.

Lisa wrapped her arms around my neck, a sound of pure euphoria catching in her throat. I gripped her waist tightly and twisted our bodies, landing her on her back. She extended her legs and embraced my waist, her grip constricting as I thrust forward with an unrelenting intensity.

The small, proverbial angel voice popped inside my head and whispered, *You forgot a condom,* while its nefarious counterpart devil voicing in a more primal urge shouted, *Keep on, keep on!*

Just as she reached her climax, I pulled out rapidly, a jolt of alarm running through me, but then I felt it—somewhere in the mix, she had managed to put a condom on me. A wave of relief washed over me. I took it off and climaxed, a bellow of victory thundering in my head: *Not today, Satan!*

I spun her around again, landing her on top of me. We continued kissing, panting as our adrenaline subsided, both catching our breath. She laid her head on my chest and closed her eyes, our breathing slowing in unison.

After a long moment, she lifted her head; her gaze was soft and direct. "That was grand," she said softly. "Ye were grand." She leaned in and placed a soft kiss on my lips before laying atop my chest once again. We breathed together, sighing in between.

When I sensed she had fallen asleep, I gently shifted from underneath her. Moving with caution, I picked her up and carried her to my bedroom. I laid her on the bed, totally fixated on her beauty. A sudden tingle, a fluttering of butterflies, stirred within me. I covered her with the comforter and left her to rest, a feeling of peaceful contentment settling over me.

Feeling utterly drained and slightly dehydrated, I scavenged through the refrigerator, my stomach a ravenous void. Having discarded all perishables earlier, I reached for a pitcher of water, and behind it, to my surprise, was a single slice of sandwich meat wrapped in cellophane. I tore open the wrapper, slapped it on the last slice of bread, and wolfed it down. Realizing I only had two hours left before it was time to wake up, I headed to the bathroom to floss and rinse. I spat out the mouthwash and lifted my head, only to be met with another freaky apparition in the mirror. This time, it was of people dressed in Renaissance-era clothing, standing silently behind me.

I blinked repeatedly, then turned to find only my robe hanging from the hook on the back of the door. "I must still be buzzed," I mumbled to myself, trying to rationalize the impossible. Shrugging off the illusion—which must have been a culmination of a night of drinking—or so I thought, I went to bed. I lay on my side, staring at Lisa, whispering softly, "Damn, she's beautiful."

Chapter 3 – Spirit of Relevance

A cloud of smoke, black as it gets when tires burn, billowed from nowhere, its oily scent sharp in the sudden silence. I turned, searching the darkened street for the source, but no fires burned. Then came the sound, a detonation so profound it rattled my head—the concussive thrum of a bomb going off a few blocks away. My heart hammered against my chest, a frantic beat of pure terror.

But it was no bomb. It was a wave, towering higher than any building I'd ever seen and wider than a dozen football fields laid end to end. The sound wasn't an explosion, but the roar of a million tons of water gathering itself for a kill. I ran, my legs pumping frantically against the pavement as I tried to outrun the unthinkable. A siren blared, a desperate shriek cutting through the noise, urging me faster. The sound grew deafening, an electric wail just as the wall of water was about to collapse on my head. I threw up my arms, a useless gesture against the inevitable, and screamed—a long, guttural cry that tore from my throat.

I shot upright in bed, tangled in the sheet, gasping, the scream still vibrating in my throat. The siren was my phone alarm ringing from the nightstand.

"*Shit*," I mumbled, scrubbing a hand over my face. "It's 7:30. I was supposed to be up over an hour ago."

The adrenaline was a live wire in my blood. I turned to the other side of the bed, reaching for Lisa, but she wasn't there. "Lisa?" I called out, but got no response.

The aroma of fresh coffee grounded me amidst my groggy thoughts. I stumbled out of bed and searched the house, calling her name, but the only evidence of her presence was the Post-it note stuck to the coffeemaker.

Myles,

Last night was magical. I hope you don't think less of me. I don't just go around sleeping with the first man I meet, you simply made me feel safe. It was familiar, if that makes any sense at all. You completely and strangely enchanted me. If you have time during your trip, call me. I would love to hear from you again. Have fun. xoxo, Lisa O'Quinn.

The note, marked with a bright red lipstick print, brought a smile to my face. I folded it carefully and tucked it into my wallet—a small, vibrant piece of the night before.

Time was flying now, and the panic of being late for the airport kicked in. I sprinted for the shower, a five-minute blur of scalding water and frantic scrubbing. I bolted through the house like a headless chicken, checking and re-checking for what I needed.

"Passport … check. Wallet … check. Credit cards … check." I rattled off the list, patting my pockets, my mind a whirlwind of details.

I made one more pass, checking the refrigerator for anything that could spoil, testing the locks on the car doors, and jiggling the windows. Leaving nothing to chance.

I wolfed down the rest of the coffee, swished the cup in the sink, and flipped off the coffeemaker. Just then, my phone buzzed with a notification: "Arrived." I grabbed my suitcase and keys, locked the door behind me, and walked out to the waiting Uber.

The driver, a tall man with a friendly face, came around and opened the trunk. "Good morning. Myles?" he asked warmly with a familiar *Nuyorican* accent.

"Yeah, that's me. And you must be Junior?"

He grinned, his eyes crinkling at the corners. "Since the day I was born." He reached for my suitcase and grunted, heaving it into the trunk. "*Coño*, this thing is heavy, yo!"

We got to the airport with plenty of time to spare. Junior pulled over, hopped out, and unloaded my suitcase onto the curb. I thanked him and handed him a twenty. "Thank you, Mr. Myles," he said with a smile before getting back into his car.

Junior had been a funny guy. Throughout the entire ride, he'd been telling me about being on his apartment complex's board. "I get my kitchen and bathroom painted every year," he bragged. "I've even been known to go over the property manager's head to her boss when they told me no. With a little haggling, I've managed to get either a new stove or a refrigerator, *¿sabe?*" The entire ride, he had me in stitches.

I rolled my suitcase into the airport and made a beeline for the airline counter.

"Good morning, sir. May I see your passport and ID, please?" the ticket agent asked politely.

I unzipped the front pocket of my suitcase and pulled out my passport, then fished my wallet from my back pocket and handed it to her. "Do I have time to grab a cup of coffee?" I asked.

"Yes, sir, you do," she confirmed. She returned my passport and ID with a quick tap on the counter. "There's a coffee shop right before the TSA, and another once you're through security, just before the gates."

I took the documents, tucking them into my wallet. "And do I check my bag here with you?"

"No, sir. For this flight, you'll need to check your luggage at the assigned gate. That'll be on your boarding pass."

I found it unusual, but simply said, "Excellent, thank you." I glanced at the towering information board, my eyes scanning the sea of departures. The Blue Wings Airline logo, a simple blue bird in flight, was listed with gates 7-10 on the northern side of the airport. An arrow pointed me toward the monorail.

The automated train arrived with a soft *thwump-thwump,* and I stepped on, my suitcase rolling smoothly behind me. A minute later, I was on the automated walkway, the gentle motion pulling me forward. I grabbed the handle of my suitcase, and that's when I felt it—one side of the extended arm wiggled, a sickening, loose tremor, then came completely out of the base.

"Great, that's all I needed," I muttered, forcing the plastic back into place. It seemed to hold, but as I walked into the coffee shop, the smooth surface gave way to large, deeply embedded tiles with wide grout. The bump was enough to do it: one wheel gave way, wobbling on its axle with a metallic clatter.

Son of a bitch, what is with this fucking suitcase? I thought, my jaw tight. "Guess I'm gonna have to buy a new one." I lifted the suitcase, the clanking noise a distraction I didn't need. I set it down with a quiet thud when I reached the counter, my face a mask of weary frustration.

"Hey there," I greeted the barista, a young guy with a smile and a name tag that read 'Luis.' "Can I get a grandé coffee with almond milk and two sugars in the raw, please?"

"Would you like a muffin or scone with that, sir?" he asked politely.

I considered it for a moment, raising an eyebrow and squinting one eye at the pastry case. My healthy eating plan flashed through my mind, and I opted out. "Just the coffee, thanks."

"There's a luggage shop right after the TSA checkpoint, by the gates, if you need to replace your suitcase. It announced your arrival."

My cheeks turned red as if a slow fire had been lit within. I offered him a sheepish smile. "Thanks for the tip," I said, and waited for my coffee.

***

After passing through the security checkpoint, a process I found confusing and unnecessarily complicated, I asked the agent for directions to the luggage shop. "Head down this passageway," he said, pointing to his right, "then turn left just before you reach the water fountain." The hallway ahead of me was a maze of sorts, a confusion of twists and turns.

I carried my battered suitcase in my hand; afraid the wheel would pop off completely or that the handle would come loose again. I walked into the luggage shop and was greeted by an elderly woman with kind, piercing blue eyes and a face etched with a thousand stories. She wore a gold-braided chain around her neck, from which hung a pendant that caught my eye. It was old but beautifully kept, a Celtic-inspired design of an ocean wave and two arrows, like the hands of a clock, curved and pointing counterclockwise.

"That is really beautiful," I said, genuinely taken with the piece.

Her reaction was immediate and startling. She grasped the pendant with both hands, her eyes narrowing as if I were about to snatch it away. "How may I help ye?" she asked dryly, with the lilting accent of an Irish grandmother.

"I need a new suitcase," I replied, taken aback by her sudden coldness. "This one fell apart the instant I got to the airport."

She turned to the window display and chose a silver-colored metallic suitcase, its sides ridged like an old New York apartment radiator. "Will this do?" she asked, handing it to me.

I inspected it, feeling the sturdy texture of the case and the solid weight of the wheels. "Yeah, it feels good," I said, a slight grin on my face. "It's *braw*."

A faint smile touched her lips. "Well, ye get a free metal waterproof case and an atlas with yer purchase."

"Oh, um … great," then thought, *An atlas? What the hell am I going to do with a paper map?*

Her demeanor changed as I handed her my credit card. The stiffness in her shoulders eased, and she became more conversational, her eyes softening. "Where are ye traveling to today, *mac*?" she asked, swiping the card on the reader.

"I'm heading to Ireland," I said excitedly.

"Ireland!" She beamed. "Ah, me beautiful country. How I do miss her so." Her eyes became distant for a moment. "Will it be yer first time traveling there, lad?"

"Yeah," I replied matter-of-factly. "First time out of the country, actually."

"Ye will have a wonderful experience. Mark me words; 'tis like nothing ye have ever experienced before!" she remarked with a strange, almost ominous quality to her voice.

The transaction completed, and she handed me the receipt. She allowed me to use the other side of the counter to transfer the contents of my damaged suitcase into the new one and kindly threw the broken one into the back for me.

Before leaving the shop, I turned to wave and thank her, wishing her a wonderful day. She waved back; her smile warm but her eyes holding a deeper, unsettling light. "Ye as well, young lad, and remember to embrace an watersfall."

The hairs on the back of my neck prickled, a sudden, cold tingle. "Um ... thanks," I managed, clearing my throat and trying to shake off the strange, haunted feeling. *Embrace an watersfall.* The phrase echoed in my mind, and I was baffled as to what she could have meant. I shook it off, just as I'd done with every bizarre experience I'd encountered over the past couple of days. It had to be a joke, a strange bit of Irish humor I hadn't picked up on.

I turned to leave the shop, so lost in my thoughts that I nearly collided with a young man entering. "Oh, I'm so sorry," I said, stepping aside quickly. "I wasn't looking where I was going."

He smiled politely. "No problem at all, sir. No harm done. Was there something I could help you with?" he asked attentively.

I gestured to the new suitcase in my hand. "The lady at the counter already helped me. I just bought this."

His smile faltered, his eyebrows drawing together in a confused frown. "What lady, sir? It's just me, Fabian, working here this morning," he revealed.

I felt the blood drain from my face. "The ... the short, gray-haired elderly woman," I stammered, my heart starting to pound. "She was right behind the counter, not ten seconds ago."

"I'm sorry, sir, but no one other than myself works in this shop," he replied, with a kind of gentle pity that only deepened my alarm.

I pointed at the empty counter. "But she was right there! I just paid for this suitcase with my credit card. I have the receipt to prove it!" I fumbled in my pocket for the flimsy paper, a desperate need for tangible proof.

Fabian, now looking just as puzzled as I felt, walked behind the counter. "This is odd," he muttered, logging onto the computer. "Can you allow me a moment to check the receipt number in our system?"

"Sure," I said, feeling dejected and more than a little insane. "Please do."

His face went slack with disbelief as the system confirmed the purchase. The transaction was real, the credit card charge valid, and the receipt number active. He then, with a shaking hand, pulled up the security camera footage, allowing me to peer over his shoulder. The camera angle was strange, showing me handing my credit card forward, but with no one on the other side to receive it. The footage then showed me transferring my belongings from the old suitcase to the new one, but the space behind the counter remained entirely empty. The elderly woman was nowhere to be seen.

Fabian looked at me, his face pale and eyes wide. "I don't believe in ghosts, sir; I never have. I've always been a skeptic." He handed me the receipt, hand trembling. "Now, seeing what can only be described as … an unnatural occurrence … I think I'm a believer." He grabbed the register key; his gaze still fixed on the blank camera screen. "You obviously paid for the luggage, so you're good to go. As am I." With that, he blurted out, "I quit!" and practically ran out the door.

I was at a loss for words, my mind a blank. I carefully folded the receipt and placed it back into my pocket, walked out of the shop, and took a huge, deep breath. My first thought—a desperate, gut-deep one—was a simple, powerful invocation: *I need a drink.*

***

After checking my bag in at the gate, I made a beeline for the nearest bar. I ordered a vodka grapefruit and downed it in one go, the bitter citrus and harsh liquor a much-needed shock to my system. A boarding call for my flight came over the loudspeaker just as I was about to order a second. I closed my tab and headed for the gate.

I found my seat, a wide, comfortable spot next to the window. The other passengers seemed to have situated themselves with unusual speed. Sooner than later, we were taxiing out of the gate and onto the runway.

Despite the utterly inexplicable occurrences of the past hour, I felt a trace of delight. Not only had the day of my long-awaited trip finally arrived, but I also had the entire row to myself. I could stretch out, get some sleep, and try to forget about the ghost of an old woman and her mysterious parting words.

Shortly after takeoff, the "Fasten Your Seatbelt" sign turned off as we reached cruising speed. The captain's voice came over the loudspeaker, calm and professional. "Good morning, ladies and gentlemen, and welcome onboard Blue Wings Airlines. We'll be traveling at a speed of nine hundred kilometers per hour, with an estimated arrival at a quarter to midnight, local time. The weather looks pleasant and cooperative for the duration of the flight, so we expect it to be a smooth one. The seatbelt signs have been turned off, so you are free to move about the cabin. Thank you and enjoy the flight."

I leaned back in my seat, listening to the purr of the engines. I still did not know what "embrace an watersfall" meant, but I had a freaky feeling I was about to find out.

I unbuckled my seatbelt and stood to use the restroom. I had completely forgotten the new metal case was sitting in my lap. It slipped, falling with a clatter and thud that was thankfully muted by the carpet, sliding underneath the seat in front of me. The atlas—one of the strange gifts from the 'spectre'—tumbled out. I reached with my foot and hooked the slick, metallic case, pulling it out from under the chair. The atlas lay open on the floor. I stared at the page.

My eyes went wide, the hairs on my arms standing at attention. The page was a detailed map of Ireland. An arrow drawn with a dark, inky pen pointed to the exact location of a waterfall. I looked from the map to the case, and back again, my mind struggling to process what I was seeing.

A wave ... a ghost ... and now this.

I wasn't sure if I was about to lose my mind or if this was simply the worst hangover I had ever experienced. Regardless, I got up and made my way to the restroom. When I returned to my seat, I reclined it and, despite the swirling chaos in my mind, drifted instantly off to sleep.

***

The clinking of silverware against ceramic plates and the savory smell of food roused me from my deep nap. *It must be dinnertime,* I thought, my stomach rumbling in protest.

A flight attendant, a man with a placid smile named Jeff, appeared by my seat. "You woke up just in time, sir. We're now serving dinner, and you look hungry."

I cleared my throat. "How long have I been out?"

Jeff's smile widened. "Just over five hours now," he replied jovially.

"Jeez, okay. Sure. What's on the menu?" I asked, holding my stomach and gesturing with hunger.

"We have baked chicken with rice pilaf and mixed vegetables, or baked lasagna with Caesar salad and garlic bread." He flipped the laminated menu, revealing a second option. "We also have a vegan choice, if you prefer: vegetable green curry with basmati rice."

"I'll have the baked lasagna," I said without hesitation. "And can I also have a bottle of water with a slice of lemon on the side?"

He nodded politely. "Coming right up." As he placed a napkin on the folding table, he added, "Would you like a glass of wine or one of our specialty spirits to pair with your meal?"

"I'll have the red wine, thanks."

Following dinner, I passed the time with a movie. Two hours into the film, just as the protagonist was about to make a crucial discovery, the screen paused and the pilot's voice came over the loudspeaker. "Ladies and gentlemen, we will soon begin our approach into Dublin International Airport. The temperature is a pleasant seventy-one degrees. We will land in approximately twenty-five minutes."

The cabin lights came on, a soft, warm yellow glow, and Jeff's voice sounded over the intercom. "Please place all tray tables in the upright position and fasten your seatbelts. We will come around to collect any trash."

The landing was smooth, a gentle touchdown that felt more like a glide than a descent. Passengers deplaned with unusual speed, a surprising feat given the number of people on the large aircraft. The flight attendants took their places by the exit, presenting animated, forced smiles as they repeated their greeting. "Welcome to Ireland! Enjoy your stay!"

I made my way down the aisle, a knot of anticipation tightening in my stomach. I was here. And whatever was happening, whatever the old woman's cryptic message meant, I had a feeling my journey was just beginning.

Chapter 4 – Caisleán Dhún na nGall

It took a little over three hours to reach the Cottages of Caisleán Dhún na nGall from Dublin Airport, a drive that felt every bit as long as the flight itself. I arrived at the ungodly hour of four in the morning, the bone-deep exhaustion of a day spent traveling finally catching up with me. The damp chill of the Irish air bit at my skin as I staggered from the bus. After the long flight and the cramped bus ride, all I craved was a hot shower and the simple relief of a comfortable bed.

"Welcome to the Cottages of Caisleán Dhún na nGall, sir. Yer name, please?" The young man at the reception desk asked with a friendly smile on his face.

"Myles Roberts," I said, trying to keep a yawn from escaping.

"Thank ye, Mr. Roberts, and welcome. We have yer cottage ready fer ye. The concierge, Kevin, will take yer luggage and transport ye there fer yer convenience. D'ye have any requests?"

"No, I think I'm all set," I said, my voice hoarse with fatigue.

He slid my ID and the key card across the counter. "Here is a pamphlet showing the amenities we offer and places of interest ye may want to visit. We also provide a complimentary full breakfast buffet in our main dining hall, beginning at seven in the morn. Is there anything else I can provide to make yer stay a memorable one, Mr. Roberts?"

"No, thank you again!" I said, collecting my things and heading out into the canopied reception area.

Kevin was waiting for me beside a round golf cart, my new suitcase already strapped to the back. "First time in Ireland, sir?" he asked, making conversation as I climbed into the passenger seat.

"Yeah, this is my first time out of the States," I responded, stifling a yawn and failing miserably.

Kevin chuckled. "Where in the States are ye from?"

"Atlanta, Georgia."

"Ah, Atlanta! I love Atlanta. I visited there twice with me wife. The first time was on our honeymoon," he said, his voice brimming with nostalgia.

I managed a tired grin just as Kevin announced our arrival. "We're here, sir." He parked the cart directly alongside the front door of a cottage that looked like it had been there for a hundred years and dashed out of the cart. He unlocked the door with a skeleton key—a surprisingly heavy, old-fashioned thing—and placed my suitcase on a wooden table next to the bed.

I handed him a €10 note. "Mighty gracious of ye, sir," he said, his eyes lighting up. "Anything else ye will be needin', Mr. Roberts?"

"Just a good night's sleep," I replied, and with that, he was gone, and I was finally alone.

***

I woke up from a deep sleep by the rushing waters of the River Eske, its murmur a constant, calming presence. For a moment, half-asleep and disoriented, I thought I was back at the Wave Shores Beach Resort. The damp air and the unfamiliar scent of peat and damp earth quickly reminded me where I was.

I'd slept for most of my first day in Ireland, but it had been the exact recharge I needed. The cottage, my home for the next two weeks, was a rustic masterpiece, with walls of actual stone and a replicated, straw-thatched roof. It was cozy and felt oddly familiar, as if I'd been here before.

I prepared for my first adventure. I placed both hand-cranked chargers, along with my wallet, three charging cords, and a pen, into the waterproof metal case. I then headed to the reception center, where the welcome breakfast was already in full swing.

The spread was a gargantuan feast, a traditional Irish breakfast laid out with impressive grandeur. *This all looks delicious,* I thought, my mouth already watering. Eggs, baked beans, and sausages sat beside mounds of mushrooms, grilled tomatoes, and bacon. A hash labeled "bubble and squeak" was next to boxty, alongside blood sausage, porridge, and white pudding. Oddly, there was also a bowl of champ, which I had always thought was a dinner side dish, along with an assortment of fresh-baked breads and a variety of beverages.

I opted for a piece of Irish soda bread and a coffee to begin with, easing my way into the feast. A dining room server, a kind-faced woman with a flour-dusted apron, approached me. "Care t' make yer coffee a proper Irish one?" she offered with a knowing smile.

"Yes, please," I replied at once. I filled my plate with a little of everything and made my way to a vacant table with a wonderful view of the town. I ate the breakfast with gusto, following it with two more cups of proper Irish coffee before heading out to get my day started. I was in Ireland. And my journey was about to get into full swing.

***

Using the small atlas I'd been given by '*Marion Kerby*', I located the waterfall and decided to make that my first adventure. Before that, however, I had to see the castle that had given my cottage its name: Caisleán Dhún na nGall. It stood as the very epitome of Irish architecture; a magnificent ruin steeped in eleven centuries of history. The O'Donnell clan, the formidable Lords of Tír Chonaill, had held a stronghold here, one of the most powerful Gaelic families in all of Ireland. The castle was a partial shell, its Jacobean-style wing of sandstone and limestone still standing proudly, surrounded by an outer wall and a seventeenth-century gatehouse.

I entered the cool, covered area of the castle and made my way up a set of narrow, winding stone stairs. The air was thick with the damp scent of old stone. Midway up, I stopped, captivated by a small, unassuming privy—a simple toilet built into a small landing. It was a mundane detail, but it brought the history to life—a testament to the daily lives of the people who had once lived here. I continued on, emerging onto the main level. The walls, thick and ancient, were adorned with historical antiques, and what had once been simple window openings were now covered in modern glass. In the center of the main hall stood a massive, ornate stone fireplace, its grandeur a silent echo of the centuries of warmth and light it must have provided. *This is truly beautiful,* I thought, feeling a profound sense of awe at the gargantuan feat of engineering.

I paused, glaring at the lute hanging above the fireplace, and let my imagination run wild. I closed my eyes and pictured what it must have been like to grow up here, to run through these halls with the O'Donnells, to live a life so far removed from my own. I thought of my students back home, their young faces eager for stories of history. I knew how much they would have loved to visit this place.

I continued up a set of creaking wooden stairs and entered a room filled with glass casings. Each one contained information plates and artifacts, telling the long, complex history of the castle. My eyes were drawn to the high ceiling, with its beautiful dark wooden beams spanning the width of the room. I spent a long while soaking it all in before making my way through a final entrance, down another set of wooden stairs, and to the exit.

Standing on the sidewalk, I turned abruptly for one last glance at the castle. I scanned my surroundings, once again imagining what it must have looked like during its heyday. I pictured myself in period clothing, feasting alongside the O'Donnell clan, a feeling of strange belonging enveloping me.

The buzz of my phone broke my reverie. I checked the time: I had to get to the welcome center by noon to catch the shuttle for the Eas Gorm i Bhfolach—the "Hidden Blue Waterfall." Intrigued by the brochure and the chilling words of '*Marion Kerby*', I felt a deep, undeniable pull to see the waterfall for myself.

The pamphlet warned that the waterfall, located at sea level, required a visit timed to the tides of the Atlantic Ocean. My shuttle would arrive just in time for me to explore before the 2:30 pm return of the tide. To reach the waterfall itself, which was hidden inside a cave, I would have to walk down a semi-grassy, muddy trail, with sheep roaming freely, before carefully stepping over slippery rocks to reach the entrance of a passageway that would eventually be swallowed by the ocean waters.

I carefully folded the pamphlet and stored it inside the metal case, along with the atlas. My exploration of the castle could wait until tomorrow.

***

Arriving with barely a moment to spare, I followed the signs pointing to Romero's Shuttle Service, a small, unassuming sign at the far end of the welcome center. I waited at the curb under a green canopy, the designated area bustling with a handful of other passengers. I handed my ticket to a broad-shouldered man and boarded the van, crouching low to make my way to a seat. The small group included an elderly couple and a Middle Eastern woman with her two young children. I settled into the rear, choosing a seat with large panoramic windows that promised a better view.

The driver, a cheerful young man, tapped on the microphone, causing a sharp, painful screech of feedback to cut through the stillness of the van. He winced, then grinned. "Pardon the noise, folks. Me name is Petey Taz, and I'll be yer driver fer the day. Unless I fall asleep, then I'll just be the sleeping lad at the wheel." A ripple of subdued laughter went through the van. "If traffic allows, I estimate our arrival at Eas Gorm i Bhfolach to be no later than a quarter to one. Please refrain from eating or drinking while onboard, unless it's a bit of pizza and a bottle of ale; then ye can pass it on up to me. And if ye need to use the toilet, well … ye'll just have to hold on until we get there!"

Petey was as much a tour guide as he was a driver, a charming raconteur who pointed out every location of historical significance. He explained the events connected to each place, weaving stories of battles and legends while navigating the narrow, winding roads with an easy confidence. As we neared our destination, the smooth pavement gave way to a primitive road of pebbles and stones, causing the van to bounce and jostle like a cork on the ocean.

"Someone back there must've been snacking on jumping beans!" he jested as the van lurched to a final stop. He was the first to exit, securing a step stool for us. "Watch yer footing, please," he said, extending a hand to aid the elderly couple first. He then informed us of the scheduled departure time and handed each of us a small card with his phone number, in case we ran late.

"Isn't this just a magnificent view?" the elderly lady said pleasantly as she tapped my shoulder and pointed toward the shore.

"Yes, it most certainly is!" I replied, my gaze fixed on the endless expanse of the Atlantic. But my eyes widened in stunned recognition as I turned to look at her. She was the absolute spitting image of the woman from the luggage shop— the specter. The same kind eyes, the same gray-white hair, the same knowing smile. A sudden cold shock ran down my spine, the hairs on my arms standing at attention once again.

"Enjoy yourself," she said cheerfully, her smile never faltering as she walked away toward the trail. I simply stood there, frozen in disbelief, a choked, confused sound escaping my throat as I watched her go. I then turned abruptly, dashing in the opposite direction.

My frantic sprint was broken by a sudden chuckle that escaped my lips. The ticket booth was something to behold. It appeared whimsical, like a dollhouse, painted a shockingly bright pink with a see-through plastic door and a big red ribbon tied just below the roofline. A young lady with a cascade of dark brown hair and a face of perfect porcelain greeted me from within. Her makeup, a bit dramatic for the remote locale, gave her the appearance of an actual doll. She wore half-inch-long fake eyelashes that fluttered like butterfly wings, a liberal dusting of rose-colored blush on her cheeks, and a perfectly drawn line of orange lipstick outlined with a tracing of red pencil. It was quite humorous.

"Good afternoon, sir," she greeted. "Will it be just yerself visitin' today?"

I struggled to repress my laughter. "Just myself, yes," I answered.

She slid a ticket across the counter. "The ebb tide will last only until twenty-eight minutes after two. The attendant will retrieve ye thirty minutes prior, so don't be late."

"Duly noted," I replied instinctively, a frisson of excitement mingling with the dread in my stomach as I took the ticket and prepared to enter.

Chapter 5 – Eas Gorm i Bhfolach

I proceeded with caution down the muddy trail, the earth soft and yielding beneath my shoes. I climbed over boulders, some waist-high, then up and around smaller, 'slippy rocks,' as the locals called them. Each precarious step brought me closer to the unseen mouth of the cave. Here and there, intricately crafted cairns—small, stacked stone tributes—lay atop larger, scattered rocks, silent prayers or memorials. I felt a sudden urge to add my own, a small offering of respect to the unseen ancestors of this land.

The entry to the cave appeared ancient, almost magical, its jagged maw framed by crags of varying shapes and colors, mostly well-bedded limestone. It radiated the illusion of being on another planet, with the natural rock formations sculpted by eons of water and wind. A few modern reflectors, however, drilled discreetly into the stone, hinted at its contemporary accessibility. I was so utterly mesmerized by its primordial beauty that I failed to notice I was the only person inside. *My God, this place is something else,* I thought, pulling out my phone. I began taking pictures, then, unable to resist, a few silly selfies.

Moving closer to the torrent for a better view, I felt the mist from the waterfall swirl and accelerate, an ethereal shroud wrapping around me. As a precaution, I quickly slipped the euros from my pocket and my phone into the waterproof case. To my pleasant surprise, I discovered the case had a hidden strap. I pulled it out, secured it over my head, across one shoulder, and under the other arm, ensuring my valuables were safe and sound against my chest.

As I neared the cascading wall of water, it discharged an even stronger wave of condensation, blanketing me, soaking my clothes to the skin. A symphonious vibration emitted in the air, a deep, resonant whine that was subtly dizzying. It was akin to the sensation one feels when a heavy train arrives at a station on an elevated platform, the ground trembling with its approach. A sudden, colossal blast erupted, pummeling me like a locomotive racing at two hundred miles an hour, striking me directly and knocking me off my feet. I fell flat on my back with a loud thud, every ounce of air expelled from my lungs in a painful gasp.

Suddenly, a terrifying perception seized me: the feeling of my cells and body parts exploding simultaneously in quick succession, all while remaining excruciatingly aware of the process. It was a sensation utterly beyond comprehension, my mind struggling to grasp what was happening. I was conscious of what I perceived to be immense pain, yet, felt nothing.

A thought, a bizarre memory, flashed through my mind, taking me back to my childhood. During one of our annual family vacations, we'd visited a water park. That summer, a new attraction called "The Flush 'n Bowl" had just opened, which was exactly what the name suggested: a literal giant toilet bowl. I remembered reaching the top and standing just before the plunge, stricken by fear, thinking if I took the plunge, I would surely drown in its narrowing vortex. How I wished now I had not backed away from that challenge; perhaps then, I might have been prepared for the utterly surreal imagery of drowning in a similar, narrowing mist that I was presently experiencing.

The whirlwind of mist and wind subsided as abruptly as it began, allowing me to stand and try to regain my composure. I shot to my feet, unsteady from the profound disorientation, my clothes drenched. "Well, I'm still breathing, so I know I didn't drown!" I muttered, gasping for breath. "My arms and legs are in place," I whispered, patting myself down, a frantic, desperate check, to make sure my limbs were all still there. After experiencing the profound feeling of having my body disassembled and reattached in waves of extraordinary rapidity, I wanted to be absolutely certain I was still whole.

The waterproof case remained strapped over my shoulder, but the linked white gold bracelet I had worn for years was gone.

Tracking back toward the entrance, my attention was drawn to the stone where I'd seen the modern reflectors. They were gone. Completely. "Wha … what … what in the world?" I stammered. *What the hell is going on?* I thought, looking around, still reeling from the bizarre incident, my mind scrambling for an explanation.

I took out my phone to check the time, stopping dead in my tracks when I saw the display: 3:00 pm. "How can this be?" I recalled seeing the time on the ticket stub when I purchased it, clear as day: 1:10 pm. *How could it be possible if I've only been inside the cave for, what, ten minutes?* I inspected my phone frantically, turning it over in my hands. It had been inside the waterproof case, and there were no visible markings, no signs of damage whatsoever.

Clearing the cobwebs from my mind, or attempting to, I exited the cave and trailed across the slippery rocks and back up the muddy trail. I reached the gate with the '*Close the gate behind you*' sign and the spot where the ticket booth had stood. They were gone. *Vanished.* The area was overgrown; the faint path I remembered from earlier barely visible beneath a tangle of weeds. *Could it be that the ticket sales stop according to the ebb tide and the concession box gets hauled away? That makes zero sense!* I said in my head as I spun around, examining the area for anything familiar. There was nothing. Just the silence of the Irish countryside, and a horrifying, dawning realization.

I stopped dead at the edge of the pebble parking area where the van had parked. It had disappeared. In its place, grass grew where stones had been, and the guardrail was nonexistent. I was completely disoriented, struggling to grasp how the landscape could have transformed so drastically in minutes.

***

Following the faint visual of the road the van had taken, I walked on. It was nothing more than a rutted track through the fields, unpaved, and what should have been a fifteen-minute journey stretched into what felt like endless miles. The soft, incessant movement of my own two feet on the damp earth was the only sound for a long time. I checked my phone again for a signal—nothing. I should have reached the paved road by now. I felt as if I were trapped in some episode of *The Twilight Zone,* the eerie theme song humming in a constant loop in my head. *Maybe I'm passed out in the cave,* I thought. *Maybe this is all a fever dream, an out-of-body experience.*

A plume of thin gray smoke rose in the distance. I quickened my pace toward it, the hope of human contact pulling me forward. The smoke led to a small cottage, a humble stone structure with a rough, thatched roof. It sat in the middle of a small farm, a herd of sheep huddled within a worn, wooden fence, their bleating the only sound. Next to them, a field of potatoes, their green leaves dark against the brown earth, stretched toward a low rise.

I approached an open Dutch door and knocked repeatedly, my knuckles reddening against the aged wood. "Hello!" I hollered. "Is anyone home?"

A middle-aged woman with fiery red hair, tied in a neat, tight bun, appeared from behind the cottage. She wore a simple linsey-woolsey gown, belted at the waist, with a starched linen apron tied over it—the kind of clothing I'd only ever seen in history books, worn by peasant women.

"*An féidir liom cabhrú leat?*" she greeted me in a soft, deep voice.

My mind scrambled to access the Irish I'd learned. "*Dia dhuit*! *An bhfuil Béarla agat?*" I asked, hoping I pronounced it correctly.

"Aye, laddie, I speak English," she responded, her accent a low burr that was a blend of Scottish and Irish.

"Do you have a phone I can use? I've been walking for miles, and I can't get a signal."

Her head tilted to the side; her brow furrowed in a confused frown. She peered into my eyes, her expression odd, as if I were speaking in a language utterly alien to her. "I'm sorry, laddie, I dinnae ken yer meaning."

I pulled out my phone, waving it in front of her. "Look, I have no signal."

She stepped forward, glaring at the phone with a mixture of curiosity and caution. She gently grasped the phone from my hand, her fingers calloused. She turned it over, inspecting the smooth, black surface. "What in God's name is that?" she asked tensely.

"It's a phone, ma'am," I responded, trying to remain calm, in desperate need of a logical explanation fighting the panic in my throat.

"Laddie, I dinnae ken what ye're sayin'," she said abruptly, a cold suspicion creeping into her eyes. She returned the phone to my hand.

"Is there a store or a gas station nearby?" I asked desperately.

She wiped a bead of sweat from her brow with the back of her hand, her expression softening with a touch of pity and concern. "Laddie, ye must be far from home. Ye look parched. Come inside, me dear, and have a wee nip."

My eyebrows raised involuntarily, the aftermath of exhaustion from walking for miles and my dehydration finally catching up to me. I nodded agreeably. "Sure."

I followed her inside, my eyes taking in every detail of the single-room cottage. Everything was a puzzle: the rough-hewn oak rafters, the central hearth with a perpetual fire, the scent of wood-smoke filling the room. I was immediately drawn to a large maple-wood table. It had beautiful, intricate carvings of oak trees and birds along the corners, with ivy vines draping down the legs—a beautiful, expensive piece of furniture. However, there were no light switches, televisions, lamps, or even electrical outlets. *Maybe she's Amish,* I thought, grasping for the only rational explanation my modern mind could offer.

"What's yer name, laddie?" she asked sternly, interrupting my thoughts.

"Myles Roberts, ma'am."

"'Tis a pleasure to make yer acquaintance, Mr. Roberts. Me name is Omibheann MacKinney."

I struggled to express a smile, not wanting to appear rude. "It's a pleasure to meet you as well, Mrs. MacKinney."

"Ye may call me Mrs. Omi. Now, have a sit down." She pulled out an old wooden chair with a cushion made from a burlap sack stuffed with straw. *This sure as hell ain't farmhouse chic,* I thought, frantic humor rising internally.

"Yer accent is a rare one; I've nae heard its like before."

"I'm not from around here. I'm from Atlanta, Georgia," I replied. "I can tell you're Scottish from the sound of your accent."

"Aye," she said, her chest swelling with a hint of pride. "Born in Dundee, but me parents moved to Donegal when I was a wee lass, nae but ten years auld, and we've settled here since."

While she poured the beverage, a rich, dark ale that smelled of barley, my eyes fell on a familiar-looking book sitting on a small wooden table. "May I have a look?" I asked politely, pointing at the tome.

"Aye, help yerself, laddie. Just dinnae lose me page, eh?" she said, a small chuckle rumbling in her chest.

I picked it up, my fingers tracing the ornate leather binding. My eyes widened in recognition. "*Don Quixote.* This is a terrific book. It looks old, but in excellent condition. You must have paid a fortune for it."

She set the cup down with a soft thud. "Ah, ye ken it? 'Tis nae old, mebbe forty-three years since its publication."

My brow furrowed. "You mean over four hundred years?" I replied with a tired, confused sarcasm creeping into my voice.

Mrs. Omi looked unamused. She clapped her hands on her hips, her eyes narrowing. "Have ye hit yer head, laddie? I ken math well." She took the book from my hands, flipping through its pages until she came to a small, hand-scribed note at the back. "See here," she said, her finger tracing the text. "MDCXVII, the year present is 1648, 'tis thirty-one years, aye?"

This lady had to be hitting the bottle all day, I thought, the absurdity of the situation almost making me laugh.

"Have ye lost track of time, eh?" she asked, passing the cup of ale to me, her face now a mask of placid amusement.

"The year is 2022, the last time I checked, Mrs. Omi."

She let out a loud, joyous laugh, so hearty that it caused droplets of beer to slosh out of the pitcher. She clearly found my comment hilarious. "Maybe ye don't need any ale after all!"

She opened a small wooden box sitting on the mantel and took out an old piece of paper. It reminded me of a school trip I'd once taken to a history museum. There, I'd seen a document from the seventeenth century, written on paper made of raw flax and hemp fiber. The paper she now held looked similar, though not quite as aged, and resembled a receipt.

Two sacks o' grain, one sack o' sheep's wool, one sack o' potatoes. Received on this twenty-first day o' May, Sixteen Hundred and Forty-Eight W.M.

My eyes widened. The shock of disbelief hit me hard, like a cold wave, making my stomach turn. "You can't be serious?" I whispered, my voice trembling.

"Aye. The year present is 1648, the third day o' June, lad," she said with quiet certainty.

Feeling a knot of pure terror, I blurted out, "I have to go!" I stood up abruptly, finding myself lightheaded.

"Well, laddie, ye need nae hurry yerself out," she said, sounding a bit concerned and bewildered.

I rubbed my temples, trying to ward off the onset of a blinding headache, and cried out once again, "I need to go; please direct me to the nearest road!"

"Aye, lad, ye ken the O'Brian farm?"

"Mrs. Omi, I don't know anyone or any place here!" I said indignantly, my hands balling into fists out of frustration.

"Dinnae worrit yeself, lad. All ye need do is walk northeast 'til ye cross a wee doire wi' patches o' shamrocks, then ye'll come upon the O'Brian farm. Mebbe they can be o' help t'ye."

I stood again, the sudden movement causing a rush of blood to my head.

"Ye okay, laddie? Wee bit too much ale, eh?" she asked while a small giggle escaped her.

"I'm okay. I just got dizzy from standing up too fast." I exhaled slowly, trying to calm my frantic heart. "Mrs. Omi, are you being sincere with me?"

"In regard to the year present? Aye, lad! I would nae speak dishonestly to ye nor to anyone else, *mo leanabh*. God teaches us dishonesty is a sin, ye ken?" she expressed with the most heartfelt conviction I'd ever heard, her blue eyes shining with an unwavering honesty.

"So, how is this possible? I, too, am being sincerely honest with you. I really am from the year 2022, from America," I declared, a tear of frustration and fear escaping and running down my cheek. "Atlanta, Georgia."

"I believe ye, lad!" she said, her voice taking on a comforting sound, like that of a mother when a child scrapes their knee. "From the looks of that strange contraption ye have in yer metal box, I ken ye're not from here. I just nae imagined ye bein' from a time and place so far away!"

After some time, with the warmth of the fire at my back and the ale taking the edge off my anxiety, I felt a sense of ease. Mrs. Omi's comforting presence was a relief, like a gentle hug, to my frazzled nerves. "Mrs. Omi," I inquired, feeling my shoulders finally relax. "Do you live here alone?"

She was reaching for a wooden bowl from a high table in what served as her kitchen, a simple but warm corner of the single room. Her hearth was tucked into the wall, a fire crackling merrily beneath a cauldron that hung from an iron chain. The table was covered with small wooden bowls of spices and honey, a half-cut loaf of a thick, white bread called Waterford blaa sitting on a solitary wooden plate.

"Nae, lad. Me husband, Williston, is out bartering three of our sheep fer a cow. We must often travel weekly fer milk and cheese, ye see. 'Tis simpler to have a cow of our own!" she explained.

"Yes, that makes sense," I said with a nod.

"Ye hungry, lad? Let me offer ye a wee bit o' stew," she said with a maternal concern. "And some o' this bread wi' honey."

"That does sound delicious. Yes, thank you," I replied, the thought of food finally breaking through my confusion.

She ladled the stew into a bowl, its savory aroma rising to meet me. The smell of root vegetables was familiar and intoxicating. "Here ye are, lad," she said, placing the bowl on the table.

I eagerly scooped up a spoonful, the hot liquid a welcome shock to my system. My eyes rolled to the back of my head as my mouth filled with an explosion of rich flavors. "Oh, my God, Mrs. Omi! This is amazing. What kind of stew is this?"

She beamed with a grand smile. "'Tis a simple *stobhach gaelach*, lad. Mutton, potatoes, onions, wi' a wee bit o' *peirsil*."

"*Peirsil*?" I asked, my brow furrowing in curiosity.

"Aye. Ye may ken it as parsley," she said.

"Oh, yes, okay. Wow, it is delicious," I said, finishing another spoonful.

"Add a wee bit o' honey to the bread and dip it in the stew; 'tis heavenly," she suggested. I wasted no time and did just as she proposed, for a moment forgetting my present ordeal as I focused only on the delicious food in front of me.

Mrs. Omi sat on the chair opposite me, her hands folded in her lap, and began what I could only describe as an innocent interrogation. "So, what does the future look like, lad?"

I set down my spoon and took a deep breath. "Well, we have roads that cars ride on, planes that transport people through the air, and phones, mainly cell phones like this," I said, showing her the device.

She looked at the phone with the same mix of suspicion and awe as before. "Lad, explain that contraption to me, please. Why does it have such significant meaning?"

"A phone is how we communicate in my time. I can speak to someone clearly on the other side of the world without having to raise my voice."

She pursed her lips, a look of skepticism on her face. "Christ, ye must have to yell rather loudly fer someone to hear ye so far away!"

I laughed at her comment. "Cars are used to travel on the ground, on roads. It's a metal box with four wheels, and it's controlled from the inside. We can travel from one place to another in half the time it would take on a horse. The speed is comparable to that of one hundred and eighty horses."

She fell silent for a long moment, her head cocked as she processed the information. "Lad, did ye come from the Eas Gorm i Bhfolach?"

My heart pounded in my chest. I looked at her, my eyebrows raised high. I simply nodded.

"Then the stories must be true," she said in astonishment. "I heard stories as a young lass, tales of trolls and leprechauns that dwelled in the cave and swallowed whole anyone that entered." The intensity was discernible in her

61

voice as she spoke of it. "But folks say 'twas nae a troll nor leprechauns, but a passageway bridged betwixt our world and time."

"Well, now we know it's not just a tale," I remarked with a tone of resigned irony. In that moment, I came to the horrifying realization that I was truly amidst something utterly unnatural. "In my time, there are many books of fiction written about time travel, but never in my wildest dreams did I ever imagine myself experiencing it. One part of me says that I'm in a dream, but a major part of my heart is telling me I'm not."

Mrs. Omi reached across the table and pinched me on the arm as hard as she could.

"Ouch!" I yelled, the pain a fiery sting. "Why did you do that?!"

"To confirm what a major part of yer heart is telling ye. Ye're not dreaming, *mac*." She released my arm. "Me husband will arrive in three days' time; he'll nae protest ye staying here. I will prepare the shelter in the stable fer ye. It has a bed and a fireplace to keep ye warm. It gets cold here at night even in the summer, ye ken."

I rubbed my arm, the sting a painful but welcome reality. "Thank you, Mrs. Omi. You are a considerate woman. I appreciate your hospitality."

"Aye, *dinnae fash* yerself with formalities, laddie. Me parents taught me never to turn yer back on a person in need, as mebbe ye'll find yerself in need one day and nae a person to help ye. God has blessed me, and I return that blessing t'ye."

"Yes, I ken, Mrs. Omi," I replied humorously.

"Come, lad, I will show ye to the shelter. Bring the book if ye wish. It be a long night."

***

Nestled in the corner of the barn was the stable shelter, a small, quaint room with a rough-hewn feel. A bed stood low to the ground, a crude wooden frame supporting a makeshift mattress with prickly straw protruding. It was a larger, more rugged version of the chair inside her cottage, and just as rustic. The overwhelming odor of horse manure enveloped my nose, a thick, earthy smell that was at first nauseating, causing me to gag slightly. *What I wouldn't give for an air freshener right now,* I thought. A small open window faced the southern part of the property, overlooking the potato field and a quiet, gurgling creek. I made a mental note to keep it open during the night, hoping to air out the persistent smell.

"Here ye go, lad," Mrs. Omi said, handing me a thick wool blanket that was rough to the touch but undeniably warm. "D'ye ken how to light a fire?" she asked, already arranging logs in the soot-filled fireplace.

"Only by turning a knob or flicking a lighter," I quipped, shrugging my shoulders.

"Turning a what, lad? ... Never ye mind, I will do it meself."

She took a small piece of iron from her apron and grabbed a flint sitting on the half-cracked mantel above the fireplace. Piling four logs onto the andiron, she stooped and began striking the iron and flint over a ball of tinder. When a spark caught, she blew on the tinder continuously, a slow, steady breath that coaxed the tiny ember into a flame. She then placed it in the middle of the andiron underneath the logs.

Ta-da, I whispered to myself, amazed at how quickly she brought the ember to life. "Maybe you can teach me how to light a fire someday."

"Ye'll nae learn overnight, ye ken. Takes practice, eh?" she explained, still fanning the tinder. "Don't ye light fires in yer time to keep warm?" she asked, wrinkling her nose and turning her face away from the growing smoke.

"No. We have central heating and air-conditioning units."

Shifting the logs with the poker, she reached for a small stool, pulled it underneath her, and sat. Being a woman of generous proportions, I found it comically endearing that her derriere covered the stool completely. "What is air conditioning?" she asked with deep interrogation.

I reached for a chair from behind the door, sat, and explained, "It's a box that blows frigid air during days and nights that are hot," then added, "while the same box expels warm air during days and nights that are cold."

"I need to visit the Eas Gorm i Bhfolach and pass through the watersfall to live in yer time, lad!" she said with a burst of laughter that seemed to shake the stable. "When me husband arrives, he will direct ye to a wise man who kens the stories of the watersfall well. He is a *Mórghinearál* in the military."

"What is a *Mórghinearál*? My Gaeilge is not as advanced."

She placed the fireplace poker back on its stand and stood to brush off the settled ashes from her skirt. With an air of immense pride, she said, "'Tis a Major General!"

"How can *he* help?" I asked, but she had already turned toward the door and disappeared into the stalls. I followed behind her, curious about the abrupt exit, but she was gone. "That was rude," I blurted to the empty stable.

Dumbfounded, I returned to the shelter and closed the door, sat on the bed, and began to undress. I pulled off my running shoes and unbuttoned my shirt, placing it on the small wooden stool. I then pulled the tank top off over my head and tossed it onto the chair, standing to pull down my pants when Mrs. Omi suddenly entered, barging through the door. "Oh, crap!" I yelled out, yanking my pants back up from around my knees. "You startled me! I thought when you rushed out that that's how people dismissed themselves in this century!"

"Nae, lad, we have manners, eh! I went to fetch a pitcher of ale and grab a wee book. I have a *scéal* to tell ye!" She took her place on the stool, settling in. "Back when I was a wee lass, me *seanathair* read stories to me of the Eas Gorm i Bhfolach. The stories say only those who enter the cave who are meant to be there, dinnae return," she explained, pouring the ale into a big cup and giving me the first pour. I placed it on the edge of the bed frame and pushed myself back toward the wall to get comfortable.

"Later in life, I learned trolls and such had nae to do wi' the disappearances. Just a chosen few were the ones that dinnae return." She gulped down her drink, followed by another.

This lady could drink Alex, Devon, Rey and me under the table any day of the week, I thought, smiling wryly.

"The ones that dinnae return were believed to be sent to a chosen moment in time to aid in an endeavor, simply to change an event in whichever place the watersfall sent them!"

"Do the stories say whether in fact it is a portal to other times?" I asked, then stared down at the ground, suddenly recalling the conversation I had with Lisa. She had referenced the bedtime stories her grandmother recounted to her and her brother, mentioning the same thing Mrs. Omi had just depicted: people disappearing into the cave, thought to be gobbled up by trolls.

Without realizing it, she had taken hold of my cup to refill it, finding it still half full. "What are ye waitin' fer, lad? Ge' on wi' it! Drink up!" she commanded. I blinked with a grin, then grabbed the cup and gulped down the rest of the ale, which she once again refilled.

"Aye, it does, but nae directly. I keep this wee book hidden in the wooden chest, fer if it were found in me possession, I would certainly *hangit* the same day, ye ken!"

"Why? Would you be seen as a witch or something?" I asked curiously.

"A witch, demon, troll, worshiper of Satan. 'Tis all the same to 'em!" Her comment triggered a memory of a documentary I watched concerning the Salem Witch Trials in 1692. To imagine that it hadn't happened yet, that it was still decades in the future, boggled my mind.

I skimmed through the pages of the small book written in Gaeilge. I felt excited to finally make use of the course I took in the language. Though imagining I would practice speaking it in a different century freaked me the fuck out.

"Me husband will translate it fer ye if ye need."

"No need. I took a class, um ... schooling, in the Gaeilge language before traveling to Ireland. I can read, write, and speak it, just not completely fluently."

"Lad, ye are meant to be here. God brought ye to this time to change an unknown." Her voice softened, becoming emotional. Having heard these stories all her life, and now being told they were indeed true and not tales of folklore, must have been overwhelming for her.

I stepped forward to offer her a hug. "I'm sorry!" she said, sniffling.

"Please don't be, Mrs. Omi. It must be profoundly odd to know that a bedtime tale told to you as a child is indeed true. I'm still trying to wrap *my* head around it." Tears welled up in my eyes as I continued the embrace.

She pulled away, taking a handkerchief from her apron and blowing her nose with a loud honk. "Okay, lad, get yerself some rest. Ye appear bone-weary. We will continue in the morn. *Oíche mhaith*!"

"Good night, Mrs. Omi, and thank you once again!"

"Aye, *ná bí buartha*. Ye're welcome in me home fer as long as ye need to be, eh!" she said, then nodded, a faint, knowing smile cracking her lips, and walked away, shutting the door softly behind her.

Chapter 6 – Life on the Farm

The days that followed became a living education, and I soon discovered that the basic rhythms of farming could be surprisingly therapeutic. Mrs. Omi detailed the daily chores around the farm, and it was clear she desperately needed the help, for her husband had still not returned. I found the distraction most welcome; it kept my mind from spinning with impossible questions, and I was more than happy to help take the load off her back, earning my keep with honest labor.

I began with simple tasks, like feeding the squawking chickens and the grunting pigs. Gradually, I worked my way to the stables, where Mrs. Omi explained the great importance of keeping a horse well-groomed. "Ye need to befriend the beast and keep it clean, calm, and fed, then trust will be built," she explained reassuringly as she handed me a wisp of hay to groom one of the sturdy steeds. I stroked its coarse coat, my hand moving in a tentative downward motion along its side. Mrs. Omi stopped me, her hand gently guiding mine. "Ye must brush with long strokes, lad," she demonstrated, her arm sweeping in a graceful arc, "in the direction the hair grows, aye!"

"Understood, ma'am," I replied respectfully, trying to mimic her fluid motion. As I continued to brush, I found myself conversing with the horse, a low murmur of questions and reassurances. I half-expected a response, just like "Mister Ed" from the old 1960s show I'd once stumbled upon while channel surfing. Given my recent experiences at the waterfall, I wouldn't have been at all surprised if the horse had answered me.

***

I wanted to treat Mrs. Omi to something special today—a slight gesture of gratitude for her unexpected kindness. "Mrs. Omi," I asked excitedly, "what method do you use to bake?"

Her brow furrowed slightly. "Why d'ye ask, lad?"

"I want to bake oatmeal cookies," I said, feeling thrilled over the thought of making something familiar. Besides, oatmeal cookies were my favorite.

"Cookies?" she repeated, the word sounding foreign to her.

"Yes, cookies. Wait ... you refer to them as shortbread. Oatmeal shortbread?"

"Aye, oatcakes. Me ma never taught me how to make oatcakes," she said, taking an iron shovel to scrape hot ashes out of the kitchen hearth. I found the ancient cooking method to be a stark reminder of the centuries separating us.

"It'll be a moment before the *oigheann* is ready fer ye. Mebbe I'll have a wee nip while I watch ye!"

"Excellent," I replied with a chuckle, delighted by her enthusiasm.

I set to work, gathering the ingredients: honey from a small earthenware pot, ground oats stored in a burlap sack, and butter from the cool, damp confines of the root cellar. Dates too, I found, dried and sweet. Using a large wooden bowl, I threw in the softened butter, poured in the golden honey, and mixed them together with a heavy spoon until they formed a creamy paste. I pitted the dates and smashed them into a thick, yogurt-like consistency, placing them in a separate bowl. Last, I tossed in the oats to complete the batter. Using a large wooden spoon, I scooped up several dollops of the thick batter and carefully placed them onto a wide, flat stone plate.

I could only fit five scoops on the plate at a time, so I set aside the remaining batter for the next batch. "Lad, ye'll need to add the cover and pour the hot ash over it!" Mrs. Omi instructed from her stool by the hearth while downing her ale. I scooped up the glowing ashes with the shovel and poured them over the cover, just as she instructed, sealing the stone plate into its ancient, natural oven.

After periodically checking and conducting several clandestine taste tests—each one a burst of sweet, oaty goodness—the cookies were finally done. I used the long metal fireplace poker to pull the hot plate out of the *oigheann* and placed it on the tall wooden table. One by one, I carefully removed the warm, fragrant oatcakes and spread them on a cooler wooden plate next to the window to cool.

"Smells lovely, lad. Do all men bake in yer time?" she asked, her eyes wide as she inspected the golden-brown discs.

"Not all men, but some do. We also cook. There are many famous male chefs in my time," I explained, watching her eyes widen further in disbelief. "Ye don't say!"

"I can manage a dish or two myself. In fact, I would be more than happy to cook for you today and allow you some time to rest. There's a chicken and potato recipe handed down to me by my mother—*'papas con pollo guisado'*—and it would be my pleasure to prepare it for you."

She tapped forcibly on the table with both hands, her eyes alight with joy, and belted out rejoicefully, "Ye need'nt repeat yerself! I will process a wee chicken from the pen fer ye!"

I smiled, my heart warming at her reaction, then turned my attention to the plate cooling by the window. "The cookies… oatcakes rather, should be cooled by now, Mrs. Omi." I picked one up, placed it on a small plate, and handed it to her.

She quickly took hold of it, inhaling the sweet, familiar smell of baked oats and honey. She bit into it eagerly, her eyes closing in bliss. "Mmm, Christ, can ye make more?!" she exclaimed, her voice muffled by the mouthful of cookie.

***

The sounds of sheep bleating, horses neighing, roosters crowing, and chickens clucking in the distance woke me. For a bewildered second, I thought it was strange to hear so many animal sounds in what I still instinctively considered "the suburbs," but then the thick smell of the stable hit me, and I remembered where and when I was. I laid my head back on the scratchy pillow, a profound ache of longing gripping my heart as I thought of home. I turned on my side to observe the room, my eyes sweeping over the crude timbers and straw. Though I had been here several days, I reverted to the thought I had when I first arrived: *How is this even possible?* It was a constant, maddening loop in my head.

As a history teacher who had watched countless movies referencing time travel, I felt a sudden grip in my stomach, a thrilling, terrifying sensation that I was actually living a fantasy. It was bizarre that such an unheard-of opportunity had been handed to me. *Screw it,* I thought, a reckless freedom settling over me. *I'll just go with the flow and see how it all plays out.*

An unexpected thought then hit me like a freight train. My stomach lurched, a sick feeling as if a dozen stones had just been piled there. The awful reality of the date settled in with a force that made me gasp: 1648. Just one year and Cromwell would be in Drogheda. The knowledge was a screaming quandary in my mind—should I warn Mrs. Omi? Am I even allowed to interfere? *Damn!*

***

A sudden, urgent need to relieve myself sent me leaping out of bed like a wild rabbit. I slipped on my pants and wrapped the wool blanket over my shoulders, shivering slightly from the chill that lingered in the early morning air. I raced toward the back of the stable, skidding across the muddy ground behind the worn wooden fence where the sheep were kept, reaching a hidden alley of sorts between the stable and a rotted shed—my usual go-to spot to tend business.

I stubbed my bare toe against a hitching post, yelling angrily, "Fuck!" as I hopped in place, cursing like a drunken sailor. My bladder was screaming in protest, so I clumsily pulled out *El Gallo* to relieve myself, wetting my pants a bit. My mind was so focused on the task at hand that I was oblivious to everything around me.

I was suddenly startled by the sound of a deep voice coming from behind. "Good morrow, laddie!" The voice caused me to turn swiftly, forgetting that I was still peeing. The stream of urine caught the stranger directly on the pants.

"Oh crap, I'm so sorry, sir!" I said, my face burning with mortification.

"Dinnae worrit, lad," he said with a nod, then looked down and suggested, with a slow, sarcastic grin, "but feel free to hide yer wee friend, eh!"

I looked down and saw my penis sticking out of my pants. "Oh, man!" I exclaimed, feeling the heat creep up my neck. I quickly tucked it away and zipped up my pants.

"The privy is on the other side of the stable. Being from the future, I thought ye'd kent that by now." In all the days I'd been on the MacKinney farm, I had relieved myself in that same spot behind the stable. It had never once occurred to me to ask Mrs. Omi where the bathroom was.

"I do apologize again, sir!" I stammered, my cheeks still burning.

"*Ná bí buartha*. So, ye're the journeyer me wife told me about, eh?"

"Yes, sir, Myles Roberts," I replied, extending my hand for a handshake.

He took my hand, his grip firm and rough. "Williston MacKinney, yer servant, sir."

Mr. MacKinney was a tall man, roughly six-foot-three, a bit on the heavy side, with a muscular build. He had the physique of a man who worked the land—assuming that's what farmers are supposed to look like in this century. His accent was more Scottish than Irish, just as Mrs. Omi's was, so I felt inclined to ask, "Are you originally from Scotland as well, Mr. MacKinney?"

"What gave it away, lad? Me red hair or me accent?" he replied with a sound of humorous sarcasm, rubbing his thick beard. "Aye, lad, born and bred in Cairnryan. Me father brought us here to escape an ongoing war with a rival clan when I was nae but a young lad, ye see."

"That's fascinating; I've read many stories referencing clans and how the rivalry between many of them caused disbandment among them."

"Aye, lad, 'tis sad but true. Go on and dress yerself and meet us at the house to break yer fast," he said, then headed to the cottage.

I returned to the shelter, my mind spinning. The phone alarm was vibrating inside the metal case, and for a fraction of a second, I felt a flash of hope that this entire time-travel experience might have been one of my frequent daydreams. The surreal noise pulled me back into my reality, a plain reminder of the world I'd left behind. I opened the box, dismissed the alarm, and stuck the phone into my pocket in case I needed to do a show-and-tell for Mr. MacKinney.

After dressing, I walked to the main house. I politely knocked on the Dutch door.

"Ye no need to knock, eh, enter, lad," Mrs. Omi responded with a mouthful of bread.

"Good morning," I greeted as I walked in, nodding and bowing. It seemed like I was finally adapting to the traditional greetings of this century, even if I was still a long way from fitting in.

"Good morrow. Sit yerself down, lad, while I serve ye some porridge," Mrs. Omi instructed. She placed a cup of tea next to the bowl of porridge on the table beside me. "Would ye like eggs and potatoes, *mac*—"

Mr. MacKinney chimed in without a pause, adding, "And nae a need fer formalities."

My eyes widened at the sight of the food, then turned to Mr. Omi. "Yes, please, thank you!" I blurted, overwhelmed with a strange, voracious hunger. I shifted my attention to Mr. MacKinney, looking directly into his eyes. "My mother brought me up to be polite in the homes of strangers."

He gave a sharp nod. "Well, lad, we no strangers. Best t'ken it now. Get used to the idea!"

"Yes, sir," I replied respectfully, as if I were being reprimanded.

He shook his head, his gruffness softened by a hint of a smile. "Nae a need to address me as sir either. I am not an old man. Ye may address me as Mr. Willis!"

Mrs. Omi placed a platter of fried eggs, potatoes, black pudding, and thick-cut bread before me, the savory scent rising in an enticing cloud. I eagerly devoured the feast, driven by a deep hunger. "This is just as delicious as all your meals, Mrs. Omi. Thank you!"

"Enjoy, lad," she said, her face lighting up with a proud, motherly smile.

I took a large swig of the tea, then, feeling a sudden need for something more, asked, "I didn't want to trouble you before, but could I ask you for coffee?"

Mrs. Omi's brow furrowed. "I dinnae ken what coffee is!"

"It's like tea, but made from beans!" I explained.

Mr. Willis took a sip of his tea, then set the cup down with a deliberate thud. "Aye, I heard of such a drink from a lad who hails from England, but no, we dinnae have yer coffee here, lad!"

"Guess tea will do," I replied with a small sigh of resignation.

Rubbing his palms together, Mr. Willis leaned forward, his voice taking on a serious tone. "Okay, lad, tell me, what brought ye here? Did ye have visions prior to arriving at Eas Gorm i Bhfolach?"

"Yes, I did," I answered, the words spilling out quickly. "I saw an ocean wave in the mirror of my bathroom, then again in a dream, as well as people dressed in vintage clothing. I also met an elderly woman who wore a Celtic pendant who turned out to be what I believe was a ghost," I babbled on, never once catching my breath.

Mr. Willis glanced over at Mrs. Omi, a questioning look passing between them, then turned his gaze back to me. "Aye, fascinating," he drawled, then inquired, "What is a ... mirror in a bathroom?"

"A bathroom is what you call a privy, and a mirror is a ... a looking glass used to see one's reflection, like this." I brought out my cell phone, clicked on the camera app and pressed the button to flip the camera over, as one would do to take a selfie. I positioned myself behind Mr. Willis, leaned over his shoulder, and placed the phone in front of him. "You see!"

He was so fixated on his reflection that his head turned from side to side with wide-open eyes. Then, like a frightened cat, he leaped from the table, rising with such intense force it caused his chair to fall backward with a crash. I jumped reflexively to avoid being hit, almost knocking over the bread and honey table. "What in God's glorious land did I just witness, lad?" he asked, almost winded, breathing as if he had just run a marathon.

"Mr. Willis, it is what we call a camera. It captures the image of a person, a place, or anything you choose to capture. It also acts as a mirror," I explained, silently giggling at his reaction while picking up the chair.

"Get that cursed thing away from me!" he commanded in a low growl.

"Bring it here to me, lad; let me see the magic of yer contraption," Mrs. Omi said, grinning mischievously as she covered her mouth, holding back a laugh.

She grabbed the phone from my hand and stared into the camera, a look of sheer admiration on her face as she saw her own reflection. She then glanced over at Mr. Willis and said to him with a tone of mock confidence, "Now I ken the reason ye married me, Williston." His expression shifted, and he burst out in a boisterous laugh.

During breakfast, I filled them in on stories referencing the future. Mr. Willis got up abruptly and headed to a trunk sitting on top of a table in a passageway next to the sleeping area. He opened it with a key hanging from a leather string around his neck, just like the one Mrs. Omi had. He took out the book Mrs. Omi showed me, and collected a quill, ink, and paper to write on.

"Lad, I am going to duplicate certain passages from this book fer ye! 'Twill nae be much information, just enough for Dujardin Brindley to ken the meaning of yer visit."

He leaned the book against the ewer on the table, flipping through it at a fast pace, as if searching for something in particular. He dipped the quill into the bottle of ink, dabbing it on the edge so it wouldn't smear as he jotted down a summary of the book.

"Who is Dujardin Brindley?" I asked with tense curiosity. Mrs. Omi was clearing the remaining cups and bowls from the table. She paused, her hands still on a wooden plate, and looked at me. "He is the *Mórghinearál*, the Major General I told ye about. He is also a wise man, ye ken, has knowledge of the book Williston is duplicating fer ye, and kens well the stories of Eas Gorm i Bhfolach."

"*Mago de Conocimiento,*" I whispered under my breath. The phrase felt appropriate for a man who possibly knew the secrets of the waterfall.

"What is the meaning of that word, lad?" Mrs. Omi inquired, her head cocked in a way that reminded me of a curious bird.

"It means 'Wizard of Knowledge' in Spanish."

"Hmm," she responded with a thoughtful look on her face, and continued with her chores. Mr. Willis, with a speed that belied his age, had a fast hand at writing. He had already completed one page and was nearing the end of the book. I assumed the second page would not have much written on it.

***

I stepped outside to visit the privy. In the distance, I took notice of a man riding in a horse-drawn wagon. I thought nothing of it, other than someone passing through, and continued with my business. Once I was done, I headed toward the house, where I overheard Mr. Willis speaking with someone.

Driven by curiosity, I approached the cottage, only to be spotted by Mr. Willis, who motioned me over with a wave of his large hand. "Mr. Roberts, there is someone I would like fer ye to meet. This is Mr. William Wexton."

The man, who was of average height with a slender build, bowed from the waist. "Your servant, Mr. Roberts," Mr. Wexton said, his English accent clipped and formal.

I bowed respectfully in return. "Nice to meet you, sir!"

"Ye'll nae get far wi' calling him 'sir' either, ken it now," Mr. Willis remarked with a shake of his head as he walked inside the cottage. I grinned with amusement and extended my hand in greeting. "Nice to meet you, Mr. Wexton."

"Call him William, ye *eejit*!" Mr. Willis yelled from inside the cottage.

I burst out in laughter and, attempting a comeback, yelled back, "Yes, sir!" I then turned to William, a playful curiosity playing in my voice. "Where in England are you from, William?"

William's face was a study in politeness. "I hail from Manchester."

"I've always wanted to visit the Manchester Museum in England," I responded hastily, the words tumbling out before I could stop them. My forehead perspired slightly as my eyes widened. *The Manchester Museum*! It hadn't been built yet, not for another two centuries.

William's polite expression morphed into a puzzled frown. "I am not familiar with the Manchester Museum." My skin felt clammy with sweat as I looked from his confused face to the cottage door. *I am such an idiot.*

Mr. Willis suddenly appeared, his face tight with concern. "He kens yer secret, so dinnae fash. Just be mindful; not everyone knows it, so be careful wi' what ye say! William will be yer guide to the Abbey of Donegal, where Dujardin Brindley is stationed. Ye'll take the correspondence wi' ye on the journey." Turning his gaze to the carriage, "William has a wee compartment hidden under the wagon where yer metal box will get stored. Ye'll leave first light come the morrow." Mr. Willis detailed.

Taken by surprise, I uttered like a ventriloquist, with teeth clenched in a frozen smile, "Thanks for letting me know!"

Mr. Willis gave a peculiar look and quipped, "D'ye think he came here fer a cup of tea?"

***

I spent the rest of the day making myself useful around the farm. After tossing leftover food from breakfast into the pig's pen, Mr. Willis summoned me to the wooden fence, intent on showing me how to shear a sheep's wool. I felt as if I were on a school field trip at a petting zoo, about to take a "Great Clips" tutorial for sheep shearing. Following the barbering, Mr. Willis led me into the stable, where he introduced me to the beautiful white horse he rode on the night he returned. I found it ironic that the horse had a marking on its shoulder in the shape of a lightning bolt, just like my running shoes. I showed Mr. Willis the similarities, but, presuming from his expression, he had no interest.

"Ye'll nae be wearing those on the journey. Ye dinnae want to attract unwanted attention to yerself," Mr. Willis said, pointing a finger at my shoes. "Omibheann will outfit ye wi' a pair of me britches and a *léine*, and ye'll need wool stockings and a pair of heavy shoes to keep yer feet warm."

Great, a makeover! I thought, sighing quietly.

The chores were completed just in time to hear Mrs. Omi holler in her commanding voice, "Come in from the dirt, it's time fer yer sup!" I hurried myself in, walking into a buffet fit for royalty. The tall table held plates filled with roasted chicken, honey-glazed carrots, beet nips, and bread pudding. No sooner had I sat at the table than William began reciting grace.

"Lord, thank you for the meal blessed upon us. We give thanks to thee and pray that thou wilt bless all who sit among us. Bless the hands that prepared this meal. Keep us in your holy embrace. In your divine name we pray, Amen!"

"Amen," we followed aloud.

Mr. Willis, who had poured a cup of whiskey for me, since I was the only one without, raised his cup to propose a toast. "To our humble guests, we wish them safe journeys. *Slàinte Mhaith*."

"Cheers," I followed with, raising my cup. Mr. Willis looked at me oddly, a quick, amused smile flashing across his lips.

Dinner was once again as expected, a welcome feast. Not a hint of processed crap, just wholesome, organic food. I found myself thinking how much healthier people in the twenty-first century would be, eating meals such as this. Following supper, Mrs. Omi cleared the table while Mr. Willis went back into the passageway, his heavy footsteps thudding on the floorboards, to retrieve a pistol from the locked chest. He then summoned me to meet him outside by the chopping block, where William had strategically placed three separate logs side by side.

"Have ye ever fired a pistol, lad?" Mr. Willis asked gruffly but attentively.

"Yes. I've been to gun ranges many times with friends. One of them is, um ... or was ... or *will* be an officer of the law," I tried explaining, the words coming out in a clumsy, tangled mess of tenses.

"I *dinnae ken* the meaning of what ye said, but here, show me yer skills!" Mr. Willis placed a heavy, ornate pistol in my hand. I took hold of it, admiring its uniqueness and in awe of how different in design and weight it was compared to modern-day guns. I remembered listening to an audio display plaque at a history exhibit, describing how pistols from the sixteenth and seventeenth centuries were prepared for firing.

"The gunpowder is poured from the powder horn into the barrel, followed by inserting the ball, and the flint should ignite the gunpowder once the trigger is pulled, thus forcing the ball to fly out at a high rate of speed."

It was something along those lines. I raised the gun and aimed it at the log. Mr. Willis looked at me with a flicker of disappointment in his eyes. "Did I forget something?" I asked, confused about his reaction.

He tugged the pistol while still in my grip, pulling out the ramrod. "Ye failed to pack the powder and ball, lad." He let go of the pistol and handed me the ramrod. I inserted the ramrod and, as he instructed, pushed it back and forth to tamp everything down.

"I knew what I was doing. I just wanted to make sure you were paying attention," I said playfully, trying to break the tension with a wink.

Aiming at my intended target, I held the pistol steady and pressed the trigger. The metal ball shot from the barrel, penetrated the log, split it in half, and sent it flying off the tree stump. "Ye'll need to continue practicing, but 'twill do!"

He's a hard man to please, I thought.

Following the long day, Mr. Willis thought it wise to rest. According to William, the upcoming journey would take about a day and a half, beginning at sunrise. Before taking my leave, I felt compelled to divulge the specifics of the impending Cromwellian invasion.

"Mr. Willis, before I go, I'd like to speak with you, William, and Mrs. Omi on a matter."

He took a seat at the table, followed by Mrs. Omi, both of them looking at me with tired, expectant faces. William remained standing by the entrance, methodically sharpening his dirk. "There are certain things that should not be known to you, but I feel the need ... no, not need; the responsibility to warn you of a battle that is to happen this coming year, specifically September 1649." I leaned against the tall table and continued, "There will be an invasion led by a man named Oliver Cromwell. He'll lead an army of thousands of English soldiers to place a firm hold on the Catholic-owned lands. The British Protestants will usurp these lands, resulting in the obliteration of much of the Catholic population."

Mrs. Omi's face manifested a look of fear and sadness, but she listened intently, her hands clasped tightly in her lap. "If I remember correctly, a vast majority of the lands will be redistributed to British Protestants, and over five thousand Irish men of the military, including women and children, will be slaughtered. This will be followed by years of famine, violence and an outbreak of the bubonic plague."

A profound silence descended upon the room. Finally, Mr. Willis let out a long, heavy breath. "Well, lad, mebbe that is why ye have come to us. Wi' God's will, it willna be fer naught. *Oíche mhaith*!"

Mr. Willis displayed a look of distress, mirroring Mrs. Omi's sentiment. He stood abruptly from the table and walked away to his bed. I stared at Mrs. Omi and William, feeling heavyhearted, and offered them a most heartfelt apology for being the bearer of such fateful news.

"*Ná bí buartha*, Myles. All will be well!" she replied, her voice soft but filled with a deep assurance.

Chapter 7 – Quick Draw MacKinney

The scent of farm animal dung, pungent and inescapable, roused me. I recalled opening the small window in the shelter before going to bed, hoping to air out the persistent stable odor, but I had failed to notice the cow Mr. Willis had bartered for was tied directly outside, below the window. I pulled myself up, groaning, and reached out to close it, hoping the stench would subside. When I lay back down on the makeshift bed, I found a curious sight positioned next to the door: a flickering image, like a ghost, that was somehow familiar. It was a television screen, tuned to an old Western movie, with a man on horseback being chased. The horse he rode had a familiar marking on its shoulder, a distinct lightning bolt, just like the one on the horse Mr. Willis had asked me to groom.

As I squinted, trying to make sense of the blurry image, I was stunned to see that the man on the horse was *me*. My face, my build, even the way I sat in the saddle. But as the camera panned out, it revealed my pursuer. It wasn't another rider at all; instead; it was simply a cow, with eyes that glowed fiery red, its hindquarters expelling a continuous stream of manure.

I rummaged frantically under the wool blanket for a remote, desperate to turn the television off. Instead, my hand closed around a wooden spoon, which I squeezed repeatedly, but all it did was raise the volume, causing the sound of cows mooing to blare through the tiny shelter. "Shit, shit, shit!" I yelled, frustrated, as I continued to stab at the spoon, trying to lower the deafening noise. In a fit of pure exasperation, I threw the wooden spoon at the screen, and to my surprise, it flickered and died. The silence that followed was abrupt and absolute.

I pulled the blanket over my head, as I usually did after a particularly bad dream, but a sound from the small window above me triggered a primal fear, forcing me to peek out. And there it was, the same cow from the television, its head poking through the open window, mooing even louder, its massive red eye staring directly at me. I let out a waking scream, a strangled gasp that expelled from my chest, panting as if I were still being chased by the cow.

I scrambled onto the bed, nearly falling off in my haste, and slammed the window shut. Just as I secured the latch, I heard a real cow moo. *"Fuck!"* I bravely, if foolishly, stuck my head back through the now-open window, and lo-and-behold, there was an actual, honest-to-God cow tied up to a hitching post, right next to the window beneath which I slept. *Puñeta!*

After tossing and turning for what felt like an eternity, sleep finally claimed me again, only to be broken once more by the cacophony of roosters crowing and chickens clucking wildly in panic. The commotion was swiftly followed by the sharp crack of a gunshot, shocking me out of bed. I grabbed my shirt and ran out to the field to investigate. I found Mr. Willis standing by the barn, his rifle raised, preparing to take a shot.

"What's going on, Mr. Willis?" I yelled from the corner of the stable.

"Bloody pine marten attacking the wee chickens!" he growled powerfully. "Run up there and see if it is dead, lad," he ordered, gesturing toward the chicken enclosure.

I sprinted toward the coop, my heart pounding. "I see a furry tail! Do they have furry tails?!"

"Aye, lad," he said, running up behind me, his heavy boots thudding on the damp earth. I inched closer to where the critter was when suddenly, the furry bastard jumped unexpectedly, a chicken still clutched firmly in its mouth. If you have ever seen videos of cats jumping in fear after being spooked by the sight of a cucumber, that's exactly how I must have looked when the pine marten scurried to escape with its potential meal. Mr. Willis, however, refused to lose another chicken. He aimed intently at the fleeing animal and, with perfect, almost casual precision, hit his mark. "Quick Draw MacKinney," I jested, clapping silently.

Though a bit grossed out, I bravely picked up the dead pine marten and tossed it into the small fire Mr. Willis had lit to dispose of the carcass. I kept myself from laughing as Mr. Willis mumbled angrily under his breath, cursing incessantly in Gaelic over the loss of his chickens. I empathized with him; he had just lost three chickens, and the fourth potential victim was about to be devoured by the pine marten, but, surprisingly, it had survived. It wasn't like he could go to a nearby hatchery and buy new ones on a whim.

Following the mayhem, Mr. Willis requested I change clothes and meet him at the cottage. I quickly returned to the shelter to discard my soiled pants and don the rustic period clothes Mrs. Omi had given me. When I arrived at the main house, William was already seated at the table, quietly drinking tea, waiting for me to join them.

"Thank ye, Myles, for helping with the mess of the wee chickens. 'Tis nae often we get these bloody martens in this area," Mrs. Omi remarked, her voice carrying a hint of the morning's frustration. She placed a bowl of thick, creamy porridge and a steaming cup of tea at my place setting. "Sit yerself down, lad."

I reached for the honey and drizzled it plentifully over the steaming porridge, but my mind drifted, a longing ache for a familiar taste. *What I would give for mami's avena,* I thought. It was a porridge of my own time, a comforting bowl made with cinnamon, sugar, and both condensed and evaporated milk. It was stirred constantly until it bubbled, then the heat was raised just enough to let the bottom burn for a moment, creating a sweet, caramelized crust. It was then served on a flat plate with a sprinkle of cinnamon powder on top.

Mrs. Omi set a plate of round bread—four loaves—in the middle of the table, beside a platter heaped with bacon, boxty, sausages, and fried eggs. "'Tis a long journey ahead o' ye, one best suited wi' a full belly," she said. With all the fuss since early morning, it had slipped my mind that today was the day of my road trip to meet with the Major.

"Mr. Willis, you never explained exactly how Mr. Brindley is supposed to help me with my situation," I commented, piling my plate with sausages and eggs. "Is he going to put me on a ferry back to the twenty-first century?" I joked, though a part of me desperately hoped it were true.

Mr. Willis gave me a hard look, utterly unamused. "Fairies are wee things, lad, incapable of carrying ye on their wee backs, ye ken!"

"Never mind," I replied with a roll of my eyes and a chuckle.

Mr. Willis took a long sip of his tea. "He has done extensive research and could offer a better understanding of the stories behind the Eas Gorm i Bhfolach. I dinnae ken if he can tell ye how to travel back to yer time, lad, but mebbe give ye knowledge of what ye are meant to do during yer time here. Share wi' im the information of the coming battle ye warned us about, and mebbe he will ken how to direct ye from there."

That gave me a better perspective of what to expect when meeting with the major.

***

Mrs. Omi gathered old clothes from a chest she kept in the main room. They belonged to Mr. Willis, and she handed them to me, suggesting I wear them and leave my "future clothing" behind. I headed to the shelter to wash up and dress. Just as I opened the camera app on the phone to use as a mirror, Mr. Willis appeared in the doorway.

"Lad, be sure ye keep yer blasted contraption in yer case, and have William hide it in the wee compartment under the wagon," Mr. Willis warned.

"Yes, sir, I will."

I followed behind, out of the shelter and into the stable, where Mrs. Omi was rummaging about the wagon, fitting a stack of folded wool blankets into a burlap sack.

"I'll store it for you, Mr. Roberts," William said, beckoning me over. He took hold of the metal case and bent low underneath the wagon. Curious as ever, I followed behind to see where this secret compartment was located. William inserted a nail into a plank of wood, pushing it in until the wooden plank beside it popped open. "That's ingenious!" I yelped. It was the same concept used when inserting the metal pin into a cell phone to make the SIM card holder pop out.

He stored the case inside, along with an added pistol and a leather pouch filled with coins. It looked spacious, bigger than a glove compartment.

"Here, lad, put this on and buckle it tight. This here will hold yer dirk," Mr. Willis said, handing me a belt embellished with leather loops and tugging the loop on the left side of the belt, "and this yer pistol," sticking his finger through the one on the right. He then handed me a sack filled with metal balls with a hook sewn on to clip onto the belt and a powder horn with a long leather strap attached. "Keep this 'round yer neck!" he instructed.

Mrs. Omi secured the burlap sack to the corner of the wagon, placing it inside a wooden crate so it wouldn't get tossed about. "I packed ye salty meats, sweetmeats, cheese, two loaves of bread, and the flasks are filled wi' whiskey. That should keep yer bellies nice and filled through the journey."

"I guess we don't need to stop at a gas station for snacks," I remarked humorously.

"What is a gas station?" she asked, her head cocked in confusion. "Never ye mind, 'tis a term from yer future, I gather, and I dinnae need to ken more than I already do!"

William Wexton and I were ready to go, but before hopping up onto the wagon, I approached Mrs. Omi and spread my arms to offer her an embrace, which she awkwardly rejected. Embarrassed, I simply displayed an uncomfortable smile. I had forgotten that women of this century did not show public displays of affection, even to their husbands, out of respect, let alone to another man. I smiled understandably with a nod, then turned to shake Mr. Willis's hand and thank him. "I hope we see each other again. You both have been so welcoming, kind, and generous to me. I appreciate the comfort you brought me during this ordeal, and I hope to someday repay you!"

"Ye have nae business repaying us, ye ken," Mrs. Omi said resolutely. Her eyes, which held a knowing, quiet strength, sought and received a quick nod of approval from Mr. Willis. She then grasped my hands in her own. "God brought ye to our time on a mission to aid us, thus forming a better future—"

"Accomplishing the task set before ye is repayment enough, lad," Mr. Willis interrupted brusquely, with an emotion he fought to suppress. He gave a gruff bow and marched inside the house, leaving us to our goodbyes.

"*Dia dhuit*," Mrs. Omi said, and to my surprise, she reached out and pulled me into an embrace. She clung to me for a long moment, a silent farewell. She then let go, and still holding my hand, led me to the wagon. I climbed up and snuggled myself in. William gave a soft click of the tongue and whipped the reins to urge the horses forward. The sudden, unexpected movement caused my head to jerk back, almost giving me whiplash.

"So long!" I shouted, waving at Mrs. Omi as she stood alone, watching us go.

"*Slán agat, dia leat*," she whispered softly, her hand raising to wave back as she patted the tears from her eyes with her apron.

Chapter 8 – Road Trip

The roads of this century—if one could even call them roads—were mostly simple trails of small stones and pebbles, often making a ride impossibly bumpy, much like the shaking I'd felt on Petey Taz's shuttle van as it entered the parking area of the Eas Gorm i Bhfolach. After we passed a fast-moving, gurgling creek, the stones on the track gradually disappeared, transitioning into a smoother path of grass, making the ride more bearable.

"We will need to stop just ahead once we pass the upcoming grove," William warned in a low voice. He pointed toward a dense thicket of trees in the distance. "Highwaymen frequent groves such as these and ambush travelers. Have your pistol loaded and ready should we chance upon any pillagers, Mr. Roberts!"

My mind wandered, a sudden dread replacing the sway of the wagon. I recalled my youth, the impulsive fistfights in high school, and the disciplined sparring sessions during both boxing and self-defense classes. Never once in those modern, controlled environments, had I ever imagined myself having to prepare for a genuine gunfight in the wilderness.

"The highwaymen are known to attack under the cover of night, but we shall not find ourselves unprepared!" William declared, handing me the reins while he loaded and prepared his own pistol. I gave him a sidelong stare, one eyebrow raised. I detected a different tone in his voice, one of confidence and steely assertion, a boldness that had not presented itself until now. He had initially come across as a passive man, but his demeanor was now undeniably that of a warrior.

He slid his loaded pistol into a cleverly designed, slanted piece of wood that also served as a footrest. It was roughly two and a half inches high and shaped like a forward-leaning triangle, with the forward-facing side a quarter-inch shorter than the other. It was hollowed out, with enough space to fit a pistol on one side and a dirk on the other.

Taking firm control of the reins once more, William whipped them, urging the horses to accelerate their stride, hoping to get past the treacherous grove at a quicker pace and reach the clearing without incident. We rode fast for several minutes, the wagon rattling, when William finally slowed the horses. I glanced at him, and he gave a nod, a silent signal of reprieve. A calmness seeped into me, a blast of relief enveloping my anxiety, knowing we had avoided the imminent danger of a gunfight, which I was learning was an all-too-common occurrence in this place and time. "We shall make camp and take our rest here," William informed me as we came to a stop at an elevated clearing facing the vast, restless ocean. We situated ourselves beside a small creek, its clear waters murmuring as it wound down from a small, wooded hill just northwest of our location, flowing into a larger stream.

William unfastened the reins from the wagon and led the horses to the creek for watering, their flanks steaming in the cool air. He then secured them to a nearby tree. He grabbed his flask and took a few long sips of whiskey as I unpacked the salted meats and bread, along with the cheese, and placed them on a large plate Mrs. Omi had packed for us, setting it all on the wool blanket.

I unwrapped the coarse cloth from the meat, wiped the excess salt from the lamb, then tore the round bread and shared half with William. "This is similar to what we call a cheeseburger in my time, William," I explained, gesturing with my hands.

"What is a... cheeseburger, Mr. Roberts?" William inquired curiously.

"It's a round, cooked patty, made from ground beef—cow's meat—garnished with onions, pickles, and cheese. It's placed between two pieces of bread, like this," I said, using my lamb and bread as an example. "French fries are served as an accompaniment, which are fried potatoes cut in the shape of squared fingers and dipped in a sauce called ketchup—puréed tomatoes with vinegar and spices added on."

William watched my demonstration intently, then mimicked my sandwich, placing the lamb between the breads and adding a thick sliver of cheese on top. He bit into it with a look of great pleasure.

***

"I'll be over by the creek washing up," I informed William, rising from the blanket.

"I suggest you take your pistol with you," William warned, as his eyes scanned the surrounding treeline.

I paused. "Why? Do you expect an incident?"

"No, but one can never be too certain in these parts, Mr. Roberts. Here," he said, handing me his own pistol. "Take mine. I have my sword and dirk on hand."

I inserted the pistol into the loop of my belt and headed to the creek. Feeling a prickle of paranoia, I looked around nervously as I washed, rushing to get done so as not to be further distracted, eager to return to full-alert status. I pulled up my pants and buckled the belt, just as a sudden, sharp sound—the unmistakable clashing of steel—erupted from the direction of the camp.

The sound tore through the serene evening. I whipped around, my blood turning to ice, and saw William. He was fighting, locked in a brutal battle with two men shrouded in black, their faces hidden by kerchiefs. One of them shoved William with brutal force, sending him staggering. His sword flew from his grasp as he struggled to regain his footing.

I felt rooted to the spot where I stood, my feet heavy as lead, but my mind screamed with the undeniable truth: William needed my help. My hand, as if acting independently, tore the pistol from my belt loop. I cocked it and aimed toward the chaotic tangle of bodies. The scuffling made it impossible to lock onto just one man without the terrifying risk of hitting William. My breath caught, a cold sweat breaking out on my forehead.

Just when I thought William had finally gained the upper hand, the second man, moving with a serpent's speed, pulled out his dirk and plunged it into William's back, just above the right-side of his waist.

"No!" I yelled frantically; a raw, guttural sound ripped from my lungs. The cry startled the attacking bandit, giving William the precious fraction of a second he needed. With a desperate grunt, he scrambled for his fallen sword, twisting as he found its hilt, and, with a fatal thrust, gored his assailant. The man collapsed, gurgling loudly as he fell hard onto the damp ground.

Overwhelming anger befell me then, a pure, unadulterated rage I'd never felt before in my life. Without hesitation or a second thought, I swung the pistol toward the remaining attacker. My finger tightened on the trigger. The shot cracked through the air, dreadfully loud, and the metal ball tore through the left side of his head, just above the temple, leaving a ragged, dark hole.

A surge of adrenaline rushed through me. I ran, stumbling over my own feet, toward William. "William! William, talk to me, man!" I gasped, dropping to my knees beside him. Thankfully, he was still breathing, his breaths coming in ragged, painful gasps.

"I'm alive, Mr. Roberts," he struggled to say.

"Okay, don't talk, just point to your wound," I commanded, my hands already hovering over his back. He reached over to his right side, tapping above his waist to indicate the spot. Blood was seeping from the wound, but not enough to make me fear the dirk had penetrated any vital organ. It was a flesh wound, deep and ugly, but not immediately fatal.

Cautiously, I laid William down gently, trying not to jostle him further. Then, I scrambled to the wagon, my movements jerky with urgency, pulling out the flask of whiskey and grabbing one of the wool blankets. I tore it into strips with my teeth, the rough fabric ripping with a satisfying sound. I knelt next to William, dousing a strip with whiskey. "This is going to sting," I warned. I pressed the soaked cloth against the wound to disinfect it, prevent infection, and staunch the continuous flow of blood. William wailed, a guttural cry of agony, but I didn't deter. I cleaned the area meticulously, ignoring his pain, with absolute focus.

He continued to lose blood, though not in concerning amounts, but enough to know I needed to try something else. A long-forgotten memory resurfaced, a flicker from my years as a Junior Forest Explorer. I'd earned the Med Scout badge, a requirement for which was learning to identify plants and their uses for medicinal purposes. *Yarrow. That's it.*

"William here," I said, handing him a dry strip of blanket to replace the soaked, bloody one. "Press hard against the cut, no matter how much pain you feel." I guided his trembling hand to the laceration and pressed hard, urging him to maintain the pressure. "I'll return as soon as I can." He nodded agreeably, his face becoming paler and drawn. I leaped up and ran as fast as I was able. I couldn't remember the last time I had run at that speed, feeling as if my legs were running independently of my upper body, a frantic blur of motion.

I knew beyond any doubt I had to reach the area of the grove where I'd previously spotted yarrow plants. *I can't let this man die; I will not let this man die;* I repeated desperately in my head.

I reached the grove, my lungs burning, and swiftly gathered handfuls of yarrow plants, stuffing them, roots and all, into every available pocket of my borrowed britches. Then, with lightning speed, I turned and made a mad dash back to camp. I came in at high speed, sliding on my knees like a baseball player sliding into home base, stopping directly beside him. "William, are you with me?" I gasped, shaking his shoulder aggressively. He remained silent, with his eyes closed, and breathing shallow. "William! William!" I yelled frantically.

"I am here, Mr. Roberts," he said in a strained whisper, his eyes fluttering open slightly. His breathing was still labored, but he was conscious.

I reached behind William to replace the blood-drenched cloth with a fresh one, tossing the used one aside. *Shit!*

I stuffed the yarrow leaves into my mouth, packing in as many as I could fit. Using my saliva and whiskey as the moistening agents to reach the desired consistency, I chewed incessantly until the leaves formed a thick, pungent paste.

Then, I spit it into my hand and kneaded the concoction until it reached the proper thickness. Taking hold of the flask again, I poured more whiskey onto the wound, causing William to yell once again in anguish. I knew that no matter how great the pain was; I needed to keep him conscious. Lastly, I applied the poultice abundantly to ensure it covered the entire wound.

I then affixed the reins to the horses, a strange, automatic knowledge guiding my hands. I was perplexed as to how I knew how to do it. Mustering all the strength I could, I lifted William into the wagon. Though William was not a large man, reaching five feet nine and approximately one-hundred and fifty-odd pounds, lifting him was like hauling dead weight; his body limb. However, with the continued surge of adrenaline, I placed him in the wagon with ease. I balled up the other half of the ripped blanket to form a crude pillow for his head and used the remaining blanket to cover him, even though the night air was warm.

I found a flask hidden in the lower corner of the wagon and brought it with me to the creek to fill with water. I could use the already torn blanket I had thrown into the wagon earlier, douse it with water to keep him cool, and avoid any chance of him developing a fever.

I rushed to the creek, rinsed out the flask, filled it with water, moistened the cloth, and returned swiftly. I gently placed the moistened rag on William's forehead and positioned the flask within his reach so that should he awaken, it would be easily accessible.

Once William was comfortable and secure, I turned to do something I had never envisioned myself doing—dig a grave and drag two dead bodies to their final resting place. Raised as a Catholic, I felt inclined to pray as I plowed the holes in the ground, which was not an effortless task. The shovel William kept in the wagon was worn, but it would have to do.

My adrenaline was still at full throttle as I went back and forth, digging the hole in the ground and continuously checking on William. I dug as quickly and deeply as I could, knowing that William needed my attention more than these two dead bodies did. It was an arduous undertaking, so the four feet I dug would have to suffice.

I dragged both corpses and tossed them into the hole, oblivious to the fact that not so long ago, these two men were living human beings—a brother, a son, a husband, or simply a friend who made bad choices. Despite the situation, the anger that dwelled within me caused me to see them as nothing more than mere trash. In the confined space, I had no choice but to disjoint the arms of the man lying on top and fold them underneath him to better accommodate them in the restricted space.

I gathered thick branches strewn throughout the ground alongside a line of hedgerows. Using the dirk, I cut one long branch into two even pieces and stripped another to form twine to use as the binder for the cross I was fashioning to place on the gravesite. I shoved it into the ground as far as it would go, then kneeled in front of the gravesite and, with tears flowing, recited the Lord's Prayer.

Aside from having witnessed a fatal fight, collecting the yarrow, tending to William's wound, digging the grave, and knowing I still had to try by whatever means necessary to help him live, I didn't have time to fathom the guilt that entailed taking a human life.

***

As night fell, I searched for a location near a creek or stream dense enough to use as cover during the night to avoid another attack. As we approached another grove, the path forked. I took a gander and pulled the reins to motion the horses to turn toward the eastern part of the path and continue riding on the side that was not so obviously a road. Further in, I spotted a stream flowing from a heavily wooded part of the grove, ideal for concealing the wagon and watering the horses.

Once we were settled, I hopped up to the back of the wagon to check on William. I felt relieved knowing that the yarrow had done its job better than I expected. Only a hint of blood seeped through the strip of rag.

I woke William to get him to drink water to rehydrate. He remained in pain, as indicated by the grunting sound he made when he opened his eyes. "Are you hungry, William?" I asked, taking out the remaining salted meats and bread from the burlap sack.

"Just a bit. I *am* still thirsty," he whispered in a dry voice, even after having just finished the water from the other flask.

"I'll refill the flask. There's a stream just yards from where we are," I said, feeling exhausted. I handed William a few slivers of cheese and a quarter of the bread still wrapped in cloth. He quickly took hold of them and devoured them with a primal hunger. I took that as a sign, a drop of hope in the grim reality.

I gathered the two wooden cups I'd found inside the wagon and both flasks, then headed to the stream. I knelt at the edge of the shore, the cool dampness of the ground seeping through my britches, and used the cups to fill the flasks. A sudden breeze, laden with the scent of something distinctly fresh, carried a hint of mint. Quickly lifting my head, like a bloodhound on a scent, I searched to find its source. The smell led me a few yards further upstream, where I caught sight of tiny purple flowers, clustered at the water's edge. Water mint. *These will serve perfectly as pain relievers for William,* I thought excitedly. I foraged several handfuls, stuffing them, roots and all, into a corner of the blanket, bringing plenty back to camp.

"William, do you have a cooking pot?" I asked urgently.

"Inside the smaller crate," he struggled to answer, sounding strained. Rummaging through the box, my hands brushing against coarse fabric and strange implements, I finally found a small, soot-blackened pot hidden below a ball of hay. I returned to the creek and filled the pot with plenty of water, enough to prepare the decoction. Preoccupied with William's well-being, a sudden, frustrating realization struck me. *Why didn't I learn how to start a fire like Mrs. Omi suggested? Shit!*

I improvised, gathering logs and piling them alongside the branches I'd snapped earlier. I broke off a thin tree branch to use as tinder. "Okay, I can do this," I muttered to myself as I scraped a rock using the metal from the dirk. I scraped continuously in a frantic, repetitive motion, but was utterly unsuccessful at igniting a spark. My frustration mounted.

Then, a soft banging noise came from the side of the wagon. I turned to find William's arm flung over the side, his hand weakly holding a piece of metal and flint. "This will light the fire faster, Mr. Roberts," he rasped, barely audible.

"Thank you, William," I said, taking the primitive lighter from his unsteady hand. I placed the tinder on a flat piece of stone and scraped the metal together with the flint, striking continuously, sparks showering the ground. After several tries, the tinder finally caught a spark. I blew on it, over and over, my breath coaxing the ember until the fire finally grew, flickering against the logs. I quickly tucked the burning tinder underneath the piled wood, and the flames roared to life.

"Who needs a lighter?" I remarked confidently, grinning triumphantly.

I poured the water mint tea into a wooden cup, the minty steam rising, and recommended he sip it slowly. William nibbled on another piece of bread, followed by several shots of whiskey after finishing the tea. The liquor, coupled with the warmth of the tea and the pain relief, instantly put him to sleep. I checked the wound once more before he was sound asleep, finding it clean and dry. *Hopefully, he will sleep well throughout the night,* I thought, pulling the blanket higher on his chest.

Feeling the cumulative events of the day suddenly catch up with me, I lay on the ground next to the fire; the warmth comforting against the cool soil. I gazed up at the sky, mesmerized by the dark canvas illuminated by millions of shimmering stars. I turned my stare toward the moon, a pale, silent disc hanging in the heavens, feeling as if I could reach up and touch it. I shut my eyes for a moment, drifting into a blissful, well-earned sleep.

***

The accumulated droplets from the morning dew on the leaves trickled down, landing on my forehead, a gentle touch that roused me from a restful sleep. The sounds of lapwings chirping their bright calls and mallards quacking in the creek filled the brisk morning air, adding to my unexpected wake-up call.

I raised myself from the damp ground, my muscles stiff and aching from the previous day's exertions, and peeked into the wagon to find William gone. "William!" I yelled sharply with sudden fear, producing an echoing silence that only amplified my panic.

"I am here, Mr. Roberts," William's voice, though strained, called out from a nearby boulder, a welcome sound that instantly eased my worry.

"Are you okay? Why didn't you wake me to help you?" I asked, concerned.

"I was able to manage on my own." He sat himself on a boulder, a bit winded, and looked up at me, his eyes solemn, yet filled with a deep gratitude. "I would like to thank you for your swift thinking and healing yesterday, Mr. Roberts. Your actions saved my life. I am highly indebted to you!"

He stumbled slightly when he rose from the rock, and I quickly took hold of his arm, steadying him, then led him back to the wagon. "No need for that, William; your healing and recovery will satisfy," I said gently.

"My brother, Topher, lives just outside of Caisleán Dhún na nGall at Wilson's Creek, just a half-day's ride from here," he explained. "His wife, Charlotte, is an ailment healer and can stitch the wound closed. Nourish yourself so we can be on our way."

Chapter 9 – His Brother, My Friend, My Brother

The course was long—a slow advancement over the rough, unpaved tracks. My back ached from the constant jarring of the wagon, and my eyes, though accustomed to the wild Irish landscape, still strained against the ancient unfamiliarity of it all. Finally, I leaned over the backrest of the wagon, tugging gently on William's shirt. "William, are we in the right place?"

William raised himself with a grunt, slowly, painfully, and peered over the side of the cart, his gaze sweeping the surroundings. "Yes, Mr. Roberts," he rasped. "Just follow the road. It will lead to the main house. There, you will ask for Topher Wexton." He slowly, carefully, lay back down.

The entrance to the Wexton estate was extraordinary, an utter contrast to the rustic MacKinney farm. The dirt road we rode on was lined with mature willow trees, their graceful branches adorned with the cheerful yellow of daffodils on both sides, creating a verdant, living tunnel. Outside the main entrance, a white cobblestone roundabout, meticulously laid, encircled a large stone fountain brimming with frogs and lily pads, all surrounded by a riot of freshly bloomed, polychromatic flowers. It was a vision of cultivated beauty, a pocket of refined elegance in the untamed, ancient past.

I stationed the wagon at the bottom of the long, stone stairs. I jumped out and placed a wooden stopper in front of the left-side wheel to keep the wagon from moving. I sprinted up the steps with haste and hammered on the heavy oak door continuously. An elderly woman appeared, her face prim, dressed in a brown, laced uniform with white trim, and with a white cloth wrapped tightly around her head, held with a thin lace.

"Are you the lady of the house, ma'am?" I asked with desperation, my eyes darting toward the wagon where William lay.

"No, sir, I am the maid of the house. Whom may I say requests to speak with the mistress?" she responded stiffly and slightly pompously, as if the very idea of a stranger at the door was an imposition.

"I was told to ask for a Mr. Topher Wexton. I travel with his brother, William Wexton, ma'am."

She looked over my shoulder curiously, her gaze sweeping toward the wagon, then turned her attention back to me at a turtle's pace. "Allow me a moment to summon the master for you. Whom may I say inquires, sir?"

"Myles Roberts, ma'am, please hurry! His brother is badly hurt!"

"Wait here," she said, escorting me inside and pointing to a dark, uninviting bench alongside the passageway of the foyer. The speed at which she walked was that of a sloth, causing my anxiety level to pass through the roof. *If it were not that I was in the home of a complete stranger, I would have gone and searched for Mr. Wexton myself,* I thought, barely restraining myself from running past her.

I felt extremely concerned about William, knowing he was alone in the wagon and still not out of the woods. Unable to keep still, I paced back and forth, peeking through the door several times, wondering why it was taking so long for anyone to return. Just as I was about to make my way into the next room, Mr. Wexton appeared, walking into the foyer with whom I gathered was his wife, Charlotte. He carried a pipe in hand with a gold ascot tied around his neck, his hair slicked back, giving him the distinct look of a pimp. During times of dire circumstances, I often sought humor to help me cope, and Topher's appearance certainly provided it.

"Mr. Roberts, I am Topher Wexton. What news have you of my brother?" he asked, his voice dripping with an affected pretentiousness, observing me superciliously, as if I were a particularly uninteresting specimen.

"Mr. Wexton, your brother William is lying outside in the wagon. We were on our way to the Abbey of Donegal and camped out for the night. Long story short, he suffered a knife wound inflicted by a highwayman—" Before I could finish my sentence, I felt a whirlwind of motion beside me. I turned just in time to see Charlotte running past me like an ER doctor when a trauma patient is brought in.

"Dear Lord, step aside, man!" Topher yelped, pushing me aside with a force that caused me to lose my balance and slam against the door. He then bellowed,

"Quintin! Out here at once, now, immediately, and bring the groomsmen with you!" The urgency in his voice was a jarring contrast to his earlier aloofness.

Two burly men hurried past the front door toward the wagon and jumped inside. They pushed aside crates and lifted William with surprising caution, taking care not to cause him any discomfort while still rushing to get him inside.

"Bring him to the room beside the parlor!" Charlotte ordered clearly with command, then shouted to the housemaid, "Marlene, bring my *mála leighis*, hurry!"

The men rushed past the threshold with such speed that they had to readjust themselves several times, struggling to keep William from falling.

Topher seized my arm and demanded, in a commanding and rather rude tone, that I explain what happened to his brother. I pulled my arm from his grip and, ignoring his rudeness, gave him a concise, detailed account of the attempted robbery and how William had bravely fought off the two would-be thieves. He turned and walked away, heading to the parlor.

He returned a moment later, holding a small leather pouch filled with coins. "Here you are, sir. I bid you gratitude for bringing my brother safely back to us."

I blocked Topher's hand, a sudden, firm gesture that stopped him from handing me the pouch. "You're confused, sir. I don't need your money. William was my guide to the Abbey of Donegal. I met him at the residence of Mr. and Mrs. MacKinney in County Donegal. They arranged for me to meet with Major General Brindley, and William came at their request."

"You must find yourself in distress if you are having to meet with the Major General?" he stated, his brows furrowed in suspicion.

"I'm not in distress, sir. The major general has information that can help get me home to the U.S... um... I mean—" I realized with a sudden, sickening punch that America wasn't known as the U.S. in this century. I struggled for a second, my mind racing, then I remembered. "The colonies." I breathed a sigh of relief, feeling as if I'd just dodged a bullet. Topher tapped me on the shoulder in acknowledgment, then motioned for me to follow him into the room where William was being treated.

"How's he doing, Mrs. Wexton?" I asked, a shaky sound of concern in my voice as I entered the room.

"I have sewn his wound. You did splendidly in keeping it clean and suppressing the hemorrhage. Are you a healer, sir?" she asked calmly and professionally as she placed a clean cloth to cover the stitching.

"No, ma'am, I learned a few things from reading medical books."

"Splendid, just splendid. You saved his life, Mr. Roberts; we are indebted to you and will bear our gratitude eternally!" she declared, smiling faintly with a nod.

William began to snore loudly, so as not to disturb him, I excused myself from the room to continue the conversation with Topher. I still needed to reach the military post, but I wasn't sure if I could find it on my own. Mrs. Wexton followed me out of the room, carrying her medical bag with her, leaving William to convalesce.

"Will you follow me into the library?" Topher asked suggestively, his tone less pretentious than before.

"Have a seat, Mr. Roberts." He placed a chair next to a small, round table propped beside a grand fireplace made of aqua-colored stones, glimmering as if covered in glitter. He poured two glasses of whiskey, handing one to me, then lit a cigar, which smelled like an old leather shoe. He raised a hand in a show of a toast. I took a sip of the whiskey, causing my eyebrows to flinch involuntarily in one quick flutter, finding the taste of sweet oak satisfying.

"I am indebted to you, Mr. Roberts. It is seldom that a stranger would tend to another during such dire circumstances, especially those concerning life and death."

"William is not a stranger to me; I consider him a friend!" I said, lifting my cup in a show of gratitude. "Thank you, Mr. Wexton."

"You may address me as Topher."

***

I was grateful to have been invited to stay as their guest. I woke up feeling rested, having slept on a mattress stuffed with feathers and pillows fitted with sheets made of soft, fine linen, giving me much-needed rest. A knock on the door, followed by a sudden burst, announced Marlene's arrival with a military march to her walk, like that of a disciplined soldier, just as I was dressing the bed. She quickly placed a tray on the table next to the window facing the rear of the estate. She then ordered me to sit after snatching the sheets from my hands to dress the bed herself.

"I brought tea and sweet bread. Once you have finished, I will escort you to the dining room."

"Thank you, Marlene," I said politely, sitting and preparing the tea. I added two irregular clumps of sugar, broken from a larger loaf, and put them into the cup. After stirring the drink, I dipped my bread into the warm drink. Dunking the bread into the tea didn't taste the same as it did with coffee, which was commonly done in Hispanic households. There's a distinct taste when bread lathered with butter is dipped into a cup of *café con leche*, with extra sugar added to sweeten the neutral taste of the butter. The thought of it brought a smile to my face.

Marlene finished dressing the bed and retrieved the tray from the table before I could finish drinking my tea. She then motioned for me to follow her, marching at a brisk pace down the stairs and into the dining area. I was met by Mr. and

Mrs. Wexton, who were already seated at a table laden with breakfast foods. I looked around, my heart giving an uneasy flutter, concerned to see that William was not sitting alongside them.

"Good morning, Mr. and Mrs. Wexton," I greeted, a little more formal than I was accustomed to.

"Good morning, Mr. Roberts; please sit. You must be hungry," Mr. Wexton said, gesturing to the empty chair across from him. The footman, a solemn-faced older man, pulled out the chair, unfolded a crisp cloth, and laid it on my lap. *I could get used to this,* I thought, smiling wryly.

"Did you rest well?" Mrs. Wexton asked elegantly as she sipped her tea.

"Yes, ma'am. Indeed, I did. Quite comfortably, I might add. Thank you," I replied matter-of-factly.

"Mr. Roberts, we have arranged for our head servant, Quintin, to escort you to your destination here in Donegal. He is preparing the horses and stocking supplies for your journey as we speak."

"I'm immensely grateful for your generosity. How is William feeling today? Will he be joining us?" I asked with a note of worry creeping into my voice. Mrs. Wexton's smile faded, and she looked at Topher with a troublesome expression that sent an uneasy flutter of fear through my stomach. *Something happened overnight.*

Charlotte set her cup down with a soft click. "William fell into a fever during the night and was tended to with wet strips of cloth to help regulate his temperature."

I sighed a long, disquieted breath.

"I do expect his full recovery, Mr. Roberts; you need not worry yourself. He will be simply fine, I assure you," she assured, though her formal tone did little to quell my fears.

"I would like to see him and say goodbye before I leave," I insisted.

Topher looked at me with grudging respect. "I am sure he would never forgive us, knowing we allowed you to leave without bidding your farewells. Charlotte will check on his progress when we are finished with breakfast, so you may speak with him then."

***

The room where William convalesced was quiet and smelled of antiseptic and damp cloth. He stirred as I entered, raising his head. "Mr. Roberts, you remained," he said, grunting surprisingly.

"How would I not, William? I wanted to ensure your recovery. Mrs. Wexton said you ran a fever during the night."

"The fever has broken. I am feeling much better." He cleared his throat as he propped himself up on the bed. "Have a seat, Mr. Roberts."

I reached for a chair and placed it beside his bed. "I am filled with gratitude not only for your bravery, but for your compassion and friendship. Your selflessness saved my life, and I know you may have heard it from my family, as you will hear from me. I am truly grateful, and I am forever indebted to you."

"We are friends, William. I may even say we are like brothers now, and by the way, I suggest you refer to me as Myles."

"Myles," he said with a tired smile spreading across his face. "I would be more than honored to relate myself to you and consider you a brother. Thank you eternally. I can count on our paths crossing again." He laughed, then let out a low moan of pain.

"Without a doubt, I know they will! I'm hoping you'll join me in confronting Oliver Cromwell when the time arises and aid in ending his tyranny," I stated as I placed a hand on his shoulder.

"I have been informed Quintin will be your escort to the Abbey of Donegal," he said, grinning dryly, clearly wanting to digress from the subject.

"You've been informed correctly," I answered. "He's preparing the horses and wagon as we speak."

"Yes, Marlene?" William said tiredly, as she tapped on the half-open door.

"Pardon me, Mr. Wexton, but I am to escort Mr. Roberts to the stables. Sir Wexton is waiting to see him off."

I stood and pushed the chair back under the desk, extending my hand to William. "My brother, I look forward to our reunion. I will pray for your speedy recovery."

William grunted as he reached for my hand. Rather than a handshake, he took a firm grip and pulled himself up. He faced me and embraced me in a brotherly hug. "Thank you, brother!"

I followed Marlene and joined Mr. and Mrs. Wexton in the courtyard, where Quintin was waiting. He informed the Wextons that all was ready for the journey. They expressed their gratitude once more, then made their way back to the manor. Quintin led the way to the stables, where the wagon William and I had arrived in had been prepared to take us to our destination.

Chapter 10 – Major General Wise One

I spent a month searching online for a new home, my enthusiasm waning with each new listing. The houses were either too small, too expensive, or required too much work. I had just about given up when, one evening, a new listing appeared. It was a beautiful house, bone white with light gray trim and a wide, charcoal-colored door. It was in the highly sought-after Summerhill area, only five miles from my work. It had three bedrooms, two bathrooms, a fenced yard, and, to my surprise, a pool. All of this was within my budget. It felt too good to be true. I contacted the listing agent, a woman named Berith, and scheduled a tour for a few days later. I secretly hoped I was the first to view the house.

Overwhelmed with anticipation, I eagerly presented all the required pre-approval documents during our initial meeting. Berith, in turn, seemed impressed by my readiness, a step that proved advantageous.

"Ready to become a homeowner, Mr. Roberts?" she asked with resounding enthusiasm.

My eyes widened with excitement. "Yes, yes!" I exclaimed, my heart pounding in my chest.

It was truly a memorable day. How I long for my home!

***

As we followed the path William and I had taken into the Wexton estate, Quintin briefly informed me of the journey's distance. His communication ceased there, his demeanor becoming reclusive and taciturn. After receiving a few concise one-word replies, I stopped questioning him. I had already learned that the house servants of this era, obedient only to their masters or the families they served, answered to no one else.

I welcomed the silence, allowing myself to revel in the breathtaking beauty of the surrounding landscape. The way the land met the ocean coast was a sight to behold. Birds filled the skies with their vibrant colors and songs. Across from us, the grass radiated a profound emerald green, its spiked blades stretching as far as the eye could see, interwoven with colorful foliage. The scene reminded me of a trip to Acadia National Park in Maine years ago. The similarity was uncanny.

Distracted by the terrain, I was surprised when we crested a hill and two-story stone buildings came into view. "We have arrived, Mr. Roberts," Quintin announced flatly as we entered a courtyard nestled between the two tallest structures. To the south, three smaller buildings appeared to be dormitories.

Quintin unhitched Moonlight, the horse with the lightning bolt mark on its shoulder, from the wagon and tied him to a hitching post, leaving the other horse tethered. He then led the way into the larger of the north-facing buildings. Crossed swords were carved into the façade beneath the roofline. A miniature drawbridge led to a red-arched wooden door. Below the bridge, a pond teemed with flowers, plants, and small frogs hopping about.

At the doorway, a soldier halted us, inquiring about the purpose of our visit. My attention was immediately drawn to his uniform. It resembled one I had seen at the history exhibit on Stafford Beach: dark green with long sleeves, knee-high britches with white stockings and cotton-laced shoes, embellished with a gold sash draped over one shoulder and tassels hanging past the waist. Though typically gold, the *cathbharr* he wore was shiny silver. A longsword hung on his left hip, while his right hand gripped a musket.

"We request an audience with *Mórghinearál* Dujardin Brindley. I am to deliver correspondence sent by Sir Topher Wexton, stating urgent news."

The soldier's reaction suggested that Topher held a position of respect in this province. At the mere mention of his name, the soldier swiftly stepped aside and unlocked the gated door. He then instructed another soldier inside to escort us directly to Major General Brindley.

We navigated a maze of corridors, ascended a staircase, and passed three open storage rooms filled with crates and barrels, each guarded by a soldier. As we approached a large chestnut-brown door at the end of the corridor, the soldier stopped us. He knocked sharply, and a deep, raspy voice from within called, "Enter."

Before we entered, Quintin stopped the soldier and handed him Topher's sealed letter. He hurried inside, gave the letter to the major general, and quickly returned, motioning for us to enter.

Quintin informed Mr. Brindley of the Wexton family's debt to me for saving the life of one of their own. Mr. Brindley broke the waxed seal and read the letter.

Though unaware of the letter's contents, I felt a sense of relief when Brindley nodded in agreement. He reached into his pocket and handed Quintin some coins. Quintin then gave me the bag containing my belongings from the wagon's hidden compartment, along with a brown leather pouch.

"I shall take my leave, sir. Your horse will remain tied to the hitching post. Mr. Wexton has instructed me to inform you that should you ever find yourself in need, all you need do is send word or present yourself at the estate." I extended my hand in gratitude, but Quintin simply nodded, turned, and walked away.

"Have a seat, Mr. Roberts."

I retrieved the summarized letter from Mr. Willis and handed it to Mr. Brindley. Whatever Mr. Willis had written in the opening lines caused Brindley's eyes to widen in surprise. He then fixed his gaze on the guard.

"Step out and close the door behind ye, and under no circumstances are ye to allow anyone to enter wi' out me permission," he commanded the soldier.

Brindley possessed an unusual accent. As Mr. Willis had explained, Brindley was born and raised in Ireland, yet his speech carried a distinct British inflection, a formal overlay, no doubt because of the many years he'd spent living in the northwest of England and attending Hutton Grammar School in Lancashire. He was a tall, thin man, approximately six-foot-four, no older than fifty, and he carried the weight of his position in the lines etched around his thoughtful eyes.

He skimmed both pages of the letter Mr. Willis had transcribed for me, his gaze, sharp and assessing, fixed on me. "So, ye say ye are, in fact, a journeyer?"

His voice was deep, raspy, yet perfectly clear. "How would I know ye speak the truth?"

I opened the metal box and retrieved my phone. I tapped the screen and played a video of a dog barking at airplanes while banging its nose against a window. "Dear Lord God in heaven!" Brindley exclaimed, crossing himself with a swift, involuntary motion, then abruptly snatched the phone from my hand. He stared at the video, utterly mesmerized, his eyes wide with an intensity that suggested he was looking at God himself. His expression suggested his very world had been shaken by the sight of a living creature existing within the confines of something no bigger than a snuffbox.

"I have read the stories and studied the folklore," he said, awestruck, "even met alleged Elder Folks. They shared tales of meetings wi' journeyers, yet I still had doubts. But now the truth sits here in front of me, and I am beyond astonished!"

He returned the phone to me, shaking his head slowly in disbelief, his stare still fixed on the device as if it might disappear. "Tell me, lad," he asked, hinting a whisper, "from which time d'ye come?"

"The twenty-first century. 2022 was, or is... or will be, the year," I replied, still finding the verb tenses confusing. I tapped the screen to open the calendar app. Brindley hesitantly reached out a finger, his hand trembling slightly, to touch the screen, causing the day he clicked on to expand. He flinched and quickly withdrew his hand as if he had touched a hot coal, his eyes wide.

"Major Brindley, have any of these alleged Elder Folks ever mentioned how to return to one's original time?" I asked with desperate hope clinging to my voice. He gazed at the letter, flipped it over, then turned and looked at me, a solemn expression on his face.

"Regrettably, no, sir. I assure ye—yer visit here is not coincidental, nor will it be fer naught. In my research, I have found that journeyers are destined to travel to a time where their knowledge is crucial and much needed—a matter of life and death. Achieving the destined endeavor is essential. Here, look at this!" He reached for a large, leather-bound book from the vast library behind him, its shelves piled with ancient texts, and opened it to a bookmarked page. He stood behind me, peering over my shoulder, with the scent of old paper and ink filling my nostrils.

"I understand ye read Gaeilge, as Mr. MacKinney noted, but allow me to explain." He inhaled excitedly, a scholar's passion lighting his eyes. "A man named Adam Towell appeared as if from nowhere near the Eas Gorm i Bhfolach and was taken into custody by an infantry regiment. He was suspected of being a highwayman." He pulled up a chair and sat beside me, his voice dropping slightly as he continued. "It occurred during the vernal equinox of 1598. He was a young lad, nae but sixteen years of age. He was escorted by the soldiers to a holding house, where he befriended a king's guard." Brindley flipped the page eagerly, the paper crackling softly. "The soldier provided Adam with intel of an invasion that was to happen in the coming months, led by Sir Henry Bagenal." He read with an intensity rivaling Mrs. Omi's passion when she described the stories from the wee book, which I soon discovered were authored by Major Brindley himself.

"Shortly after sharing the privileged information with Mr. Towell, the soldier met his demise, hanged for his transgressions. Mr. Towell, having foreknowledge of this battle, bartered for his release by offering to disclose the confidential information that would lead to a guaranteed victory against the English."

Pausing for sips of ale from a tankard, Brindley continued reading aloud, his excitement growing with each word. "He met with the 2nd Earl of Tyrone, Hugh

O'Neill, and provided him with the precise date and location of the imminent battle. The earl agreed to his freedom, but only if they were victorious."

Noticing my empty cup, Brindley refilled it and his own, grinning with a spirited expression. "The Battle of the Yellow Ford, which followed two months after meeting with the earl, brought victory as foretold by Adam Towell. Hugh O'Neill promptly ordered the release of Adam Towell and declared that if it weren't for him, the troops led by Sir Bagenal would have decimated thousands of Irish soldiers."

I recalled the lessons I had taught at school about Sir Henry Bagenal and how many of his military campaigns had ended in failure, including his last—the Battle of the Yellow Ford, where he was mysteriously killed by an unknown gunman.

"Whatever became of Adam Towell?" I asked curiously.

"I dinna know, lad. Believers of the falls, the Elder Folks, say that once the battle was over, he was never seen again. But others claim he may have returned to the waterfall and back to his time or simply disappeared after completing his said destiny."

Overcome with a sense of dizzying hope, I felt that I, too, might have the chance to return home once my destined mission in this century was accomplished.

"The letter Mr. MacKinney transcribed mentions a matter ye have knowledge of, something that is to happen next summer involving Oliver Cromwell?" Brindley inquired, his tone suddenly grave.

"Yes, Mr. Brindley," I said low, the magnitude of the coming tragedy settling upon me. "Oliver Cromwell will lead an army of English Protestant soldiers into Ireland. His intention is to force a mass conversion from Catholicism to Protestantism. The town of Drogheda, under the leadership of Sir Arthur Aston, will be held under siege by Royalists and the Confederation of Irish Catholics, only to be *besieged* by Cromwell and his army on the eleventh of September. Thousands will be slaughtered, including children and their mothers." I paused, momentarily overcome with emotion, the images flashing through my mind from history books. "Lands belonging to the Irish Catholics will be seized through deadly force, and the English Protestants will govern those lands. The tragedy will continue with years of famine that will bring on years of disease."

Brindley abruptly rose from his chair, his face pale with alarm. He walked to the liquor table and refilled our cups, his movements stiff with suppressed disturbance. "He will become king in 1653, dethroning King Charles II and forcing him into exile."

Brindley's thick brows furrowed, his expression one of confusion mixed with profound curiosity. "What of King Charles I?" he asked raspily.

I opened the phone, my thumb swiping across the screen until I located a downloaded folder containing information on European history. I knew the story of Oliver Cromwell was in that folder because I had used the subject of the Cromwellian conquest in the recent quiz for my students.

"Mr. Brindley, look at this," I said, showing him the screen. "This is what we refer to as a folder. It stores a copy of our history books. This one details the coming battle of Oliver Cromwell, which will be known as the Cromwellian Conquest." Brindley stared at the open folder, a look of absolute disbelief on his face, before mustering the courage to take the phone from my hands.

I enlarged the font and showed him how to scroll, my finger moving up and down the screen. "Christ, this is remarkable! How can something so wee hold so much information?" He continued to scroll, reading word by word, the history of his future unfolding before his eyes. His initial excitement quickly turned to shock. "King Charles beheaded the year next! Is this true?!"

I nodded, my throat tight with the grim reality of it all. Brindley continued reading, his face filled with horrified fascination. I picked up the two letters from Mr. Willis and began reading. The writing on the second sheet, I noticed, ended abruptly. My heart skipped as I skimmed down to the signature. It was the same page I had seen on display at the Irish American Heritage Museum during the field trip with my students. In place of the signature were the initials W.M., for Williston MacKinney. *Well, I'll be damned!* I thought, shivering at the coincidence.

He returned the phone to me, his hand shockingly calm. "I'll take a screenshot for quicker reference when you are ready to continue."

"Aye. Whatever that means, lad!" he said with a groan, looking confused.

I chuckled, but a sense of panic settled as I noticed the battery indicator on my phone. It was blinking ominously. "Is something amiss, lad?" Mr. Brindley asked with concern.

I explained, "The phone runs on what is called a battery, and it's almost depleted. It needs to charge to continue working when this,"—pointing to the battery percentage on the screen—"reaches the lowest number. It needs to be given energy to continue displaying the contents." I hoped he understood what I was trying to convey.

A colleague had told me about a hand-cranked phone charger and recommended I bring one on the trip, just in case I found myself without electricity. I'm glad I bought two.

I connected the charging cord to the hand-cranked charger and spun the handle clockwise. It made a low whizzing noise as it rotated, meeting little resistance. The battery indicator jumped to the next percentage in under two minutes.

"Do all the contraptions from yer time require this box with the spinning handle to get 'energy'?" Brindley asked, pointing to the charger with a look of astonishment.

"No, sir. We have cords such as this," I explained, tugging on the charging cord, "with metal prongs on one end that are inserted into outlets built into walls. They generate almost unlimited electricity."

"Electricity?" Mr. Brindley asked inquisitively.

"It's a form of energy that allows light to illuminate and gives power to all forms of contraptions, as you call them. We don't require candles or fire to give us light or heat. The electricity generates it."

"Amazing, absolutely amazing!" he exclaimed in wonder.

Mr. Brindley suggested I hand him the phone for safekeeping in a locked chest hidden within a compartment under the floorboards in his office. I placed the phone inside the metal case, secured the lock and handed it to him.

He sat on his chair, lifted his leg, and stomped down with excessive force, a hollow-sounding thud that triggered a hidden compartment to open. He pulled out an armada chest with two latches and a keyhole in the front and an additional keyhole on top. Inserting a key into each hole, he simultaneously turned them— one clockwise, the other counterclockwise—creating the sounds of a complex mechanism before raising the lid.

He neatly tucked the metal box under a stack of papers tied together with a thin rope and closed the lid, repeating the sequence he had used to open the chest, but this time, he turned both keys in the same direction. Once the chest was secured under the floorboard, Brindley led the way out, and I followed. We passed through the corridor I had originally entered; this time, however, we took a detour in the opposite direction, which led us directly to the courtyard.

When we reached the hitching post where Moonlight was tied, I checked on my newly gained horse. "Can we stop for a minute, Mr. Brindley? I'd like to check on Moonlight." Brindley seemed lost in thought as he continued walking, perhaps overwhelmed by the information he had just absorbed.

"Who is Moonlight?" he asked, turning abruptly, snapping out of his distraction.

"It's the horse, I mean, my horse."

He glanced at Moonlight. "It has no saddle. Are ye to ride it bareback?" Unfamiliar with the customs of this time, I replied, "I didn't think about that. Quintin unhitched Moonlight from the wagon and tied him to the hitching post, but he left no instructions." I paused, thinking, then said, "I'm guessing I'll need a saddle then."

Mr. Brindley nodded and quickly added, "No need to fret yeself, lad. I will have one fetched for ye."

"Thank you, Mr. Brindley."

We entered one of the smaller, one-story buildings on the south side of the compound. Judging by the foot traffic, I presumed it was a commissary. "Come, lad. 'Tis time we ate. I am hungry, and ye look like ye can do wi' a *boxty* or two."

Soldiers were eating, playing cards, and drinking. We walked past several tables to an area cordoned off from the rest of the dining hall. The sentry saluted Mr. Brindley and ushered us through an open door. It appeared to be the Major's private dining quarters. A memory resurfaced from the Pub on Peachtree, when Devon and I had rented the VIP area for Alexander's twenty-second birthday. We had found it inconvenient to walk through the crowd of dancers and weave around tables to reach the roped-off section.

Here, we were welcomed by a friendly servant. She curtsied and then approached Mr. Brindley to pour him a drink. "The usual, Major?"

"Aye, Caira, and bring the same for me friend." I looked at Caira and shrugged agreeably, following up with a nod.

Caira returned shortly, carrying a large tray with two plates, each with roasted chicken, a stack of boxty, parsnips, two medium-sized rolls of bread, and two small bowls—one filled with honey and the other with butter. "Thank ye, Caira. That will be all."

"Lad, I have sent word to have a bedchamber prepared for ye at me estate. I will need to get as much information from ye about Oliver Cromwell, with dates and such."

"Is this a safe place to discuss the matter of the falls?" Brindley, his mouth full of chicken, shook his head. Swallowing the food, he washed it down with ale, then explained, "Me estate offers better privacy and discretion. There are soldiers amongst us thought to be spies and Judases, so we canna risk sharing such knowledge here!"

***

After lunch, Brindley and I returned to his office to collect a satchel of sensitive documents from a wardrobe. He stomped on the floor to open the secret compartment and retrieved my case. He then securely locked his office door with two exceptionally large padlocks before we headed back to the courtyard.

I untied Moonlight from the post and led him to the stables, where Brindley, whose horse had already been prepared by a groomsman, waited by the entrance. He presented a brown mahogany leather saddle. It was equipped with saddlebags on either side, secured with a belt and buckle, and included a thick knitted blanket to provide cushioning and prevent sweat buildup on Moonlight's back. Brindley handed me the saddle to hold while he placed the blanket over Moonlight. He then took the saddle and strapped it on while I secured the bit and bridle, making sure it didn't cause Moonlight any discomfort.

Moonlight's beautiful white coat and scattered black markings reminded me of my car, which was white with a black leather interior. Not to mention, the distinctive lightning bolt mark above his right shoulder was similar to the Thor bumper sticker on the rear bumper of my car.

Having never ridden Moonlight, I risked injury. So as not to startle him, I slowly placed my foot in the stirrup and mounted slowly, watching for any sudden reaction. He fussed briefly, but quickly settled down. It was then that I felt that peculiar connection, like the one you feel when you first meet a puppy or dog at an adoption kennel. When it is meant to be, you know.

Chapter 11 – Paramour

The journey took two hours, a slow, rattling progression along a crude trail formed by the frequent passage of horses and wagons. Our path led southeast, running parallel to the coast, and I found myself gazing at the coastline, marveling at the natural, unspoiled beauty of the land. The small, scattered population was evident in the few houses that dotted the route, leaving large stretches of the country uninhabited and wild.

We reached a paved trail composed of small, broken stones with edged grass on either side. Fully grown birch trees intertwined overhead, their branches forming a leafy green tunnel that led directly to the house, similar to the Wexton residence. The estate was grand, a two-story stone structure surrounded by a wild, untamed forest, with the south side of the property facing the vast, wild ocean. The eastern side, where we had entered, held a beauty I had only seen in books and television, embellished with manicured hedges and a stable framed by a vine-filled lattice that connected to the main house.

Two groomsmen and a lady servant waited attentively at the bottom of the steps to the main entrance. The groomsmen took the horses to the stable as the lady servant collected Brindley's satchel and cloak. The Major led the way inside, his boots echoing on the polished wooden floor, where we were welcomed by a beautiful woman in the foyer. Judging by her fine dress and jewelry, I assumed she was Mrs. Brindley.

"Mr. Roberts, I present to ye me wife, Triona Brindley," the Major announced. She offered her hand with a graceful curtsy. I bowed and kissed her hand, a gesture I was quickly learning was expected.

"'Tis a pleasure to make yer acquaintance, Mr. Roberts," she said softly and melodiously. "I received word of yer arrival and had the servants prepare the guest chamber fer ye." I nodded with gratitude and thanked Mrs. Brindley. "Please excuse me. I am needed in the keeping room." She excused herself with a polite nod and headed into the kitchen to oversee the preparations for dinner.

***

Following a high tea of venison, cabbage and potatoes, Brindley ushered me into the parlor. *What a magnificent room,* I thought as I entered, admiring the enormous oil paintings of horses and landscapes adorning the walls. One oil painting in particular, hanging over the grand fireplace, caught my interest. It was an exact replica of the Major's estate and the surrounding forest, painted with astonishing, almost photographic, detail.

A valet, a silent, efficient middle-aged man, filled our cups with wine. Mr. Brindley then ordered him not to allow anyone into the parlor and to ensure no one from the house staff was listening. "Would there be someone making sure the valet would not be listening?" I asked with a hint of humor, a habit I was trying to suppress but was still a part of me.

"No, lad. Mr. Adderley has been in me employ for twenty years, and I trust him with me life. Now, I will need whatever information ye can provide for me."

Before I could divulge any intelligence, Mr. Brindley excused himself to retrieve paper, quill, and ink. This gave me time to bring out my phone and prepare the folder containing the history of Oliver Cromwell. I found the file labeled TCC, "The Cromwellian Cause," but mistakenly opened the folder below it, also labeled TCC, "The Crys Concert." It was a recording of a concert Rey, Devon, Alex, and I had attended in Central Park. The music—familiar dance-house songs—saddened me; I missed my home, my friends, and my own time dearly. I closed my eyes, losing myself in the music, which brought both joy and sorrow in equal measure.

Fully immersed in the sound, I didn't hear Mr. Brindley walk into the room and call my name. "Mr. Roberts, Mr. Roberts, are ye mad?!" Startled by his sudden reappearance, I fumbled my phone, nearly dropping it on the Persian rug.

"My apologies, Mr. Brindley. I was searching for the folder containing the information to provide you and mistakenly opened the wrong file."

He entered quickly, shutting the door behind him. He looked uneasy but composed himself as he sat behind his desk. "I can make no sense of what ye've muttered, but let us be on wi' it." I imagined how my students must have felt when I reprimanded them in class. *I wonder if he's going to put me on time-out,* I thought, a small, closed-mouth grin forming on my lips.

I continued narrating the campaigns led by Oliver Cromwell, those that resulted in the Cromwellian Conquest, as well as the outcomes for Parliament, King Charles I, and the relevant events that followed. Brindley was particularly amused when I mentioned that Cromwell's body would be exhumed from Westminster Abbey three years after his death and his head displayed on a pike for thirty years as a show of the King's power. "Serves the bastard right," he said vehemently, continuing to listen.

Hours of reciting history, or history to be, seemed to have worn out Mr. Brindley, as evidenced by his snoring after falling asleep, his head resting on his desk. I checked the progress of his notes, took a screenshot of the page we were on, and decided to continue where we left off at another time. My throat felt dry after the hours of narrating, so I headed to the kitchen for a drink of water. I was surprised to find Mrs. Brindley sitting at a small dining table, reading her Bible.

"Evening, lad. May I offer ye a measure of whiskey?" she offered politely while closing her Bible and reaching for a cup on the counter behind her.

"Yes, please, I'd be grateful," I said.

She placed her Bible on the mantelpiece and poured the whiskey. "Here ye are, Mr. Roberts," she said, handing me the cup.

"Please call me Myles," I requested, a small, hopeful gesture of camaraderie.

"I would prefer to address ye as Mr. Roberts if it pleases ye." She said this with a prim, unyielding politeness that made her appear distant.

Taken aback by her unexpected reply, I simply nodded. "Of course."

"Forgive me, Mr. Roberts. I hope ye dinna find it intrusive, but I overheard ye giving information to me husband, and a name ye mentioned is familiar to me."

I took long sips of the raw spirit, feeling its potency flow down into my chest, all the while quenching my thirst. I assured Mrs. Brindley that she was not being intrusive. "May I ask to whom you refer?"

"Adam Towell."

"The journeyer... I mean... Mr. Towell?" I stammered, surprised by her knowledge.

She giggled softly. "Sir, I know of the Eas Gorm i Bhfolach whence ye came and its tales. I may portray the quiet and obedient wife, but I have stories of me own."

"Care to elaborate?" I asked, intrigued.

She seemed eager to recount her story, so she smiled, sat, and began. "Before Dujardin and I wed, during our courtship, I chanced upon a stranger in a village in Ballure, near me childhood home in Ballyshannon. Me mam and I often traveled there to purchase fabrics at the cloth merchant, and we occasionally visited the local blacksmith." She paused briefly to refill my cup, then motioned for me to sit while she continued. "One afternoon, while me mother remained at the smithy, I visited the cobbler to reinforce the buckles of me shoes. A slightly older, and might I add, rather handsome man, entered the cordwainer's shop with his eyes fixated on me. I blushed and quickly turned away from his gaze." She placed a hand over her mouth to hide a giggle. "At first glance, I thought him to be a pauper, but then I noticed the full coin pouch he presented from the slit on the side-seam of his britches."

Listening to her story, I couldn't help but wonder if this was a tale of a budding romance. My modern sensibilities told me that a young woman's story of an insistent suitor might not end well, but her bright eyes and smiling lips suggested a different outcome. "So, he intended to make a purchase?" I asked, further intrigued.

"By all means, he did," she replied. "Strangely, he inquired with the shoemaker about acquiring a set of silver girandole earrings. The shoemaker suggested McGavans Bijoux across the way."

"That *is* odd," I said.

"Aye, 'twas," she added. "He left the shop only to return a short time later, though I did not see him enter. I found meself distracted by an interesting article in the Northwest Irish Corantos."

She rose abruptly to prepare another cup of tea for herself. I gallantly took the cup from her hand and served it to her. "One sugar clump, please," she requested.

I set the cup on the table and returned to the chair across from her, a feigned fascination on my face as I waited to hear the conclusion of her story. "The gentleman stood before me, with a posy of flowers in hand and a small white satin box, which he quickly tucked into the pocket of his cloak." While stirring her tea and taking sips, her mouth twitched, forming a smile. She appeared enchanted, reminiscing about the stranger, and seemed eager to carry on with the romantic tale.

"I informed him I was already spoken fer, which he respected, but insisted I take the flowers, which I did. Mother and I returned a sennight later, having forgotten the laces fer the dress she was preparing fer me twentieth birthday celebration."

"Don't tell me he appeared at the cloth merchant?" I asked, acting genuinely surprised.

"While me mother exchanged pleasantries and teatime gossip with the shop owner's wife, I visited the sugar maker's shop to purchase sweetmeats. Would ye believe he was inside the sugar shop, purchasing sweetmeats as well?"

"You don't say!" I responded, raising an eyebrow.

"Aye. I was flabbergasted. Though I should have been ashamed, as I was already being courted, I seemed to have become smitten with the lad." It was seldom, even in my own time, that a woman with her pedigree would disclose such a secret sentiment for another man so openly.

"I presume he became smitten with you as well, Mrs. Brindley?" She blushed, a delicate shade of pink rising on her cheeks, and giggled girlishly. "'Twas discovered later!"

"Ah," I said with understanding.

"With the soirée soon approaching, mother and I and several servants visited the town fer last-minute embellishments. Mother insisted on having the servants handle the errands, but I wanted to ensure every single adornment matched the theme—and secretly, I wanted to meet with the stranger again."

This is getting good. What I'd give for beer and chips! I thought, my mind lost in the compelling narrative.

"Mam felt slightly flushed, so I suggested she return home and have the carriage driver return fer me later in the afternoon. She complied but insisted on leaving the servants behind, so I handed them each a coin and instructed them to return to the manor discreetly." She paused for a moment, her gaze drifting down the corridor toward the entrance to the Major's office, then stood abruptly. "Pardon me fer a moment, Mr. Roberts. Let me check on Dujardin."

The entrance to his office was visible in my line of sight. I watched as Mrs. Brindley peeked inside the room to check on her husband. She went inside to blow out the candles, then returned hastily to continue her story.

"Me apologies, Mr. Roberts, fer me abrupt exit."

"No need for apologies, Mrs. Brindley," I replied sincerely. "I appreciate you feeling comfortable enough to share your story with me. I'm practically a stranger to you."

Her eyes narrowed with a deadpan expression. "Ye are our guest. Mr. Brindley has taken kindly to ye. He is not one to favor just anyone. His sentiments are mine as well."

"That's very kind of you both, Mrs. Brindley!"

"So, back to me *scéal*," she said, her expression brightening again. "Once the servants returned to the manor, I filled me basket with all the trinkets I sought and made me way out of the shop to await the carriage." She blew lightly on her hot tea and took a sip. "I waited but only a moment when the stranger finally appeared. He stood before me and bowed. A gracious gentleman he was. He kept me company until the carriage arrived. We met many times after that and talked at times until one day... Oh, my Mr. Roberts. This is something I should not find meself sharing wi' ye."

"You don't have to go into details, Mrs. Brindley. Not to sound ill-mannered, but I assume you were intimate with him?"

Her cheeks turned a light shade of red, and she nodded. "It was not intended to happen. He was quite charismatic and charming. He chanced upon me one day when I was in a vulnerable state, and that is when it happened."

I grinned slightly, looked away, then back at her, asking in a bold but subtle way, "Were you not afraid Mr. Brindley would know that you... ahem... that you were not... ahem, um...?"

"A *maiden*?" she blurted unreservedly.

"Yes, that!" I said with a light chuckle.

"After turning seventeen, a stranger posing as a groomsman attended to me Welsh cob. He told me the regular groomsman had taken ill. I later found that the groomsman was lying behind the stables, unconscious, after being robbed by this stranger. The bandit dragged me inside the stable and violated me."

"Wow! I'm sorry you had to experience that," I said sympathetically.

"It was dreadful fer me, but I managed to pull meself from the abyss of sadness. I revealed the ordeal to Dujardin. He was sympathetic rather than condemnatory."

"Was the bastard ever found?" I asked.

"Aye. He was castrated, then hanged a few days later for the wickedness he brought upon me and several other women."

To lighten the conversation and appease my curiosity, I switched back to the topic of the stranger. "Did you ever see the village stranger again?" She sighed with contentment, a wistful smile on her lips.

"Aye, years later. Dujardin and I attended a dinner party hosted by the former Earl of Ormond, James Butler. He was an invited guest. We exchanged pleasantries, but after that, I never saw him again." I looked at Mrs. Brindley with narrowed eyes, then glanced at her silver girandole earrings, a perfect, elegant match for the ones she mentioned. Trying not to appear overly surprised, I commented, "So that is why the name Adan Towell was familiar to you. He was the stranger."

The Waters Fall-A Journeyer – Rob Mylo Vazquez

Chapter 12 – Missing Persons Report

Detective Garda Flynn O'Sullivan knocked persistently on the grime-stained door, causing the woman inside to yell furiously, "Just a moment, hold yerself!" The door creaked open, and a pungent, stale cloud of cigarette smoke billowed out, so thick that both Flynn and Agent Tirad instinctively stepped back and gasped for air. The woman who appeared, a lit cigarette in her mouth and a teacup clutched in her hand, mumbled, "What can I do fer'ye?"

Flynn, professional and unfazed, held up his tablet with Myles's picture on the screen. "Good afternoon, ma'am. I am Detective Garda Flynn O'Sullivan, and this is Agent Reymond Tirad. He is an FBI officer from the United States, and we are searching for this man. Have ye seen him of late?"

The woman, with a dismissive flick of her wrist, took a long drag of her cigarette. "No, I'm afraid I havena seen the lad. Now, go on wi' yerself," she demanded rudely, slamming the door shut with a final thud. O'Sullivan, being persistent, slipped a business card under the door and called out, asking her to please call should she come across any information about Myles.

"What now, O'Sullivan?" Rey asked, his shoulders slumped in a posture of despondency.

"Well, we've searched the residential neighborhoods within the vicinity of Caisleán Dhún na nGall—"

"Wait a minute," Rey said, interrupting Flynn mid-sentence as he pulled out his phone, a sudden flash of insight illuminating his tired face. He had just recalled the witness account from the concierge of the Caisleán Dhún na nGall Cottages, which he had documented.

"See here. The concierge, Kevin, said Myles bought two tickets, one for Caisleán Dhún na nGall and another to the Eas Gorm i Bhfolach to visit the day after. Would it be possible he visited both places on the same day?" Rey returned his phone to his pocket, feeling optimistic. "Let's pay Kevin another visit and confirm if our hunch is correct. Then we can expand the search to the area of the waterfall."

The date was June 28, 2022, and Myles had vanished without a trace, a disappearance that was utterly uncharacteristic of him. He was a man known for being solicitous, always checking up on everyone through social media, text messages, or phone calls. En route to the Cottages at Caisleán Dhún na nGall,

Rey received an email notification from the deputy assistant at FBI headquarters, granting him permission and providing the necessary credentials to access Myles's account and retrieve his most recent location. Just as he thought, it pinged Myles's last phone location between the areas of the castle and the waterfall.

"My hunch was right!" Rey told O'Sullivan as they arrived at the welcome center. "I just received word from my deputy assistant confirming the same information about his last known location."

Rey asked O'Sullivan to question Kevin again while he discussed his findings with the assistant director. O'Sullivan hurried inside and approached Kevin, pulling him aside to begin his interrogation. Minutes after the questioning, Flynn, his face alight with discovery, dashed back to Reymond, exclaiming, "Mr. Tirad, Mr. Tirad! Kevin confirmed that Mr. Roberts did indeed take the shuttle at twelve noon on the third of June to the Eas Gorm i Bhfolach after leaving Caisleán Dhún na nGall early that day. He also mentioned that the same shuttle runs daily at noon, which, coincidentally, arrives now."

Rey turned to look at Kevin, who was standing in the doorway, and yelled, "Thank you, thank you so much!"

They both ran toward the green canopy where Romero's Shuttle Service picked up and waved down the driver as he drove in. Rey was overcome with the urge to cry, but he suppressed his emotions, knowing he had to stay in control. He and Myles had been best friends since grade school and had even attended college together. The realization that Myles had disappeared without a trace made his heart ache.

He approached the van and climbed inside, eager to question the driver. "Hello, sir. My name is Reymond Tirad. I'm an FBI agent from the United States. Do you recall seeing this man around the first week of June?"

"Petey Taz at yer service, sir!" Petey replied jovially. He grabbed the tablet from Rey, looking closely at Myles's picture. He seemed unsure at first, but then a glimmer of recognition dawned. "Aye, aye! He was on the Eas Gorm i Bhfolach excursion. He insisted on sitting at the back of the van to get a better view." Rey spontaneously grabbed Mr. Taz by the shoulders and pulled him in for a hug, a gesture of profound relief.

O'Sullivan's phone vibrated repeatedly, pulling him away from the immediate investigation. "I apologize, Mr. Tirad," Flynn said, his voice laced with remorse as he glanced at the message. "This is a matter I urgently need to attend to, related to an ongoing case."

Reymond, though having to continue alone, waved a dismissive hand. "It's quite alright, Flynn. You've done so much already. I'm grateful to you." He offered, with a hint of his natural warmth returning, "Let's meet later for dinner or drinks if you're available—my treat."

"Aye, that sounds grand," O'Sullivan replied. "There's an excellent pub I frequent just twenty minutes from here. They serve the best Guinness and an excellent coddle. Say, at seven p.m.?"

Rey instinctively looked at his watch. "Seven p.m. sounds perfect. Text me the address."

Just as Rey walked past the entrance of the resort, Kevin, the concierge, called out to him. He handed Rey a pamphlet with a detailed map and directions to the waterfall. He then offered Rey a ride on a round golf cart to the far side of the complex, where his rental car was parked—a small gesture of Irish hospitality.

***

It took Rey less than half an hour to reach the Eas Gorm i Bhfolach. He gazed at the surrounding area, captivated by its wild, untamed beauty. Remembering his purpose, he quickly grabbed the tablet from the car's center console, locked the door, and headed to the ticket counter, where a young woman with an eclectic appearance—her hair a riot of bright colors, her clothes a patchwork of textures—greeted him graciously.

"Welcome to the Eas Gorm i Bhfolach, sir. Just yerself visitin' today?" she asked.

Rey swiped open the tablet and showed her Myles's picture. "Have you seen this man recently? Say, around the beginning of June? He supposedly visited the waterfall, arriving in a shuttle van from the Caisleán Dhún na nGall Cottages, and may have been alone."

The young woman took the tablet, her eyes sharp, thoroughly inspecting Myles's picture. She returned the tablet to Rey and nodded. "Aye, I remember the lad quite well. He was the only person from the excursion who bought a ticket into the cave that day, and I found it strange I never saw him return."

A cold knot tightened in Rey's stomach. "Are there any cameras nearby that might have recorded him?"

"No, sir. We havena cameras in the area, not fer many kilometers."

Rey rubbed his face, a weary sigh escaping him. "Will you allow me to enter the cave to search for any hint of a clue?" he asked, trying to conceal the desperation that clawed at his throat.

"I highly doubt ye'll find anything in there, sir. During high tide, anything left behind unfortunately gets washed into the ocean. The attendant, William, usually fetches any trash left before the tide returns—"

Rey cut in quickly, his voice quick with a sudden hope. "Is he here? William? May I speak with him?"

"No, sir. He is not working today, and the day yer mate visited, William was on leave. This I undoubtedly recall, having entered the cave meself—which I rarely do—to direct yer mate out before the tide returned, but I did not find him inside." She paused in thought, her brows raising, gazing distantly for a moment, then continued, "I assumed he had already made his way out. Yer more than welcome to go in and search, but I caution ye, the tide is due to return at 15:44."

Rey checked the time. With only two hours remaining to conduct his search, he hurried down the muddy path, cautiously leaping over the slippery stones. Heedless of any potential injury, he was determined to reach the cave. Rey didn't consider himself a nature enthusiast, but he found the natural vibrations emanating from this place to be both amazing and surreal. He now understood why Myles would have visited. Rey opened the camera app on the tablet to record every inch of the cave's interior. He could always use the footage to review later, should he have missed any clues.

He searched vigilantly, examining every rock and stone, sifting through the pebbles of a trickling, snake-shaped stream running from the cave entrance into the waterfall. As he inched closer to the waterfall, a shiny object wedged beneath a small stone submerged in a puddle caught his attention. Closely inspecting the object, a wave of nausea washed over him as he recognized the bracelet Myles had bought after losing a similar one he had inherited from his late mother, Aida Luz.

The brief moment of panic turned into a flash of fierce certainty as an overwhelming feeling overtook him: his search had brought him closer to possibly finding Myles. He continued investigating the cave, trying to ignore the gnawing unease that comes with being so close to finding something, yet feeling it's beyond reach. But drawing upon his innate optimism, he forced down the rising tide of despair and focused on the next step, sifting through every memory he could resurface, filling himself with enough resolve to continue searching without giving up hope.

An old memory crept into his thoughts of a yoga class he and Myles had attended together in college to earn extra credit. It had taught them both how to think and feel positively, even during the direst of times. For Myles, it had also taught him not to eat before class; he had been prone to gas back then, and Rey had made sure everyone in their dorm knew about it. He had once sent a blast email with an edited video of Myles letting out a loud fart, complete with cartoonish green gas. Myles had been mortified. Now, thinking about it, he felt a great deal of regret for distributing that video, but promised to seek recompense once he found Myles.

He inched closer to the waterfall, determined to be thorough in his search. His shirt dampened as the heavy mist sprayed against his face like tiny grains of sand. Light gusts of wind began blowing in his direction. He contemplated investigating beyond the waterfall itself, hoping to find an entrance, but the rock formation on the opposite side was clearly visible through the transparent wall of water and showed no evidence of anything beyond it. He had a growing suspicion that there was more to this place than it appeared.

A sudden, dizzying sensation of lightheadedness, which he attributed to hunger from not having eaten since early morning, caused him to cease his search. When he turned, the head rush returned, accompanied by a wave of nausea. Remembering the hard candy offered to him by the front desk clerk at the resort, he popped one into his mouth to ease the urge to vomit. Suddenly, a violent squall hit him with the force of a quarterback tackling a player. He landed on his back, gasping for air, gazing at the spinning ceiling of the cave. Despite his best efforts to stand, he fell back repeatedly, blinking rapidly to clear the haze, then he blacked out.

The Waters Fall-A Journeyer – Rob Mylo Vazquez

Chapter 13 – Parliamentarian Joan

Weeks had passed since I arrived at the Brindley estate, and for the first time since my arrival in this century, I was beginning to feel a sense of permanence. My bedroom, with its high ceiling and large windows, overlooked one of the two ponds on the south lawn of the manor. It was a beautiful, tranquil scene, but my twenty-first century mind found it difficult to comprehend the lavish lifestyle of military men in this era. This was radically different from my time, where veterans are fortunate to receive any kind of stipend, let alone a grand manor.

I spent a major part of the day in my room, diligently recording my experiences using the primitive writing implements I had found on the desk beside the bed. I was determined to document every detail, every emotion, every chilling realization of my predicament.

When a knock came at the door, I quickly hid the papers under a wooden slate, abiding by Brindley's strict orders of discretion. I opened the door to find Mr. Adderley, the valet, standing on the threshold. He held a tray with a small, round plate of goat cheese, a few pieces of flatbread, and a cup of wine. He also held a large white box, which he carried under his arm.

"Thank you, Mr. Adderley," I said, taking the tray from him as he walked inside. Adderley placed the white box on the bed and returned to take the tray from me, setting it on the table next to the fireplace.

"Master Brindley requests your presence in the library at 5 p.m.," Adderley informed me while opening the white box.

"What is that?" I asked, pointing at the box with a curious finger.

He reached inside and pulled out a rather sharp-looking suit. "The master has requested this be your attire for the evening, sir," he replied flatly and formally. He carefully laid the clothes across the bed, placing a pair of shoes by the bedroom entrance as he left the room.

I picked up the new clothes, inspecting the white linen *léine* first, admiring the ruff collar and matching ruffled cuffs. I held it by the shoulders and spun it around, giving it a once-over. Neatly folded underneath, wrapped in a soft cloth, I found a black velvet, long-sleeved doublet with matching britches and white stockings. *If Alex and Devon were to see me wearing this outfit, they would have brought out their phones at lightning speed and snapped as many pictures as they could to post immediately on social media,* I thought, smiling at the thought of my friends.

***

As I descended the spiral staircase, I heard voices coming from the library and saw servants bustling in and out. Before I reached the doorway, Sadie, Mr. Adderley's second, stopped me with a message.

"Sir, you are requested to join Master Brindley in the parlor rather than the library." I nodded and headed to the parlor, where Brindley sat looking visibly uneasy, his expression both gruff and pensive.

"Is everything all right, Mr. Brindley?" I asked with concern.

"I am far from all right, Mr. Roberts. In fact, I am utterly disturbed," Brindley replied, a dark look in his eyes. "It appears Oliver Cromwell's exploits have been set into motion, at me front door of all places!"

My head cocked, peering at him with interest. "What makes you think that?"

"Does the name Elizabeth Alkin have any meaning t'ye?" I scratched my forehead, my eyes squinted in thought, struggling to recall the name. Then it came to me: Parliamentarian Joan!

"Yes! Parliamentarian Joan. She was—" I paused for a moment, rethinking the verb tense. "She *is* a spy for the Parliamentarians, originally hired by both the Earl of Essex and Sir William Waller. If I recall correctly, following the earls' and Mr. Waller's tenure, she was employed by Cromwell's right-hand man, Thomas Fairfax."

Brindley pounded his fist on the desk, bellowing, "Good God, man, she's here in me home, uninvited, I might add."

Before joining his invited guests, Brindley ordered Mr. Adderley to keep a close watch on Ms. Alkin. Adderley's expression showed he was familiar with the reason for the request.

I followed Brindley into the library, grabbing a glass of wine from a servant's tray on my way in, then situated myself by a window to observe the crowd. I was excited and fascinated to be among figures who seemed to have popped out of a history book. It felt like being in the Haunted Mansion at Disney World, surrounded by socializing apparitions.

Several guests exhibited expressions of surprise as a known official entered the library, holding a walking stick in one hand and escorting a mature, dainty woman with the other. Brindley rushed over to me, his voice a scandalous whisper. "That is Denzil Holles with Elizabeth Alkin in tow, not his wife, Jane!"

"The notorious Parliamentarian spy, otherwise known as Parliamentarian Joan," I whispered comically. At first glance, she appeared to be an average debutante who frequented balls and elite dinners. However, according to history, she was known to be a ruthless and dangerous spy.

"I sensed malice exuding from her mere presence the second she entered," Brindley expressed, a scowl emanating from his face. "Why would he arrive with that jezebel in hand and not his wife? I am puzzled!"

I bit my lip to contain my laughter, amused by his portrayal of a bitter and angry woman. "Denzil Holles was known for visiting brothels incessantly, so he must be under the assumption that his companion is a courtesan," I explained. "She may have befriended him to gain his trust and extort information to bring back to Thomas Fairfax, or even to Cromwell himself."

Still indignant, Brindley excused himself, bypassing the wine and going straight for the whiskey to calm his nerves.

Parliamentarian Joan gawked at me from across the room with a look of familiarity, possibly believing she knew me from somewhere. She tapped Denzil Holles's arm, excused herself, and made her way toward me. She stood before me, her gaze scrutinizing me from head to foot like a dog inspecting a new bone. She extended an arm for a hand kiss, then remarked expressively, with a flirtatious tone, "Are you related to Henry Rich of Holland House?"

I raised an eyebrow and promptly replied, "No, ma'am, I come from the... the colonies. Myles Roberts at your service."

She glanced at me, smiling beguilingly. "The resemblance is uncanny. I dare say you were cousins," she said, chuckling ingratiatingly. I gave a smile to match her falseness, recognizing her audacity. She may have sensed my expression and that any attempts at extorting information would be futile. So, with a whispered "hmm," she curtsied in dismissal and rejoined the crowd.

I chuckled and stepped out of the library and into the garden for a breath of fresh air. I found myself in the company of Brindley and Mr. Holles. "Mr. Roberts, Mr. Roberts, come here, lad. Allow me to introduce ye to Denzil Holles, one of the eleven members of the House of Commons of England." He then turned to Holles for introductions. "Mr. Holles, this is Myles Roberts of the House of... Atlanta."

I bowed, then offered a handshake, turning to look at Mr. Brindley, who gave an awkward smile and a wink.

"House of Atlanta? I cannot say I have heard of it; my apologies. What brings you to Ireland, Mr. Roberts?" Holles inquired.

I froze for a moment, unsure of what to say. My lips pursed as I thought of an answer. "Harvard... Harvard University. I collaborated on a project with Henry Dunster at Harvard University in the colony of Massachusetts and came to Donegal for research."

"I met Mr. Dunster on a pilgrimage to Cambridge in early 1641 with my late wife, Dorothy," Holles replied excitedly. "He is an exceptional clergyman and an equally aggressive leader."

Awkwardly agreeing with an "if only you knew" grin, I simply replied, "Yes, that he is." My heart fluttered, thinking of what would happen should Holles, Dunster, and I ever find ourselves in the same room. *That would really suck!*

Mr. Brindley chimed in, suggesting we return to the library before dinner was served. He now displayed a joyous expression; likely due to the number of drinks he had consumed since the afternoon.

I remained observant of Ms. Alkin, as requested by Mr. Brindley. Upon informing him of her reputation as an enticer—or, as he later put it, a succubus— he overemphasized the need for discretion to avoid the risk of revealing my true identity.

"Mr. Brindley, with all due respect, I'm an adult and capable of safeguarding secrets, especially those of my own!" I strongly declared. Brindley stared icily with a vexed expression, then swiftly changed his demeanor, tipping his head forward in a show of agreement. Major General Brindley, a leader and an enforcer, was not accustomed to having anyone, especially a near stranger, disobey an order, but he surrendered this time.

I caught sight of Elizabeth Alkin parading around the library, striking up conversations primarily with men of prominent nobility and military influence. "She's ruthless at digging for information. I'm sure she's eager to take anything remotely incriminating back to Mr. Fairfax," I whispered to Brindley.

"Yes, I have been observing her like a hawk, and I do have the perfect solution to remedy that shrew!" he claimed expressively. He scampered out of the library undetected, on what appeared to be a secret mission.

I continued my reconnaissance mission, keeping a close watch on the English spy while Brindley completed his. She appeared to be deep in the drink, moving from guest to guest, striking up brief conversations and laughing rather loudly and obnoxiously.

After some time, I stepped into the hallway to search for Brindley. I headed down the corridor and found him coming out of the servants' quarters with Sadie on his arm. Sadie was radiant, dressed like an aristocrat. She wore a gold and white gown laced with silk embroidery, and her hair was rolled up in a bun, tied with an embroidered ribbon.

"Wah-how," I expressed, surprised.

"Sadie has been instructed to keep Ms. Alkin distracted and separated from the men until it is time to move into the dining room," Brindley explained.

"Smart move, 007!"

The Waters Fall-A Journeyer – Rob Mylo Vazquez

Chapter 14 – Tastes Like Chicken

The dinner bell rang, its deep, sonorous clang drowning out the loud conversations in the library. "Dinner is served!" Mr. Adderley announced with the authority of a town crier.

During my time at the Brindley estate, I had dined in the dining hall many times, but the arrangement for this event was astonishing. The table was impossibly long, able to accommodate twenty-four guests or more. It was a vision of opulence, adorned with blue and white ceramic vases and plates, and crystal candleholders that threw dancing light across the room. Glass goblets were used for the wine, along with gleaming silver dinnerware. Assorted trays filled with pastries were spread throughout, while others held a colorful bounty of pears, apples, and grapes. An elevated rectangular platform sat in the middle of the table, embellished with bowls of hazelnuts, cinnamon sticks, and aromatic pomander balls. *I can't believe I had to travel over three hundred years into the past to attend such an elaborate dinner as this,* I joked to myself, rolling my eyes.

The servants entered the dining room in formation, each carrying serving trays. Some held large, deep soup bowls, which were placed on long tables lining the walls, all in a precise serving order. The soup bowls were filled with a thick, creamy Irish mushroom and potato soup, and the trays held an array of side dishes: rumbledethumps, roasted potatoes, colcannon, cole slaw, caramelized carrots, bread, and sides of rich gravy, sweet honey, and butter. All served as an accompaniment to an undisclosed main dish. I, being a self-proclaimed observant person, seemed to be the only one protesting the absence of a protein. *Do these people think I'm a vegetarian?* I wondered, thinking of refusing to taste any of the food in silent protest.

Just then, another set of servers entered the dining room, hauling two immense silver trays holding... peacocks. Freaking multicolored peacocks, with their full feathers and tails still attached. My first thought was that they were just decorative, and the meat was being kept warm inside. I was quickly disabused of this notion.

The massive trays were carefully laid on the elevated platform. The servers then grabbed the peacocks—it took two of them to manage each bird. One took hold of the neck while the other held the tail from its stem, and they simultaneously lifted them to reveal what I dreaded seeing: an actual gilded roast peacock inside. I was momentarily mortified but also astonishingly intrigued, having never eaten peacock meat. I never knew the fowl was even edible, but having been stranded in the seventeenth century, I threw caution to the wind and decided to take the plunge.

The carver delicately sliced the feathered creature into thick servings, plating the bird in a wing-shaped pattern, and then poured Burgundy over the meat, which was meant to tenderize it. I, however, remained hesitant about consuming it.

"Is the bird not to yer liking, Mr. Roberts?" Mrs. Brindley asked softly with a hint of concern.

"I've... never had it this way before," I expressed with an awkward grin, trying to sound convincing.

Mr. Holles, seated across from me, chimed in, "Give it a try, chap. 'Tis divine!"

I smirked dryly and, with a heart full of courage, grabbed the knife and fork, cut myself a hefty sliver, doused it with a bit more Burgundy, brought it to my mouth, and hesitantly, delicately bit into it.

"Wow," I expressed with awkward enthusiasm. "It does taste quite good," I added, savoring the morsel.

"Are ye now pleased with the flavor, Mr. Roberts?" Mrs. Brindley inquired.

"Yes. In fact, it tastes like chicken."

***

The guests conversed among themselves, enjoying the fine wine and food. For a moment, it brought back memories of Christmas Eve dinners with my family at my childhood home. My reverie was broken by none other than Scrooge herself. Elizabeth Alkin. She was sounding off vile comments about Catholicism and how the Protestant church should be the governing religion in all of Ireland.

"Catholicism and Protestantism both espouse faith—aye—I agree," Brindley countered, keeping his voice steady but firm. "but not solely *sola fide*. Equally honorable deeds are also rewarded by our Lord and Savior, madam."

"Rescuing a sheep from being slaughtered or releasing a butterfly from the mouth of a snake is not the means of reaching salvation. *Justificatio*, by *sola fide* and riddance of the vile swine ruling these lands presently is, by all accounts, the means of bringing upon eternal salvation!" she declared, her voice rising in a furious, self-righteous rant.

"May I remind ye this is a social gathering, madam," Mrs. Brindley remarked in a low, dangerous growl. "'Tis neither the place nor time to be discourteous nor condescending, so if ye are to continue with yer ridiculous ranting, I demand ye leave me table at once!"

"Oh no, she didn't," I whispered in jest. *Mrs. Brindley is not a woman to cross*!

"Will you be the one to remove me, Mistress Major? I will allow it if you so wish," Alkin replied, her eyes narrowing into dangerous slits.

Mrs. Brindley responded to Alkin's invitation by sliding back from her chair. She dashed around the table toward her, a peacock leg raised high in the air, intending to bash it on her head. Mr. Brindley quickly reached out and restrained his wife's arm, an action that oddly agitated Alkin even more. Obviously intoxicated and truculent, she grabbed a handful of potatoes and tossed them at Mrs. Brindley. Understandably alarmed, the guests swiftly exited the dining area, while those who remained were genuinely concerned and scrambled to de-escalate the situation as Alkin continued to hurl food toward Mrs. Brindley and them.

"Ms. Alkin, you need to calm yourself," I shouted, stepping out of my chair and bolting in her direction. I came up behind her and held her in a restrictive hold, causing her to gyrate her body rebelliously against my grip. She freed an arm, brandished a knife, and flailed it, catching my forearm and inflicting a gash, causing me to lose my grip on her.

Denzil Holles created a distraction by clanking a goblet with a spoon, the high-pitched sound piercing the chaos. This allowed Brindley to approach Alkin from behind and quickly restrain her. He then pulled her away from the dining room. This gave Mrs. Brindley the chance to tend to my wound. She poured whiskey on the cut, the sting a sharp, cleansing fire, then doused a cloth to use as a bandage. "Are ye in discomfort, Mr. Roberts?" she asked while tightening the knot on the cloth. "Is the pressure excessive?"

"It feels fine. Thank you, Mrs. Brindley," I assured her. I excused myself to follow the noise coming from the foyer, where I stumbled upon a group of soldiers from Brindley's Infantry Regiment taking Alkin into custody. She thrashed about like a reeled-in fish, heedless of her actions.

"Women should be flogged for merely touching a cup of wine," Brindley expressed, clearly angry and uneasy, his face filled with furious contempt.

"There's never an excuse to beat a woman, Mr. Brindley. She was plainly acting out against her failed attempts at extortion, that's all!"

"Aye, lad. Ye speak truth," Brindley said, his anger giving way to a hint of regret. "I should never have suggested such an act of violence. Anger overcomes me when I am in the presence of buffoons such as she."

Mrs. Brindley calmed the remaining guests, directing them to the parlor and instructing Mr. Adderley and Sadie to provide them with wine, whiskey, and hors d'oeuvres, hoping to salvage the evening. After freshening up, she joined them in the parlor, apologizing for the calamity and reassuring them that the instigator had been removed. She also disclosed that Alkin would face repercussions for her misadventure. Brindley and I rejoined the guests as well. They were concerned about my wound, but I reassured them I would recover.

"What is to become of Ms. Alkin?" Lady Montgomery asked in her high-pitched, crisp English lilt.

"She will sleep herself into sobriety and will be ousted at once come morn. I recommended Denzil Holles keep watch of her and oversee her immediate return to England!"

"She should be cast out of Ireland permanently!" Lady Montgomery proclaimed strongly while wiping the stains from her silk gown, having been one of the few to receive the brunt of Alkin's storm.

"She has certainly become a leper in this house," Mrs. Brindley expressed, as she handed another napkin doused with lemon water to Lady Montgomery.

The events of the evening had worn on me, so I excused myself and headed to my room to change out of the "Halloween costume" and meditate. I reflected on Alkin's actions and wondered if the events that had just taken place were the fuel for Oliver Cromwell's fire. Whether or not they were, nothing was going to stop the bloodbath that was to come.

Chapter 15 – Honor of My Word

The attendant at the exhibit handed me a pair of latex gloves, their thin, white film stretched taut across my fingers. It was an unspoken honor to be allowed to handle the Saxon wheellock on display, as typically no one other than the curator was trusted to do so. It was one of the unexpected benefits of being a history teacher and having a best friend who was an FBI agent. Rey had called in a favor to the curator—whom he knew from prior exhibits—to allow me to hold the piece.

The handle was embellished with separate silver plates on either side, and a pear-shaped pommel at the end, worn smooth by centuries of hands. A small, oddly placed brass plate, original to the weapon, was fixed to the butt of the grip, with the initials "A.T." carved on it. It was a sizable pistol, and the various added plates and pommel made it quite heavy for a handgun, its weight a surprising heft in my gloved hands.

I asked the curator to provide a verified authenticity of the pistol's origins, but all he could produce was an authenticated certificate with a simple date. There was nothing concrete showing its original owners. The cogs of my academic mind began spinning, turning over every piece of information I had absorbed about the era. I found myself trying to connect a sixteenth-century Saxon wheellock to a historical figure whose name fit those enigmatic initials. It was a puzzle I couldn't solve, but one that stayed with me long after I had left the exhibit.

***

August 3, ~~2022~~, 1648

Two months have passed since my bewildering arrival in this century, and for the first time, I was beginning to feel a strange, unsettling sense of permanence in this epoch. I have saved a man and killed another. My arm had been slashed with a knife by a madwoman, and I still can't figure out what strange and unnatural anomaly brought me here. I feel a growing need to set out and find answers to the insistent questions of why—why me, and why this specific time. I acclimated myself to this time in a short period, so I feel confident to venture out and seek the answers on my own. I would be...

"Mr. Roberts, are ye presently occupied?" Brindley bellowed while pounding boisterously on my door, making the very timbers of the manor seem to shudder.

"No, come in, come in," I called out, a bit bothered by his uncivilized knock, which seemed more suited to a stable door than a gentleman's chamber. "Is everything all right with you, sir?"

"Yes, lad, why d'ye ask?" he replied, a clueless look on his face.

"Never mind," I said, grimacing. "What can I do for you today, sir?"

He abruptly brushed aside the notes lying on the desk, scattering them, and unrolled a large parchment map of what looked to be Ireland. "I thought about yer concerns and desire to explore fer answers, so I brought ye this wee map of Ireland from me library and took the liberty of circling various localities in which trusted colleagues reside who may be of help to ye," he exclaimed, his face alight with an almost boyish optimism. "I have assigned trusted men of me regiment to deliver word of yer arrival and have given them me personal orders to keep watch over ye should ye encounter any malefactors!" he added, rolling up the map with a flourish and handing it to me.

"Thank you, sir. How soon before I'm to go?" I asked, staring at the rolled map. "To be honest, I'm beginning to get cabin fever!"

Brindley looked unsettled by my words, his brow furrowing as he reached out and placed a large, warm hand on my forehead. "Is something amiss, lad? Are ye unwell? Shall I call on the physician?"

I burst into laughter, quickly replying, "I'm not with fever, sir. Cabin fever is a term used in my time to describe being inside a place for too long."

"Well, that is good to know, lad. Canna have ye falling ill if ye are to embark on yer journey in a fortnight," he responded, sounding visibly relieved.

"Oh, that soon?" I asked, a bit staggered by the swiftness of his plans.

"Yes, lad. If the invasion is to begin next August, according to yer history books, ye must make yer way expeditiously and discover if yer destiny *is* indeed woven into the coming battle!"

"Agreed. I'll get myself prepared then," I said, reaching to collect the map. "I'll need to read and familiarize myself with it. I'm a quick study, so I should be able to maneuver myself… hopefully without getting lost."

"As the time grows closer, Adderley will make the needed preparations for weapons and provisions for ye to take on yer journey," Brindley proclaimed, echoing with authority as he exited the room, leaving me alone with my thoughts and the vast, unknown map.

***

I spent the better part of the day studying and acquainting myself with the geography of the land, meticulously tracing the routes with my finger, strategizing the best paths to follow. Feeling both nervous and excited, a mix of apprehension and anticipation, I poured myself a generous glass of whiskey. Then, I powered on my phone and played meditation music I kept stored in an offline folder. Hopefully, this would help take the edge off and allow me to *whoosah. Sláinte.* Here's to my next adventure!

***

Overwhelmed by a sudden wave of anxiety, I woke up before sunrise and prepared early to join my hosts for breakfast. The two weeks had passed with disorienting swiftness, and I couldn't help but feel a sense of sadness as I prepared to leave. The Brindleys had become parental figures to me during my stay, showing great attentiveness and care, much like the MacKinneys. Their presence had made my time here not only bearable but truly enjoyable, which is why bidding farewell to them now proved to be so challenging.

Watered and fed, Moonlight looked stouthearted, just as I felt, eager to step out and venture forth. I had spent these past few weeks acquainting myself with the steed, gaining his trust by grooming him daily and providing him with treats such as apples and carrots—apples being his clear favorite. Brindley had insisted I get familiar with Moonlight should the time arise when I would have to leave, not realizing the time would come so soon. Now, knowing without a doubt that the time had arrived, I felt blessed and fortunate to have such a dependable companion.

Galway was the first stop marked on the map Brindley had provided. It was located southwest of Murvagh, near the shores of the North Atlantic Ocean, where a man by the name of Oistin Killian, rumored to be an Elder Folk, lived. According to Brindley's notes, Killian was purported to be the first to discover Adam Towell as a journeyer. It was said that Mr. Towell took up residence for many years with Killian and his family, earning his keep as a farmhand, but I found that story questionable. After all, Adam Towell was rumored to have disappeared right after the death of Sir Henry Bagenal.

Could it have been that the Earl of Tyrone, Hugh O'Neill, had extracted Towell and placed him in a 'witness protection' program of sorts? I thought. There was a strange disconnect, a gap between the world of the story and my own. *Maybe I'll find the answers I need in Galway.*

***

Traveling for most of the day, I stopped to check the map and searched for a safe place to hunker down for the night. Veering less than a mile eastward from the trail, I came across a heavily wooded grove with a creek just off its edge, a spot dense enough to keep me undetected throughout the night. Though water was easily obtainable, I realized that fruits, vegetables, and hay for Moonlight were not. The Port of Sligo was near the grove, so I planned to visit it in the morning to acquire provisions, just as Mr. Brindley had suggested.

Sleeping outdoors alone for the first time was a burdensome reality. The constant rustling of unseen wildlife kept me on edge, and the snap of twigs falling from trees as critters scampered about on the branches felt like a drumbeat of danger. I paced around trying to find a rhythm, hoping sleep would finally overtake me. Finally, feeling heavy-eyed and drained, I lay down between the campfire and Moonlight, the horse's warm presence a slight comfort against the cold ground, and drifted off.

I found myself adrift on a log, bobbing up and down on the ocean as the waves swayed. I kept a tight grip on the log to avoid falling into the cold, dark water. That's when I caught sight of a castle in the distance with a female figure dressed in a white gown, her flaming red hair billowing in the wind. She stood waving on the shore. Though the sound of her voice was faint, I could discern, "Bring the fish, bring the fish!" My nose was suddenly filled with a strong, fishy odor I surmised came from the port, which roused me from the dream. "Man, that stinks," I said, covering my nose as I stirred, trying to escape the stench. "Guess that's my cue to get up!"

***

Entering the port, I found a post beside a watering hole, dismounted Moonlight, and secured him. The port was teeming with anglers boarding and disembarking their *currachs*, hauling scores of fish with their nets. *It seems like catching fish is best done in the early mornings in any century*; I thought. I approached a young angler who looked to be no older than fifteen and asked politely, "Good day, young man. Can you tell me where I can find a merchant who sells fruits and hay to feed my horse?"

"Aye, sir. Walk past the Ouzel Galley just there," the young angler replied, pointing at a sizable vessel, its sails furled against the mast. "A merchant by the name of Geary Alymer will aid ye and yer horse!"

"Much obliged, young man," I responded, then handed him a silver sixpence.

His eyes widened, and he took the coin, turning it over in his hand as if it were a rare jewel. "Thank ye, sir, thank ye, thank ye so much. God bless ye!" he expressed with gratitude.

I patted him on the head and continued down the dock toward the merchant's shopfront, recognizing it by the multiple stacks of hay and crates neatly piled.

"Good day, sir. I was told I can purchase provisions for my horse from you."

"Good day, lad. Geary Alymer at yer service," he cheerfully responded warmly. "What will ye be needin' this fine *maidin*?"

"Just a bushel of hay and a sackful of fruits and vegetables, preferably carrots and apples if you have them."

He bustled about, packing the produce into a sack, then dragged the bushel of hay and set it by my feet. "Three copper Irish pennies for the hay and another three copper Irish halfpennies for the produce, me friend!" Sifting through my pouch, I took out one shilling and gave it to the merchant. Mr. Alymer then ordered someone, who I presumed was his son, to fetch the sack and carry the hay for me.

"I can manage it on my own, Mr. Alymer, thank you," I said, then picked up the sack with one hand and lifted the hay with the other. I refused to accept the remaining coinage from the shilling I paid with, prompting Mr. Alymer to lay one hand on my chest, a look of heartfelt gratitude on his face. "This will allow me to take a few days to spend with me family, sir. Greatly generous of ye!"

"Enjoy your well-earned rest, Mr. Alymer." I responded. I flung the sack over my shoulder, held the hay by the bound rope, and strolled down the dock toward the hitching post.

I dropped the sack of produce abruptly, my heart lurching with a sudden, cold panic. Moonlight was gone. I hollered, "My horse! Where on earth is my horse?!"

I then saw the young angler helper running toward me, yelling, "Sir, sir, the horse, the white one. Was that yer horse?" he asked, panting.

"Yes, did you see someone take it?"

"Aye, sir! I saw a man untie him and lead him in the direction of the Ouzel Galley, just off the north dock—"

I interrupted, "Yes, I know which one. Please keep watch over my things. There's another shilling in it for you!"

"Aye, sir. I'll be keepin' guard!"

I made a frantic dash toward the Ouzel Galley. Spotting a plank used to lead animals onboard the ship gave me a sickening feeling. I was afraid Moonlight might have been taken on board. I then saw Mr. Alymer walking toward me. He approached me, asking with concern, "Mr. Roberts, ye look troubled. Is something amiss?"

"A young angler helper has just informed me he saw my horse being led toward the Ouzel Galley."

"Say *nil* more, Mr. Roberts. The captain of the Ouzel Galley is a good patron and a friend. I will personally take ye to 'im and inquire about yer horse!"

Overwhelmed with relief, I reached inside my pouch to hand him a coin, but he stopped me. "Mind ye sense, Mr. Roberts. Ye've done plenty fer me. Allow *me* to help ye now," he said, then turned to his son and ordered assertively, "Go and mind the merchandise, Digul. I will return shortly."

Mr. Alymer and I headed up the gangway, the aged wood groaning under our weight. We made our way onto the ship, where we were confronted by a crew member standing guard. Looking sour-faced, he exclaimed unmannerly, "State ye business!"

"Let them through," the captain commanded, his voice a deep, resonant rumble.

"Thank ye, Captain Boyle." Geary Alymer pulled me by the arm and guided me to the captain. "Allow me to introduce me friend, Myles Roberts. It has come to his attention that one of ye men may have come into possession of his horse. A young angler helper witnessed it."

"Yer servant, Mr. Roberts. Ye have me sincerest apologies fer any wrongdoings on the part of me men. I am an honorable seafarer, and I expect the same of me crew." He bowed, placing a hand over his heart. "I am ashamed to know that ye belongings have been trespassed upon. Let us visit the stable and see if yer horse is there."

I was pleasantly surprised, despite the misconceptions in history books, to encounter a seventeenth-century sea captain who appeared to be a decent man. "I appreciate you, Captain Boyle."

I hope this is not a too-good-to-be-true scenario; I thought, my apprehension still warring with my relief.

We made our way below the creaky deck. I noticed an unusual number of horses being kept inside the ship's stables, but I felt instant relief when I saw Moonlight. He neighed the minute he saw me, shaking his head excitedly. I approached him, reaching out to comfort him. "There, there now, buddy, you're okay. I'm here with you now."

I turned to shake the captain's hand, but I noticed the friendly smile he had worn when we first met had vanished, replaced by a cunning look that caused a prickle of unease to crawl up my spine. "Thank you, Captain Boyle," I expressed hesitantly, pulling back my hand slightly as he ignored the gesture. "Is something wrong, Captain?"

"How much is yer horse worth t'ye, lad?" the captain asked; a note of warning resonated in his low tone. I stared at him for a moment, dumbfounded by his response. I examined the faces of the men in the room, all of whom mirrored the captain's shrewd expression. Then, like a puzzle coming together, the pieces clicked into place. My first instinct was to bash the captain's head open, but, outnumbered and outmatched, I kept my composure, responding swiftly, "What do you mean, how much is he worth to me? He's my horse, and his worth should not even be a matter to discuss."

I turned to Mr. Alymer, who expressed a wry, unapologetic grin. "Were you in on this?" I asked through clenched teeth.

He cocked his head with a shrug, replying dryly, "*An captaen* pays better!"

"You son of a bitch!" I bellowed.

In some odd way, the scenario played out in my head as if it were a "whodunit" movie, in which the unfolding scheme was revealed. The young angler helper had watched as I dismounted Moonlight. Taking notice of the mahogany leather saddle, he had run to Mr. Alymer's son, Digul, who in turn informed his father that I sought to buy produce and hay. Assuming I carried a considerable number of coins, he had instructed a crew member, on orders of the captain, to untether Moonlight from the post and hold him for ransom.

"You shady bastards won't get a damn cent from me. I'll guarantee that!" I voiced angrily and took hold of Moonlight's reins in an effort to lead him out of the stable.

One henchman, a brutish man with a missing tooth, pulled the reins from my hands and twisted my arms behind my back, forcing me to stand in front of the captain as he proclaimed, "Unless ye're ready to pay a sizable number of coins, yer horse will remain here on me ship."

Feeling a hot flush of anger rising to my head, I snapped, "The only sizable thing you'll receive from me is my foot up your crusty ass, motherfucker!" Finding amusement amid my anger, the captain ordered the men to remove me from the ship and ensure I wouldn't return unless it was with a full purse to offer.

As the men dragged me down the gangway, I managed to pull one arm free, taking hold of the man's neck in a guillotine choke. I seized the opportunity and punched the other henchman, breaking his nose, evident from the gush of blood spewing, and instantly knocking him out. Two other crew members hurried down the plank to aid the one still in my hold. Seeing this, I quickly changed my stance and hooked him under his arms. I hurled him toward the other two like a battering ram, causing them both to fall overboard.

"Take hold of him at once," the captain ordered from the deck, prompting me to swing the man still in my clutches overboard. This allowed me to run onto the dock, cross the pier, and search for a place to hide and gather my bearings.

I stumbled upon a storage shed filled with fishing nets and hid inside, hoping to remain undiscovered. I then heard movement just outside the door, so I reached for my *sgian-dubh*, preparing myself once again for the possibility of taking yet another life. As the door swung open, I lunged forward, but I was suddenly intercepted by someone I perceived to be a crewman. Fortunately, he ended up being one of Major General Brindley's men.

"Mr. Roberts, no cause for alarm. I am First Lieutenant James Olson of the General's regiment, sent by Major General Brindley himself to keep watch over you. I am aware of your encounter with the captain and his cohorts, which will be remedied," he explained in a single breath. "Your horse will be safe and returned to you, honor of my word, sir!"

Though not unheard of, I found it odd to hear a trusted lieutenant of an Irish regiment speak with an English accent. I recalled how, throughout history, English redcoats sided with the opposing country. Whether it was with the Scots or the Irish—certain redcoats were raised as Catholic and didn't share the same beliefs as the Protestant church; therefore, they fought to support the supposed enemy.

Lieutenant Olson led the way to the back of the storage shed, climbing over empty, discarded crates strewn in the alleyway. We reached a covered area where a group of plainclothesmen waited. I assumed they were part of the regiment as well, as they saluted the lieutenant and then guided us to a shortcut leading back to the Ouzel Galley.

We spotted two guards at the bottom of the gangway and a third at the top, with their muskets and swords at the ready. I imagined they were waiting for my return. The soldiers split up into groups: one to canvas the area, three to scale the pier just below the gangway, and myself, the lieutenant, and two others to stand watch, awaiting the signal from the sentry canvassing the area to alert us when it was safe to move ahead once the crewmen on watch were distracted.

The three-regiment soldiers hiding below the gangway tapped on the plank to attract the attention of the two men on lookout as the one standing guard at the top of the gangway advanced to investigate. When he reached the bottom of the plank, the lieutenant's men popped up over the gangway and grabbed the crewmen by their ankles. Using considerable force, the soldiers pulled on their legs, causing them to fall forward. They were then dragged underneath the pier, where the soldiers placed them in chokeholds, rendering them unconscious.

The lookout whistled, a piercing sound that signaled the coast was clear.

We crept quietly up the gangway. The soldiers kept their pistols and swords drawn, and I had my *sgian-dubh* in hand, having left my pistol stored in the under-pouch of Moonlight's saddle. The captain and his crewmen were unaware of our surreptitious infiltration, giving us the upper hand to surprise and incapacitate them. "Take the west passageway, and we will follow the east," Lieutenant Olson commanded in a gravelly whisper as we inched toward the stables. Maneuvering to the eastern side, I found it peculiar that it was now only the lieutenant and me on the prowl, having lost sight of the soldiers heading west.

"Where did the men go, Lieutenant?" I asked, feeling a bit bewildered.

"No need to fret over that, sir. We have the situation under control. Continue behind me!" he ordered with a stern tone.

Reaching the entrance to the ship's stable, we saw that neither the captain nor his crew were in sight, so we entered discreetly. Unbeknownst to us, the captain and his men were lying in wait, buried under piles of hay. "You thought ye and yer friend could board me ship without me knowledge and attempt to take hold of me property, eh?" the captain mocked in a growl. He pointed a pistol at me and motioned to one of his thugs to relieve the lieutenant of his pistol. "I intended to sell ye me horse for one pound; the price just went up to four!" he exclaimed with a callous smirk.

"You fucking insane Anne Bonny wannabe!"

"I'm not familiar with whom ye refer, but it does not change the fact that I have forbidden yer presence on board me ship, so I will allow ye and yer friend passage, unharmed, once I reach the count of ten, then I canna guarantee yer safety!"

"Come on, Mr. Roberts, let us do as the captain commands," Lieutenant Olson suggested, tugging on my shoulder and signaling with a subtle wink.

Once we turned to exit the stables, the lieutenant shouted, "Get down, Mr. Roberts," taking hold of the back of my neck and shoving me to the ground.

The lieutenant's soldiers appeared as if from nowhere, with pistols drawn and aimed intently. Without hesitation, they shot at the crew, knocking the pistols from their hands with precise marksmanship.

Lieutenant Olson lunged forward, performing a dive roll toward the captain, snatched the pistol from his hand, and stood firm in front of him, the barrel buried into his forehead. "I suggest you stand down and command your men to do so as well, or you all will see your last sight of light," he commanded with a dangerous edge to his tone. The captain slowly raised his hands in surrender, signaling his men to do the same.

"How did you manage that, Lieutenant?" I inquired, feeling as if I had just become part of a scene in a spy movie.

"As you and I took the eastern route, unbeknownst to you, my men entered an unguarded artillery room and rendezvoused with the soldiers that were headed west. Then they kept themselves in hiding, awaiting the proper time to reappear."

"Freaking ninjas!" I cried excitedly.

As the lieutenant and his men tied the crewmen to the posts lining the stables, I noticed the captain scratching his thigh, stealthily reaching lower as if searching for something. He tugged on a strand of lace sticking out of his britches, exposing a flap with a concealed weapon. He reached inside, brandished a pistol, and aimed it at the lieutenant.

Leaving me no choice, I yelled out frantically, "Look out, Olson!" then snatched the lieutenant's pistol from him, which was still cocked. All else faded in the background; the only focus being the captain's chest. I aimed and pressed the trigger, striking him dead center. He toppled forward onto the pile of hay he had previously hidden under.

"No, no, not again," I whispered, feeling the wretched emotion of having taken yet another life. I remained frozen, my arm stretched in front of me with the pistol still pointed at the captain.

Lieutenant Olson, his eyes holding a stern, unwavering gaze, reached for the cold steel of the pistol and forced my arm down. "He made his choice, Mr. Roberts. Do not struggle with yourself. It was inevitable." I closed my eyes and nodded in agreement, a single silent tear running down my cheek.

"You have saved my life. Know I will be forever indebted to you, sir," Lieutenant Olson proclaimed decisively, as he took a knee before me. "From this day onward, you command my armament and my actions, honor of my word!"

I glanced down at him, the sight of a seventeenth-century soldier kneeling before me a surreal shock. I placed a hand on his shoulder, and for a moment, I was transported back to my living room, having beer and chips with Alex and Devon. We were watching a movie based on King Arthur with a scene about Arthur crowning his knights. Mimicking the scene, Devon had used a plastic bat and begun pounding Alex and me repeatedly on our heads.

"Thank you, Lieutenant," I said, my voice steadying. "I did what was right by you, just as you did for me. I am the one indebted to you."

The lieutenant rose, gazing directly into my eyes. "Honor of my word has already been bonded to you, sir. For the remainder of the days that I draw breath, it shall remain sealed!"

"So shall it be!" I replied, the words feeling heavy with a significance I was only beginning to comprehend.

The soldiers gathered the weapons off the ground, fortified the ropes around the wrists of the crewmen, and released the horses. This allowed them proper transportation, as they had arrived crammed in an artillery wagon.

I led Moonlight out of the stall, eager to get him watered and fed. "I'm sure you're craving sunlight after being cooped up in that stall, my friend!" I said, stroking his mane. As soon as we reached the pier, Moonlight pranced in place like a child playing in a sandbox, delighted to be under the warmth of the sun and ready to bolt.

"I need to get another sack of fruits and hay for my horse," I informed the lieutenant as I placed a bucket of water in front of Moonlight.

"No need, Mr. Roberts. I've already sent one of my men to fetch all the nourishment your horse will need for your journey." Reaching into his pocket, Lieutenant Olson added, "I would like you to carry this." He handed me an emerald-green Irish Claddagh patch with a horseshoe stitched into the heart. "If you ever find yourself in the clutches of a malefactor within any of the Irish provinces, present this to them. It will guarantee your safety."

"Thank you, Lieutenant. It will remain with me always."

Once Moonlight had his fill, I thanked the soldiers for their heroics and offered them each a coin, which at first, they refused, but with some persuasion, I got them to accept.

"It isn't much, but it's the least I can do. Thank you, gentlemen!"

The lieutenant arranged accommodation for the night at an establishment just five miles past the port—across a bridge—allowing time for both Moonlight and me to rest. The soldiers guided us back to the trail I had followed into Sligo, directing me on a straight path to Galway, hopefully without being forcibly detained by marauders this time.

Chapter 16 – A Future from Long Ago

Adam felt a surge of exhilaration as the airplane soared, his first time experiencing such a marvel. He pressed his face against the window, fixated on the vast expanse of the ocean below, experiencing what he imagined being a bird's-eye view of the world. His family had always traveled by car during vacations, an enjoyable ritual, save for the inevitable overcrowding in the backseat with his siblings.

He recalled his first trip at the age of eight, shortly after being adopted by the Towell family. They had journeyed from their home in Alexandria, Virginia, to South Dakota to visit Mount Rushmore. The drive had taken two arduous days, with an overnight stop in Whiting, Indiana, at a hotel on Whihala Beach. Their room had faced Lake Michigan, and he remembered standing on the balcony, watching the sun dip below the horizon, painting the sky in fiery hues. He had imagined himself looking out at the ocean then, never having been to a real beach. The following day, they had checked out of the hotel before noon, allowing them a brief moment to dip their toes into the cool edge of the lake before their dad, always pressed for time, ushered them swiftly back into the car.

The eight-hour flight to Ireland made the endless hours they had spent in a car feel like a mere stroll. During their first days in Ireland, they visited local museums and castles, their ancient artifacts a noticeable and significant difference to Adam's modern sensibilities, and spent time at the resort's indoor pool, taking the occasional swim. One afternoon, Adam picked up a pamphlet at the brochure stand. It featured a captivating picture of an ocean seashore with a cave and a cascading waterfall as the backdrop. He ran to his dad, waving the pamphlet excitedly, and begged to be taken there. It was not only near a beach, but Adam assumed it would be the closest they would get to being on one for some time. His dad, Paul, passed the leaflet to their mother, Rachel, a subtle gesture that implied they should make this a destination during their stay. She responded with an agreeable nod, prompting Adam and his siblings to express their delight with excited shouts.

The following day, his parents woke them early and announced that after breakfast, they were going to visit Caisleán Dhún na nGall. This disheartened the children, as they had been hoping to go to the Eas Gorm i Bhfolach instead. Not having much say in the matter, they boarded the shuttle, settling into their seats with visible disappointment. Adam, however, noticed his parents whispering, a conspiratorial murmur they only ever indulged in when they had something up their sleeves. A glimmer of hope ignited within him, suggesting that the actual destination might, in fact, be the waterfall.

Entering the pebble-covered parking lot, the children glanced at each other, their eyes widening in eager recognition. They yelled with delight, realizing where they were. They expressed their gratitude to their parents as they headed to an area patched with grass near the shore. Feeling intrigued and adventurous, Adam opted to visit the blue hidden waterfall.

"Go ahead, Adam, we'll be lounging out on the grass," his father said, pointing to his mom, who was already laying out blankets and setting down the picnic baskets. "Just don't stay in there for too long."

"I won't, Dad, thanks," Adam responded, a sudden, heartfelt urge compelling him to add, "I love you!"

"Love you too, buddy. Be careful!" his father said.

"Will do, Dad!"

He bought his ticket and made his way to the cave, cautiously trailing around the slippery rocks. He was amazed at the variety of cairns displayed atop the flattened boulders, each reflecting the passage of countless visitors. He entered the cave, instantly mesmerized by its ancient beauty, marveling at the surrounding stones that spanned from the half-covered ceiling down to the walls and ground. He felt oddly nervous, sensing a deep vibration he initially assumed came from excitement as he reached the cascading wall of water. Much to his dismay, the vibration began reverberating intensely the closer he got, growing in power until he reached for the side of the cave to balance himself. Like a sudden, unseen force, he felt himself slammed to the ground, an experience best described as being struck by a colossal, invisible hand.

After what seemed like an eternity, his eyes opened, and he instinctively reached to rub the back of his neck, tilting his head to dispel the cold droplets that poured into his eyes. Seized by a sudden, overwhelming surge of panic, he shot to his feet and darted out of the cave, scurrying over the stones, past the muddy, sloped trail leading to the grassy clearing by the waterfront. He came to an unexpected halt, his breath ragged.

"Where did they go?!" he yelled frantically, calling out to his family. "Mom! Dad! Luke! Jasmine!" There was no response. He raced back toward the muddy trail and crossed the pebbled parking area, searching desperately for the ticket counter, but it too was gone. The world around was altered, subtly but terrifyingly, and he was utterly alone.

A man riding a moped stopped when he saw Adam in distress. "Hey, lad, what's wrong? Are ye lost?"

"I can't find my family; they were sitting over by that patch of grass near the shore, and now they're gone!" Adam's voice was intense with fear.

"D'ye think they might be out searching for ye?" the man asked in a comforting tone.

"They know I was inside the cave. I went to see the waterfall, but then a gust or squall of some kind knocked me down. I blacked out for a moment, then came to. I ran outside, and the ticket booth, along with my family, had all disappeared!" he exclaimed, the words tumbling out in a panicked rush.

Feeling concerned for the boy, the man offered him a ride to the nearest Garda station, a place where he would have a better chance of finding his family.

***

Days later, Adam found himself on a plane, heading back home to Alexandria. His mind, still reeling from the events at the waterfall, clung to the hope that with the continued help from the USAID, he could contact his grandmother and stay with her while they searched for his family. Arriving at Washington Dulles Airport, Adam was confused. The people seemed oddly dressed, their clothes a strange mix of retro fashion and futuristic attire he assumed was part of a convention of some sort happening in town. He made his way into the city, where his grandmother worked as a general manager at a hotel on Connecticut Avenue.

The entrance to the hotel was blocked off with barricades, and several Secret Service men stood guard, their impassive expressions showing no emotion. *President Bush must be visiting,* he thought, then pondered a way to get word to his Nana, letting her know he was outside.

He waited by the side entrance along the T Street NW exit, hoping to bump into an employee who would recognize him and send word to his grandmother. He was suddenly distracted by the muffled sound of voices emitting from walkie-talkies inside the Presidents Walk corridor. The excitement of possibly seeing a President of the United States in person for the first time distracted him from the present ordeal. He grew anxious as the voices over the radios drew closer, so he threaded past the crowd for a closer look.

Finding a spot that offered a better view, he nearly lost his footing as a man standing next to him shoved him forcibly aside. The man, a boorish figure with a wild look in his eyes, stared at Adam with an evil scowl. Adding to the strangeness, the man knelt just as a man with a familiar, handsome face walked past. "Wait, what... who? That's not President Bush, that's former President Reagan, but younger," he muttered, the realization a dizzying, sickening blow.

His head spun with a sudden, overwhelming lightheadedness, causing his weight to shift against the barricade, but he quickly took hold of it and balanced himself. Suddenly, the sharp cracking sound of gunfire rang out from beside him. Everything seemed to go in slow motion as the gun emptied in rapid succession.

With a flash of reckless bravery, he kneed the man in the shoulder, causing him to topple to the ground just as the last gunshot exited the barrel.

The Secret Service, their movements a haze of executed precision, shoved Adam aside, piling themselves on top of the gunman and incapacitating him. In the confusion, Adam felt someone grab him by the ankles, a disorienting, desperate pull, dragging him away from the crowd and hauling him into a dark alleyway.

"What the hell just happened?" he asked the old man standing over him, still shaking from the excitement.

"Dinna fret over the incident. 'Twas yer destiny to be here," the old man conveyed mysteriously.

"What do you mean by my destiny?" Adam asked nervously.

"Here, smell this!" the old man suggested.

He passed a balled-up, slightly moist cloth across Adam's nostrils. The vapors caused his head to spin, and he quickly succumbed to their effect and passed out.

***

His mind in a fog, Adam blinked continuously to clear his vision, waking to the sight of a mesh-like material hanging above him, likely a canopy or tent. "Hello, hello," he yelled, his voice filled with a sudden fear, but there was no response.

He propped himself up, slightly dizzy but able to muster the stamina to stand. He darted out of the tent to observe his surroundings. The area looked familiar yet completely foreign, as if he had been there before—a feeling of powerful déjà vu. He followed a trail of muddy dirt surrounded by stones and large rocks, coming to an embankment leading to the grassy area where he had last seen his family. "I'm back in Ireland?!" He clutched his chest, his words emerging as a strained whisper between gasps for air. "Hello, lad, good to see ye up and about," the elder man said with a warm, low voice.

"I know you! It was you who pulled me from underneath the pile of Secret Service agents. How did I get back here? Did you find my family?" Adam asked, panicked.

"Easy, dinna worry yerself about that, lad. Ye have stumbled upon a grander opportunity, not a frequent occurrence." He turned towards a clearing leading to the path into the cave. "Ye'll be able to see yer family again once ye have fulfilled what ye are meant to."

"What the hell are you talking about? To accomplish what? What exactly am I supposed to fulfill here?" Adam asked, clearly irritated.

"Do ye think ye ended up in front of that hotel by coincidence? It certainly was not to see ye grandmother, lad. The watersfall chose ye to be there."

"You're a crazy old man. I'm going to find the cops and report you for kidnapping."

The elder man smiled with a look of deep consolation, motioning for Adam to follow him in the cave's direction. "You expect me to follow you back in there? That's where this whole damn nightmare began!"

"Lad, ye'll need to go back into the waterfall if ye expect to return to yer time, the year ye first entered the Eas Gorm i Bhfolach."

"Now I know you're freaking nuts!" Adam snapped, then he promptly recalled the weirdly dressed people on the plane and at the airport in Washington. And then there was President Reagan.

"The Eas Gorm i Bhfolach is a bridge betwixt time and our world, lad, with no knowledge or understanding of how folks are chosen and unaware of its origins. All I can presume is certain folks are appointed to take part in significant moments in time."

Adam rubbed his head in frustration, his mind struggling to process the information the elder man had just revealed. Yet he struggled even more with the fact that he sensed the truth in his story. "So, if you're such an expert, tell me where I am now. What year are we in?" Adam asked sarcastically.

"We are in the year 1981, lad; ye fell twenty-one years into the past!"

"Twenty-one years? I haven't even been born yet!"

The elder man chuckled, then went on, "Aye, lad. It doesna matter to the watersfall, just know that ye appeared where ye were supposed to, at a place where a pivotal moment in history was destined to occur."

"What are you talking about? Do you mean to say that what happened in Washington was the result of a changed future?" Adam responded, shocked.

"Aye, laddie. It was the fulcrum. If it were not fer yer interference, that man would have succeeded in the president's assassination, prompting a change of leadership, eventually culminating in a nuclear demise of the world as we know it."

"So, you mean to say that I just averted some sort of dystopian future?" Adam responded, the words a strained breath.

"Aye. Now, I'm not precisely sure where the watersfall will take ye next, but what I do know is if yer destiny has been fulfilled, ye will reach yer own time and be reunited with yer family."

Feeling uncertain about his story, Adam hesitantly responded, "So, you're not sure that I'll reach my time, then? It's all uncertain."

"Ye'll not know either unless ye return to the cave and allow the watersfall to guide ye!"

Exhaling in frustration, Adam marched back inside the cave, dauntlessly yelling at the waterfall, "I'm here! Now take me home, dammit!" He turned and faced the cascade, standing motionless, waiting for the vibrating squall to strike him like before, saying loudly, "Beam me up, Spock, or whomever," but nothing happened. The air then turned thick and misty, like when fog rolls in, but nothing like his first experience days ago.

Waiting for what felt like an eternity, with the silence of the cave pressing in, Adam finally surrendered and turned to exit. A sudden wave of lightheadedness and nausea washed over him, and then, without warning, the intense, hurricane-like squall struck him. It hit him with the force of a battering ram, almost knocking him to the ground. He reached for the rough cave wall to support himself, but the powerful vibrations emanating from the anomaly overtook him, and he fell, blacking out the moment his head struck the ground.

Coming in and out of consciousness, his head throbbing, he shook it to clear the cobwebs, the world still spinning around him. He sat briefly, his stomach churning as if it had been torn to shreds, before slowly making his way out of the cave. *Please tell me I made it home, please!* he pleaded silently in desperation.

His heart pounded as he darted over the rocky turf, each step fueled by despair. The grassy patch, warm with memories of his family only days before, was gone, replaced by sharp, overgrown weeds and a tangled brush thick with buzzing insects. A biting panic, like the metallic tang of fear, began to set in. He retraced his steps, trekking up the muddy hill leading to the road. Once he reached the top, he found himself standing on the grass where the pebbled parking lot had been. There, he encountered an unexpected and terrifying sight: a group of men on horseback, wearing what appeared to be historical uniforms, their steel morions gleaming in the harsh light.

Gripped by fear as the riders approached, their horses' hooves thudding ominously, he scrambled to hide behind a wall of boulders, hoping to avoid detection. Leaning against one of the larger rocks, he waited nervously, pressing his sweaty palms against his forehead. Suddenly, he felt a pair of powerful hands grab his wrists and pull him up and over the boulder, dragging him roughly to the other side. "Thought ye could get away from us, did ye?" a gruff voice snarled, its accent thick and foreign. "We heard of ye exploits, laddie, stealing from travelers in these parts!"

He gazed at the officer with wide, frightened eyes. "I have robbed no one, sir, I promise. I'm just lost."

"Ye can explain that to the keeper of the gaol at the holding house. Pray fer ye sake he is in a forgiving mood," the soldier sneered, his grip tightening.

Adam's hands were tied to the end of a long rope anchored to the saddle of a soldier's horse, and he was dragged along, falling constantly during the three-hour journey. Still stunned, it did not cross his mind to question where or when he was, knowing with a chilling certainty that he was neither in the twentieth nor the twenty-first century.

***

They arrived at a small stone building with two windows in the façade, each fashioned with thick metal bars. It appeared to be a jail or a holding house, as the soldier had called it. They led Adam inside a grim room with a rickety wooden door and an opening covered in metal bars. Inside was a rough wooden bench lined against the wall, with a bucket on one end and a person stretched out on the ground underneath the bench, covered in a red coat.

Refusing to accept the situation, Adam asked the soldier once again, "Why am I being arrested? I did nothing, sir," he declared, his voice cracking, as the soldier shoved him inside.

"We recognize ye to be a highwayman, laddie. Images of ye on the circulars dinna lie."

"How can that be? How can there be a flier... ah, um... circular with a pic... image of me?" he asked, trying to contain himself and avoid any further allegations. Though the question might seem far-fetched, he built up the courage to ask the soldier, "Can I ask a strange question?"

"Go on, ask away!"

"What year are we in?" The soldier, finding humor in his question, turned and walked away in laughter, never providing an answer.

The person under the redcoat emerged, raised himself from the ground and sat on the bench, scrutinizing Adam with weary, intelligent eyes. "Young man, it is best to remain silent when surrounded by those ruffians. They will only ridicule you," he advised, his voice deep with a proper English accent.

"Can you tell me what year we're in?" Adam asked in a whisper.

The man sighed as he put on his redcoat, a long, drawn-out sound. "I make it a point never to counter-question. It is the year of our Lord, 1598."

If it hadn't been for the small confines of the jail cell, Adam would have surely passed out, stunned by the answer. *Could the elder man have been mistaken, not having reached my time, or was he correct that I was to fulfill yet another destiny in this century?* The question hung in the stale cold air of the cell, a terrifying, unattainable truth.

Chapter 17 – Guilty of Innocence

Adam spent several months confined to the cell alongside the redcoat, Henry Williams. The cold stone walls and the rank smell of straw and confinement became a new normal for them. They made the best of their time, exchanging stories of their respective lives. Adam, of course, had to modify his accounts to accommodate the present era, a task that became a strange sort of game. Henry often pointed out the similarities in their upbringings, but little did Mr. Williams know just how profoundly different they truly were.

Explaining how he had come to be in Ireland, Henry Williams recounted the circumstances that had landed him in the holding cell. He claimed to have traveled there as a dispatcher to deliver correspondence to the estate of an Irish infantry commander. He was found wandering the halls of the home and swiftly apprehended on suspicion of being a spy. In his defense, he declared, with a wry, weary smile, that he was merely searching for a servant to provide him with a chamber pot.

"*Are* you in fact, a spy?" Adam asked, intrigued.

"No, lad, I am merely a courier," Henry replied.

The present century, Adam quickly learned, was notorious for condemning innocent people without cemented law. It was a brutal reality, a world where innocent people were put to death for the crimes of others or simply for being misunderstood. For all intents and purposes, they were guilty of innocence.

Henry Williams's face hardened with a grim resolve. "It might serve you right to gain confidential knowledge of a planned invasion being put into place as we speak, Mr. Towell."

"What do you mean it might serve me right?" Adam asked, his brow furrowing in confusion.

"My execution soon approaches, despite my declarations of innocence, to no avail. What I have knowledge of might buy *you* your freedom."

He thoroughly detailed a planned English invasion that was to reinforce the fort at the Blackwater, a matter of great significance in the ongoing Nine Years' War that was to happen in the county of Armagh before the fall equinox. It suddenly dawned on Adam—the battle he referenced. During his sophomore year in high school, Adam had learned about a battle that occurred during the tumultuous time of the Nine Years' War in Ireland—the Battle of the Yellow Ford, in August 1598.

In mid-July, after providing Adam with as much information as he could recall about the approaching conflict, the soldiers hauled Mr. Henry Williams away to meet his impending doom at the gallows. His declaration of innocence remained unheard, falling on deaf ears, right up to the moment he drew his last breath.

***

Thinking of the coming battle, Adam felt a sense of excitement. A thought, both daring and desperate, crossed his mind: *If I meddle in the Battle of the Yellow Ford, it might be the culmination that could win my return home.*

Granted the freedom to wander outside of his confinement twice a day to perform janitorial duties, Adam was often escorted by a young soldier, Private Gideon, to ensure he carried out his assigned tasks. While performing his chores, Adam caught sight of a regiment hauling carriages filled with artillery. He presumed the infantry to be that of the Earl of Tyrone, Hugh O'Neill, as the chatter of his arrival had spread throughout the camp the past few days.

"Is it possible for me to have a word with the earl?" Adam asked Private Gideon doggedly.

"What need d'ye have to speak with the earl?" Gideon asked suspiciously.

"I have vital information that can gain him victory in the coming battle at Blackwater River," Adam replied solemnly, hoping to convince him he spoke earnestly.

"I will see what I can do. Now finish burying that shite," he commanded, pointing with his foot at a pile of refuse.

Adam completed his duties, his mind now focused with a singular purpose, and then was escorted back to his holding cell, where he found a loaf of bread sitting on the bench. As Gideon shut the cell door, he glanced at Adam, a friendly grin on his face, and simply remarked, "Enjoy!"

***

The next morning, Private Gideon abruptly woke Adam and ushered him to an enclosed pavilion where Hugh O'Neill awaited. Adam's heart pounded in his chest as he approached the earl, ceremoniously extending his hand in a formal gesture. "Good morning, sir. My name is Adam Towell."

The earl, a formidable man with a hawk-like gaze, ignored Adam's handshake and grunted commandingly. "I know well who ye are, Mr. Towell. I have a full day ahead of me, so speak ye mind hastily," he said in a gravelly voice.

"Mr. Henry Williams revealed pertinent—" Adam began, but the earl quickly cut him off.

"Who is this Henry Williams, lad?" he asked assertively, with a tone of impatience.

Private Gideon, who had been standing silently by the entrance, chimed in, revealing the identity of the English redcoat. "Are ye to waste me time with foolish stories of a dead English soldier, lad? Be gone wi' ye," the earl snapped, his patience wearing thin.

"Sir, wait, please, please let me explain," Adam begged desperately. He knew this was the only viable way of gaining his freedom.

The earl sighed. "I'll give ye a moment to explain yerself, lad, then off wi' ye!"

Adam seized the opportunity, his mind a whirlwind of information. "Mr. Williams revealed to me a planned invasion that is to come on the fourteenth of August, next month, near the Blackwater River in the county of Armagh."

"We have heard rumors of such an invasion. Go on!" the earl said with a genuine interest in his eyes.

"Well, with all due respect, please don't ask how I know this. Just be assured that I speak truthfully; you *will* be victorious, I guarantee it with my life."

The earl peered at Adam with deep skepticism. He then asked unexpectedly in a faint voice, "Have ye met an Elder Folk?"

Adam's eyes widened in shock, stunned by his impulsive question. "Yes, sir. I have," he responded hesitantly, his heart racing.

The earl rose from his seat, his massive frame a towering presence, and bellowed at his soldiers, "Leave the room now, the lot o' ye!" He commanded Adam to sit on the chair beside him, then stepped outside to give instructions to his soldiers, who seemed surprised by his sudden change of behavior. He then returned to the pavilion, a small, polished wooden cup of ale in his hand, which he forcibly set on the table, the clatter echoing in the sudden silence.

"Tell me, lad, what d'ye know of the Elder Folks?"

Feeling apprehensive, Adam swallowed noisily, pondering whether he should answer truthfully. He then felt a peaceful conviction in his heart that if he were to have any chance of returning home, he needed to be honest. "An old man, or Elder Folk, told me to enter the cave of the waterfall—"

"The Eas Gorm i Bhfolach, aye, go on."

"Yes, sir. I was on vacation with my family in 2002, visiting Donegal—"

O'Neill suddenly flew from his seat, the sound of his fist landing on the table a sharp, splintering sound. "I knew the stories were true. Go on, lad, go on. How did ye come to be about in this time?"

"The first time I entered the cave, I emerged in the year 1981, where I met the old man. He advised me that if I expected to return home, I was to go through the waterfall once again, warning that it wasn't guaranteed in which year I would emerge, and that is how I appeared in your time."

"So, how did ye come to be in the holding house then, lad?" the earl asked with a keen inquisitiveness dissimilar from his earlier demeanor.

The Waters Fall-A Journeyer – Rob Mylo Vazquez

"When I came out of the cave, I reached the dirt road where your soldiers spotted me and mistook me for a thief... um... a highwayman, as you call them. I was apprehended and brought here."

The earl stood beside the table, pacing back and forth anxiously. "What exactly did the redcoat tell ye, lad?"

"He said he came across correspondence he was delivering to Thomas Maria Wingfield and found the seal had been tampered with. Curious, he opened it and read the contents, which detailed the plans of how the invasion was to be executed, along with the date of the planned invasion. As he recounted the story, I was reminded of a subject regarding a battle I studied in my history class during my junior year—"

"Lad, if I am to understand anything ye say, ye must explain it in present terms. I dinna understand the language of the future," the earl said in annoyance.

Frustrated, Adam paused for a moment, thinking how best to explain in terms the earl would understand. "During my schooling, one lesson taught entailed stories of various events that occurred throughout history. One such event was the Battle of the Yellow Ford; a battle fought between the Irish and the English. According to the history books, the defenses led by yourself and your soldiers brought victory to the Irish."

"Aye, I am in history books, ye say?" he expressed, a look of absolute honor on his face.

"Yes, sir, you are," Adam replied with an innocent chuckle. "So, would you allow me to return to the waterfall to return home, sir?"

"Aye, lad, I will—once we claim victory!"

Adam felt his stomach sink, a knot of dread forming at the thought of having to wait, secluded inside that cage, for another month. *Then again, it might just be a brief delay, and then I can finally go home.* He held on to the hope that by

200

disclosing the particulars to the earl and its impending outcome, he might fulfill his destiny in this century and secure his ticket home.

***

Though still considered a prisoner, the Earl arranged for Adam to accompany his garrison to help set up the encampment on the hill of the Boggy Ford in Armagh. Adam examined his surroundings, feeling a thrilling sense of awe, because in a short time, he was going to be a part of history. After stocking the wagons with additional artillery and provisions, they began the arduous journey to County Armagh. He felt nervous but equally excited, thinking of how cool it would have been to have brought a camcorder to record the battle. It took two days to reach the desired location for their encampment. The soldiers put Adam to work at once, setting up tents, organizing ammunition for the firearms, digging privies, and feeding the livestock.

Private Gideon had become a guardian of sorts to Adam, instructing him on how to organize and prepare essentials, becoming more of a friend, which brought him a deep sense of comfort. Though they had developed a bond, Adam still had orders to follow, which meant Private Gideon would need to continue to be stern and command Adam about when necessary.

There were only two days left before the battle. Private Gideon instructed Adam to meet him atop the small hill where the soldiers had set up a range for target practice. He handed Adam a pistol, intending to coach him on how to use it. "Lad, if ye are to keep safe, ye'll need to learn how to load, aim, and fire the pistol," Gideon instructed.

"Um... yes, sure. But you'll have to teach me how," Adam replied nervously, having never held a gun before in his life.

"Ye'll take the wee pouch—smell the sulfur, now—and pour it into the barrel. Next, add the metal ball. Feel its weight, then ram the ball and powder down tight. Aim. Shoot," Gideon demonstrated smoothly. It sounded easy enough; all Adam needed to do was calm his nerves and keep himself from shaking. "Okay, lad, are ye ready?"

"I think so."

"Eye the wee target just there," Gideon instructed, pointing at a wooden cup balancing on a rock a few yards away.

Adam closed his eyes and took aim, his hands trembling slightly. He was abruptly stopped by Private Gideon, who forced his arm down. "How d'ye intend to hit the target wi' ye eyes closed?" he asked with a chuckle.

"I'm sorry, man. It's first-time jitters," Adam replied, his lips quivering with embarrassment. He loosened his hand and cocked the pistol once again.

Gideon advised, "Keep ye eyes solely on the target. Dinna look at anything other than the wee cup." Adam took a deep breath, then exhaled, his gaze laser-focused on the wooden cup. He blurred out all other distractions, cocked his head with one eye squinted, and then, with surprising steadiness, pulled the trigger.

"Aye, lad, well done," Gideon cheered as he walked to retrieve the cup, which, to his surprise, had a hole in the middle of it. "Ye have done this before, eh?"

"No, Private Gideon, I have never even held a pistol before in my life. Luck of the Irish, I guess?" he remarked, shrugging his shoulders.

They continued practicing throughout the rest of the afternoon. Adam was then summoned by a garrison soldier to the main pavilion at the earl's request.

"You wanted to see me, sir?" Adam asked confidently.

"Aye, lad, have a seat. I have received news that Henry Bagenal and his foot soldiers are marching in from Dublin as we speak, planning an onslaught on our encampment, proving ye story true. Ye have me word, lad, once victory is ours, freedom *will* be yers," he proclaimed. He then walked over to a table draped with a long cloth that reached the floor. He bent underneath, pulled out a small wooden chest, and handed it to Adam.

"What is this, sir?" Adam asked, taking the heavy box in his hands.

"'Tis a wee gift fer ye, forged by me personal blacksmith, lad. I saw ye shooting on the hill. Ye's a natural marksman." Adam opened the box to find a beautiful Saxon wheellock.

Having missed a few months of school during his sophomore year after a car accident, Adam had taken a makeup class during the summer, studying historical artillery, which is how he recognized the pistol. "Sir, this is very thoughtful of you. Thank you. It's a Saxon wheellock, correct?" Adam inquired as he inspected every angle, impressed by its artistry.

The earl pulled his dirk from its sheath and handed it to Adam. "Aye, 'tis a Saxon wheellock; it will be yer first weapon, lad, one that ye'll take back wi' ye to ye time when the moment arises. I want ye to use the dirk and carve ye initials, claiming ownership," he commanded, his eyes fixed on Adam with a look of absolute trust.

Adam used a cloth to hold the dirk by the blade and forcibly scraped against an oddly placed brass plate above the pommel. He traced his initials, "A.T.," slightly crooked, but clearly legible.

"Continue practicing wi' it, lad, the day soon approaches!" the earl urged.

"Yes, sir, I will. Thank you again. I will cherish it, I promise."

Adam felt suddenly obligated to warn the earl, a heavy responsibility settling on his shoulders. "Sir, there will be certain campaigns led by you that will result in loss. In some battles, you will emerge victorious; however, in most others, you will not."

"Do I lose me life soon, lad?" he questioned, sounding suddenly downhearted, the earlier triumph fading from his face.

"No, sir, you will live on, until... I'm sorry, sir, I didn't mean to—"

"No... Aye, lad, aye. When... when will it happen? Tell me!" the earl insisted, his eyes wide with a desperate need to know.

"Sometime in 1616, sir," Adam answered with heaviness in his voice and heartfelt sadness.

"Lad, I will live a full life; 'tis fine. I will be fine. Thank ye. Now go, practice ye aim," he said, a forced cheerfulness in his tone, but his eyes held a distant, somber look.

Adam left the pavilion and met up again with Private Gideon, who was waiting outside the mess hall tent, gesturing for him to join him on the bench seating. "'Tis yer duty to continue practicing ye aim, so once ye fill yer belly, we will go back up to the hill."

***

The day had finally arrived—the infamous Battle of the Yellow Ford. Adam had slept little the night before, tossing and turning anxiously, the weight of history pressing down on him. Private Gideon had assured him he would be kept away from the lines of fire, on the opposite side, beyond the small hill, but Adam knew he couldn't simply stand idle.

Sounds of pistols and cannon fire reverberated in the early morning, echoing in the distance. The cries of wounded soldiers were accompanied by the brutal clanging of swords. Adam knew the battle was growing closer to the trenches where he was ordered to remain, but, tempting fate, he snuck away and entered the artillery tent to supply himself with metal balls and gunpowder should the time arise when he would need to defend himself. He felt strangely overcome with courage and bravery where fear had once existed, a cold resolve hardening his gut.

Venturing behind the encampment, completely disobeying Private Gideon's orders to remain unseen, Adam scanned the area and spotted a regiment of over one hundred redcoats. They were all armed to the teeth with muskets, pikes, cavalry, and artillery. Leading them was a man wearing a shiny *cuirass* and a lobster-tailed pot helmet, his armor gleaming ominously. Adam quickly ducked to avoid being detected. Suddenly, he was taken by surprise when a set of hands clutched his shoulders and forced him flat to the ground.

"Private Gideon, you shouldn't sneak up on a man in the middle of a battlefield that way. You nearly scared the crap out of me!"

"Did I not instruct ye to keep out of sight and remain in the trenches?" he whispered angrily, reprimanding Adam, his eyes narrowed.

"Yes, I'm sorry, but I felt useless just sitting there," Adam quickly added, changing the subject. "Who is that man wearing armor?"

"'Tis Sir Henry Bagenal, the bastard that leads this invasion," Gideon said with contempt.

Adam's jaw dropped, and his heart raced. "Follow me back to the artillery tent—"

"Be quiet and get down, Gideon," Adam muttered, pulling him down just as the regiment changed its stance, weaving in their direction. "They're heading this way!"

Private Gideon shoved Adam aggressively, yelling, "Ambush, ambush!" trying to get the attention of the front-line captains stationed at the back trenches.

The actions of the redcoats and the defense of the Irish soldiers all played out as if in slow motion, cinematically, as Adam lay hidden behind an oak tree, avoiding the exchange of gunfire. He mustered the courage to prepare his pistol, ready to fire.

Unable to find a clearing for an escape, Adam remained hidden behind the tree, alert for any sign of danger. Private Gideon ran past him with his gun drawn, pausing and pointing his pistol at him. At second glance, he lowered his gun, realizing who Adam was, but was distracted by movement coming from behind a brush. A loud popping sound echoed nearby, close enough to make Adam's ears ring, disorienting him. Pinpointing the source, Adam turned to find Private Gideon doubled over, falling to his knees, clutching his stomach, and toppling over with his face crashing against the ground.

Disregarding his own safety, Adam reached out to pull him safely out of harm's way. Gideon's eyes remained open, staring at Adam with a look of shock, but Adam, in his innocence, did not perceive that he was dead.

Adam got on one knee to stand, intending to lift and carry Private Gideon to the medic tent, when the man who fired the fatal shot appeared from behind the brush, standing over him. "Sir Henry Bagenal," Adam whispered. He remained kneeling, lifting his head to meet Bagenal's eyes as Bagenal extended his arm, pressing the barrel of his pistol against Adam's forehead. Then, a gunshot echoed.

Chapter 18 – Malus Sylvestris

The verdant, undisturbed lands of Ireland unfolded before me, a breathtaking panorama of rolling hills and ancient forests. Yet, with every mile Moonlight carried me, my mind was haunted by the bloody carnage and suffering that would soon befall this beautiful country, a gruesome scenario brought to life by the nefarious Oliver Cromwell. *I have to reach Brindley's sources fast and gain the answers I need;* I thought as I tugged gently on Moonlight's reins.

After traveling for most of the day, pushing Moonlight and myself to our limits, I stopped only out of sheer necessity, trying to make up for the time I had lost back at the port of Sligo. My eagerness to reach Galway, hopefully by the next day before sundown, was a constant goad. I arrived in Ballyhaunis just before dark and found a riverbed with a boma-like rock formation, its curves offering a secure enough hollow to keep me hidden from any lurking thieves. I felt disquiet, struggling to grow accustomed to sleeping outdoors, with unseen insects crawling on me and the rustling of unknown creatures creeping around in the darkness. I finally settled in, wrapping myself tightly in the wool blanket, and plunged into a deep sleep, resting well through the night. As the sun rose, painting the sky in soft hues of pink and gold, I was rudely awakened by the unwelcome splat of bird droppings landing squarely on my head from a passing bird overhead.

***

I approached the cool riverbed to hydrate and wash, as well as to water my faithful companion. It felt mildly cool for an August day, making it ideal for traveling without having to stop as often to water Moonlight. I replenished the flasks, doused the embers of my small fire, and prepared us to ride nonstop, determined to arrive at Knocknacarra before nightfall.

The unseasonably cool weather made for a comfortably pleasant ride. We passed through small villages; their whitewashed cottages nestled amongst the green. Friendly locals, their faces stamped with the hard realities of their lives, unexpectedly handed me bread and salted meats as Moonlight and I rode by. It was a welcoming gesture, and I pondered if Lieutenant Olson had anything to do with their generosity, a subtle network of support Brindley had put in place.

I crossed paths with a gentleman tugging a wagon filled with bleating goats, their long beards swaying. Catching his attention, I inquired, "Good afternoon, sir. May you be so kind as to tell me how far it is before I reach Galway?"

"Ní far, lad. Once ye cross the River Corrib, travel west as the crow flies, níl more than three to four miles," he kindly replied with his thick Irish brogue.

"Much obliged, sir!"

I estimated it would take another hour to reach Galway, and then I would make my way into Knocknacarra, a direct route according to the map. There, I could search for the cattle farm, the only one like it for miles, according to Brindley's detailed notes.

***

After a few hours of vigilant searching, my eyes scanning every distant cottage and every grazing animal, I finally spotted a herd of cattle roaming behind a large, low-slung cottage. I assumed it to be the place I was looking for, so I dismounted Moonlight, secured him to a sturdy hitching post, and made my way to the front door, knocking persistently. "Hello, is anyone home?"

I received no response, only the distant lowing of cattle and the gentle sigh of the wind. I headed over to an open window on the opposite side. "Good afternoon. Is anyone home?" I called out, my voice echoing slightly in the silence, but was met with only the gentle whirr of the countryside.

Assuming no one was home, I returned to Moonlight, my initial hope beginning to wane. I rode down a dirt path lined with tall, whispering Scots pine trees, their needles rustling softly in the breeze. Just as I passed a trail of hedgerows, I heard a voice, rough and ancient, coming from the far side of a copse. "Is there something ye need, lad?"

"Hello, yes. Good afternoon, sir. I'm hoping you can tell me where I may find a gentleman who goes by the name Oistin Killian. Do you know where I might find him?"

An elderly man, sporting a long white beard that flowed like a winter stream, popped out from behind the bush. "Aye, lad, I would be he. Who asks?"

"My name is Myles Roberts. I have been instructed to find you and deliver this," I said, handing him a sealed letter, its red wax seal still intact. "It was sent by Major General Brindley."

"Oh, aye, I received word from Sir Brindley and have been expecting ye," he said, his eyes, intelligent, assessing me with a keen gaze. He gestured for me to follow.

He snapped open the wax seal with a flick of his wrist and read the contents of the letter, his expression growing more solemn with each line. He stopped abruptly, his stare lifting from the parchment to settle on me. "My dear child. Never in me lifetime had I imagined such a thing existed, but now I meet a second journeyer while I still draw breath on this earth. 'Tis truly an enchanted blessing."

We strolled leisurely along the narrow trail leading back to the house. Mr. Killian walked with a pronounced limp, using a carved wooden walking stick for balance. It was sizably taller than him, its gnarled wood giving it the semblance of a wizard's staff. As we approached the door, Mr. Killian requested I keep my voice low, as his wife was asleep, having fallen ill; not wanting to disturb her rest.

"She has been ill nigh on three days now with a hardened belly, unable to relieve herself," Oistin explained with a worried voice. He pulled out a rustic seat at his table and gestured for me to sit.

"Has she been able to eat at all?" I asked, my mind already sifting through the limited medical knowledge I possessed.

"Just the occasional cup of tea, nothing solid except fer cheese, which she devours daily." My college science studies, specifically an epidemiological paper I'd once written on the links between dairy products and constipation, surged to the forefront of my mind. Cheese, with its negligible fiber and high-fat content, was a notorious culprit for severe constipation.

"Sir," I began with a sudden certainty, "I noticed the hedgerows near the road, the ones with the small, berry-like fruits. They are known as *Malus sylvestris*, or crab apple—a fruit high in fiber."

Mr. Killian looked at me with a puzzled expression, his brow furrowed. "What is fiber, and what does that have to do wi' me sickly wife?"

"Fiber is a nutrient found in certain foods that helps the body easily relieve itself of excrement, or 'shite,' as you call it," I clarified, trying to simplify the explanation. "Your wife is suffering from constipation; in other words, the shite has built up inside her belly, probably because of the excessive consumption of cheese. If she consumes enough of the fruit, the fiber will allow her to have a bowel movement, relieving herself of the shite."

Mr. Killian gazed at me with a look of dawning anticipation, his eyes widening. He exclaimed brusquely, "Then what are ye waiting fer, lad? Go on and collect the fruits!"

He handed me a hand-woven *sciob*—a small basket—and shooed me away with an impatient wave of his hand. I hurried out to the field, my steps quickening, and filled the basket with the small, round, yellow fruit, gathering enough to fill a bowl to create the sauce, easy for Mrs. Killian to consume.

***

"Nuala, Nuala, wake up, me dear. We have a visitor," Mr. Killian said urgently to his wife, nudging her gently on the shoulder to rouse her from sleep.

A frail, whispered voice responded from the bed. "Forgive me, darling. I must have overslept, me love. Allow me a moment to ready meself, and I will prepare a meal fer ye both at once." She struggled to lift herself, her movements weak. "Did I miss Nolan's arrival?"

"Keep still, me love. Nolan will arrive shortly. This is Mr. Roberts. He is acquainted wi' Dujardin Brindley."

"A pleasure to make your acquaintance, Mrs. Killian," I said softly with concern. "Allow me a moment while I collect the sauce that I prepared for you."

I waited for the sauce to cool, the tangy scent of crab apples filling the small cottage, then brought it to Mr. Killian. He placed the bowl on the table beside the bed, quickly dipping a wooden spoon inside. "Mr. Roberts has prepared this sauce to aid yer ailment, me love. Ye will remain in bed, and I will feed it t' ye!" Mr. Killian expressed joyously, his face alight with hope.

He nourished his wife, one spoonful after the other, as she conveyed an expression of contentment, her eyes fluttering closed with each taste. "She will need to drink plenty of water," I advised, "anticipating she'll feel relief come morning."

"Aye, lad, I will ensure it," he replied, then, his tone becoming more conversational, he asked, "Tell me, how long has it been since ye arrived in this time?"

"I arrived on the third of June, over two months ago, sir. Please tell me you know of a way for me to return to my time?" I asked desperately.

"Lad, no, but I am convinced ye *can* travel back through the watersfall, just ní sure if it is t' ye time."

My eyebrows tensed, a sinking feeling settling in my stomach. "So, I assume I will be stuck in this century with no way back, or ahead... I just have no *fucking* way back home!" I snapped, the words rough with frustration, feeling less optimistic than when I first arrived. I quickly collected myself, then looked at Mr. Killian curiously, apologizing for my abrupt outburst. "What of Adam Towell? Did he ever manage to go back, or did he just disappear into the Eas Gorm i Bhfolach?" I inquired, a sneer involuntarily parting my lips. The thought that Adam Towell might have already returned to his own time made me a tad jealous.

"Aye, he did, in fact, return to the Eas Gorm i Bhfolach. Every day fer years, he entered that cave, each time walking out whence he came."

"Is he still alive?"

"Aye," Mr. Killian answered instantly, his eyes twinkling. "He dwelt here fer many a year. He now resides at Cong Abbey, in the northern part of Lough Corrib." He continued, "He often travels on pilgrimage to Galway and here regularly during *Nollaig,* bringing trinkets and such to Nuala, Nolan, and me."

"How far away *is* Cong Abbey?" I asked, subconsciously intending to ride there come morning, a new hope blossoming in my chest.

"Nigh on twenty... twenty-five miles or so."

***

My intended overnight visit turned into days, a stretch of time I spent recounting the coming Cromwellian Conquest to Mr. Killian and his adopted grandson, Nolan. I also revealed the outcome of slavery, the coming World Wars, how the union of the colonies would form the United States of America, and how the colonies would gain their independence from English rule.

Killian was fascinated to learn that rulers of the Americas would be known as presidents, and he was most astounded to hear that there would be both a Black president and a Black-Asian female vice president governing alongside a Caucasian man in my time.

"What a grand time ye live in, lad," he expressed, his eyes wide with joyous wonder.

"You might say, *lived* in?" I replied anxiously, the weight of my predicament settling on me once again.

"*Ní gá a bheith buartha*, lad. All will work itself out," he said, his hand, gnarled but gentle, coming to rest on my shoulder. "I will see ye properly prepared fer yer journey to Cong Abbey come first light."

"Did Adam ever recount anything pertinent to the future?" I inquired, a sudden curiosity striking me.

"Níl. He was a recluse. Shared pleasantries, 'tis all."

As the time quickly approached, I once again felt lighthearted, a sense of nervous excitement replacing my anxiety, knowing that I would soon meet the alleged other journeyer.

Chapter 19 – Presently in the Past

The journey took less than half a day, and as I approached Cong Abbey, I was overcome by the sheer beauty of the structure. Constructed in the ecclesiastical style, it was founded in the seventh century by Saint Feichin and had seen its share of destruction and restorations since its inception. The current parish abbot, Father Patrick Prendergast, along with members of the church, including monks, had helped to rebuild the abbey, which had fallen into ruins after 1542, making it a haven for Catholic parishioners.

I made my way into the beautiful and eclectic structure, a perfect example of medieval architecture. Though I hadn't been in the seventeenth century for long, every complex I saw left me in awe. They were all a testament to the fact that I was living presently in the past.

I stumbled upon a friar, who greeted me inquisitively with a friendly face. "Good day, sir. Are ye in need of a helping hand today?"

"Hello. Well... not quite. I'm here to inquire about a man who goes by the name Adam Towell. I've been informed he takes residence at your beautiful abbey."

His eyebrows furrowed with a questioning expression. "Me apologies, sir. I know no one by that name in our abbey. Might ye have been misguided?"

"I'm sure I'm in the correct place, sir. A gentleman by the name of Oistin Killian directed me here."

"Oh, ye refer to Brother Don," the friar quickly replied. "Aye, he is present in the abbey. We do not call our brothers by their given names; the parish priest appoints one fer them. Come, follow me."

The friar led the way, walking down a narrow corridor, through an archway, and up a flight of stairs leading to a galleried room with rows of cots strewn across the open flooring. I was instructed to wait at the top of the stairs, by the rails with the strangely shaped balustrades.

I waited patiently, taking the time to admire the altarpieces that decorated the walls alongside the lancet windows and the grand pieces of art that adorned the hall. The friar reappeared a short time later alongside an elderly man who sported a long white mane and an equally long beard. His eyes, though timeworn, held a youthful sparkle.

"Brother Don, this is... Me apologies. Ye dinna disclose yer name, sir."

"I'm sorry. I'm Myles Roberts," I swiftly responded. Brother Don conveyed a look of skepticism, and his eyes revealed a sense of great familiarity.

"Your accent—you don't have one," Brother Don remarked.

"No, sir, I do not. Neither do you, Mr. Towell."

"You know my true name?" he asked, a look of surprise on his face.

"Yes, sir, I do," I responded. "You and I have something important in common that we must discuss urgently!" His expression softened with relief. He quickly grabbed my forearm, squeezing it tightly, tears welling in his eyes.

"Will you excuse us, Brother Cian?" Adam requested. "Let's go to the reflection garden, Mr. Roberts," Adam said, motioning for me to follow him down the stairs.

He should be close to sixty-six years of age by now, I thought, recalling the story Mr. Brindley had recounted of Adam's arrival in 1598, at sixteen, though he still walked with the stride of a young man.

We situated ourselves on a circular wooden bench midway into the garden beside a cascading fountain. "I received word from Mr. Killian of a possible fellow journeyer. I never expected you to show up here." He grinned with a sigh and asked, "What's your story?"

"Not to go into much detail, but I came through this past June, and I simply want to go home."

"If it were that easy, do you think I'd be here sitting and talking with you?" he remarked dryly. "You haven't been here that long. You're still a baby," Adam said.

I exhaled and responded, "No, sir, I haven't. It's only been three months. I understand you've been here a little over fifty years."

"Yep. I have spent my entire adult life in this crazy town," he quipped.

"I'm assuming I'll be stuck here as well, then," I said, a grimace forming on my face.

Adam's gaze, which had been fixed on the cascading fountain, lifted to meet mine. "This isn't the first place I was transported to, you know, Mr. Roberts—"

"You can call me Myles," I interrupted.

"Myles. I first traveled when I was sixteen years old, just shy of turning seventeen, while on vacation with my family," he said, cupping his hands and reaching into the cascading fountain for a sip of water. "I first entered the cave in 2002 and emerged in 1981."

"1981? Seriously?!" I exclaimed; the anachronism of the year an absolute shock.

"Seriously! Have I got a story for you!" he said, a grin spreading across his face, his eyes lighting up with an impish gleam. "When I arrived in 1981, I traveled on my own to Washington, D.C., from Ireland. I made it to the downtown area and found myself in the presence of none other than President Reagan himself, saving his life to boot..."

"Wait... you... who... *what*?!" I stuttered, my mind racing to connect the dots.

"Yeah, yeah. I thought the same thing," he said, the grin still on his face. "I stood beside John Hinckley Jr. and watched him take aim, firing off a couple of rounds before I could nudge him on the shoulder with my knee, causing him to lose his footing. He missed his target, hitting the limo instead. He then got trampled by the Secret Service. I kid you not."

Highly intrigued, I responded, "I'm guessing you thought at the time that it was your pivotal moment?"

Grinning, he replied, "So I thought. I see you know about the moments in time we're supposed to change?"

"Both Mr. Killian and Mr. Brindley mentioned that the Elder Folks were the ones who would guide a journeyer into the place of their pivotal moment."

Adam got up and began pacing, his agitation evident in the nervous energy of his stride. Then, with a tone of excitement, he continued, "An old man, who I presumed was an Elder Folk, dragged me out from underneath the pile of security officers after the assassination attempt, then doused my nostrils with chloroform. When I regained consciousness, I found myself back in Ireland, inside a tent near the cave entrance."

"How did he manage to bring you to Ireland from Washington while keeping you sedated?"

He looked at me, a puzzled expression on his face. "I ask myself the same question, though I should've asked him!"

"So that is how you came to be in this century?"

"Yep. The old bastard said I needed to go back through the waterfall to return to my time, though there were no guarantees. Something having to do with the waterfall choosing the journeyer's destiny."

Understandably upset, he rebuked loudly, "Fuck you, waterfall," while giving the middle finger in no particular direction.

"So, it's safe to say that you're still searching for the definitive moment in this century?" I asked, curious to know.

A deep crease formed on his forehead, and he looked at me with frustration. "I freaking thought I did. When I first arrived, I was arrested—"

"I quickly chimed in, "for being a highwayman...""

His eyebrows frowned, and he continued, "Yes, yes, a fucking common thief. I was just a damn kid, you know." His voice cracked, sounding emotional. "I shared a jail cell with a redcoat who mentioned the name Henry Bagenal, which jogged a memory of the Yellowstone National—some crap..."

"The Battle of the Yellow Ford, you mean," I said, chuckling as I corrected him.

"Yep, that's the one. I revealed the outcome of the battle to the Earl of Tyrone, Hugh O'Neill. He claimed to have heard the tales of the watersfall and, long story short, he figured out I was a journeyer from the future." I sat listening to Adam, engrossed as he recounted the story Brindley had read from the book at the military post.

"The earl was an avid believer in folklore, so naturally, he was overjoyed to know that the tales were true. He promised that once he was victorious, I would be free. And indeed, he was victorious. I, in turn, killed someone significant whom I thought would be part of the pivotal moment, but obviously turned out not to be!"

"Who did you kill?" I asked instinctively.

"Sir Henry Bagenal, right after he killed a kindhearted soldier I befriended, Private Connor Gideon."

I stood abruptly, shaking my head and exclaiming, "You're A.T., the initials on the Saxon wheellock! Oh my God, why didn't I figure this out sooner?!"

He glared at me as if I were a madman. "What are you babbling about, kid?" he asked, continuing to stare, completely lost.

"I'm a tenth-grade history teacher, and a month before traveling to Ireland, I visited an exhibit at Stafford Beach in Georgia, where artifacts of Irish history were on display. One piece that caught my attention was a sixteenth-century Saxon wheellock. It had a brass plate above the pommel with the initials A.T. carved in. It was labeled as the pistol rumored to have taken the life of Sir Henry Bagenal."

"I will attest that I'm indeed A.T., owner of the aforementioned Saxon wheellock, and I can also affirm that it was unquestionably used to kill Sir

Bagenal. The pistol was gifted to me by the earl himself," Adam declared with a triumphant look on his face.

"No shit! Wow!" I yelped. "I struggled for a time, trying to figure out to whom those initials belonged."

"You mean to say my pistol made it to the twenty-first century?" Adam exclaimed, his eyes wide with a mixture of disbelief and wonder. "I should've carved an SOS message instead of my freaking initials. Care to see it?"

"You mean to say you still have it in your possession?" I asked, a surge of excitement making my heart pound.

Adam rose, a silent signal for me to follow, and led the way back up the stairs to his sleeping quarters, a small, private room separate from the open-floored dormitory. He opened a brown wooden box, its hinges creaking softly, and placed it in my hands.

"Jesus Christ, I can't believe it. The actual Saxon freaking wheellock," I inhaled, my fingers tracing the cold metal. Inspecting the brass plate closer, I noticed a symbol of a cross just below the letter "A," a detail I distinctly recalled seeing the first time I inspected the piece at the exhibit. "I remember this cross," I said, pointing below the initials. "The curator at the exhibit explained it was possibly carved after the near decimation of the Irish Catholics during the mid-seventeenth century."

Adam offered a look of dry sarcasm, adding, "Apparently, he didn't do his research thoroughly." He chuckled at his own remark, a sound that held a hint of bitter irony.

The longer Adam and I spoke of our respective futures, which were his past and my present, the more apprehensive I grew that neither he nor I would ever make it back to our own times. Though I was deeply concerned about my own predicament, a weighty empathy settled over me for Adam. He had traveled twice through the waterfall, futilely trying to make it home both times, only to be flung into yet another unfamiliar era. I felt a growing sense of obligation to do what I could to guide Adam and me on the right path, to achieve our selected destinies, whatever they might be.

***

Cong Abbey, I soon learned, was more than just a haven for Catholic parishioners. Several practitioners of Druidism, allowed to practice their ancient religion freely within the confines of the cloister, resided here. Others were leaders and lore keepers, men who carried the arcane knowledge of the alleged Elder Folks and the enigmatic Eas Gorm i Bhfolach.

During my stay at the abbey, I heard many stories referencing the tales of these mysterious Elder Folks. Unsure of their true origins, Fionntán Ó Domhnaill, an archdruid hailing from Rathlin O'Birne, explained that they simply *"tháinig le bheith"*—came to be—through creatures from Celtic mythology who dwelled in the Otherworld. He described a mold forged using oak branches, coated with their saliva, sweat, and tears, along with *salvsangre*— soil from the Otherworld blessed with human blood—thus forming the Elder Folks. It was a fascinating, chilling piece of lore.

Adam, I discovered, had befriended Fionntán when he first reached Cong Abbey, learning about Druidism and Celtic lore. Adam confessed his original intent in befriending Fionntán was to gain any possible detailed knowledge of the waterfall, desperately hoping for a way home.

Adam revealed that for twenty years he had traveled randomly to Donegal, each time entering the cave, searching vigilantly for a cycle of sorts, anything resembling the ambiance he experienced both times he crossed through. But each attempt was useless. Yielding any lingering sense of hope, he had finally surrendered and returned to Cong Abbey, swearing never to visit the waterfall again.

Fionntán Ó Domhnaill, with a quiet, somber tone, recounted the years it took for Adam to come to grips with the fact that he would never return to his time. Though it came as a shock, I knew in my heart of hearts that I, too, would likely never make it back to my home. The only thing keeping me from losing hope was, strangely, the coming Cromwellian Conquest. I sensed deeply that this was the ruling event, the pivotal moment that would indeed return me home.

Chapter 20 – Class of 2019

One of my daily highlights was retreating to the teachers' lounge to indulge in a freshly brewed cup of coffee. With a free period after lunch, I would often sprawl on the couch in the quiet, dimly lit corner of the room, allowing myself to zone out undisturbed.

The principal, Mrs. Galson, bustled into the break room, distracted by the towering stack of pamphlets she carried, completely unaware of my presence. "Good afternoon, Mrs. Galson. How are you?"

Startled by my abrupt greeting, her arms flew up in the air, sending the leaflets scattering throughout the room like startled birds.

"You stealthy bastard! I didn't see you there. Are you trying to give me a heart attack?" she exclaimed, clutching her chest dramatically.

I stifled a laugh at her reaction and quickly sprang from the couch to help her collect the pamphlets from the floor. "My apologies, Mrs. Galson. I didn't mean to startle you. I thought you saw me lying there on the couch."

Still seemingly agitated from the scare, she sighed. "It's my fault. I should be mindful of my surroundings, no matter *where* I am."

"Yes, you're right about that," I whispered quietly, agreeing with her assessment.

Handing her the first batch of flyers, she suggested I keep one for myself. "What's on the schedule that requires all these leaflets?"

"Where's your head at, Mr. Roberts? It's the program for the graduating class of 2019, which you seem to have forgotten about," she responded dryly. I groaned inwardly. I had inadvertently failed to check my emails and completely forgot to turn in the suggestions for the roster as required by the creative committee I was part of.

"Oops!" I replied humorously.

I handed her the last remaining flyers and returned to my place of Zen, sprawled across the couch, continuing to sip my coffee. I opened the pamphlet to familiarize myself with the schedule and was delightfully surprised to find a name dear to my heart written in big, bold letters: **Zoe Clive**. The commencement speaker.

She was a gorgeous, brown-skinned beauty. We met in college at a dive bar I frequented near the dorms. We dated throughout most of my junior year, but then she graduated and moved out of the country to pursue her career in medicinal chemistry, thus ending our relationship. Though she wasn't a petite redhead, I thought at the time she would be my future wife.

Because of her experiments, I became just as fascinated with science as I had been with history, prompting me to switch my minor from business management to environmental science. I was grateful to have been part of her exams and class demonstrations, but I never got a chance to express my gratitude for her appointing me as her official guinea pig.

Anticipating her visit to the school, I felt a rush of excitement. After so many years, I was finally getting the opportunity to thank her in person. She had inspired me not only to pursue my career goals but also to excel academically, shaping me into the educator I am today.

I found a notice posted on the bulletin board in the teachers' lounge requesting the faculty to attend a meet-and-greet social gathering at the gymnasium that evening at seven. I nearly flew out of my seat when I read Zoe was among the attendees who had already RSVP'd.

I checked my watch and realized I had just enough time to make it home to change into my Sunday best and return to the school nonchalantly, in case I ran into her.

I rushed home after school and ransacked my closet for something trendy to wear. Once I was showered and dressed, I hopped into my car and headed back. By the time I reached the school, the guests were already arriving. This allowed me time to enter the gymnasium unseen. I scampered up to the top row of the bleachers, perched like an eagle at the highest peak, searching for its prey. I caught sight of Zoe entering on the opposite side of the gym, still exuding the same beauty she had when we first met.

I quickly raced down the stairs, pausing for a moment to catch my breath, coming to terms with the fact that I was behaving like a juvenile. I slowed my pace and walked gracefully across the floor, introducing myself to some invitees I did not recognize, subconsciously avoiding detection by Zoe.

"Evening, stranger!" a voice whispered behind me. My body tensed, and my butt cheeks clenched as a surge of excited electricity raced throughout my body. It was Zoe. *Busted,* I thought, a rush of mortification overcoming me.

"Zoe, hey, what a surprise! What brings you here?" I asked nervously, my palms perspiring and my hands shaking from a mixture of tension and excitement.

"You have the roster in your hands, Myles. Has your vision deteriorated at your age?" she replied with a smile. "Didn't you recognize my name at the top of the list?"

Feeling red-faced and not knowing where to look, I let out a tense laugh, followed by an indiscernible response. "Um… uh… well… uff!"

Amused at my awkwardness, Zoe giggled, then planted a familiar kiss on my cheek, whispering into my ear, "You're off the hook."

We laughed at the quirky reunion. I motioned for her to follow me and led the way to the beverage station to share a toast. "Here's to old friends and fresh memories!" I toasted clumsily, clanking her cup a bit too heavily, causing half her drink to spill.

"Myles, why are you so nervous?" she asked cheerfully.

"I have no clue. The minute I read you were going to be here, I got excited, having not seen you in so long. I simply melted like butta."

"Is that why you snuck in here and ninja'd yourself up on the bleachers?"

Slapping myself on the forehead, I responded, embarrassed, "Oh man, you saw that? I don't know, Zo—your presence brought out the nervous high school teenager in me!"

We were interrupted when Mrs. Galson stood on the stage and tapped on the microphone, followed by a high-pitched feedback noise. We turned to listen to her speech. Following her address, she called out the names of the invited guests, requesting them to come to the stage and give a brief description of their profession and trade in their respective fields.

Zoe was the first invitee onto the stage. I beamed with pride, listening intently as she shared her experiences in Africa. She described the people and places passionately, making me want to travel there.

Following her introduction, the remaining speakers continued to make their way onto the stage in the order listed on the roster, allowing Zoe and me a moment to sneak away and continue catching up. We left the gymnasium, as the acoustics made it difficult to hear each other clearly, and went to the makeshift reception area in the hallway.

"So, what brought you back to the States, Zo?" I asked. "Anyone would think from the way you made it sound that you would never want to return!"

"I accepted a position with a pharmaceutical company in Virginia," she explained, then added hesitantly, "I also needed to handle a personal matter that I couldn't fully manage alone back in Africa!"

"Hopefully, nothing extremely worrisome!" I said, expressing my concern.

"No, it wasn't anything majorly worrying, but it *was* major!"

"How so?"

"Well—"

I intentionally interrupted her. "I know what it was. You found me on social media, and seeing how handsome I still looked, you couldn't help yourself; you still find me irresistible!" I said in jest. I grabbed her hand, caressed her soft palm, and slowly trailed my fingertips up her forearm.

I assumed it was sheer reflex when she unexpectedly retracted her hand, disguising her rejection by looking into her purse. Taken aback by her reaction, I reached for my socks and pulled them up, a counter-reaction to her unforeseen response.

"I'm sorry. I didn't mean to react that way, especially with you, Myles. It wasn't cool; it's just…"

Reaching for her hand once again, she rose instantly, her eyes widening. She then cried out nervously, "Honey!"

I replied with a comically overconfident smile, "Yeah, baby?"

She curled her lips suggestively, signaling for me to remain silent just as someone walked up behind me and took Zoe into a tight embrace, followed by a kiss on the lips. The man turned to me and introduced himself.

"Hi, I'm Mark, Zoe's husband. And you are?"

I looked at the man, then at Zoe, and the only words that escaped my mouth were, "Aw, crap!"

Chapter 21 – Don't Go Chasing Elder Folks

Using the map Mr. Brindley had provided, Adam and I mapped out a route less traveled, hoping to keep ourselves undetected from bandits should we find no alternative but to sleep outdoors. We felt the need to venture out in search of the alleged Elder Folks, who I had concluded were merely made-up characters created to amplify the stories of the waterfall. Still, any information they might provide could help our efforts to succeed.

It took us three weeks to course a favorable route when Adam abruptly fell ill. Despite being inoculated against most diseases, the constant vomiting and diarrhea concerned me, not solely because of his age, but primarily because dehydration through dysentery could lead to his demise. I concocted an oral rehydration solution to prevent him from dehydrating severely by mixing salt and sugar with water, recommending that he sip it steadily. I continued preparing the mixture for the next several days. Though no longer appearing pasty-faced, Adam could not keep food down. It occurred to me he would not fully recover quickly enough, so I decided to take the journey on my own.

Overnight, a dense fog rolled in, filling the air with a mist that limited visibility. As I considered venturing out on my own, I found it would be difficult to navigate, particularly in this area that was still foreign to me.

Anxious and avoiding any further delays, I went to visit Adam to announce my intentions. "Are you holding up okay today, Adam?"

"I could go for a Philly cheesesteak with fries," he responded feebly.

"Don't worry, man, you'll be up and about in no time. I promise," I assured him.

"I'm hoping so. I'm not accustomed to lying down for so long doing nothing. I'm used to being in constant motion." Tears welled in his eyes as he confessed, "I'm scared, Myles. I want to make it home, back to my home. If I'm to die, I'd rather it be in my century." He kept a firm grip on my hand, showing his despair.

"I'll take you home if it is the last thing I do. You have my word, Adam."

"You look like you wanted to tell me something. Are you leaving?"

I unrolled the map and spread it on the table next to Adam's bed and revealed, "Yes. I planned to leave today to avoid any further delays. I'll travel southeast," pointing at the map, "to Kilkenny. Brindley drew a half-circle to denote a contact from his list that may or may not be alive. If the former, he goes by the name Lorcán O'Quinn, but in the latter, he said his kin could be trusted."

"Will you be able to navigate on your own in this fog?" he asked, raising his head to peek out of the window.

"It's letting up. I stepped outside before coming to you, and it had begun to clear."

"I'll wait here in hopes of your return, and I promise you I'll be fully recovered by then," Adam said.

"I'll hold you to your word, Gramps," I replied in jest.

"Call me Gramps again, and I'll skip recovery and get up from this bed and kick your ass," he replied humorously, giving me hope that his recovery would be a speedy one.

"I promise you, Adam, you'll make it home to your family, alive and well. You have my word!"

***

I was grateful to the friars for the preparations they made for my journey. They put together basic rations consisting of salted meats, cheese, bread, and flasks filled with whiskey and water, while others groomed, fed, and watered my trusted companion. They fashioned a separate saddlebag and stuffed it with hay and berries to keep Moonlight nourished along the way.

I rerouted myself from the original course, heading just a few miles southeast to a town called Oranmore. During one of our conversations referencing the tales of the Eas Gorm i Bhfolach, I remembered Oistin Killian mentioning an alleged Elder Folk, though not by name, who lived in a castle on the shores of Galway. Looking at the map, I calculated the castle to be approximately twenty-eight miles from the abbey, so it would take no longer than eight hours to reach it.

The weather was shifting, growing cooler, as it often does in northern coastal countries. Fortunately, I had brought two wool blankets, one for Moonlight and one for myself, knowing the temperature could drop sharply after sunset. Adam had warned me that even if the air wasn't bitterly cold, the ocean breeze could make the nights feel as frigid as a winter dawn sometimes.

***

Oranmore Castle sat on an inlet at Galway Bay, its ancient stones overlooking the vast gray expanse of the Atlantic Ocean. Like most places I had visited since my baffling arrival in this time, Oranmore Castle appeared just as formidable as the others I had encountered. At first glance, one might mistake it for a fortress or a *gaol*, with its stark rectangular façade, iron-covered windows, and a heavy, gated entrance. I discovered an open, unguarded gate, its hinges groaning softly, leading to an unkempt path that wound directly to a main entrance flanked by two weathered statues of stone lions, rampant and watchful.

As I approached the half-open wooden door, I heard a cacophony of voices and the clinking of tankards from within. I let myself in, stepping into a large, dimly lit hall, stumbling upon a group of soldiers, their laughter echoing off the stone walls as they drank and caroused. "Evening, gentlemen," I greeted. All conversation ceased. Every head in the room swiveled, their eyes, some impassive, others openly curious, fixing on me.

A soldier, short in stature but broad in the chest, stood before me, drinking straight from a pitcher. He squared his shoulders, his head held high, a challenging glimmer in his eye. "What business d'ye have entering here uninvited?" he demanded.

"Forgive the intrusion," I replied. "I'm searching for an elderly wise man, rumored to live within this castle. Would any of you know who I am referring to?"

His eyebrows furrowed with a questioning expression, then a cunning look entered his eyes. "Aye, Seanfhear Ciallmhar, we know of him. Who inquires?"

"My name is Myles Roberts. Oistin Killian informed me I may find Mr. Ciallmhar here." The inebriated men around him exchanged glances, their expressions showing little interest in Oistin or the nature of my visit.

"I can tell ye where to find the *sean gabhar Gaelach*, but it will cost ye!" the soldier declared, a greedy look emerging in his eyes.

Having left my money hidden inside the under-pouch of Moonlight's saddle, I reached into my pocket and offered the soldier the only two shillings I had on my person.

"Is that all ye offer fer information from us, lad?" he scoffed. "That gold horsehead ring on ye finger looks to be worth a pretty penny, eh!"

"The shillings are all I can offer you, sir, nothing more," I stated, my patience wearing thin. His arrogance chafed. I brazenly stepped closer, standing mere inches from his face. "Here are the two shillings," I snapped furiously. "Now, tell me where the fuck to find Mr. Ciallmhar!" With that, I threw the coins in his face. He flinched, and his hand instinctively went for his sword.

Despite the room being filled with armed soldiers, a primal instinct took over. I shoved him with a force that sent him toppling backward, bringing down with him the others standing behind him like dominoes. The sudden distraction offered me a desperate chance. Rather than exiting through the main entryway, I changed direction, dashing through a narrow corridor just left of the main entrance. It led into a smaller room with an enormous fireplace and, to my dismay, more soldiers.

"Fuck!" I muttered under my breath.

As the other soldiers pursued me, their shouts echoing behind, I was unable to retrace my steps. I scrambled, sliding across a large wooden table that stood in front of the fireplace, and made my way to a narrow set of stairs. Not knowing where they led, I grabbed a chair and several crates I found piled next to the passageway and hurled them onto the steps, hoping to create a temporary barrier and put some distance between me and my pursuers.

I reached another hallway at the top of the stairs; its walls lined with several doors on either side. I checked each one, my hands fumbling with the primitive latches, hoping to find somewhere to hide, but they were all securely locked. The barricade I had made didn't hold for long, and I could hear the soldiers' boots thundering up the stairs behind me. I hurried toward the end of the hallway, turning corners through what seemed like an endless maze of corridors, finally coming to a dead end with a solitary door. "Shit," I muttered to myself, pushing hard on it, hoping against all reason it would open.

"Thought ye could get away, eh? Now ye'll know what running from a soldier will bring ye!" the soldier's voice snarled from behind me.

A sudden, desperate thought flashed through my mind—a memory of the Claddagh Lieutenant Olson gave me, and his warning to use it in a life-or-death circumstance. I reached into my pocket to retrieve it, but the soldier already had his sword drawn, lunging forward to impale me.

The tip of the blade came millimeters from piercing my chest, but as luck would have it, the door behind me flung open, causing me to fall flat on my back. I lay gasping for breath, the wind knocked out of me, then heard a familiar, commanding voice cut through the chaos. "Stand down, Private!"

I looked up, and lo-and-behold, it was Lieutenant Olson.

"Man, are you a welcome sight! What are the chances?" I said with a mixed rush of relief and adrenaline surging over me.

The lieutenant helped me off the ground, his face harsh with concern. "Mr. Roberts, are you hurt?"

"No, Lieutenant, not now that you're here."

"What is amiss, Private? Why have you assaulted this man?" the lieutenant demanded sternly, with authority.

"Lieutenant, me apologies, sir," the private said nervously, his eyes darting from me to the lieutenant. "The lad entered uninvited and attacked me, shoving meself and some of the other lads to the ground."

"Think carefully, Private. Do you really want to deceive your lieutenant?" I warned. "First, you tried to extort money from me, then wanted to rob me of my ring, and now you lie to your commanding officer about it?"

"I will deal with you shortly, Private; you are dismissed, the lot of you!" the lieutenant commanded, his scowled stare never leaving the private's face.

The soldiers turned and paced down the corridor in a hurried, defeated manner.

"Someone is in trouble," I teased sarcastically as they walked away.

"Mr. Roberts, come inside. My apologies for the soldier's incompetence."

I followed him down a narrow corridor and entered through another door, which led into Olson's office. I observed a man standing in front of the lieutenant's desk, facing me with a look of extreme disbelief. The lieutenant looked at us. "Mr. Roberts, may I present to you..."

***

As a young boy, my friends and I would carelessly venture throughout the neighborhood, the concrete canyons of the Bronx our sprawling playground. Our parents, with both love and wisdom, warned us never to enter any of the abandoned buildings on the block. Yet, growing up as Puerto Ricans in the Bronx, defying our parents' wishes and doing exactly what we were told *not* to do was less an act of rebellion and more a cherished rite of passage.

Across from the apartment building I lived in on Walton Avenue, an entire block lay scarred and gutted, lined with abandoned buildings, most ravaged by the hungry maw of fires. Drug dealers and addicts, shadows in the urban decay, frequented the neighborhood, concealing themselves from the police within the decrepit structures, using bolt cutters to breach the flimsy metal barrier gates.

There was one particular building, a brown brick hulk standing in the middle of the block, less trafficked by the peddlers. My friends and I chose it to be the headquarters for our group, the "Titaneers." We were resourceful, running two connected extension cords from a nearby light post into the room we had appointed as "Titaneers Hall."

***

One Saturday afternoon, as I strolled down the street, I encountered a kid who was new to the neighborhood. He was short and stocky, his shoulders hunched, and he was known to be bullied at school because of his physique. He was fiercely intelligent, but equally sensitive, his eyes often downcast. I felt a pang of empathy for him, seeing him sitting alone outside the building, lost in the pages of a book. I approached and introduced myself.

"Hey, how's it going? What are you reading?" I asked, initiating the conversation, hoping to break through his shell.

He replied in a low, faint voice, barely audible above the street noise. "*Spirit of the Berserkr.*"

"Oh, cool, what's it about?"

"Vikings!"

"Oh man, sweet! I like anything that has to do with Vikings. My name is Myles. What's your name?"

"Norman, but everyone calls me Gordi."

"Hey, Gordi, my friends and I have a group called the Titaneers. You can come and hang out with us if you want. We have a spot across the street in that building," I said, pointing at the brown brick building with streaks of smoke traced across its façade. His face brightened, a sudden, radiant smile transforming his features. I perceived from his expression that he had never been invited to be part of a social group before. He called out to his mom, yelling surprisingly loud, to get permission, which she granted with a wave. He quickly returned, exuding an air of contentment and excitement.

We ran to meet up with the others, making a quick stop at the *bodega* along the way to buy potato chips and soda to snack on while we watched a movie. Michael had borrowed his brother's portable Mini-TV/DVR combo, while Anthony had sneaked into his older brother's R-rated movies. Gordi looked nervous as we passed through the broken fencing, hesitant to enter the abandoned building. I assured him it was safe and gave him reassurance by walking through it, telling him we had been in and out of the building countless times and that he had nothing to worry about.

"Are you sure, Myles? The floors look like they're going to collapse the second I step on them."

To boost his confidence, I stepped in again and jumped up and down theatrically, giving him consolation that the worn wooden boards would not crumble beneath him. Gordi nervously stepped inside and slowly paced, his eyes wide, appearing relieved that he did not fall through.

***

The other boys arrived, their boisterous energy filling the hall, and all quickly took a liking to Gordi, who seemed to fit right in. Joel brought out a makeshift name tag and wrote Gordi's name on it with a sharpie, but before pinning it onto

Gordi's shirt, he informed him, "You can only wear this pin and become an official Titaneer once you pass our initiation test."

Gordi's eyes widened, the joyous expression he previously wore quickly turning to fear. "Wh... what do I have to do?" he stammered, biting his lower lip to keep it from quivering.

"First you need to run up to the roof, where you'll find a box full of toys. Inside, you'll uncover a green hot rod car at the bottom of the box." Gordi appeared relieved that the task at hand was not as demanding as he had expected. "After you collect the car," Joel continued, a mischievous grin appearing on the corner of his lips, "you'll need to go inside one apartment on every floor and gather nine different lettered blocks to spell out the word 'Titaneers."

Gordi's brows tensed, showing his anxiety, but he was not deterred. "Okay, it sounds easy enough," he remarked reluctantly. Anthony grabbed the bag full of blocks and ran upstairs to place them in the selected apartments. He lived up to his nickname, "Speedy Gonzales," making it back in less than ten minutes. Joel took out his pocket watch and warned him he had only fifteen minutes to complete the mission. "Only fifteen minutes? You have to be kidding me. You do know it's six floors up, right?"

Waving his pocket watch, Joel teased, "Time's a-tickin'!" We all yelled, egging Gordi on, "Go, go, go!"

We followed behind as he raced up the stairs, then slowed to a crawl when he approached the unstable-looking steps, their wooden planks groaning under his weight. "You're fine, keep going," we shouted, continuously urging him on.

"You think he'll find all the letters?" Michael asked, doubting Gordi.

"I doubt he'll even make it up to the roof," Anthony remarked humorously.

"Cut him some slack, man!" I said compassionately. "Let's just cheer him on."

Gordi yelled over the railing, his voice sounding winded. "Okay, I've got this, just two more floors to get to the roof!"

I yelled back optimistically, "Yes, you've got this, Gordi!" The door to the roof scraped against the cement floor with an echoing screech, bringing a wave of relief, knowing he had carried out the first part of the test. I then heard the door scrape a second time, so I yelled out, "Did you find the car?"

"Yes, yes, I got it. I'm heading through the hallway, checking apartment 6C."

"Woo-hoo, you go, boy!" we yelled encouragingly. "Don't forget to shout out the letter of each block you find and the floor where you found it."

A few minutes of silence passed before Gordi hollered, "Found an E!"

"Okay, now hurry. You have eleven minutes left!"

"I'm hurrying, I'm hurrying!" Less than a minute later, he shouted, "I'm on the fifth floor now!"

I was surprised at how quickly he reached each floor and how swiftly he searched through every apartment. With only four apartments per floor, it was easy for him to find the blocks, as they were placed on counters, clearly visible upon entering each apartment.

"I found the letters A and T."

"Eight minutes to go!" Joel screamed.

"Fourth floor now, and I found another two letters, a T and an E," Gordi shouted, panting audibly.

"Six minutes to go!" Joel continued.

A crashing noise, the sound of splintering wood and metal, echoed throughout the hallway, causing panic. I ran up to the second floor, crying out, "Gordi, are you okay? What happened?"

I then heard a banging sound, quickly followed by Gordi shouting, "I'm alright, I just tripped over a chair."

To be safe, I waited at the top of the stairs leading to the third floor in case Gordi needed my help.

"How much longer does he have?" I shouted over the railing.

"One minute!" Joel responded.

"Gordi, what floor are you on now?" As I waited for his response, Joel yelled out abruptly, "Time's up!"

I dashed through the corridor, reaching the landing of the stairs leading to the fourth floor. "Gordi, where are you?" As I was about to run up to the fourth floor, a frightening sound of breaking window glass echoed throughout the building, prompting the boys to join me on the stairs. They appeared just as frightened as I was.

"What was that noise?" Anthony asked, fear resonating in his voice.

"I don't know!" I replied, my voice matching the tone.

We all shouted, "Gordi, Gordi," but there was no answer. The silence was deafening as we waited for a response, so I instructed the guys to run and get help. I sprinted up to the fourth floor, where Gordi had last checked in. I searched the first apartment at the top of the stairs, finding the door halfway open, assuming Gordi was inside.

"Gordi, are you in here?" I yelled, panic-stricken.

Getting no response, I made a quick sweep of the apartment, then headed to the next, but that one was locked. I bypassed the third door after spotting a lettered block peeking out between the threshold and the door of the fourth apartment. I reached down to pick it up, horrified when I found it soaked with blood.

I began hyperventilating, fearful thoughts of a macabre scenario filling my head. I kicked open the door and encountered the most horrific sight I had ever witnessed.

Gordi lay on the ground with his throat cut open, his jugular continuously spewing blood. There were shoeprints trailing from where Gordi lay, leading directly to the fire escape window, with pieces of shattered glass strewn about. I braved my fears and ran to the fire escape window, hoping to identify the culprit who might have caused this atrocity. I caught sight of someone running across the alley, but the person quickly disappeared around the corner.

I turned my gaze back to Gordi's body, staring at his blood-stained clothes. My hands went numb, and I felt an overwhelming sense that my knees were about to buckle beneath me. Beads of sweat formed on my forehead, yet I couldn't tear my eyes away from him.

I did not understand it at the time, but I now realize that at that moment, I was going into shock. Although the distress I was currently experiencing in the lieutenant's office was not as intense as seeing Gordi's body lying in that puddle of blood, the intensity I presently felt was equally profound.

***

"Am I freaking dreaming? Rey, is it really you?" I stammered, my mind struggling to reconcile his familiar face with the impossible reality of the seventeenth century.

"Myles? Oh my God, Myles!" Rey cried, launching himself into my arms. He hugged me with an intensity that felt like he was clinging to a lifeline, weeping uncontrollably, refusing to let go.

"Rey, but how?... Why?... When?... Ho... how?" I managed.

Grasping my shoulders, Rey pushed away from me, his eyes, red-rimmed and glistening with tears, searching my face as if to reassure himself that it was indeed me. His ragged sobs overpowered his ability to talk. He struggled to regain his composure, taking a shuddering breath before he explained, "Myles, I went to Caisleán Dhún na nGall and then to the waterfall, looking for you after you went missing. That's when I got caught in the…."

Rey stopped mid-sentence, his gaze flicking to Lieutenant Olson, who stood quietly observing us. He held back from blurting out the big secret, then offered the lieutenant an awkward, apologetic grin.

"The Major has informed me of Mr. Roberts' special situation, so I assume you share the same secret," Olson stated. Rey and I looked at each other, nodding in agreement, confirming the lieutenant's summarization.

"I'll excuse myself and allow you both a chance to reacquaint yourselves, as I must confront the private and berate him in front of the other soldiers to teach him a lesson," Olson said, a light chuckle escaping him.

"Thank you, Lieutenant Olson. I appreciate you. You have helped me a second time, and I am forever grateful to you!" I said, shaking his hand cordially.

"Cheers, Mr. Roberts. I shall take my leave. I will have a servant bring ale and bread if you so desire."

"That would be excellent, Lieutenant, but before you go, are you familiar with someone who presumably resides in this castle and goes by the name Seanfhear Ciallmhar?"

With furrowed eyebrows, deep in thought, Olson shook his head. "No, but I will inquire with the men and inform you upon my return."

Lieutenant Olson left the office, the door clicking softly shut behind him, finally allowing Rey and me time to talk freely. "What brought you here to Oranmore Castle?" I asked, staring in disbelief at my best friend.

"I met a friendly couple the day I went through the waterfall at a potato farm."

"Don't tell me—Mr. and Mrs. MacKinney?" I exclaimed excitedly, a sense of warmth washing over me at the mention of their names.

"Yes, yes. They were extremely nice, though there were times I almost suggested to Mr. MacKinney to get laid or something; he sure was capricious."

"You're not kidding, man. He really needed to!" I agreed wryly.

"I was there just a few days," Rey said, sifting through the satchel he carried over his shoulder. "Mrs. Omi said if I found you, I was to give you this."

Rey pulled out a book, its familiar leather binding bringing tears to my eyes. "*Don Quixote*, oh man!" I exclaimed, flipping through the pages of the book that had unexpectedly bonded Mrs. Omi and me.

"Why does the book make you emotional, Myles?" Rey asked with a grin.

"When I first met Mrs. Omi, before I knew what century I was in, we debated the year this book was published. That's when she and I figured out I was a journeyer."

"A journeyer? You mean to say we have a title?" Rey remarked playfully, a spark of his old humor.

"Yup. A fantastic man named Dujardin Brindley, who is also a Major General in the Irish Army, authored a book referencing the waterfall and the people known as the Elder Folk. Based on his years of research trying to justify the tales, he refers to the people who disappear inside the cave as journeyers."

"Mrs. Omi mentioned the book to me, saying it was written in Irish, but her husband refused to translate it for me. He said if we were to cross paths, I was to ask you for the summary he provided you with."

"I guess he liked me better than he did you!" I replied teasingly.

There was a knock on the door, though it sounded more like a foot kicking rather than a polite hand knock. I opened it to find the private standing on the threshold, carrying a large tray with ale, cheese, bread, and grapes. "Oh, okay," I sneered sarcastically. "Come in, Private. You can set it on the table there, just beside the desk."

"I am to apologize to ye fer me disobedience and disrespect, sir. Should ye wish, I will take permanent leave of the regiment." The private bowed his head remorsefully for his insubordination. I assured him there would be no need for him to take leave.

"I'll put in a good word with the lieutenant on your behalf, Private. You may remain. Just remember to treat no one else with disregard."

"Thank ye, sir. Ye have me word. I willna be an oaf ever again!" I shook his hand and then dismissed him.

"What was all that about? Are you some sort of high-ranking commander in this century?" Rey asked, his eyes wide with surprise.

"Nah. But I feel like one sometimes. The guy was a jerk when I arrived. He tried to extort me for my money and ring in exchange for information I needed."

"Myles, you're going to be happy now that you mentioned your ring," Rey said, digging through his waist pouch, having to pour out the contents onto the desk, unable to find whatever it was he was searching for. Sifting through the coins, he picked up and displayed the white gold bracelet I had lost in the waterfall.

"Rey, is that my bracelet?" I asked in a whisper of disbelief. I gently took the bracelet from his hand, turning it over to inspect its familiar, intricate links. I latched it onto my wrist.

"When I went searching for you at the waterfall, I examined that place for clues to your whereabouts," Rey explained. "I spotted a shiny object wedged under a rock, and boom, there it was!"

"I thought it was gone forever. Thank you, Rey. As always, you are there to the rescue." I couldn't help but smile, a grin so wide it felt like my face would crack.

"What's with the clown face?" Rey asked, grinning teasingly.

"Rey, do you remember the Saxon wheellock I told you about? The one I was allowed to handle at the exhibit at Stafford Beach?"

"Yes. The pistol with the carved initials!"

"That's the one. Well, the reason I'm here is that the initials A.T. belong to a man named Adam Towell, a fellow journeyer. He arrived here in 1598, but get this—he journeyed from 2002 to 1981, *then* to 1598. He visited the waterfall over and over but couldn't make it back."

"No shit," Rey exclaimed, grimacing. "Do you think we'll be stuck here as well, Myles?"

"I'm almost sure we won't," I replied, putting a hand on Rey's shoulder to comfort him. "I met an alleged Elder Folk, Oistin Killian, discovering later that he was just a man with a vast knowledge of the waterfall. He said that journeyers are chosen to change a pivotal moment in whichever time they're in, something inevitable. Even though Adam changed two noteworthy outcomes, he was still unable to travel back to his original timeline, so it makes me wonder."

"So, what makes you think our attempts would be any different?" Rey asked indignantly.

"That's just it," I replied. "As I see it, his fate may be joined to mine—well… now ours, I presume."

"You may be right, Myles. Where can we find this Adam Towell?"

Confidently, with a raised eyebrow and a sly smirk, I swiftly responded, "Funny you should ask, my friend. What I failed to mention was that the person I spent the past few weeks with, before venturing to Oranmore Castle, was Adam Towell himself!"

"Then what are we waiting for? Let's go!"

***

Days after our reunion and Rey and I departed Oranmore Castle. Having had no luck finding the alleged Elder Folk, Seanfhear Ciallmhar, we had to move on. We had worked out a route that would lead us first to Kilkenny in search of Lorcán O'Quinn—if he were still alive. Though it would entail substantial travel time, once we reached Kilkenny, we would return to Cong Abbey, meet up with Adam, and prepare him to travel back with us to Donegal, and eventually back into the waterfall.

The first leg of the trip to Kilkenny would take approximately two days; therefore, we needed to stop somewhere in between to rest the horses and ourselves. Rey pointed out a town located approximately forty miles midway between Oranmore and Kilkenny, near the River Shannon, just a few miles west of Carrigahorig, which he said he had visited on his way to Oranmore.

We traveled well into the night, finally having to camp and rest as the horses were lagging in their pace. We found a suitable spot, dismounted, hid our satchels and my metal case nearby, and tied the blankets between two wide trees to block the wind. Once we were settled, Rey was the first to drift off as I stared in disbelief that he was actually here.

***

The distant thud of horse's hooves, muffled by the damp earth, roused me from a fitful sleep. The sound grew steadily closer. I tugged on Rey's shoulder, shaking him hard several times before his eyes finally drifted open. "Rey, there's someone on a horse heading our way. Ready your pistol while I douse the fire!"

Rey sprang to his feet instantaneously. "Shit, where did I put my pistol?" he whispered loudly, rummaging frantically through his satchel, coming up empty. Then, a flash of memory: he had hidden it under his blanket before falling asleep. "Got it!" he murmured, pulling the weapon free.

"Shhh! They're getting closer. Get behind the tree; I'll hide behind the bush across from it!" The thought of preparing for a gunfight, or even the possibility that I might have to take another human life, turned my stomach. Though my adrenaline was now coursing through me, I took a moment to say a quick prayer, asking for forgiveness. *Dear Lord, please forgive me for my sins. Please understand that I did not choose to be here, and I am left with few choices but to take actions that are beyond my control. Please forgive me!*

"Rey, is your pistol loaded and cocked?"

"That's what she asked!" he joked nervously.

"This is not a time for your dumbass jokes, Rey!" I hissed impatiently.

"Sorry, Myles. Oddly enough, I'm nervous." Though he had many years of experience as an officer of the law, Rey seemed unable to adjust to the harsh difference between the law and order of this present century and the realities of our own.

We stood hidden, waiting, both of us uneasy, realizing that the sound of the horse's hooves had stopped. I grew concerned, as the sound of the hooves was what I had used to determine the distance between us and the approaching stranger. After moments of uncomfortable silence, I could make out the squelching sound of footsteps in the mud, just a few yards behind where we hid. I tossed a pebble at Rey to catch his attention and signal him to walk quietly in my direction.

"I heard footsteps just a few yards that way," I whispered, pointing behind him. "Stay attentive and don't react impetuously in case it's one of the lieutenant's men."

"I should be the one barking orders at you, Myles. I'm the FBI agent here. *You* relax; we've got this, bruh!"

As the footsteps drew nearer, I leaned in and whispered in Rey's ear, instructing him to be ready and wait for my signal. A faint voice then emerged from the direction of the footsteps. The closer the figure in the darkness approached, the clearer the sound became. It was someone singing Vanessa Carlton's song, "*A Thousand Miles*"!

"What the hell?" Rey whispered, a bewildered look on his face.

"Adam, is that you, Adam?" I yelled out, unable to contain my surprise.

"Who the hell else would it be that knows that song in this century?" Adam replied with his usual sarcastic dry wit.

I followed his voice, navigating through the darkness. When I reached him, I pulled him into a tight embrace. I was overjoyed and relieved to know he had survived his battle with dysentery. "You have no idea how happy I am to see you, Adam! How are you feeling? The last time I saw you, I honestly thought it would be the last time I'd lay eyes on you."

"I may trip, but I won't fall! Never underestimate me."

"How did you know where to find me?" I asked.

"I have many acquaintances in these parts, Myles. I asked around if anyone had seen a young man traveling on a white horse with a distinctive marking on its shoulder. You sure know how to leave a trail behind, especially back there in Oranmore." I reached for the flask and poured Adam a drink. "I spoke to Lieutenant Olson. He pointed me in the direction you told him you would be traveling..."

He stopped mid-sentence and turned to look at Rey, inspecting him from head to toe. "Why the hell is this guy staring at me like I'm the ugly girl at the prom?" he asked, displeased.

"Adam, you will never believe it. This is my childhood friend, Rey, the one I told you about, the FBI agent. Long story short, his search led him to the waterfall, and he ended up here as well."

"Holy crap, sucks to be you, Rey!" Adam remarked comically. "Word of advice: if you are going to hide yourself using the cover of night, learn to extinguish the fire before going to sleep. You might be cold, but you won't be dead!"

"I will definitely heed your advice, Grandpa!" I shot back with a grin.

"I'm assuming you're wanting to cash in on that ass-kicking I've been saving?" Adam said, his eyebrows furrowed in a mock frown.

"Ha-ha, sure. Let's get the fire restarted. Are you hungry, Adam?"

"Just a bit, yes. I caught and gutted a rabbit before sunset, but I didn't want to slow my pace and risk you disappearing from my radar." He nodded suggestively to his horse. "It's hanging off my saddle. Go fetch it, doughnut hog, while I get the fire started!"

We sat by the campfire as the rabbit roasted, sharing the whiskey and ale Adam had brought along, and reminisced about our century and the things we missed most. Rey and I filled Adam in on the details of movies, songs, and current events he had missed after he traveled. I leaned back against the large tree; my eyes fixed on them. Just then, I surmised that however improbable it might seem, together we stood a greater chance of returning home.

Chapter 22 – Law of Entanglement

They say that as an adult; you tend to forget many childhood memories; they become flashes, like brief clips from a newsreel. What is also forgotten are the memories that came before we were born, like the sounds we heard in our mother's womb and the memorable events from the life we lived before being conceived.

Yes! Our past lives.

If you have ever met someone who, in your heart of hearts, you felt connected to but just could not pinpoint where you had met; it is said that that person is someone with whom you have been linked in past lives. If you reunite with that person once again, inevitably, love will be tethered, as that is the same soul you have been conjoined with throughout all your lives.

It might sound foolish, but that's exactly how I felt when I first met Lisa. As we sat in that pizza shop, talking for hours, it became increasingly easy to believe that I had known and loved her for many lifetimes. Her words, both during our conversation and in the note she left by the coffeemaker, solidified that feeling in my heart.

***

Adam, having traveled through these parts for so many years, was familiar with the lay of the land, so naturally, he took the lead as we headed toward Kilkenny. He was a familiar face throughout the towns we passed through, and we found ourselves welcomed by the locals and treated like royalty.

The last residence we were invited to stay in before reaching our destination in Kilkenny belonged to the former twelfth Earl of Ormond, James Butler, who was now known as a Marquess. He was a well-known supporter of the Parliamentarians and a Royalist supporter of King Charles I. Following the death of King Charles; he continued his support of the throne by rallying Confederates of the Catholic Church and Protestant Royalists for King Charles II after the Cromwellian Conquest. I found him to be an opportunist and somewhat of a betrayer to the Irish, which left me staggered to know that Adam had agreed to lodge at his estate.

I caught up to Adam, riding alongside him, and questioned him about why he would suggest staying in the home of this defector. "I have met the Marquess on my earlier visits to Nenagh. We were introduced by the Earl of Strafford, whom he has been acquainted with for many years."

"You do know the history behind this man, don't you?" I asked, stating the obvious.

Adam seemed puzzled at first, conveying a look of skepticism, then he clapped back, "Whatever, kid, at least we will sleep comfortably tonight and with our bellies full. We have a long ride ahead of us to Kilkenny tomorrow. Once we leave there, we don't have to deal with the Marquess anymore!"

I pulled on Moonlight's reins and slowed my stride, positioning myself behind Adam, trying to keep my cool. Observant of my demeanor, Rey paced alongside me, curious to know the reason for the look of anger I was projecting. "What's wrong, Myles?"

"I'll tell you about it later. Nothing to worry about right now!" I replied, feeling vexed.

"Keep calm, man. I've seen that look before, witnessed it for many years, and it's one that nothing good ever comes out of!"

"I'll get over it," I replied as I clicked my teeth and jerked on Moonlight's reins once again to slow my stride and pace behind them. I questioned myself about why I felt so strongly against this man, never having met him, only knowing of him from what I had read in history books. There was some sour, deep-rooted sentiment I felt toward him. Knowing he was a treacherous snake in the grass made him a thorn in my side, but I could not explain why.

Passing Lough Ourna, we traveled less than thirty miles before arriving at the Marquess's estate. To pass the time, I hummed a song I had come across on YouTube by an Irish group called Seo Linn. It was titled "*Óró 'Sé Do Bheatha 'Bhaile.*" It was an Irish folk song I had listened to repeatedly the week before flying out to Ireland. It became my vacation mantra. It not only helped to ease my mind, but I imagined myself, in some bizarre way, singing it aloud in a battle charge.

I returned from my brief trance, catching sight of a steeple atop St. Mary's of the Rosary Church peeking over a copse of mature rowan trees. Nenagh Castle was near the church, but we still had some time before arriving at the Marquess's residence.

The song played on an endless loop in my mind, leading me into a state of mindlessness as we galloped across the semi-barren land. Beyond one of the many hills we passed, we came upon a ridge where I noticed two towers rising above a three-story manor nestled behind a bawn. The bawn wall stood six feet tall and stretched out to what I imagined being the size of a football field. "We're here, Myles," Adam announced.

We crossed over a river on a stone bridge leading directly to the manor's entrance. A trail of cone-shaped hedges adorned the entrance of the home, opening to a cascade of steps where several groomsmen and servants stood in formation with their heads bowed and eyes locked to the ground.

As soon as we dismounted the horses, the groomsmen grasped the reins and led Moonlight and our other horses to the stables. Adam led the way up the wide, oval-shaped steps to a set of grand double doors crafted of oak wood with iron handles. A valet escorted us inside and instructed us to wait in the foyer until the Marquess was ready to greet us.

It was incomprehensible to me that a man such as the Marquess could live so lavishly, having a home showcasing marble flooring and massive paintings encased in frames made of chestnut wood, yet somehow find himself in such dire financial straits. *I can almost guarantee that many of his colleagues are oblivious to his monetary circumstances*, I thought.

A servant, who introduced herself as Maureen, escorted us into the drawing room to meet the Marquess. He was seated in a grand Sligo chair of solid mahogany, upholstered in an Edwardian fabric, adorned with a pattern of green wild shamrock clovers, trimmed in gold lace. As an antique enthusiast, I was in awe of the well-crafted fixture.

He rose immediately the instant we entered the room, quickly placing his unlit cigar on a tray. He didn't appear to be very tall, though the heeled shoes he wore suggested otherwise. Nevertheless, he presented himself graciously and politely. *At least I can say that much for him,* I speculated. He first greeted Adam, having met him on earlier occasions. "It's a pleasure to be in your presence again, Mr. Towell. It has been some time since we last shared the same room."

"Yes, my lord, it *has* been quite some time," Adam replied.

"How was your journey here?" the Marquess questioned.

"It was enjoyable, to say the least. I stumbled upon old friends I had not seen for a while." Adam then turned to acknowledge Rey and me, making introductions. "Speaking of which, I'd like to present to you two longtime confidants, Reymond Tirad and Myles Roberts."

"A pleasure to make the acquaintance of you both, your humble servant!" the Marquess said, the words delivered with a formal, Anglo-Irish lilt.

I bowed respectfully, then nudged Rey on his back to suggest he do the same. "The pleasure is mine, Mr.… My Lord!" Rey stammered, replying sheepishly. I stepped back and watched the Marquess make his way to the liquor table and pour himself a drink. He didn't offer us one. Before I could pass judgment, the valet entered carrying a tray with three cups, placing them on a trestle table with gold leaf edges.

The Marquess raised his cup in a gesture of proposing a toast with a simple nod. "Please, gentlemen, have a seat." He snapped his fingers to summon the servant, ordering her to bring in the canapés prepared for us. "What takes ye to Kilkenny, might I ask?"

Caught off guard, Rey and I remained silent, allowing Adam, quick-witted as he was, to answer. "We are visiting a past acquaintance I met at the monastery during his passage from Belmullet to Kilkenny some years back, Lorcán O'Quinn. Our arrival at his estate is expected the day after tomorrow."

The Marquess leaned his head back skeptically. "Has the nobleman been made aware of your intended visit, Mr. Towell?"

"Evidently so, my lord!" Adam responded. "Why do you ask? Are you familiar with him?" Rey and I quickly glanced at each other, both suppressing a smirk. Then we turned our gaze toward the Marquess. "We sent notice several weeks back."

"The reason for my questioning is that Nobleman O'Quinn and his family are en route here as we speak on a business matter, and are intended to stay for a sennight. I sent word at once upon receiving notice of your arrival, requesting he arrive today to dine alongside yerselves."

Anxiety struck, an uneasy flutter flaring in my stomach, thinking we might have been caught in a lie. Adam, thinking fast on his feet, responded, "He may not have received our correspondence in time. Fortunately for us, we can deliver the news to him in person."

The Marquess's eyebrows were furrowed. He rose abruptly from his seat and walked over to the liquor table to refill his cup, quaffed the fine spirit, then poured himself another, never once uttering a word. He turned and looked at us individually with a dry smirk. "I suppose I saved ye all the trouble!"

From the look on Rey's face, I was sure he felt just as relieved as I did. It made me laugh, though, thinking Adam wouldn't have given a shit if he were caught in a lie. He could wiggle himself out of any circumstance at the drop of a hat, I presumed. It was no wonder he made the perfect ally.

The next few hours were spent chatting with the Marquess. Aside from Adam, Rey and I had little to say concerning our "renewed" lives in this century, so we made up stories as we went along, following each other's lead. Maureen appeared and announced the arrival of Nobleman O'Quinn, prompting Lord Butler to excuse himself and greet his expected guests.

As I analyzed the Marquess's plans, I knew that while some would come to fruition, others of greater importance to him would not. Nevertheless, he would achieve several of his desires, notably becoming a permanent fixture among the royals. Based on my studies, I knew he would succeed in various endeavors throughout England and Ireland. Yet, despite his well-intended actions, that persistent thorn continued to poke at my side.

Before I could discuss my issue with Lord Butler with Adam and Rey, the "prick... ling" returned to the drawing-room with his invited guests. "Gentlemen, may I introduce to you Nobleman Lorcán O'Quinn, his wife, Isleen, and daughter, Eilis."

I froze, my eyes wide as saucers, staring at her as if I had seen a ghost. I clung to the corner of the trestle table, fearing I might topple over. Shocking situations had become a trend for me in this century. Unexpected circumstances and unforeseen run-ins with people I wagered I would never see again appeared before me once more. "Lisa?!"

***

Lisa and I left the pizza shop, the breezy evening a welcome caress as we wandered through the lively Friday night crowd. We delighted in each other's company, each exchanged word knitting our stories together as if they had been shared in some otherworldly, cosmic manner. I was rendered speechless when she asked, "Do ye believe in fate, Myles?" just as the thought, *Maybe this is fate,* crossed my mind.

In response to her question, I used the maieutic method, asking, "Do *you* believe in fate, Lisa?"

"I certainly do. Growing up in Ireland, I heard many tales about how finding a four-leaf clover was tied to fate. When one is found, it isn't meant to bring riches or glory, as some might think, but rather, it is destined to grant fated love."

I remained silent for a moment, captivated not by the myth itself, but by the passion she exuded while recounting it. There was so much more I wanted to learn about her—her favorite foods and movies. She radiated an energy that could only be described as truly special. I longed to be with her, not just tonight, but in some strange, inexplicable way, forever. Despite having dated other women, none had affected me in such a uniquely profound way.

"Do ye have family living here in Atlanta, Myles?"

"No, it's just me. Aside from my sister Jessica, who lives in Massachusetts, my immediate family is all in Florida."

"Well, for the most part, ye're not very far from them. Ye can see them as often as ye'd like." She glanced at me briefly, flashing the sweetest smile I had ever seen.

"I visit them occasionally. I'm assuming your family still lives in Kilkenny?"

"Aye, me parents do. I have several cousins who live here in Georgia."

"Are you an only child?" I asked.

Her eyes narrowed with a somber grin, and with a doleful tone, she replied, "I lost me twin brother several years ago."

"I'm so sorry for your loss. My condolences. I too lost my older brother Randy earlier this year; it was quite sudden."

She held my hand gently, her soft touch offering a comfort that felt far more intimate than a simple gesture of condolence. While most would limit their hold when consoling someone, her continued grip brought me not only ease, but a tingling within my soul, a sense of rightness.

We stood in awkward, momentary silence. Sensing the somberness, I quickly broke the ice and randomly asked, "Unicorns or pink rabbits?"

She stared at me, her lips pursed in confusion, then suddenly burst into hysterical laughter. "That is the most brilliant way to lighten a mood!"

Curious to learn more about her life, I asked about her childhood. She reminisced about the times she spent with her grandparents. "Me brother and I would stay with them on the weekends to allow me parents to take on overtime hours at work. I later found out that they simply wanted some private alone time," she said, chuckling. Then she continued, "Me grandmother would read us tales of this place in Ireland, a magical place, she would say. It was of a waterfall in County Donegal."

I looked at her and smiled, struck by the coincidence in her mention of the waterfall, which I had recently read about in an email from the Cottages at Caisleán Dhún na nGall Resort.

"Have ye ever heard about the stories of the watersfall before, Myles?"

"I'm familiar with it, but I've heard no tales or stories referencing the place. Now that you mention it, I recently received an email confirmation from the resort in Ireland where I'm staying. One amenity offered is an excursion to the secret waterfall—the Eas Gorm i Bhfolach, if I'm not mistaken; Hidden Blue Waterfall."

"Good pronunciation, Myles. Yer accent is natural to the Gaeilge language."

"I've been practicing. I took a course in the language earlier this year to impress the locals in Ireland. Are you fluent in Gaeilge?"

"*Cén sort Éireannach a bheadh ionam mura mbeinn líofa ann*?" she quipped.

"You would just be an Irish lady who spoke English," I remarked humorously in return. "It is a beautiful language. It came easily to me when I began the course. I picked it up rather quickly, understanding it in all aspects—reading, speaking, and such. In a short time, I managed to learn slightly more than the basics."

She asked curiously, "Do ye speak Spanish as well?"

"*Sí, señorita, con fluidez*. I grew up in a *Spanglish* household. I guess you could say I'm trilingual now!"

She giggled, a hint of blush coloring her cheeks.

"What about the story your grandmother read to you and your brother? What made the waterfall so magical?"

"She called it grand and magical, but when I was a wee girl, I found it purely terrifying. In her stories, she'd say that some people who went into the cave would just vanish, gone without a trace. I just used to imagine that some troll had gobbled them up, so I did."

"For a young child, I can see how that might be a scary story!" I commented.

"I later recalled, during me late teens, having dreams about it. In those dreams, I'd see meself staring at the cascading wall of water. A vibrant mist would lift me, guiding me in a whirl of wind through the torrent. At the other end, there was always someone—a man, I should say—reaching out to catch me. As I fell into his arms, I would find him dressed in period clothing."

"That's interesting. Who was the man?"

"Ye'll never believe me if I tell ye!"

I extended my arm and stuck out my pinky. "Indulge me! I promise to keep an open mind; pinky swear!"

"Don't be put off now, but the fella in me dreams was always ye."

Chapter 23 – Betrothed to a Swine

Looking genuinely concerned, the Marquess stepped up to me. "Mr. Roberts, is something amiss?"

I was unable to acknowledge him, still dumbfounded by what I thought to be the pre-incarnation of Lisa. Questions swirled in my mind, wondering if she, too, had traveled to Ireland searching for me, just as Rey had, and got caught in the unnatural grips of the falls. My mind couldn't quite make sense of the past and the future I was living in.

"My apologies, Marquess. For a moment, I thought I was looking at a ghost." Thinking quickly to avoid further questioning, I added, "The Nobleman is the spitting image of my deceased uncle, my father's brother."

"Have a seat, Mr. Roberts. Ye appear a bit pale. I will have Maureen fetch ye a cup of water."

"I'm fine, Marquess, thank you," I said, though my knees felt weak.

Rey cocked his head, his eyebrows furrowed, silently asking what was wrong. I winked and shook my head to indicate, "Nothing!"

After Adam, I greeted Lady Isleen with a bow and a hand kiss. Eagerly expecting my turn, I felt like a child about to board an amusement park ride after waiting for hours in line to officially meet and kiss Eilis's hand. "Your servant, Lady Lis—Eilis, Lady Eilis." Her hand held a scent of soft lavender and roses, sweet and blissful to my senses. The soft texture of her skin was like Lisa's, if not the same—smooth and milky white.

"A pleasure to make yer acquaintance, Mr. Roberts," she replied, bowing formally in a gracious manner.

The Marquess rudely stepped between Eilis and me, placing his hand on the middle of her back, and led her to the seat closest to his at the table. We settled into our places and listened as the Marquess stood, making an announcement. "It is of the greatest delight to have you all here finally. I have been looking forward to this long-awaited occasion."

I found his behavior slightly over the top, as the visit of the nobleman was intended solely as a business trip. Curiosity churned in my head, as I have always been skillful at reading people's body language. My analysis of the Marquess was that of someone silently screaming, "I'm up to something!"

"Marlene, have the valet bring both the Bordeaux for the ladies and my sealed *Uisce Beatha* Emerald Isle from the cellar," he ordered, presumably trying to impress by requesting to have a rare, sealed Emerald Isle Whiskey opened for the occasion.

Marlene returned rather quickly and immediately poured the drinks. The Marquess asked everyone to stand, cups in hand, as he proposed a toast. "To good health and fortune to us all—friends, acquaintances, and my soon-to-be betrothed." The forced semi-smile on my face turned into a grimace, not out of anger, but more so of disappointed surprise. I couldn't help but veer my gaze away from the Marquess to Eilis, whose expression turned enigmatically bland.

"Cheers!" Adam exclaimed as he raised his drink. Rey followed suit, cheerfully saying, "Congratulations." I simply continued to gaze at Eilis, then turned to the Marquess, lifted my cup respectfully, and nodded my head without uttering a word.

After the announcement, Rey and I went into the garden, giving him the chance to finally interrogate me after his ineffectual attempt to catch my attention in the drawing room. "Myles, what's with this whole lost and distant look you've had since the nobleman and his family arrived?"

"Rey, do you remember my impromptu date? The girl I met at the pizza shop the night before I left for Ireland?"

He ran his hand through his hair, narrowing his eyes as he struggled to remember. Then he quickly responded, "Yes, yes. The one you described as being your forever love!"

"It's her, Rey, it's Lisa!"

"Are you referring to Eilis?" he asked in a whisper.

"Yes, yes, yes. Eilis is her doppelgänger. Lisa had the same crescent moon-shaped birthmark on the left side of her neck that Eilis has on her cheek. When I first saw her here, my mind instantly went into a fog. I thought Lisa might have traveled to Ireland to find me, just as you did, and somehow got caught in the waterfall."

"Myles, you're nuts!" Rey exclaimed, his eyes wide with disbelief.

"I'm not crazy, man. Honestly, Rey, it's her, but *not* her. I mean, not the Lisa that I met, but—*fuck*—you know what I mean!" I expressed fervently, my hands gesturing wildly.

"Maybe she's an ancestor, her great-great, however many great-grandmothers it might be, or just a manifested result of *23andMe*. I don't know!" Rey retorted.

"What are you two Chatty Kathys blabbering about?" Adam asked, cutting in intrusively.

"Myles thinks Eilis is the ancestor of a girl he met before his,"—Rey raised his hands in air quotes—"vacation."

Adam stared blankly, appearing deep in thought, then looked at me. "It's not unheard of. The Elder Folk that guided me to this century described how, in diverse ways, the watersfall made the experience of every individual who journeyed through unique. However, one thing is always a common factor."

"What is the common factor?" I asked, leaning forward curiously.

"Connections of the past, present, and future; a link in tenses."

"What does that even mean, Adam?!" I exclaimed, my frustration mounting.

"I don't have an answer for that, Myles. The only conclusion I can draw is that the three of us are now living in the past—the past has become our present, and the future is our past. This paradox seems to allow us to exist in all tenses. Whatever your connection is, it could somehow be tied to Eilis."

I remained silent, pondering the thought. However confusing and improbable it sounded, it still made a strange, unsettling sense.

***

Maureen entered the garden, ringing the dinner bell with an insistent clang and announcing, "Please follow me to the dining hall." Her abrupt appearance impertinently disbanded the huddle between Adam, Rey, and me. Unbeknownst to us, the Marquess had already gone ahead, dragging Eilis along with him.

Maureen led us to the dining room, informally allowing us to sit where we desired. I chose a seat directly across from Eilis, giving a better view and a more intimate conversation. She seemed pleased to see me seated so close, smiling as I sat down—perhaps even blushing a bit, though it might have been my wishful imagination.

The servants entered the dining room, carrying trays laden with steamed cabbage soup, caramelized carrots, roasted potatoes, and pheasant pie. Once again, the body of a bird was used to embellish the main dish. *If it tastes anything like the peacock I ate at the Brindley estate, then I can overlook the appearance of the mangled bird,* I thought. The dish was paired with an Italian Sangiovese, which I found refreshingly earthy and fruity.

The Marquess called for another toast—his fourth one that evening—revealing his fondness for more than the occasional drink. We rose with raised cups, waiting for our mumbling host to complete his toast. He staggered from his seat, attempting to kiss Eilis, which took her by surprise. She turned away in rejection, seemingly embarrassed, which angered the Marquess. He slammed his drink on the table, then grabbed her roughly by the back of her head and forcibly planted a kiss on her lips, oblivious to her protest.

I quickly rose from my seat, intent on putting an end to his belligerence. Adam grasped my arm, restraining me from confronting the Marquess, well aware that if I did, Lord Butler would have me detained by his private guards and imprisoned without hesitation. The nobleman, Lorcán O'Quinn, came to the aid of his daughter—not aggressively as one might expect, but timidly. He draped his arm over the Marquess's shoulder, attempting to escort him back to his seat. He met resistance as the Marquess aggressively shoved his arm away, staggering back to his place at the table on his own.

"Here is to my betrothed. She *will* be willingly obedient once I teach her the particulars on how a husband is to be obeyed! Slainté!" the Marquess bellowed, his words slurred.

Eilis excused herself and hurried out to the garden, followed by Lady Isleen. I remained seated under Adam's watchful eye to avoid any unnecessary confrontation. I made a considerable effort not to appear as the overly eager hero wanting to rescue a damsel in distress. The Marquess clumsily refilled his cup, gulped it down, and consumed two more. He was slowly becoming irrational, taking a sliver of the pheasant pie and consuming several bites before tossing the remaining piece into the large bowl of cabbage soup, causing the hot broth to splatter across the table and land on Rey's arm.

Rey's face turned crimson with anger, and he sprang from his chair, lunging at the Marquess and tackling him to the ground. The Marquess lay motionless on the floor, his legs dangling from the seat.

"Rey, are you mad?" Adam shouted, his eyes wide.

"This son of a bitch is out of control. Someone had to slow his roll!" Rey rebutted, his chest heaving.

Nobleman O'Quinn swiftly rose from his seat and rushed to the aid of the Marquess, bellowing in a cowardly voice, "How will we explain this? Now he will have me head fer certain, and me family will be left destitute!"

I looked at Mr. O'Quinn, curious as to why he would condemn himself to the extent that the Marquess might want his head. Clearly, there was more involved than just a betrothal. "Do not overreact to the situation, nobleman. We will make it right," I reassured him.

Concerned about his well-being, I leaned over the Marquess. He was still breathing, but aside from a golf-ball-sized lump on the back of his head from the impact on the marble floor, I found no blood. Adam acted quickly, dragging the chair away before splashing water on his face to bring him back to consciousness. "We need to keep him responsive—we cannot risk a concussion," Adam insisted, as he continued to douse the Marquess's face.

"What are you doing, Mr. Towell?" the Marquess yelled.

"My Lord, you fell back on your chair and bumped your head."

"Get your hands off me, ye wretched invalid! Fetch me a whiskey to ease this dreadful pounding in my head," he commanded arrogantly.

"My Lord, let us get you seated in the drawing-room. I recommend you drink water to ease the ache. We would not want you to concuss; you need to remain awake and alert."

As Rey and Adam attended the Marquess, I found a moment to check on Eilis. I gestured to Rey to meet me in the hall. Acknowledging with a wave, he took a detour around the opposite side of the dining hall to avoid being spotted by the Marquess should he have a moment of clarity and later question the reason for our "brief conversation."

"Talk to me! What's up?" Rey asked with interest.

"I need you to keep Sloppy Joe there occupied while I speak with Lady Isleen and Eilis."

"Talk to them about what?" Rey asked sharply.

"There is more involved in this business trip than the Marquess is letting on. I want to ensure that the ladies and the nobleman are safe—that's all!"

"Fine. As always, I've got your back, bruh. Keep me in the loop!"

***

I made my way to the garden, finding Eilis sitting alone on a stone bench beside a bush of Irish heathers. She twirled a branch, plucking the small purple petals one by one, a sorrowful expression on her face.

"A penny for your thoughts?" I asked softly, standing before her.

"Pardon me, Mr. Roberts?" she asked curiously, startled by my sudden appearance.

"I'm sorry that you had to endure the idiocy of that halfwit. I hope he didn't hurt you."

"He placed níl harm upon me. I just wished I..." Appearing resentful at beginning the sentence, she placed her hand over her face to disguise the welling tears.

I seated myself beside her to offer comfort, then got to the point. "Are you being forced to marry the Marquess, Lady Eilis?"

She dabbed her eyes with her kerchief, nodding in agreement. "Me father owes Lord Ormond a substantial amount of money that he canni repay."

"Is your father being forced to offer your hand in marriage to this bastard as a way of repaying the debt?"

"Aye. I begged him excessively, but he would'ni listen," she said indignantly.

"If it doesn't trouble you, may I inquire as to why the Marquess is owed so much money by your father and why he would resort to using his daughter as repayment?"

"Me father is a fabrics merchant. The last two shipments of fabrics, which me father acquires quarterly from Bilbao, Spain, were seized by pirates somewhere in the Celtic Sea. The Marquess purchased nearly the entire shipment to offer as a gift to King Charles and Queen Henrietta Maria." She paused for a moment, her lips pursed as she took a deep breath, then continued, "He told me father that there was a newly constructed ship designed to travel faster. It was longer and wider than the standard ship, so he used the money he received up front to pay for that ship, rather than using the one he often used."

"Something seems out of the ordinary. Your father is an intelligent man and has made his fortune in the sale of imported fabrics, correct?"

"Aye!" she replied with certainty.

"Then why would he invest in a nonexistent ship that hasn't been invented yet and risk losing out on an even bigger profit? Your father is an intelligent man and should know that logically and financially, it makes no sense."

"Me father is unaware that I have knowledge of this, but I overheard a conversation between the Marquess and him pertaining to the investment in that ship."

"Aha, go on!"

"Lord Ormond told him that the shipment needed to be delivered with haste, and he knew of this ship that was made to coast the oceans faster." Her eyebrows furrowed in thought as she rose. "He told me father he would make the investment himself, and all me father need do is send the order and request for it to be shipped on the..."

She paused again, grappling to remember... "*El Gallo*! The name of this new ship is '*El Gallo*'."

My eyes widened at the irony, which made me giggle inwardly. *If only she knew!* I thought with a wicked sense of amusement.

"I am sorry—níl '*El Gallo*'. 'Tis named '*El Galeón*'!"

"Would you be inclined to have my friend Rey join us in this conversation? He is a constable in our country and could better help us figure out this whole calamity."

"Aye, if ye so see it fit!" Eilis said determined.

"Great. Allow me a moment while I fetch him," I said. I hurried back to the drawing room, through the hallway and into the dining hall. They were gone. "Rey!" I shouted, a low panic rising in my throat. I searched in the parlor behind the dining area. I then heard muffled chatter coming from the south side of the room, so I returned to the hallway, finding a door at the end of the corridor. I entered the room and found Adam struggling to keep the Marquess at bay while Maureen, her eyes wide with terror, watched.

"I've got you, Adam," I said, rushing to grab the Marquess's legs to keep him from falling off the settee, while Adam struggled to keep his arms still. "Where's Rey?"

"He went to fetch the watchman, hoping he would know of a way to sober up this moron. We don't need him charging us with assault!" Adam grunted, straining against the Marquess's flailing arms.

"How dare ye attack me in my home! I will have all your heads for this," the Marquess shouted. He continued thrashing about, yelling like a madman, "Maureen, bring me a whiskey this instant!" Maureen felt conflicted. Though she had witnessed her master's actions in the past, she feared the repercussions she would face if she did not obey his orders.

"Maureen, he doesn't need any more whiskey. He needs to sober up. It would be best to bring him water. The hydration will help speed his sobriety."

"As ye wish, Mr. Roberts," she said respectfully, then curtsied and swiftly turned to retrieve the ewer from the kitchen.

Rey returned with a groomsman rather than the watchman, who was nowhere to be found. The stableman was fully aware of the dilemma, as his actions in aiding in suppressing his master proved. I pulled Rey aside and asked him to follow me back to the garden to meet with Eilis. "Can the groomsman be trusted?"

Rey glowered at me and responded, "Do you not see him tying up his own master? The groomsman assured me we would not suffer any consequences for our actions. He often sees his lordship pissy drunk, and he and the watchmen are usually the ones to ease him into submission when he becomes combative."

"Perfect!" I exclaimed, then turned to Adam. "Hey old man, want to join us? We're going to meet with Eilis. That prodding thorn that's been poking at me has finally revealed itself."

"Nah, you two go on. This dumbass wore me out. I'll stay here with the groomsman."

Rey and I returned to the garden, finding Lady Isleen in the company of her daughter. Unsure if she knew of the discussion Eilis and I had; I signaled for Rey to remain silent until I confirmed it was safe to continue the conversation.

"Hello again, Mr. Roberts and Mr. Tirad. Me sincerest apologies to ye both for leaving the table so abruptly—"

I interrupted, "There is absolutely no need for you to apologize, Lady Isleen. The one who should express regret is Lord Ormond. He was rude and completely out of line. It was unacceptable behavior on his part—especially by someone of his caliber—not to mention your daughter's supposed suitor!"

"I gather ye speak the truth, but I fear fer me daughter's safety!"

Eilis took hold of her mother's hand, reassuring her that everything would work itself out. "Mother, will ye allow me a moment with the lads? Mr. Tirad is a constable in the colonies, with knowledge of the law. He may know a way out of this predicament."

Lady Isleen reached out and embraced her daughter as only a mother would. "I believe it will be resolved. I will pray that it does. I am off to attend to yer father. He took a lie down after the commotion."

Eilis placed a kiss on her mother's cheek, releasing her from the embrace. "Thank ye, mother. I wil' ni be long."

"Okay, Rey, here's the synopsis: Lord Ormond paid for Nobleman O'Quinn to buy fabrics as a gift to the royals, the King and Queen. Then, he instructed Lorcán to hire a vessel that travels faster than modern-day ships—a ship that, by firsthand knowledge, we know does not exist yet—only to have it captured by pirates?" Rey looked hard at me with piercing eyes, then erupted, "Who the hell does he think would believe that bullshit?"

"I dinnae understand yer meaning, Mr. Tirad."

"I'm sorry, Lady Eilis. It is vulgar language from my time—my country, I meant to say. It escapes my mouth only when innocent people suffer because of untruths spoken by others."

I interjected, "What he's trying to convey, Lady Eilis, is that if the vessel were indeed as swift in the waters as the Marquess claims, why couldn't it have outrun the pirate's ship? I presume the Marquess hired a common ship along with someone to command it and had the shipment redirected to England and delivered to the King and Queen. By doing so, he would be left to pay nothing, saddling your father with the obligation, making him think the cargo was stolen. By incurring that debt upon him, knowing your father could not afford repayment, he seized the opportunity to force him to offer you as payment of the said debt."

"I thought I was the detective here!" Rey blurted out.

"Ha, you have competition, man. It just came to me, like déjà vu," I responded with a smirk.

"Are ye implying that Lord Ormond deceived both me father and me? That bastard of a whore! He will ni own me, nó me body. Does he think of me as livestock to claim fer his own? This is one soul that wil' ni be usurped by that ruthless swine!" Eilis declared with a fiery, righteous fury.

Rey and I exchanged glances, surprised by her unusual language. "Well, all righty, you go, girl!" Rey quipped.

"Now that ye've clarified the situation, how do we avert the ramifications of it all?" Eilis asked.

"I will speak with Adam and consider a solution. I might have something in mind." I turned to Rey. "Do you mind giving us a minute? I'll fill you in on the details later."

"You got it. I was about to excuse myself anyway and check in on Adam. I'll see you later." He took Eilis's hand and placed a kiss, bidding her a good evening. I sat beside her again on the stone bench and faced her, but before I could speak, she said, in a non sequitur, "I feel I have met ye before, Mr. Roberts."

For a few quick seconds, my body went numb, experiencing déjà vu once again. A flash raced through my mind, recalling the conversation Lisa and I had about her recurring dream. I blinked repeatedly, clearing my throat. "I definitely would have remembered meeting you, Eilis. My apologies... Lady Eilis."

"Ye may address me as Eilis, if ye wish."

My heart pounded, as it does when a sentiment is reciprocated positively. "You can call me Myles, if *you* wish, *Eilis*!" She smiled, the tiniest of dimples forming when she grinned that way. I couldn't help but return the smile, feeling a strong urge to kiss her. Overwhelmed by emotion and curiosity, I revisited her earlier comment about having met me before. "So, Eilis, when and where exactly did we meet?"

Chapter 24 – Absent

The musty odors that accumulate when a home has been sealed shut and uninhabited for some time still lingered, a blanket of foul humidity that clung to the air. Devon, Alex, and Tina entered each room, flinging open every window to air out the stagnant house. While doing so, retching sounds echoed throughout. With the power still off, the resonating odors were difficult to tolerate, assaulting their senses.

"Devon, get the generator started and turn on the air conditioner—oh, and don't forget to open the garage door," Alex ordered from the other room, his voice muffled by the walls.

"Already on it." Devon turned to Tina. "*Mamita*, go outside if the smell gets to be too much for you."

"I can handle it, *papi*," Tina said assertively as she reached for the handle of the garage door. Sunlight, warm and golden, flooded the room, brightening the darkened space. Devon looked around, seeing things that looked familiar, yet somehow they were all foreign, each object a ghost of the life Myles had left behind.

Alex joined Tina and Devon, the three of them sorting through boxes and bags to pack Myles's belongings, a grim task that no one had wanted to undertake. "I'll start with the toolshed," Alex offered.

"Do me a favor and climb up to the garage truss to see if he has anything stored up there?" Devon asked. "I'm sure it's sweltering in there, so open it first and let it air out."

Devon pulled on the red cord, which had a wooden, multi-colored Puerto Rican flag attached by Myles, serving as a handle. The ladder connected to the hatch glided down slowly, allowing Devon to grasp and unhook the extender. Then, the sudden sound of a crash startled both Tina and Alex.

"What the hell was that?" Tina shouted.

"I lost my grip on the ladder when a bird flew out and scared the shit outta me," Devon responded shamefully.

Tina and Alex burst into laughter—a welcome release of emotions they had held in since entering Myles's home. It had been four months since he left for Ireland and disappeared without a trace, and three months since Rey had gone missing.

"The stench in the kitchen should have dissipated, so I'll take care of things in there to get it out of the way," Tina said, walking toward the kitchen. She grabbed the refrigerator handle and opened it with trepidation, afraid that either an intense odor would assault her nostrils or a critter would lunge out at her. Much to her surprise, neither scenario played out.

Myles was always meticulous, vigilant to the smallest of details. From what she saw, he had cleared the refrigerator of all perishables. The only items that remained were jars of spoiled jam, along with containers filled with moldy, melted butter and melted ice cream in the freezer. Tina took one of the larger boxes, lined it with an industrial-sized garbage bag, and began to empty the contents of the refrigerator.

Devon entered the kitchen carrying additional boxes for Tina. "Thank you, love. *Papi*, can you reach up into that cabinet and bring down the cups? It's too high for me to reach."

"Sure, babe." Devon dragged a chair from the breakfast table, positioning it directly below the cupboard, but it was not high enough to give him the maximum reach he needed to get to the upper shelf of the cabinet. He cupped his hand over his mouth and yelled out to Alex, "Bruh, can you please bring over the ladder from the garage?"

"What are you, handicapped?" Alex shouted back teasingly.

"Bitch, just do as you're told."

Being an avid jokester, Alex entered the kitchen, came up from behind, and poked Devon's butt with the top corner of the ladder, causing Devon to fall off the chair. His cat-like reflexes landed him safely on the ground without incident.

"Asshole!" he snarled at Alex.

"Hold the ladder and place that box," he said, pointing at a medium-sized box on the counter, "on the paint can holder, please."

Devon reached the top of the cabinet and began collecting the cups, taking hold of them three at a time. He passed them to Alex, maintaining a flow like a conveyor belt, as Alex safely placed them, neatly stacked, inside the box.

Suddenly, the steady flow came to a halt. Devon, left with his arm extended, asked, "Why'd you stop?" Getting no response, he looked down and found Alex sitting on the chair, his head bowed, holding a single mug. Devon climbed down to console him, realizing he was sobbing.

"What happened, man?" Devon asked with concern.

Alex stared blankly at the ground, his face a still mask reflecting the pain of loss. He raised his hand and passed the ceramic mug to Devon. Devon stared at it, remaining silent for a brief period, his throat tightening with emotion. He turned away from Alex and Tina, and rushed out of the kitchen. Tina followed him moments later, finding him on the floor of the foyer, weeping fervently, the mug still clutched in his hand. As Tina gently turned it, she recognized a photo of Alex, Devon, Rey and Myles dressed in period clothing at a Renaissance fair the previous year. Alex tapped her on the shoulder, a silent suggestion that he sit beside Devon. They both held the mug, their eyes filling with tears as they stared at the image. They hugged, and both wept intensely.

Drained of the pent-up emotions that had been building over the past four months, they remained on the floor for a while, held in a silent, shared grief. They held each other by the back of their necks and nodded, a wordless agreement that they had to continue with the task at hand. Alex was the first to stand. "Come on, we have to get as much done as we can today," he said, extending his arm to help Devon up, adding with a chuckle, "And you have snot dangling from your nose."

They started with Myles's office, which had several bookshelves filled with textbooks and novels he had collected over the years. Myles was an avid reader, always finding time to curl up with an enjoyable book and a cup of "toxica." Alex quickly emptied the large shelf holding the bigger textbooks, which Myles used as references when preparing assignments and tests for his classes.

Devon walked in, tugging a red wagon Myles used to ride his young nieces and nephews in when they visited. "If we put them in boxes, they might be too heavy to carry, so let's use this wagon for the larger books."

"Good idea. Think fast," Alex said unexpectedly, tossing a massive textbook at Devon.

"Bro, are you trying to give me a hernia?"

"Suck it up, cupcake," Alex quipped.

As if by magic, from the mere mention, Tina appeared at the door with a tray filled with none other than assorted cupcakes and Myles's favorite, espresso coffee. It gave them the added kick they needed to continue sorting through the books, piling them in subject order, as they had promised to donate them to the school.

What kept it from being an arduous chore was that Myles was a minimalist. Many of the closets and other rooms were filled with just the essentials, making it an easier undertaking. They cleared out the office, along with the guest room and guest bathroom. Tina continued with the kitchen while Devon and Alex tackled Myles's bedroom and ensuite.

Devon checked the drawers of the nightstands, finding Myles's tablet, which was always kept plugged in to stay charged. Although the power had been turned off, it kept a charge—still at forty percent. "Hey Alex, come here."

"What's up?"

"I found Myles's tablet. Should we be nosy?" Devon asked as he swiped on the screen.

"Does it need a password or PIN number?"

"Nope." Quickly grabbing the tablet from Devon's hand, Alex began swiping, then commented, "I'm sure Myles won't mind!" They both laughed and sat on the bed, feeling unashamed about snooping through someone else's belongings.

To be fair, Myles was once caught by Devon scrolling through Alex's phone—so fair-is-fair. Alex tapped on the photos app, and the first picture to appear was taken the morning Myles left for Ireland. It was of a redheaded girl placing a kiss on his cheek as he slept.

"Do you think that's the girl he mentioned meeting at the pizza shop?" Devon asked.

"Fits the description—red-haired with smooth, milky-white skin, just as he described. He did say in the last group text that she spent the night. Maybe she left it as a reminder of what to expect when he returned."

"She *is* beautiful. I'll give you that much. Definitely his type to a T!"

"Okay, I'm feeling guilty," Devon confessed. "Let's put this away and continue."

***

It was getting late, and they had been at Myles's house since early morning. They decided to stop for now, agreeing to return early the next day. Tina grabbed one of the smaller boxes labeled "European History," which Myles had stored in the closet of his office, to load into the back of her SUV. She planned to deliver the donated books to the school on Monday, the day before the beginning of the school year, as it was on her route to work.

As she took hold of the box by its sides, the bottom flaps suddenly gave way, causing several books to spill onto the driveway. She collected them off the ground. The last one she picked up was a volume titled *Full World History, Volume 3*, which had fallen open. She flipped it over and read the title—"Siege of Drogheda"—and instinctively turned the pages. Four pages into the chapter, she came across hand-painted portraits depicting historical figures significant to that era. Tina looked at the photos with interest, admiring the details of each painting, as she was an artist herself. Her silence suddenly broke with a bloodcurdling scream. Devon and Alex ran out of the house to find out what had caused her to scream.

"Oh my God, oh my God, please tell me I'm seeing things!" Tina yelled frantically.

"*Mamita*, calm down. *¿Qué pasó*? What are you screaming about?" Devon asked in a panic-stricken voice.

"Look, look!" she yelled, pointing to the open book sitting on the bed of the trunk. "Please tell me that's not who I think it is!"

Alex picked up the book and flipped it over, his face turning pale. His eyes widened, unable to blink, locked in a frozen stare as he blankly extended his arm to pass the book to Devon.

Devon appeared puzzled at first, then looked at both Tina and Alex with furrowed brows before turning his focus to the page. "Lord God Almighty!"

***

The first day of the school year at Sweet Peach High School was usually filled with excited students and teachers clamoring in the halls. The corridors would be teeming with students searching for their new classes, roaming aimlessly for their respective classrooms. Today was unlike the past. Heaviness filled the passageways. Several students were seen walking with tears in their eyes, and several teachers wore blank expressions.

It took just under an hour to get the students situated and placed in their assigned rooms, with the help of volunteers from the office of the grief counselors. It had been some time since the school suffered such a loss. The last time grief counselors were called in was after the 9/11 attacks in 2001.

It was eerily quiet throughout the school, other than the usual muffled chatter coming from inside the classrooms, which could only be heard if you were walking in the halls. The first set of counselors was assigned to classroom #228.

It had been Mr. Roberts's classroom since he first began at the school, just fresh out of college. The new history teacher taking over that room, Mr. Cohen, had big shoes to fill. He was aware of the love everyone had for Mr. Roberts, especially his students.

"Good morning, class. My name is Mr. Cohen, and I'm your new history teacher here at Sweet Peach High School. I know we all have a lot on our minds—not only because it's the first day of the school year, but also because of the heaviness some of y'all feel from the loss of Mr. Roberts. We have invited grief counselors, who you see here with us and would like to introduce themselves before proceeding to the other classrooms." He motioned for the counselors to come to the front and exchanged places with them.

"Good morning, everyone. My name is Madeline, and this is my colleague, Felix. We want you all to know that we empathize with you regarding the loss you are currently dealing with. Many of us here have suffered great losses—myself included. I'm sure you all have questions surging in your minds—some of which we'll try to answer, though some we may not. We *will*, however, do our best to help you understand and cope." She turned to her colleague. "Would you like to add anything?"

Felix held a sympathetic grin, simply remarking, "We will try our best to help you manage. We'll be in room," taking a quick glance at his notes, "#614 starting tomorrow for the next two weeks. If you need to talk or just vent, we are here for you."

Mr. Cohen walked the counselors to the door and shut the door behind them. He returned to the front of the room, sat at his desk, and opened his briefcase with a crisp snap. He took out a manila folder and set it on his desk, his movements deliberate.

"I was fortunate enough, just as y'all were, to meet Mr. Roberts right before the end of the school year. He had no intention of leaving the school; however, he had just been moved up to teach the eleventh-grade history class. I know most of you were in his class last semester. I was supposed to take over the tenth-grade class, but due to the current circumstances, they saw fit to place me with the eleventh-grade students." Shuffling through the papers, he took out a sealed envelope that Mr. Roberts had left inside the desk drawer, marked in capital letters "FOR MY STUDENTS."

"I have a letter here left by Mr. Roberts. I assume it was a message for y'all." Tearing open the envelope, he read the contents first to himself, a small, sad smile touching his lips, and then read aloud, "I have a surprise quiz today, as well!"

Several of the students found it amusing, aware of Mr. Roberts' sense of humor, while others simply bowed their heads to hide the sadness on their faces. To ease the lingering heaviness, Mr. Cohen walked up to the chalkboard and wrote, "*Full World History, Volume 3.*"

"You will find this book inside your desks. I would like for y'all to turn to page 108, 'The Siege of Drogheda.' As I understand, this is where y'all left off last semester with Mr. Roberts."

Sounds of "uh-huh" and "yup" filled the room. They opened their books and sat them on their desks, flipping through the pages.

Mr. Cohen read aloud, "The coastal town of Drogheda was under siege from the third to the eleventh of September 1649 by English Royalists and the Irish Catholic Confederation, serving under the command of Sir Arthur Aston. The defenders held strong for nine days until Oliver Cromwell ordered his regiments to charge through the breached walls. He took control of Drogheda, resulting in the deaths of thousands of Irish soldiers. Cromwell then directed his army into the homes of civilians and their churches—an action that led to the slaughter of innocent people."

"Mr. Cohen," Kaylani yelled out, her hand raised.

Looking down at his seating chart, Mr. Cohen identified the student in seat number 4 and faced her. "Yes, Kaylani?"

"I didn't mean to get ahead of what you're reading, but I was glancing through the pages and came across some photos on page 111." She burst into tears, suddenly emotional.

"I know, Kaylani. It's difficult for you and any of us."

"But I'm freaking out!" she said, sobbing.

"Do you need to go to the restroom and wash your face, maybe get a drink of water from the water fountain?"

"No, just look. Look at page 111," she urged eagerly. "Mr. Roberts brought his friend to the school to visit us during career day. His name was Agent Tirad," she explained, appearing distraught, fighting against her uncontrollable sighs.

"How is that relevant, Kaylani? Help me understand," Mr. Cohen replied gently.

There was a sudden outcry of students voicing over her sobbing—some yelling "Oh shit!" while others yelped, "Oh my God," and the rest simply gasped aloud. Kaylani held her composure for a moment, then shrieked, "That's Mr. Roberts and his friend in the portrait!"

Chapter 25 – Obstructed Scheme

The plans we laid out to visit Lorcán O'Quinn obviously never panned out, having the nobleman as an already invited guest of the Marquess amongst our company. Oblivious to his actions, the Marquess, having no recollection of the previous night, allowed us to remain in his home as originally intended, which might work to our advantage.

After breakfast, I approached the nobleman and asked him to meet me in the garden. I went ahead, taking a moment to figure out the best way to reveal my true identity and those of my fellow journeyers. The nobleman followed shortly after, still looking stunned from the previous night's chaos.

"Mr. Roberts, why have ye called upon me?" Lorcán asked.

"If you'd kindly take a seat, nobleman," I suggested. "With all the chaos yesterday, I didn't have time to speak with you privately."

"What need have ye fer a private audience with meself?"

"What I'm about to reveal might sound a bit far-fetched, so I'll try to explain as subtly as possible."

He raised an eyebrow, his curiosity evident. "Go on, lad."

"I met with *Mórghinearál* Dujardin Brindley at the Abbey of Donegal and spent some time at his estate before coming here. He gave me a map of Ireland, marking the locations of trusted men he met while researching the Eas Gorm i Bhfolach, including yourself."

Lorcán stared at me, open-mouthed, with a dawning comprehension in his eyes. "The watersfall? Aye!"

"Do you take a keen mind to where I'm leading with this information, Mr. O'Quinn?" I asked, narrowing my eyes to convey assurance.

"'Tis only tales, bedtime stories," he remarked. I reached into my pocket, pulled out my phone, powered it on, and showed the nobleman a glimpse of the future.

"Jaysus, Mary, and Joseph, saints behold!" he exclaimed, leaping from the bench like a startled kangaroo. He crossed himself, staring wide-eyed. "Say 'tis not so?"

"Adam, Rey, and I are all from the future, sir."

Visibly stunned and aghast, he exclaimed, "Allow me a moment, Mr. Roberts. I require a measure of whiskey." He quickly went inside to fetch a whiskey, disappearing for a moment, then returned just as fast with a drink in hand, resuming his seat on the stone bench.

"Mr. Brindley warned you might react this way," I said with a grin.

"Well, ní a tale after all, eh?" he said, his voice spiked with bewilderment.

"No, sir, not a tale!" I replied.

I explained to the nobleman the circumstances leading to my arrival in this present century, as well as those of Adam and Rey. "I have known the stories since I was a young lad. I aided the *Mórghinearál* in his research, even crossed paths wi' alleged Elder Folks. Never dreamt it all being true."

"That's the same comment made by those I've revealed myself to."

Emptying his cup, he added, "What need have ye of me, Mr. Roberts?"

"I was hoping you might know a way for us to return to our precise places in time."

"Lad, I dinna possess that knowledge, so I canni tell ye fer certain. I can, however, only offer an assumption—'tis possible. The information was presented to me years after meeting with the *Mórghinearál*. The reasons why or how were never shared, other than a telling of astronomy and phases of the moon. There must be an alignment of sorts with the sun or moon. So, find it to be true; ye *can* return to yer respective times."

Phases of the moon? I wondered silently. Without a doubt, I heard the sincerity in his voice. It was more than I expected to hear—more information than I expected overall—but, most importantly; it gave me hope.

***

A few days after the big reveal, Lorcán was asked to accompany the Marquess on a venture to meet Sir Arthur Aston, a professional soldier and another loyalist of King Charles I. Adam had also been invited but declined the invitation, not wanting to involve himself in matters we journeyers knew were to come.

Finding myself idle, I took a stroll through the grounds, following a stone trail surrounded by a bounty of plants, herbs, and trees. Irish heirloom apple trees—notably Blood of the Boyne—lined the path surrounding the garden. As I approached a lattice adorned with rows of foxglove plants and scattered shrubs of lady's bedstraw, I stopped to listen to the humming sound coming from behind the crossed wooden wall.

"Is that the voice of an angel I hear?" I asked gently, my heart already quickening.

"Myles, me apologies. I dinnae hear ye approach."

"No need for apologies, Eilis. It's I who should apologize for coming upon you so stealthily."

"I was plucking medlars and picking gooseberries. Care to try one?" She scooped a handful of the red and purple berries, handing them to me. "They are quite sweet, d'ye think?"

I filled my mouth, savoring each bite. "They're not as sweet as the person who picked them!"

She blushed shyly, placing a hand over her mouth and giggling youthfully. "Someone is quite the flirt," she remarked.

"I speak with affection."

A tingling sensation spread through my stomach—that same unexpected emotion I had felt for Lisa, who, in many ways, was Eilis.

"I didn't mean to be so forward with you, Eilis," I admitted.

"Nil a need to apologize, Myles. *Ná bí buartha*," she said softly.

"I couldn't help but blurt it out, to be honest. You remind me of someone I once had feelings for."

"How long has it been since ye parted from her?" Eilis asked, a hint of interest in her eyes.

"It's a long and complicated story—one I will share with you when the proper moment presents itself."

She drew herself closer to me, holding onto the *sciob*. "Well, I dinnae mean to be so forward with ye either, Myles, but I shall thank her."

I grinned, one eyebrow raised. "What will you thank her for?"

She let go of the basket, allowing the fruits to scatter on the ground, and raised herself on her toes to meet my eyes. She wrapped her arms around me in an affectionate embrace, and we kissed passionately. I requited her caress by firmly gripping her waist with one arm, while the other hand cradled the back of her head.

We held onto each other for some time, giving me that rare feeling once again, the same passion I felt for Lisa—an oddity that made me believe we had loved each other for many lifetimes. The severed connection that kept me from what could have been my forever love following the unexpected journey through the waterfall was now restored. As we kissed, a memory of Lisa's straightforward personality surfaced, making me certain that it had been passed down through generations and was now manifesting before me.

"Myles, ye's a wonder with ye lips!" she said bluntly.

"I can say the same of you, and just as sweet as the berries you picked." She smiled and then quickly turned, startled by the sound of twigs snapping on the ground.

"Myles, are you here?" Rey called out.

"I'm here behind the lattice… with Eilis."

I was cautious in making Rey aware that Eilis was with me, unsure if he might blurt out any talk about the future. Rey had a reputation for being a talker, always negligent of his surroundings—a habit he must have picked up from Alex.

"Good afternoon, Lady Eilis," Rey greeted politely, bending to kiss her hand.

She curtsied in return. "Good afternoon, Mr. Tirad. I hope ye had a joyous start to yer day!"

"I definitely have, Lady Eilis, thank you."

Rey nodded ceremoniously, then turned to me. "Can I have a word with you, privately?"

"Would you excuse us for a moment, Eilis?" I asked, taking hold of her hand and caressing her fingers, my eyes fixed on hers, lost for a moment.

"Aye, níl worry. I will collect the scattered fruit and gather more."

I nodded respectfully and walked alongside Rey, asking, "Is everything okay?"

"*Iz* all good!" he replied playfully. "Adam needs to see you, *pronto*. He's thinking of leaving this place and heading north to Donegal."

"Tell him I'll join him shortly. I'm in the middle of an interesting conversation with Eilis."

Rey looked at me with puckered lips and one eye half-squinted. "Seems like you're conversing more with her tongue, judging by the red shade around your lips." I felt my face turn red as I smiled. "Damn, bruh, you work fast," Rey joked.

"We've been checking each other out these past few days."

"I know, you big stud. I've noticed, but so has the Marquess, so be careful and don't set off any unwanted alarms."

"Has he really?" I asked, surprised. "I'm usually good at spotting things like that—reason I'm called *JAFO*," I joked.

"Yeah, yeah, just another fucking observer. You know I'll always have your back, keeping an eye out for you, but you need to stay attentive too," Rey warned.

"Yes, Dad!" I quipped, a playful jab at Rey's protective streak. "But thanks for always looking out. Tell Adam I'll meet him shortly. Let him know I'm handling a personal matter, but *please* don't tell him what you know. I don't need a lecture from him!"

"Will do, Romeo. Mum's the word on your 'dear diary' moment," Rey teased.

"Fuck off!" I retorted with a laugh.

Rey blew kisses at me as he walked away, teasing continuously until he was out of sight. I returned to Eilis, finding her refilling the *sciob* with added cherries and greengage plums to the assortment of fruit.

"Let me carry that for you," I offered, reaching for the basket.

"Ye ever so the gentleman, thank ye, Myles," she replied courteously.

"It's my pleasure." I took hold of the basket as Eilis plucked the last remaining pears within her reach. With my free hand, I picked the ones hanging from the upper branches, beyond her grasp.

"I think these three will suffice," she said. I placed them inside the basket.

"I now have plenty to prepare a healthy compote for me ma. She genuinely enjoys it."

"You are a selfless woman, Eilis."

"What made ye draw that conclusion?" she asked, smiling softly.

"Just because you are. And you have a beautiful smile to boot."

She placed the back of her hand on my cheek and caressed my face, a feather-light touch that sent shivers through me, prompting me to pull her closer. I kissed her once again, more passionately than before. I lost myself anew, feeling an affection that was fresh and invigorating, yet intimately familiar. I didn't want it to stop, yearning for more. It wasn't with a sexual connotation, but rather a deep, soul-stirring need to be ever in her presence.

We were startled by the sudden sound of a fallen object. I found a half-rotten pear lying on the ground near the rear gate.

"Shall we return to the house?" she asked suggestively. "I am afraid if we remain, me ma wil' ni get to eat the compote before dinner."

"Absolutely. You're the boss."

As we started down the path, I instinctively glanced back at the rear gate. I frowned at the half-rotted pear before returning my gaze to Eilis as we walked together toward the main house.

"I hope I get to taste the fruit salad."

"There will be plenty fer ye."

We arrived at the empty manor, except for the few servants roaming about. I escorted Eilis to the kitchen. "Thank ye fer a wonderful afternoon, Myles. Ye allowed me a blissful moment, which lingers." She looked around, her demeanor changing. "Entering this house brought back thoughts of the horrid arrangement with the Marquess." Enthralled by her presence, I had completely forgotten about the bastard and their betrothal.

"I will speak with Adam and your father to see if they've come up with something to sever that plan, or I'll just come up with one myself."

"Would ye be so brave as to take such action?" she asked excitedly, her eyes wide with hope.

"Yes, I am. You have my word, Eilis," I expressed gallantly. "Can we meet again this evening in the garden after dinner? That is, if the Marquess is distracted with drink?"

"Aye, I would like that very much." She scanned the room, quickly stole a kiss, and headed into the pantry to prep the compote.

I made my way up the stairs to my room to wash up before meeting with Adam. As was the daily routine, a servant followed behind to tend to any of the guests' needs—closing doors, clearing dinnerware, and such. "May I get a bucket with warm water and a clean wash linen brought to my room, please?"

"Aye, sir." I continued to my room, waited briefly for the bucket, then refreshed myself. I looked out of the window, smiled, and reflected on the delightful afternoon with Eilis.

The echo of a stick pounding against a tree stole my attention. I spotted movement where Eilis and I had been, just a few feet away from the rear gate. It was the Marquess, beating a thick branch against the pear tree. He appeared angry, judging by the force he was exerting on the tree. *Could he have seen Eilis and me kissing?* I wondered, then realized, *if he did, I'm sure he would have confronted us on the spot.* I shrugged off the thought and turned to head back downstairs to meet with Adam.

I walked into the drawing room, finding Rey and Adam with drinks in hand, deep in conversation. "Evening, ladies!" I said as I poured myself a drink to join my companions.

"Call me a lady again and you'll find yourself screaming like one!" Adam blurted out the playful threat.

"Grumpy, are we?" I asked cheerfully.

"No, I'm just ready to leave this place. I'm getting that sinking feeling," Adam said, his gaze drifting towards the grand doors of the dining hall.

I raised an eyebrow and asked, "Of what?"

"You've been exchanging looks with Lady Eilis, both with twinkles in your eyes," Adam replied. "The Marquess may have noticed it."

"I've been informed by Rey," I interjected.

"Yes, Myles," Adam confirmed, his tone low and serious. "You need to put an end to it, and I say that with absolute certainty."

I exhaled. "Well, I can't help what I feel and what I know she feels. She has no desire to marry that man, especially under false pretenses," I expressed, feeling that all-too-familiar tingle within me, the one that continuously reassures me.

"Enough with this *telenovela* crap," Adam demanded. "I'll speak with the Marquess after supper and tell him we received word from the town courier that I'm needed back at the Abbey. You both will be my escorts."

"Sounds like a plan to me!" Rey exclaimed, a broad grin reflecting his relief.

"I'm not ready to leave just yet," I said quietly, refilling my cup with ale, my gaze drifting toward the garden.

Adam stared at me in disbelief. "You must be fucking kidding, Myles! All because of Eilis? You know the position that bastard holds. You have no viable way of ever being with her." His voice rose in anger, with a dangerous edge to it. "The only place you'll find yourself is in a *gaol* cell, if you're lucky."

"If I'm lucky?" My voice hardened, echoing my challenge as I repeated the words.

"The man is not always in his right mind," Adam insisted, "and you know that firsthand. He has influence in this province and wouldn't hesitate to see you hang at the gallows!"

I met Adam's gaze, my resolve unwavering. "I'm meeting with Eilis later this evening, in secret. I gave her my word that I—rather, *we*—will find a way to dissolve this sham betrothal."

"How the devil are *we* supposed to do that, Myles?" Rey blurted out with concern.

"Leave it to me," I said firmly, my eyes landing on Rey. "I'm the one who gave my word."

Suddenly, a hush fell over the room as a figure appeared in the doorway. Adam shot to his feet, his earlier anger forgotten in the face of the unexpected visitor. "Good evening, Lord Ormond!"

"Lord Ormond, hello," Rey echoed, scrambling to his feet as well, with a hint of awkwardness in his greeting.

"Marquess," I said dryly.

The Marquess's face mirrored mine, an impassive mask, giving nothing away. "To whom have you promised your word, Mr. Roberts?" he inquired sharply, like the edge of a newly honed blade. My mind raced, searching for a plausible lie. "To Adam," I replied, resolutely. "He has asked Rey and me to accompany him back to Cong Abbey tomorrow. He doesn't wish to travel alone, so I gave him my word that we will go with him."

"I see," Lord Ormond replied dismissively. Reaching for a drink, I noticed a bandage wrapped around his hand, stained with blood about the knuckles. It seemed that whatever angered him had caused him to use more than a branch to vent his frustrations.

"Did you hurt yourself, sir?" Rey asked bluntly, but his concern genuine.

"It does not take a scholar to figure that out, Mr. Tirad," the Marquess snapped back with narrowing eyes.

I raised an eyebrow, giving Rey my 'not-today-kiddo' look, aware of his short temper. Adam shifted in his seat to attract both our attention, silently pleading with Rey to let it go.

"Rey, fetch the satchel from my quarters, if you please," Adam requested, hoping to prevent an irrecoverable incident. I looked at Rey and gave a slight nod, encouraging him to leave. I had more self-control than he did, and it was best for him to remove himself before any regrettable actions could occur.

"Lord Ormond," Adam said smoothly, "as Myles explained, I received word from Cong Abbey today. Certain matters require my attention. I have asked Mr. Tirad and Myles to escort me back, and they have agreed."

"When is your expected departure?" the Marquess inquired coldly, his distant stare cemented on Adam.

"We need to begin our journey at daylight," Adam replied.

The Marquess remained silent and rudely walked out of the drawing-room with a scowl on his face, the heavy door thudding shut behind him. "He is not in the best of moods!" I commented, stating the obvious.

"You think?!" Adam grunted, a dry, exasperated sound. "To hell with him. We are out of here tomorrow," Adam declared, a grim look settling on his face. "I'm sensing uneasiness. Something foul is afoot."

Rey returned with Adam's satchel. "Here you are. Did mommy dearest check himself?" he quipped, unable to resist a jab.

Adam forcibly grabbed the satchel from Rey's hand. "What the hell, man! What did I do to *you*?" Rey bellowed, his temper reigniting.

"I'm sorry, kid. It's not your fault," Adam said apologetically. "I'm just a bit on edge. Let's gather our things after supper. Once the sun rises, we'll move forward on our horses and leave this place behind us!"

"I get the urgency," I said hesitantly.

"Please don't follow that with a 'but'," Rey added, reading my mind.

"I'm meeting with Eilis this evening," I stated firmly. "I gave her my word, and I refuse to back down from it."

Adam grunted unintelligibly, stomping out of the room with the satchel in hand.

"Whatever, man," Rey said, clearly displeased, then followed behind Adam.

I sighed, running a hand through my hair. *Why did everything have to be so complicated?* I had given Eilis my word, and I intended to keep it, no matter the cost. But with Adam on edge and Rey's temper simmering, I knew this wouldn't be easy. *I needed a plan, and fast!*

***

Dinner was a peaceful affair for a change, the Marquess having been called away to attend to some matter, accompanied by his two watchmen. Though Adam was absent, everyone else at the table seemed to be in a cheerful mood. Rey, who had been uncharacteristically quiet, excused himself early, wanting to rest and nurse an oncoming headache, leaving just Eilis, her parents, and me at the dining table.

"The Irish stew was delightful," Lady Isleen remarked, her voice soft and content. "The cuts of venison made it most heartily."

Lorcán chimed in, "Aye, 'twas. 'Tis a long day come morrow, so I bid ye good evening, Mr. Roberts." He stood and walked to the opposite side of the table, extending a hand to Lady Isleen. "Come, me dear. Ye appear weary." Turning to Eilis, he added suggestively, "Dinna keep yerself from sleep."

"Aye, father," she replied respectfully. "I will be in the garden briefly for reflection." He nodded and walked hand in hand with his wife toward the stairs to retire for the evening.

I remained at the table a bit longer with Eilis, laughing and conversing. Aware that her time was limited, I asked, "May I walk you to the garden, *señorita*?" extending my hand to help her from her seat, mimicking her father's gesture.

"Aye." Just then, an unfamiliar servant rushed past me, handing Eilis a note. She unfolded the paper, her eyes quickly scanning the contents.

"Allow me a moment, Myles," she said. "Me ma has asked to see me before she retires. The timing falls perfectly."

I grinned. "How so?"

"I intended to retrieve a gift I made fer ye."

"You don't have to gift me anything, Eilis," I said, my smile widening. "Your company alone is a gift in itself."

She matched my grin. "'Tis me pleasure, Myles," she said, placing her hand on my chest. "I will return shortly."

I held her hand for a fleeting moment. "I will meet you in the garden." I watched as she excitedly ran up the stairs, her beautiful hair bouncing with each step. She seemed almost to skip with joy. I refilled my cup with wine and stepped into the garden, following the path leading to the trellis.

I stopped midway to admire the dark sky with its orchestra of stars dancing around the full moon. I suddenly recalled Lorcán's mention of an alignment with the phases of the moon. *If I can find a book on astronomy,* I thought, *as primitive as some of the information may be in this century, I might find something useful that hints at such an alignment.* I continued stargazing, lost in my thoughts.

Then I heard footsteps approaching behind me. At first, I thought it was Eilis, but then I realized there were multiple footsteps. I turned swiftly. "You're not Eil—"

But before I could finish saying her name, I felt the impact of a blunt object striking my head with considerable force, causing me to lose consciousness.

Chapter 26 – A Prayer for Myles

It had been three days since Adam and Rey searched vigilantly for Myles. Rey moved with the meticulous precision of a seasoned investigator, focusing specifically on the garden area where Myles and Eilis were purported to meet. He paced between the rear gate and the back entrance of the manor for hours, thoroughly examining the ground for the smallest detail, anything that might provide a clue to Myles's whereabouts, just as he had done at the waterfall.

As the sun began to set, a final streak of light shone through a brush, illuminating a patch of grass and revealing red streaks across it. Rey, with his keen eye, bent down to grab a sample and took a whiff.

"Blood," he whispered, the single word a grim pronouncement. He inspected the area, finding several shoe imprints in the surrounding soil. Judging by the size of the impressions, they all belonged to men's shoes. He returned to the manor, bellowing, "Adam, where are you?"

"Where's the fire, man?" Adam replied calmly, a counterpoint to Rey's panic.

"Adam, look. I came across this midway between the entrance to the house and the rear gate." Rey placed the patch of grass on his hand. "Smell it."

Adam took a hard whiff. "Iron! It smells of iron. Is it blood?" he asked, his alarm now discernible. "Oh my God, could that be Myles's blood?"

"Did ye just say blood? Where, where did ye find blood?" Eilis asked, her voice shaky, eyes watery.

"Easy, Eilis. It does not mean the worst," Rey said reassuringly. "I found several shoe prints throughout the garden—three different but related impressions. One set belonged to Myles's shoes, that I can be sure of."

Anxiously pacing, finding it almost impossible to keep still, Rey reached for a lantern, excused himself, and hurried outside, wanting to make use of whatever sunlight was left. He lit the candle inside the lantern and passed it over the tracks. He followed the only two sets leading to the back gate, and there he found a third imprint clearly visible by the wall. They were heeled.

"Adam, come out here. Walk on the stone path, not on the soil."

Adam walked hastily down the walkway, followed by Eilis pacing quickly behind him.

"Adam, look there," Rey said, pointing to the heeled prints. "Those look like they may have come from the Marquess's shoes."

Adam stooped for a closer look. "They do appear to be, but that proves nothing. This is his property, so he will roam around the grounds at any given time."

"True, but if you take notice, the narrowed heels are facing the rear gate, meaning his back was facing it, and the heels of the other two prints are facing the house, which means they were facing him. The heeled shoes seem to turn here," Rey explained, using a branch to trace the outline of the print, "and the other two sets turn there, heading back toward the manor. Whoever wore the heeled shoes clearly did not want to be seen, so they exited through the back gate."

He brought the lantern lower to the ground, following the footsteps of the other two prints. "They separate... there." He followed one set, leading to the spot where he found the blood-stained grass.

"Someone must have come up behind Myles from this side. It looks like he turned abruptly and got caught off guard. If you look closely, the backs of the shoe prints are elevated. See how the front impressions deepen?"

"Dear Lord, you're right," Adam exclaimed. Eilis let out a sob, running back inside the manor.

"Why would anyone want to abduct him?" Adam asked.

"Not only was he struck, but was carried off and presumably... kidnapped," Rey exclaimed.

"Who would want to kidnap him?"

"I dare to say the Marquess." Rey and Adam turned to find Nobleman O'Quinn walking toward them. "Eilis revealed her feelings fer Mr. Roberts. She had become smitten with the lad since the day we arrived, which I wil' ni protest, as I found him to be an honorable man. I overheard ye and Mr. Towell conversing some time ago, with a mention of the Marquess having witnessed interactions between them. Lord Ormond is a man who should' ni be crossed. He will go to great lengths just to exact revenge."

"All the evidence I found suggests what you are implying, nobleman. Myles was indeed taken!" Rey uttered.

"Has the Marquess even acknowledged his disappearance?" Adam asked with interest.

"He has spent much of his time at the home of Sir Arthur Aston since the disappearance. The few times we exchanged words, I never heard a mention of Mr. Roberts's name spill from his mouth—ni an utterance," the Nobleman expressed.

"I will request a private audience with 'im and discreetly ascertain any information he will be willing to disclose. I will be sure to bring a bottle of *uisce beatha*. He will be partial to imparting more particulars wi' drink in 'im."

"Great idea," Rey said. "A few glasses of whiskey will make the interrogation go smoothly. Just be careful not to endanger yourself."

"I understand ye meaning, Mr. Tirad. *Ná bí buartha!*"

"I'm always worried," Rey responded.

The nobleman left the room, leaving Adam and Rey deep in thought. They shared a sense of hopelessness.

"Adam, would you be able to make your way through town tomorrow, as you are familiar with the area and the people? The smallest bit of information could be the most crucial," Rey asked as he placed a handful of grapes and a few wedges of cheese on a plate.

"Maureen, may I have some bread and wine?" he asked politely.

"Aye, sir!"

"Absolutely," Adam replied. "I will leave early in the morning after breakfast. I know two merchants who are married to the biggest busybodies in the town of

Dunmore. I chanced upon them two days ago in the village. If anyone had seen anything, it certainly would have been those two."

Adam reached for a wedge of cheese, biting into it with a hardened expression. "I will tear the town and this house into pieces if I must. I will do whatever it takes to get him back."

Maureen, who had been listening from the periphery of the conversation, dropped the tray of bread and bottle of wine, the sound of shattered glass echoing in the tense silence. Rey looked at her with a questioning expression.

"You know something, don't you, Maureen?" Rey asked with intent. "Do not be afraid to say something if you do. Mr. Roberts's life could be in grave danger."

"I dinnae want to risk being flogged, Mr. Tirad," she expressed, now sobbing with fear emanating from her eyes.

"You have my word, Maureen," Adam declared. "No harm will come to you, we promise."

Using her apron to clear her eyes, she recounted, "On the same evening Mr. Roberts disappeared, just before he was taken, Master Butler handed me an unsealed letter and ordered me to be discreet. I was instructed to find the groomsman and immediately hand it to him." She paused to pick up the bread from the floor, a habit she could not break.

"Leave the fucking bread alone. Take care of the damn thing later," Adam yelled in rage.

"Adam, relax," Rey said assertively. "You're just going to make her more nervous than she already is."

Adam stood from his seat and reached to pick up the bread. "My apologies, Maureen. I did not intend to blow up in that manner. Myles is our friend, and we are extremely worried, that's all."

"Nil a need to apologize, Mr. Towell. I understand yer worries."

Placing his hand on her shoulder, Rey said, "Thank you," then asked, "Now, did you get a chance to read the contents of the note?"

"Aye, sir. It read that the groomsman was to find the watchman, and that he and another guard were to remain hidden in wait by the rear gate of the garden."

Rey slammed his hand on the table. "I told you those were the imprints of the Marquess's shoes. Shit." He looked at Maureen. "I'm sorry, go on," he apologized.

She continued, "They were to remain hidden until he gave the signal. Once Mr. Roberts was found to be alone in the garden, they were to incapacitate him and deliver him to a ship named the *White Seahorse* at the Port of Kilkenny."

Adam stared at Maureen intently, looking as if he were about to explode once again, but instead, he grabbed her by the shoulders and planted a gratuitous kiss on her cheek. "Thank you, Maureen, thank you. We are so grateful to you."

Rey dug into his pocket and pulled out a coin-filled pouch. "This is for you, Maureen. If you ever feel unsafe here, there is more than enough money to take you and your family wherever you need to go."

"'Tis kind o'ye, Mr. Tirad. Now please make haste and find Mr. Roberts!"

***

Rey was awakened by a loud knocking on his bedroom door. "Who is it?" he asked as he planted both feet on the floor and stood to pull up his pants.

"It's Adam," came the reply in a loud whisper. "Hurry yourself and get out of bed," he ordered, barging into the room and catching Rey half-naked with his britches just below his knees, fully exposed. "Good morning, Tiny Tim. Get to it. The Marquess arrived late last night and is still asleep. Maureen packed provisions and readied the horses for us. I collected Myles's belongings and placed them in my satchel. Let's get out of here before he wakes up."

Rey dressed hastily, and they both fled the manor.

Adam followed a route that would lessen their travel time by an hour or so. It was not a considerable amount of time, but given the dire circumstances, every second counted.

"How long will it take to reach the Port of Kilkenny?" Rey queried.

"We are not going to the Port of Kilkenny; we're headed to the port at Dunmore East. That is where a ship as large as the *White Seahorse* would have to dock."

"How do you know for certain?"

"The *White Seahorse* is too large a vessel to navigate through the River Barrow," Adam explained. "She would need to drop anchor at Dunmore. It's the only port large enough to accommodate such a sizable boat. We should be there before noon."

Appearing relieved, Rey exclaimed, "Wow, that soon?! Here I thought we would be traveling throughout the night."

"We are, Sherlock. Noon tomorrow," Adam replied sarcastically.

"How far is the journey?" Rey asked hesitantly, knowing Adam could be quick-tempered at times.

"Under thirty hours, I'd say."

"Ahh. Once we arrive, how do we find out if Myles is indeed on the ship, if it hasn't set out to sea already?"

"You're the FBI agent; *you* figure it out. We have some distance ahead of us, so that should give you plenty of time to solve the puzzle."

Rey chuckled loudly. "You're a barrel of fun, Adam."

The day's events, which had begun early in the day, were wearing on Adam. He looked tired. He and Rey rode for most of the day, having to stop and rest just before sundown. Rey, a man of action, wanted to continue, but he felt compassion for Adam, knowing he had risen before sunrise and had barely anything to eat. As if reading his thoughts, Adam waved at Rey to grab his attention.

"The Killamery Church is not too far from here. A friar from Cong Abbey serves the priest there and can give us refuge for the evening."

"Yes, sir," Rey said, his eyebrows furrowed in thought. "I accompanied Myles a few years back to the Irish Hunger Memorial in New York City, and there was a display that mentioned the Killamery High Cross. Is that one and the same?"

"Yes, the same one. The cross is but a few yards from the church," Adam replied. "We can walk over and see it if you'd like."

"That would be nice. I would like to kneel before it and say a prayer for Myles."

"Don't feel so anguished. All will work itself out. We *will* find Myles; I can promise you that."

Rey felt tears stream down his face, experiencing once again that sense of desperation he felt while searching for Myles at the waterfall. That was his best friend, his brother, and having to relive that hopelessness was becoming difficult to bear.

They arrived at the church just before sunset and were met by the friar, who escorted them to a shed at the back of the property. It appeared small from a distance, but once inside, it seemed more spacious. Surprisingly, there were three cots, a chair, and a small stone hearth with a vibrant fire alight.

"May I prepare tea fer ye, Brother Don?" the friar asked.

"Yes, Brother Ryan, for my friend as well, if you please."

"Certainly. There is still some stew left from supper and plenty of bread. Can I bring some fer ye both?"

Rey answered "yes" almost at once. "I will as well, Brother Ryan," Adam said.

"What brings ye this way, Brother Don?" Brother Ryan inquired.

"We are in search of a friend. He was taken rather abruptly, against his will, from the residence of the Marquess James Butler. We believe he was brought on board a ship named the *White Seahorse*, which may be docked at the port of Dunmore East."

"Aye, I have heard of such a ship. 'Tis governed by a pirate, O'Malley, no?"

Adam, reaching for his cup, nodded his head. "Yes, it is. Would you know, or even possibly have heard, if it is still anchored at Dunmore?"

The friar handed Rey his cup. "No. I haveni heard any chatter of it."

Adam sighed in frustration. He sipped his tea and lay on a cot, deep in thought. Then he turned to Rey. "We need to take some rest once we are done with supper. I want to arrive at the port before daylight."

Rey brought out his watch. "You said Dunmore East is another eight or nine hours from here. If you want to arrive before daylight, we will need to leave here no later than ten p.m. The time now is seven."

"Well, you better eat fast!" Adam responded.

"Aye, aye, Captain," Rey replied in jest.

He and Adam finished their tea and gobbled up the stew. Then, as promised, they walked over to the Killamery High Cross to say their prayers for Myles.

***

Moonlight was left in the friar's care to lighten their load. Adam warned Rey to leave anything deemed unnecessary behind to allow them to travel faster. The cool night air made the conditions perfect for their horses to gallop at a quicker pace, reducing the need to stop as often for rest.

They arrived at the harbor of Dunmore East just as the sun peeked over the horizon. Several anglers were preparing their boats for the early catch of the day, which suited them perfectly, for if anyone knew anything about O'Malley's ship, it would be they.

Adam approached a lone angler. "Pardon me, sir. Good day. My apologies for interrupting you, but could you tell me how long ago the *White Seahorse* set sail?"

The fisher tied his net to the stern of his *currach*, trussing it, then climbed onto the dock. "Good morrow. Mhaol's ship, ye say? Aye. She spent two days anchored. 'Twas a burdensome task to prepare me own *currach*, *leis* taking up nearly the whole of the dock."

"When did it set sail?" Adam asked with urgency.

"Ah... yesterday. It sailed with the tide sometime after dawn. I meself had set out just as the sun appeared over the horizon, north, but had to return, having left me catch-net stored on me horse's saddle. It had already set sail south by the time I returned."

Rey, his face contorted in anger, slapped his head in frustration, and walked away.

"I'd wager she made sail to Hugh Town on the Isle of Scilly. There is a port in the southwestern part of the island at the Garrison Walls. 'Tis an ideal place fer pirates to trade, as 'tis located off a mainland." Adam handed the angler a coin, a habit of the journeyers, and thanked him, then caught up to Rey. He, too, felt angered, but venting his frustration would not bring Myles or the ship back.

"Rey, stop," Adam yelled, walking at a fast pace to catch up to him. "We need to find a ship that is sailing to the Isle of Scilly."

"What's on the Isle of Scilly?" Rey asked, appearing defeated.

"Just after you had your little bitch fit, the fisherman said that the *White Seahorse* was sure to have set a course there to trade."

Rey chuckled and hugged Adam, feeling a surge of relief. "You're not my type," Adam commented, then tapped Rey on the shoulder. "Listen, the men I mentioned with the wives who have wagging tongues, they live nearby. We can leave our horses with them once we find a ship."

They walked along the port, inquiring with every angler and merchant for information on ships that were set to sail to Maypole in the Isles of Scilly, but to no avail. Rather than surrendering, they made their way to the home of the "wagging tongues," as Adam referred to them, and as luck would have it, they were able to help them find a ship, the *Spirited Wind*, scheduled to set sail the following morning. They secured their passage, and just after daybreak, they would find themselves on their way to rescue their brother.

The Waters Fall-A Journeyer – Rob Mylo Vazquez

Chapter 27 – An Ocean Filled with Emptiness

I lay on the wooden board that had been my makeshift bed for the past few days. The only comfort between me and the splintered wooden slab was a tattered blanket, folded in half, and a handful of hay, stuffed into a burlap sack, which I used as a pillow. While the ship was docked at the port, I had pondered various ways to escape from that decrepit box, but all my hopes vanished once the ship departed and set out to sea.

For the first time since my abduction, my nerves seemed to have gotten the better of me. I was completely clueless about where I was headed and by whom I was being held prisoner. Leif, a cabin boy no older than seventeen, was the only person I had interacted with since the beginning of the ordeal. He brought two meals daily, and from time to time, collected the chamber pot.

I was prone to occasional bouts of claustrophobia in the windowless cell. The air circulation was minimal at best in the eight-by-eight space, save for the tiny cracks at the bottom of the door, offering a meager breeze. Having been imprisoned on board for what felt like ages, I began finding it difficult to tell the difference between day and night, losing all track of time.

Needing the chamber pot collected as the stench was becoming unbearable, I called out for Leif, but was ignored, as I so often was. I yelled myself hoarse for what seemed like hours, until finally, he appeared, unlocking the door.

"Quiet, man, ye'll wake the dead wi' all ye ruckus!" Leif bellowed, his words heavy with annoyance.

"I need to know how long I'm going to be held in this hellhole, Leif. You must let me speak with whoever is in charge," I demanded, feeling desperate for freedom.

Leif stared at me, blank-faced. "What makes ye think Captaen Ó Maillé will want to speak wi' ye?"

"Please, just tell him to give me but a few moments of his time," I pleaded.

Leif placed my breakfast on the bed, picked up the used chamber pot, and replaced it with a fresh one, still with no response to my request. He walked out and then turned before closing the door.

"I will convey ye message t' er."

Consumed by my anger, the full weight of his words didn't hit me until a few moments later. *"I will convey ye message to her?"* My thoughts raced, just as they did when I struggled to figure out to whom the initials A.T. carved into the Saxon wheellock belonged. *"Who in the seventeenth century was a female captain of a ship with the surname of Ó Maillé?"* I asked myself the same question repeatedly, with each response coming up blank.

I put my meditation practices to use, utilizing the breathing techniques I learned in the yoga class Rey and I took during college. *Sit tall, spine aligned, front of body inhalation, compress while exhaling, move only during suspended breath, breathe effortlessly.* I inhaled and exhaled; eyes closed. My body and mind reached a point of deep relaxation, feeling like I was having an out-of-body experience. It was as if I were immersed inside a box filled with liquid oxygen, suspended within, yet breathing freely. With the sounds of the waves crashing and the distant voices of crewmen becoming muted, I focused on just the sound of my lungs expanding and contracting.

Just as I reached a peak of bliss, my thoughts came crashing down on me like a tsunami. "The Pirate Queen, Grace O'Malley of Connacht!"

My mind reeled, becoming pages from a book, flipping, all filled with various names of historical figures. Some were commonly known; however, there were others that were not so often heard of but were significant. Undoubtedly, Grace O'Malley fell into the category of notable. One lesson I lectured my students on included the pirate as the primary subject. It was during Halloween, and I wanted to integrate the holiday with a history lesson. With witches being too cliché, I decided to go with a pirate theme.

"Open your books to page 73, 'Gráinne Ní Mháille.' Who wants to volunteer to read aloud the entry of Grace O'Malley?"

Isaiah quickly raised his hand. "I will."

"Go ahead, Isaiah."

"Grace O'Malley was the daughter of Lord Eóghan Dubhdara Ó Máille of the Ó Máille clan from western Ireland. She was his only daughter, with a paternal brother, Dónal an Phíopa Ó Máille. Following her father's death, she took over the leadership of the dynasty, overseeing all aspects related to the family, both by land and by sea." Isaiah paused, then asked curiously, "Wouldn't her brother be the one to take over the lordship of the family?"

"Good question," I replied. "She was married to Dónal an Chogaidh Ó Flaithbheartaigh when her father passed away. Having sole ownership of many lands and proprietorship of hundreds of horses and cattle—something not easily achievable back then—made her an extraordinarily rich and influential woman. Her familial status was superlative in itself, and her marital status further elevated her above her half-brother, thus entitling her to the leadership role."

"Wouldn't a position such as that be difficult for a woman to hold during those times?" Arantsa asked, her curiosity stimulated.

"Yes, especially for a woman. It would have been equally difficult even for the most ambitious of men to hold." Flipping through the pages, I instructed, "Take a look at page 75. It reads that she was considered an astute politician and an even fiercer seafarer. Men were not quick to cross her."

"That's because women rule!" Evie yelled excitedly, rousing the rest of her female classmates as they followed suit.

"They absolutely do," I noted, followed by a wink and a smile.

As Isaiah read on, I turned to lean against the desk and found myself sitting on the rickety wooden board I detested. Time seemed to have passed during another one of my ever-present daydreams, with Leif standing before me in the place of Isaiah, holding an empty tray.

"I have come to collect ye, *babhla*. Dinnae fancy yer *leite*, eh?" he asked as he scooped up a spoonful of the cold, mushy porridge, then plopped it back into the bowl.

"Leif, were you able to convey my message to your captain?"

"Aye," Leif responded, his brows furrowed. "Captaen Gráinne Ní Mháille wishes to have ye join her in her quarters fer supper. Best t'get yerself cleaned and presentable. Ye dinnae want to meet wi' an captaen smelling the way ye do."

Leif stepped outside of the cell. He returned with a bucket filled with water and a large piece of soap wrapped in a washcloth. "I'll fetch ye fresh *arán agus im* while ye wash yeself, if ye desire."

"Bread and butter does sound good right about now," I replied matter-of-factly, my stomach rumbling in agreement.

Leif collected the untouched bowl of porridge and left the room, his footsteps echoing in the corridor, allowing me a moment of privacy. The water was warm and soothing as it trickled down my body. I combed my fingers through my hair, scraping off dry blood, and realized it had been days since I had a proper bath. I took my time, passing the damp cloth through my scalp and then across my chest and abs. I dipped the cloth once again into the tepid water and scrubbed my face vigorously. The overgrown stubble on my chin and neck had become unbearably itchy due to the lack of cleansing.

Leif returned to find me standing naked, still cleansing myself. "Just how dirty were ye, eh?" he asked with a teasing tone.

I ignored him, wringing the cloth and dipping it into the bucket of water one last time for a final pass. Leif collected my fetid clothes off the floor and tossed a pair of clean britches and a *léine* on the wooden board for me to wear.

"Thank you, Leif. You have been very kind," I said gratuitously.

"I dinnae know what offense ye may have committed, but I assume it was' ni extreme if an captaen has accepted audience wi' ye."

"That's just it, Leif. As I told you before, I have committed no crime at all. I was assaulted and kidnapped, presumably because I was in the wrong place at the wrong time. That is how I ended up on board this ship," I explained as I dressed.

"D'ye know by whom?" Leif inquired.

"I have thought about it, and I believe that, given the timing of it all, the Marquess, James Butler, was behind it." I sat and spread butter on the bread, while continuing, "There's a young lady who is betrothed to him—"

Leif interrupted, a knowing look on his face. "Aye, if there is a *bhean* involved, there is fer certain always going to be some form of jealousy."

"We grew fond of each other during my stay at the Marquess's manor. Before my abduction, she and I planned to meet in the estate's garden. I recently conceived a way of severing their betrothal and was going to inform her of it."

"So ye thinks the Marquess may have discovered of ye encounter?"

"I believe he may have witnessed our kissing in the garden that same afternoon. It could not be just mere coincidence," I conveyed, my eyebrows furrowed in suspicion.

"Well, *ná bí buartha, a chara*. 'Tis me understanding that Captaen Ó Maillé is ní fond of this Marquess. I have often overheard her speaking ill of him. I dinnae know an reason, just know that she does, so it may benefit ye."

I looked at Leif with a slight grin, a small ember of hope flickering in my chest. "That comes as a relief. I appreciate you, Leif." I extended my hand out in gratitude, and he reciprocated with a firm forearm shake. Leif turned to leave the room and closed the door, but I heard no sound of the padlock clicking closed. I took that action as a sign of trust from Leif. As curious as I was, I did not want to break that newly formed trust, so I remained still within the confines of the room.

***

Having been lulled into a deep sleep by the rocking of the ship, I was awakened sometime later by Leif. "Lad, an Captaen is ready fer ye."

I rose rapidly from the sleeping board, eager to be free from the confined area I had been sequestered in. Leif led the way, keeping a considerable distance ahead. I felt a bit off from the constant motion of the ship and the lack of circulation to my legs, causing me to pause and recover my steadiness.

"What's amiss, lad?"

"Being confined in that room with no constant mobility has caused my legs to stiffen."

"Ah. Well, best regain yer movement and make haste. Dinnae want to keep an captaen waiting. She can become testy when put off."

I hopped in place to promote circulation to my legs and regain movement. I then continued behind Leif, now able to keep pace with him. Making our way to the upper deck, I was once again captivated by the architectural details so often found in the countless structures of the present century. I came across carvings of ocean scenery, mermaids perched on rocks, and the like. The relief carvings, meticulously crafted into the walls of the hull, all told a story.

Beyond the stairs, I saw the outside world for the first time since my abduction through a porthole. I presumed it was the starboard side of the ship because of the setting sun. The captain's quarters were located on the port side, requiring passage through the mess hall to reach them. The hall was filled with crewmen and deckhands indulging in their evening meal and quenching their thirst with ale, some appearing inebriated.

They placed their cups down on the tables and stopped to gawk at me with looks of revulsion, knowing I was a prisoner. They taunted me, yelling obscenities, some even spitting at me. Leif pounded his fist on a table to get their attention.

"*Eh, calma sibh féin*, calm yerselves. He is to join an captaen as her invited guest fer supper."

They quickly settled themselves as best they could, given their present state, but not before hurling handfuls of food at my face, falling into my shirt.

"Enough!"

The room grew instantly silent. I turned to find the Pirate Queen, Grace O'Malley, standing at the entrance to the mess hall. She looked statuesque, with fists planted on her hips, giving her the cliché appearance of a pirate. Her presence alone commanded respect. She was tall, slender, and curved in all the right places. Uncommon for a woman of the time, she wore britches, a puffed-sleeved ruffled *léine*, and a long green velvet vest that reached just below her waist. The black leather boots completed her attire. Her amber hair was tied up in a messy bun, with a thin silk lace around her neck. She was a beautiful woman, and way ahead of her time.

She approached and handed me a kerchief. It felt like a reversal of roles; the pirate queen playing the hero and me, the damsel in distress. I wiped my face and *léine* and expressed, "Thank you, Captain."

She looked at Leif. "I will take it from here," she said and gestured with a wave for him to go on his way. Then she turned to me. "Follow me, Mr. Myles."

I trailed behind her, not too close, unsure whether there were any protocols set in place against walking alongside a person of her authority. We entered her quarters and were met by two crewmen who were preparing the table.

"Have a seat, Mr. Myles. Is that ye surname, nó ye given name?"

"Myles is my first name, Captain," I responded with a respectful nod.

"Aye. Well, I will continue to call ye Mr. Myles. It has grown on me," she said assertively. She then added, "Ye may continue to refer to me as Captaen."

I nodded once again with a smile, feeling eased for the first time in days. She filled both our cups with wine and placed a tray of bread in front of me.

"*Cad é do scéal*, Mr. Myles? Tell me ye story and what brought ye onto me ship."

Clearing my throat, I began, "Well, I ask myself the same question, Captain. To shorten the '*scéal*,' one moment I was partaking of a drink in the Marquess James Butler's garden; the next, I was ambushed by two strangers, one of them crashing an object against my head."

Captain O'Malley stopped abruptly before biting into a piece of venison. "Ye say James Butler, d'ye?" she asked, a loathsome sound in her voice.

"Yes, Lord Butler, Earl of Ormond, Marquess, all one and the same."

"Why would he go through all the trouble of making ye a prisoner on me ship? He could easily have had ye imprisoned in any one of the jails within his province. Why bother bringing ye here?"

"That troubles me as well," I replied.

She placed the fork down and looked at me curiously. "Why *did* he have ye abducted in the first place? What grievous crime have ye committed?"

I stared back at her with pursed lips and one eyebrow raised. "I am almost sure it has to do with the young lady he is betrothed to—a forced betrothal at his request, might I add, not hers."

"I take it ye took a shining to the *cailin*, aye?"

I tittered at her comment, "Yes. It was mutual admiration between the two of us. Her engagement—ah... um... her betrothal, I should say—was the culmination of a deceitful procurement."

"How so?" she questioned, her eyes narrowing with a keen interest that seemed to burn through the wine.

"Her father is a fabrics merchant, and the Marquess acquired a sizable shipment of his goods to give as a gift to King Charles and the Queen."

She quickly interrupted, her fork clattering onto the table. "What does that have to do wi' an betrothal?"

I gestured with my finger while I took a sip of the wine, allowing the rich taste to settle on my tongue before explaining. "The Marquess, in a desperate attempt to impress the royals, spent more than he could afford. With the help of his henchmen, he made Eilis's father responsible for all the costs."

She exclaimed, her teeth clenched, "That seed-swallowing gobshite! *Cad* I would give to drive me sword up his shite hole." Her intense hatred of the man was evident. As a perceptive man, I knew that her loathing of the Marquess could be a powerful tool for me.

"The Marquess," I continued, "then suggested to the nobleman that he'd be willing to take his daughter's hand as payment for the debt."

"So, ye dinnae commit any crimes, then? Ye are just here eating me venison and *ag ól mo fhíona*," she said, letting out a mirthless chuckle.

"I can always repay you for drinking your wine and eating your venison," I responded suggestively, offering a slow, confident smile.

We continued conversing and partaking in drinks, the easy flow of the conversation a striking difference to my earlier apprehension. She spoke of her ambition to free Ireland of any English hold by whatever means necessary and of how she planned on conceiving ways to upend the English sea trade through plundering. With a few too many cups of wine and ale in her, her inhibitions were lowered, and she confessed the details of her current mission to the Isles of Scilly.

"A ship is expected to reach the western port of the Isles of Scilly in a sennight. It holds a shipment of the spoils of old, meant for some Englishman's cabinet of wonders. The king's men will be swarming the port, and me men are eager to take on the lot of them," she proclaimed, stomping her fist on the table. "I have me eye on several precious items, namely the longsword rumored to have belonged to King Harald Hardrada, the last king of Norway. 'Tis encrusted with rare emeralds and gold, ye know."

"Is that the port outside of the Garrison Walls at St. Mary's?" I inquired, the name recognizable in my thoughts.

"Aye, 'tis," O'Malley replied. "Ye familiar wi' it?"

"Yes. I am a history teacher back in the colonies, and I have lectured on the Star Castle that lies within the Garrison Walls. It is a heavily fortified fort and is strategically built for heavy defenses."

"Aye. 'Tis an reason we arrive under the guise of flaxseed traders. Me plans are to reach port just after midnight and allow me men to disembark in secret before dropping anchor at port."

"You could find yourself caught in an onslaught, even under the cover of night," I warned, my mind racing with all the historical facts I knew about the area.

"Ye keep yerself looking pretty and lemmi manage the logistics!" she retorted, her eyes twinkling with amusement.

The Waters Fall-A Journeyer – Rob Mylo Vazquez

Chapter 28 – Conflicted

There comes a time in a person's life when they must make decisions that could compromise their integrity. That person can become guilt-ridden by the outcome of those decisions, depending on the severity of the act. I was raised to be an honest man and to deceive no one, though now, since my emergence in this century, there had been many instances where I was left with no other choice but to forfeit my beliefs and stray from the ways of my upbringing in order to simply survive, leaving me in a quandary with a heavy sentiment weighing on my heart.

***

Grace O'Malley had taken a shine to me, inviting me to her quarters to share supper with her every evening following the first—more times than I felt comfortable with. Though I was not in a traditional relationship with Eilis, my heart was still intimately connected to hers. I felt as though, in some unorthodox way, I was being unfaithful to her.

On the evening before our expected arrival at the port of St. Mary's, I was once again summoned to the captain's quarters to sup with her. She appeared to be in a buoyant disposition, a marked difference from her usual stern demeanor.

"I am grateful to you for allowing me to dine with you all these evenings, Captain," I said neutrally. "I am truly appreciative."

"Are ye now?" she replied coquettishly, her eyes beaming. "'Tis ní often that a prisoner gets the opportunity to dine with their captor." She then reached over and took hold of my hand, her grip particularly firm. "There are other ways ye can show ye appreciation."

My initial instinct was to withdraw my hand from hers, but I did not want to appear rejective. She had shown signs in the past of becoming unhinged at the drop of a hat, so with the mixture of spirits she was consuming, she was sure to blow up if dismissed in any way. I smiled politely and subtly reached for my cup, hoping to make it appear like a natural movement rather than a rejection.

"Is there something you need me to do on the ship?" I asked, feigning cluelessness about her intentions. "I can help scrub the decks if that is what you are referring to."

The captain gawked at me, a lustful look in her eyes. Then she stood impulsively, walked to the door, and summoned Leif.

"Aye, Captaen?" he asked attentively.

She commanded him in Gaeilge, though in a faint voice, almost a whisper, "*Nil aon duine chun cur isteach orm!*" I leaned over, inching closer to make out what she was saying. What I was able to decipher was something along the lines of "do not disturb." I knew at once what she was implying.

She returned to her seat and quaffed down her cup of whiskey, then ogled me with narrowed eyes, her tone openly flirtatious. "How would ye like to win ye freedom, Mr. Myles?" she asked as she stood once again, making her way to my side of the table.

"I... yes... I would like it... *that*... like that very much, Captain," I stammered, my heart thrumming a frantic rhythm as she slid her hand inside my shirt, her fingers caressing my chest. I felt nervous, never having had a woman come on to me so aggressively before.

"Whoa!" I exclaimed with a nervous laugh as she pulled back my chair and straddled me, placing her firm backside on my thighs. I wasn't so much shocked as I was conflicted. Knowing now what the price was for me to win my freedom, I knew that guilt was going to linger in my consciousness, a bitter taste in my mouth.

O'Malley continued to caress my chest through my shirt. Then, with a sudden, forceful motion, she ripped the linen open, exposing my skin to the cool air. Her soft lips found their way to my nipple. Even with my mind still focused on Eilis, my body, unbidden, responded. My excitement, a testament to my body's betrayal, strained visibly against my britches. Her hand found its way there, and with a firm grip, she toyed with me as she rose. She pulled me from my seat, and in a single fluid motion, she tugged my britches down to my knees, leaving me exposed.

The last woman I had been with was Lisa, and the memory, bittersweet, flashed through my mind. I knew then that I had to do whatever was necessary to get back to Eilis, even if it meant sacrificing my sense of integrity. I pulled off my ripped shirt and stepped out of my pants. I took Grace by her waist, propping her up on the table, and positioned myself over her. I pulled open her *léine* and took hold of her breasts. As I savored one nipple, I squeezed the other, causing her to gyrate her hips and moan. She grabbed the back of my head and pushed me toward her lips, kissing me with a fierce hunger that felt both exhilarating and terrifying.

As I pulled down her britches, she managed to overpower me, shoving me against the table where I landed flat on my back. She seized me, and with a low growl of pleasure, mounted me. She settled onto me, her body swaying in a slow, deliberate rhythm that quickly became a frantic, intense motion. She leaned forward and nibbled on my neck, finding my weak spot just below my left ear. Realizing the reaction it evoked from me, she continued softly gnawing at it, a sensation that heightened my arousal. I thrust upward with such intensity that it caused her body to tremble. Knowing she was close to climax, she dismounted and repositioned herself.

I looked at her, panting, and with a final grunt, I came up behind her and thrust inside, a furious, almost desperate release of my anger at the circumstances that had brought me to her. Her body went taut, and she let out a cry of pure pleasure. I continued my deep, powerful thrusts, an unconscious way of punishing her for making me go against my heart. I knew I couldn't hold myself any longer. I was about to withdraw when Grace reached behind and held onto my backside, restricting my movement. With the assist of her long limbs, she kept me in place, leaving me no choice but to empty myself inside her. A wave of panic washed over me, and I pulled out, gasping for breath. "Why the hell did you do that?" I yelled furiously with sudden fear.

She turned, legs spread open, and faced me with a cunning grin on her lips. "Ye paid fer ye freedom wi' ye seed."

I remained silent, my face blank as I stared at her, then jumped off the table, wiped myself with a rag, and threw it angrily on the ground.

"*Ná bí buartha*, Mr. Myles. If ye seed sprouts, ye'll have a braw and bonny lad wi' me red hair and ye pretty, green eyes!" she mocked lightly, grinning naughtily.

I yanked the ripped shirt from the chair and pulled up my britches, my anger not at her foolish action, but at the potential repercussions of it. "Am I free to go back to my cell?" I asked, unable to make eye contact with her. I have always been a docile man, but whenever provoked or deceived, my way of containing my temperament was by avoiding eye contact with whomever I was confronting.

"Ye dinnae want to finish ye meal wi' me, Mr. Myles?" she asked, a callous expression manifesting. "Nil a need to feel cross wi' me. 'Tis all in good fun."

I stared at the ground for a moment, then slowly raised my eyes to meet hers. "Are you not afraid of the consequences that may arise from what you have just done?"

"*Cad*? Sprout a lad? Nil, Mr. Myles. I have delivered four *babógs* in me life. I highly doubt I will grow another in me belly. I have already crossed that age. Me *buachaillí* are old enough to have *babógs* of their own once they find an proper wife. Tibbot hasni reached an age yet, but me *iníon*, Méadhbh; she is already married to Richard Bourke and has *babógs* of her own."

"What about your husband, Captain? What would Mr. O'Flaherty say if you came home to him with a baby in your belly?" I asked with a slight tremor in my voice.

She laughed, a harsh, unexpected sound. "If that were to be the case, Mr. Myles, then I would be the one surprised. Donal died some years back, ambushed and killed by a rival clan."

I cupped my hands and stood silent for a moment, having remembered that Grace O'Malley had been a widow for some time until she married her second husband. As much as I tried, I could not recall his name, so I improvised, "My condolences, captain. Your children must miss their father immensely."

She turned to reach for her britches from the ground, slipping one leg in. "Aye, they did at first. I then got married fer a second time. His name is Risdeárd Bourke."

"*An Iarainn*, the Iron. I have heard of him. The 18th Mac William Íochtar."

Her eyebrows raised, a look of surprise and respect in her eyes. "Aye, ye know 'im then."

I tipped my head from side to side. "I *have* heard of him. Back in the colonies."

"Me husband's name travels across the oceans then. I have done well!" she responded with overconfidence.

I felt myself settle, the panic and anger beginning to subside. The thought of becoming a father to a child conceived with a pirate from a past century suddenly sounded so absurd that it was almost humorous. It was my present truth, but the notion was a far-fetched one, and with her words, the weight lifted from my back. I felt a sense of ease, a mix of relief at my newfound freedom and the release of pent-up sexual frustration. I was relieved to know that soon I would return home—wherever that was—and be free from yet another bizarre situation.

***

I had finished dinner with the ever-vocal captain. I excused myself, exercising my newfound freedom and feeling a need to rest before the soon-approaching invasion at the port of St. Mary's. An uncertainty settled in my gut; at some point, I would either be called upon to join the fight or find myself inextricably involved.

Passing through the mess hall, with the scent of stale ale and sweat thick in the air, I came upon several crewmen testing their strength in an arm-wrestling challenge. The low roar of encouragement filled the room. I stopped to watch the match, my gaze drawn to the flexing muscles and strained faces. A lone deckhand, perched on a barrel in the corner, eyed me with an unsettling interest, which I pointedly ignored. My intention of being a mere spectator was abruptly interrupted when the crewman next in line for the challenge fixed his gaze on me, his eyes narrowed in a challenging stare.

"Eh, wench. Bring ye pretty self here," the crewman grunted, a sneer twisting his lips.

I stared back, one eyebrow raised, a silent challenge in my stare. "Which part of me convinces you I'm a wench, rose petal?"

"Argh, a battle it seems ye desire. Bring yerself here and see if ye can match me strength," he growled, pounding a fist on the table.

"I wouldn't want you to break a nail, lass," I retorted, a playful jest in my tone. "Are you sure you want to embarrass yourself in front of your lads?" With the indulgence of a hearty meal and a romp in the hay, I felt strong, rejuvenated. My adrenaline, still humming from the earlier skirmish with Captain O'Malley, was eager for another challenge.

The crewman, a large man with a leathery face and a thick, dark beard, smiled, revealing several cracked teeth, some blackened by decay. "Care t' wager a coin?" he asked, his eyes glistening.

"Let's make it two coins," I countered, reaching into my pocket. I pulled out my coin purse—which Leif had returned to me—and presented two shillings. I placed them on the rough wooden table as I settled onto the bench across from my opponent. "Now, place your bet."

The crewman, who introduced himself as Brutus, matched the wager, placing his two shillings next to mine. He filled his own wooden cup with ale and, with a nod, ordered one of the other deckhands to fetch another cup for me—a surprisingly friendly gesture. We clinked the cups in a brief toast, the clack of wood against wood—then set them aside. I used a corner of my tattered shirt to dry my palms, ensuring a firmer grip on my opponent. Brutus was a formidable man, towering over six feet, four inches, with broad shoulders and massive, calloused hands. But his size did not deter me. I had taken part in arm-wrestling challenges in the past, in various dive bars with Rey, Devon and Alex. My strategy, honed over years, was always the same: ensure my opponent was deep in drink, which naturally would alter their perception and dull their strength.

I made a request before the challenge. "Can I get two double shots of whiskey?" I asked, knowing that the potent mixture of ale and *uisce beatha* would quickly buzz him up.

The deckhand returned with the bottle of whiskey, a puzzled expression on his face. "Dinnae know what a double shot is, lad," he admitted.

I chuckled and stood to pour the drinks myself, offering a simple demonstration. "All you need to do is fill the cup with the whiskey more than halfway." The man's eyes widened in disbelief, uncertain how anyone could manage such a large serving of liquid courage. I proposed another toast with a simple, indirect gesture—a nod and a raised cup—then emptied my cup in a single gulp.

Brutus, initially eager, hesitated. He eyed the whiskey-filled cup, then glanced at the other crewmen, who watched him with intense interest. Not wanting to appear a coward in front of his lads, he took a deep breath, placed the cup to his mouth, and drained it. "Arrrghh, uff," he grunted, a strenuous sound that ended in a cough.

It was exactly the reaction I had been waiting for. I snapped my neck from side to side, then entwined my fingers and cracked my knuckles, drying my palms once more with the torn shirt. "I am ready!" I declared with confidence.

Brutus, his eyes now slightly glazed, grinned. "Dinna want to hear ye cry like a lassie when I snap ye arm in half, so be prepared," he warned, his words slurring slightly.

I laughed cunningly, nodding my head repeatedly with one eyebrow raised, my 'not-today-kiddo' expression shining through. "On your go, sweetheart."

We positioned our elbows with a forceful thud on the table, then linked our hands together, our grips tightening. I looked into his eyes, which appeared glossy from the drink. I knew at once that the man was deep in his cups. We grabbed onto the side of the table for balance and stability, our fingers wiggling to tighten our grip. My plan was simple: a quick, upward flick of my wrist would bend Brutus's wrist backward, breaking his strength and declaring him the loser. I put my game plan into action, and seconds after the deckhand raised his hand to initiate the match, our fists landed on the table with a crash, declaring me the winner.

"Ye son of a whore, ye tricked me," Brutus roared in a fit of rage. He stood abruptly and shoved the table with such force that it toppled over, its rough edge scraping my thigh.

I landed against the wooden wall; the wind knocked out of me for a second. I checked my leg for blood, finding just a trace of a scratch. The whiskey and ale, a warm haze in my head, loosened my tongue and my fear. I laughed, a low, mocking sound. "Sore loser, are you now? I won fair and square. Shall I fetch you a rag to dry your tears?"

My taunts, born of reckless adrenaline, only served to enrage the big man further. Brutus took a wild swing at me, but my reflexes, unhindered by the drink, were quick. I ducked just in time to hear the man's fist crash against the wooden wall, followed by a bellow of agony. *Good thing he missed,* I thought, the sound of splintering wood echoing in my head.

Brutus, huffing with fury, stormed out of the hall, his hand likely harboring a few broken bones. I looked down at the ground to collect the coins, only to find the sole deckhand with a predatory look in his eyes, tossing them up and down in his palm.

"I believe those are mine," I said calmly, as I reached for them.

"Ye would think they are, would ye now?" the man rudely responded, tightening his grip on the coins.

I gave him a grimacing look, cocking my head and inching closer. "You really do not want to go there with me, sir." I balled my hand into a fist. "Last chance, man."

"I know who ye are, Mr. Roberts," the man said low in a venomous hiss. "Ye took the life of me brother."

I stared blankly at him, blinking, then cocked my head again, my heart suddenly thudding in my chest. "Who are you, and *who* is your brother?" I asked, a sudden, unexpected unease gripping me. Deep within myself, I knew that no matter where or when you were, the accusation of murder, especially by someone akin to the victim, would cause even the most confident of men to tremble.

"Me name is Odhran Boyle, brother to the Captaen of the Ouzel Galley, Patrick Boyle."

The memory rushed through my head, recalling the dreadful day when Lieutenant Olson and I infiltrated the ship to regain possession of Moonlight. "I was there, being tied to a post, and watched ye take aim wi' ye pistol, ending me brother's life."

"You know I had no choice," I declared. "I could not allow him to take the life of an honorable soldier."

"Honorable soldier, me arse. That bastard of a whore had every man under me brother's command hanged. If it were not fer a poorly tied rope, I would have surely hung at the gallows meself," he imparted indignantly.

"I never intended to take his life or be the cause of the loss of life of anyone else," I replied bluntly. "If he had not been such a shithole of a man, he might still have been breathing right this day."

The man glared at me grudgingly, a look of pure hatred on his face. "Ye can have ye coins," he said, tossing them at my feet. "Just remember to sleep with one eye open!"

Chapter 29 – Spoils of Plunder

The faint squawking of seagulls in the distance told me we were close to land. I hadn't slept much, with little time to even try. The anticipation of the coming raid at St. Mary's kept my mind racing, a whirlwind of strategic ideas and theories. Using Carl von Clausewitz as an unlikely guide, I mentally rehearsed scenarios, meticulously planning an assault that, in my ideal world, would require little to no actual fighting. I recalled the captain mentioning the use of a flaxseed trader disguise to penetrate the defenses undetected—an idyllic strategy if the men would only comport themselves with the necessary discipline.

Free to roam the ship, I headed to the deck for a breath of fresh air, only to find the crewmen chosen for the raid already rappelling down ropes onto *currachs* bobbing on the water. There seemed to be four men per vessel, and a maximum of eight *currachs* in total.

The coast was a considerable distance away, about a mile, giving them ample time to reach shore, unload three men, and return to the ship for another group. They would ferry back and forth until enough men were hidden at the port. With a crescent moon overhead, there was little light, and their attempt to hide under the cover of darkness worked well. The plan was to position them near the port where the supply vessel was expected to dock.

The *White Seahorse* was to drop anchor in the northern section of the port, forcing the supply vessel to dock on the southern sector, closest to the caves where O'Malley's crewmen would lie in wait, ready to plunder the treasure with ease.

It took the crew less than an hour to get to shore, ferrying crates filled with pistols, metal balls, gunpowder, and several barrels of ale and whiskey for liquid courage. O'Malley ordered the remaining crew to hide pistols in the sacks of flaxseed as reinforcements. She anticipated only two stevedores at the docks at that late hour, ensuring a swift unloading process and eliminating the need for close inspection. With most of the crew hidden on shore, the minimal crew left behind would deter the soldiers from suspecting anything amiss.

Grace O'Malley's plans were now in motion. The helmsman and quartermaster expertly navigated the ship into port. Once the anchor was dropped, the crewmen immediately began moving the flaxseed sacks from the cargo hold down the gangway. Captain O'Malley, however, had underestimated the number of stevedores, as they were met by four dockworkers at the bottom of the gangway, joined by seven of the king's soldiers.

Grace rushed down the gangway, her boots thudding on the wood, and commanded the boatswain, "Be sure the artillery is brought down last. We cannae risk discovery by the soldiers."

"Aye, Captaen," he replied, picking up the first two sacks, knowing pistols were hidden inside, and hauled them back on board. The dock master, assessing the inventory, took notice of this, finding it odd that the merchandise was being taken back onto the vessel. He motioned to the commanding English soldier to him.

"Isn't it a strange thing, them taking the goods back on the ship?" the dock master asked. The soldier looked at the piled stock, then up toward the entrance of the ship, shouting out to the crewman, "Oi, you there! What is the purpose of returning the stock back to your ship?" The crewman remained silent, unsure of how to respond, and nervously gestured with his eyes for the captain to come to his aid.

"Aye, soldier. Is something amiss?" O'Malley asked sternly, her hands on her hips.

"Is there a reason your men unloaded merchandise simply to haul it back onboard?"

She walked down the plank to meet face-to-face with the soldier, scrutinizing him thoroughly. "Aye, sir. He was abiding by me orders. We are to sail to the port in Dublin, and he mistakenly unloaded a shipment that is meant to be delivered there." The soldier glared at her, his eyes locked with hers, then turned to the dockmaster and nodded with approval and marched away.

I stood on deck overlooking the port, watching the men running down to the cargo hold and returning with multiple sacks stacked over each shoulder. They made their way up and down the gangway plank like ants, appearing eager to unload themselves of the goods and reap the spoils of plunder that awaited them.

Finding myself restlessly idle, I approached Captain O'Malley. "Is there something I can help with, Captain?"

She looked at me lustfully, then grinned. "Aye. Ye're strong enough to carry sacks, though I'd rather have ye carry me to me bed." I bent my head, rolling my eyes. "Ye can line the remaining bags," she said, pointing to the exit, "alongside there. Make sure ye loosen the ropes, but make it appear as if they are tied." I nodded and turned right away to lift the sacks, thinking to myself how the roles had once again been reversed. It was the first time I had ever contemplated speaking to someone in HR and filing a complaint for sexual harassment.

An older gentleman, whom I recognized as part of the kitchen crew, approached me and handed me a cup of broth with bread and ale. I took hold of it. "This is kind of you, sir. Thank you," I said appreciatively.

"Rían Ó Broin at ye service, Mr. Roberts."

"Seems like you already know who I am," I commented.

"Aye, sir. Yer the lad brought on board as a prisoner. Leif told me all bout' ye. He suggests treatin' ye kindly."

I looked curiously around. "Where *is* Leif? I haven't seen him all day."

"Aye. He left with... um... hem." He moved his head suggestively toward the shore.

I confirmed with a nod. "Yes, yes. Okay. No need to say anymore."

"Eat ye broth and bread; I will pick up the slack fer ye. Nil a thing to do in the kitchen, so might as well make meself of use." I leaned against the mast, thanked Mr. Ó Broin again, then dipped the bread into the broth, savoring the taste.

Distracted by the midnight snack, my attention strayed away from Rían, preoccupied with the meal, taking less than five minutes to consume it. Though the captain hadn't been specific about lining the bags in any particular way, my internal need for organization made me question if they were being placed correctly, so I turned my attention back to the sacks and took notice of two missing bags, along with Rían.

"Mr. Ó Broin," I called out clearly with a sudden suspicion. I placed the cup down, walked to the plank, and looked over to see if Rían might have gone down to the docks. All I saw were the same crewmen who had been running back and forth the past hour since docking. It struck me as strange that the man would just disappear without a word, but I forced myself to continue with the assigned chore.

Feeling a prickle of unease, I went into the cargo hold and checked to see if there were any more bags left inside to unload. I stopped at the entrance, finding Rían hovering over a bag, which Odhran was searching through.

Rían tapped Odhran on the shoulder, a silent warning. "I believe we are being watched." I proceeded inside to confront them both.

"Is that one of the missing sacks, Rían?" I asked firmly, noticing the mauve string. Odhran quickly reached for the other end of the bag, keeping a secure grip, pulling it away from me in a sort of tug-of-war.

"What is your problem, man?" I shouted, positioning myself between Rían and Odhran.

"Me problem is yerself, Mr. Roberts," he responded, his tone dripping with condescension. Without hesitation, he reached inside the bag, brandishing the hidden pistol. "I warned ye to sleep wi' an eye open, eh? I promised to avenge the death of me brother, so now shall it be."

Rían pushed me aside, placing himself between us. "'Tis ní the agreement we made, Mr. Boyle," he said, raising his voice, staring at the gun with defiance.

"Best to remove yerself whence ye stand, Ó Broin. I'll ní tell ye again." Rían reached for the pistol, intending to take it from Odhran's hand, but that caused it

341

to discharge. I caught Rían after his legs went numb, losing my balance, resulting in Rían falling on top of me.

I carefully laid Rían on his back, then stood instantly and took hold of the pistol while Odhran attempted to reload. He inserted the ramrod but could not pack the ball and powder. Keeping a firm grip on the pistol, Odhran freed his other hand and sucker-punched me. Taken by surprise, I initiated retaliation, only to be distracted by Captain O'Malley and her deckhands storming inside the storage bay in a frenzy, drawn in by the sound of gunfire.

"Boyle, put an pistol down nó face me sword," she hollered menacingly.

Rebelliously, Odhran stood with the pistol pointed at me, hell-bent on ending my life. "Put an pistol down, Boyle. I wil' ní say it again," O'Malley threatened.

With the ramrod still inserted inside the barrel, Odhran packed the pistol, then aimed it at me once again, declaring, "He disnae deserve to breathe. Me brother was robbed of his breath, so why should he retain his?" he shouted aloud as he pulled back on the striker. O'Malley brandished her knife from the holster and flung it in his direction with force. The knife met its target, entering the side of his neck, severing the jugular vein. He dropped to the ground, bleeding out profusely, and died minutes later. I stared at his wound, reliving the moment I witnessed Gordi bleeding out in the abandoned apartment in the Bronx.

"What brought about this chaos?" O'Malley questioned as she kneeled unfazed to pry the knife out of Odhran's neck. As the edge exited the wound, the blood spewed out in a stream, landing across my face. I raised myself from the floor, grabbing a piece of garment from my pocket to wipe off the blood. I ignored the captain to check Rían's pulse, finding none. "Is he alive, Mr. Myles?"

"I'm afraid he's not," I answered, a bit saddened.

"Can ye explain how I come to find me cook lifeless on the ground?"

"Rían brought over bread and broth and organized the sacks as I ate. I was distracted by the meal and failed to notice his disappearance, along with two of the bags," I explained. "I came to the cargo bay to search for him and found him and Odhran rummaging through the bag. That's when Odhran brandished the hidden pistol."

"So where is the other sack?" she asked, scanning the room.

"I do not know, Captain," I responded. "I was just about to question Rían when Mr. Boyle became unhinged."

Looking displeased, Captain O'Malley ordered the deckhands to scour the ship for the single missing bag. She knew that if it fell into the hands of the dock master, the soldiers would involve themselves and their cover would be blown.

I returned to the deck, then made my way down the gangway to the area where the unloaded sacks were kept. I inspected the bags covertly, looking for a sack with a mauve-colored string the boatswain used to indicate the ones holding the hidden pistols. As I headed back onto the ship, I caught sight of the dockmaster digging through a bag, which was the missing sack, as it had the mauve string tied to it. I rushed up the plank and ran straight to the captain. "I found the bag," I said, catching my breath, "but I could not retrieve it in time."

"What d'ye mean ye were ní able to retrieve it?" she asked, a wandering look in her eyes.

"I spotted the sack from afar. It had the mauve string, but the dockmaster had already opened it and was digging through it."

"'Tis ní good," she said in a growl, then turned to the master gunner, Cináed. "Signal the men in wait to prepare themselves. They wil' ní make a move until they receive me word." She hurried to her quarters in anticipation of a conflict. She prepared her pistol, filled the powder horn, and packed extra ammunition into a leather pouch strapped to her belt. She pulled out the knife she had used to kill Odhran and sharpened it with a whetstone, leaving nothing to chance.

She reached the deck, finding herself in the company of two soldiers in wait as the dockmaster approached. "Captaen, a word wi' ye, please."

"Aye, *cad is féidir liom a dhéanamh ar do shon*?" she asked, her voice subtly calm. He tossed the bag at her feet, seeds spilling out.

"What ye can do for me is explain why there is a pistol hidden inside this sack of flaxseed!"

She glared at him with a puzzled look. "Did ye say a pistol inside the sack, dockmaster?" she responded evasively.

"Captaen, dinnae take me fer a dolt. 'Tis yer own stock and ye dinnae know what ye carry?"

Putting up a front, she lifted the sack and searched inside, pulling out the unloaded pistol. "I have a mind to say ye placed this there yerself, dockmaster. The many times we have crossed paths in the past, ye have never failed to protest me authority in one form or another," she exclaimed as she tossed the pistol at his feet.

The dockmaster, appearing angry, signaled to the soldiers. "Start searching this vessel immediately. Look fer any hidden weapons. Ye may meet opposition from the crew, so I suggest ye summon the rest of the king's soldiers." The commanding officer ordered one of his men to summon the guards keeping watch over the storage shed. Just as the private hovered over the side of the vessel to discharge his orders, a gunshot rang out from the darkness of the ocean.

The gunshot cracked through the night, echoing across the water. Instantly, soldiers, their weapons drawn, swarmed up the gangway, surrounding Grace O'Malley and her deckhands. She frowned, teeth clenched, her gaze sweeping the scene with fierce intensity. "Halt! That dinnae come from me ship. Look there!" she commanded, pointing at the faint, bobbing glow of a nautical lantern illuminating the water. It was the vessel she and her men had been waiting for.

It appeared to be approaching at a speed far greater than a ship of its size would normally manage. A collision seemed imminent. Fearing that it would collide with her own ship, she commanded her men to evacuate. "Dinnae leave any of the cargo behind!" They scrambled to the cargo hold, placing the heavy sacks over their shoulders, three at a time. With the ship fast approaching, they were left with little choice but to leave some of the merchandise behind. Just as the crewmen reached the bottom of the plank, the speeding vessel slowed enough for its bow to veer south, allowing the port side to collide against the dock with minimal damage—a jarring thud that vibrated through the wooden planks.

As the soldiers, the dockmaster, and his crew were distracted by the sudden commotion, the deckhands of the *White Seahorse* swiftly strayed away with the pistol-filled sacks and hid them behind the storage shed, where they would be within reach for the men in hiding to grasp should they find themselves in need of extra artillery. I remained nonchalant, sitting on an empty barrel, my face carefully neutral, knowing that soon there would be a battle ensuing or a simple, non-conflictive robbery. I prayed for the latter.

The crew of the fractured ship disembarked in haste, rushing to assess the damage to their vessel and that of the dock. In the confusion, O'Malley ordered Cináed to ready the men in hiding and be prepared to make their way into the cargo room of the stranded ship. She advised that she herself would keep the crew distracted, using her femininity to hinder their attention.

She walked through the crowd of men, her hips swaying, enhancing her sensuality to draw their eyes upon her, giving her crew the opportunity to make their move. She headed toward the aft of the ship, finding the captain investigating his vessel. "Oi, ye must be the captaen of this fine beauty," she hailed. He turned almost instantly, drawn by the unexpected sound of a woman's voice. His eyes were immediately drawn to her exposed cleavage; his mouth opened in a shameless stare, utterly mesmerized by her beauty.

"*Já*, Madame. Aksel Rasmusson, captain of *The Vasa*, at *din* service. And who might you be?" he asked, his gaze ogling her insatiably.

"I am Captaen Gráinne Ní Mháille of the ship ye see before ye—the *White Seahorse*," she said proudly, pointing at her vessel. "Did yer cargo suffer much damage?" she questioned with intent, hoping somehow that he might hint at how heavily the shipment was being guarded. He divulged little information, but she thought it best to continue digging.

With the captain and his men preoccupied with the investigation of their ship and the facade Captaen O'Malley was putting on, as per her orders, Cináed gave the signal to the crew in hiding. They traversed boulders and jagged edges, trailing their way to the dock, which was a quarter of a mile away. The shore was a mere seven feet wide, but they thought it best to trek over it rather than get on the *currachs*, which would have taken them longer.

Once they reached the lower part of the dock, Leif snuck onboard *The Vasa* and released a rope ladder as one-half of the group dove into the frigid water and swam to the starboard side of the ship. They took hold of the rope and, one by one, clambered onboard, creeping down into the cargo hold, relieved to see not a living soul guarding the grand prize. They inserted iron rods through the shackles of the padlocks, and with a twisting motion, snapped open the bolts. Their eyes homed in on the treasures. They each took on individual crates, quickly prying them open. The others used iron rods to break into the oversized trunk concealing the prized sword, along with several other notable treasures. The men returned to deck with the treasure trove, having used empty sacks to store them in, making the climb down the ladder less taxing. There were not as many items as originally thought, but the few items they pillaged were worth more than a vault filled with treasures.

They made their way up to the dock, just steps away from the extraction ladder, when the watcher waved, signaling that someone was approaching. They tossed the sacks overboard, warning the men to retrieve the treasure and make for the shore. There was no time for them to hide, so they improvised by grabbing hold of rags and began scrubbing the deck. Fortunately, the approaching men were called back, allowing the plunderers the chance to make a getaway.

Just as the last two of O'Malley's crew climbed out of the water, they were spotted by a king's soldier who was taking a piss along the southern part of the dock by the bow of the ship. "Oi, you there! Halt!" Ignored, the soldier waved frantically to alert the other guards.

O'Malley's men dashed onto the shore, yelling out to their fellow raiders, "Run like the devil! We have been exposed!"

The commotion brought on by the soldiers attracted the attention of Captain Rasmusson. He summoned his first mate. "Find out what's gone awry, Finnis." Distressed by the ruckus, he mustered a deckhand. "Go check on the cargo, now, *skynde deg.*"

"*Já*, Captain." The deckhand raced inside, hurrying as commanded, pushing anyone aside that stood in his way. He noticed at once that the door was unlocked and the padlocks had been tampered with. He checked the cargo hold to find empty crates strewn about. Just as fast as he made it below deck, he returned, yelling frantically, "The treasure is gone! The treasure is gone!"

The crew of *The Vasa* scrambled throughout the dock, some running onto the ship to retrieve weapons as others waited for the captain to bark out a command. He ordered the others to collect their pistols and swords and join the soldiers who were already on the hunt for the pillagers.

Captaen O'Malley casually walked away from the chaos, her back straight, and returned to her ship in search of Cináed. He came upon her from the deck below, his face gloomy. "What do we do now, Captaen?"

She stood still for a moment, thinking, blinking fast as she pondered a revision of her original plan. "Meet *leis na fir* at the rendezvous point. Have them hide the treasure in the caves, then scatter themselves about but ensure they remain armed." She inhaled deeply. "I anticipate a major battle will ensue."

The sounds of pistols firing and swords clanking in the distance resonated throughout the port, a grim symphony of impending conflict. I knew at some point I would need to defend myself, so I raced onto the ship and retrieved the pistol left in the sack the dockmaster had discovered. I turned the bag upside down, emptying the contents in search of gunpowder and balls. At the bottom, I found a pouch filled with ammunition. I readied my pistol and put the remaining balls in my pocket, but kept the gunpowder in the pouch.

I headed back onto the dock, taking every precaution to avoid direct conflict. Though my initial plan was to remain within the relative safety of the ship, my instincts told me to take the passageway beyond the storage shed, leading to the border of the Garrison Walls. As I climbed the sloping trail, the air crackled with tension, and I suddenly encountered crossfire. I ducked behind a hedgerow, the thorny branches scraping my borrowed clothes, waiting for the firing to cease. The sounds of footsteps rushing across the grounds lessened, allowing me a moment to maneuver my way farther up the slope.

I wasn't sure why I chose to head in that direction; it was as if an internal guide, a primal instinct, was leading me there. I drew a shaky breath, knowing I would have to go in charging like a wild boar if I was to survive any assault. Pushing forward, I found myself in the crosshairs of another clash of gunfire, taken completely by surprise.

Finding nowhere to hide, I fired back. I dropped a metal ball into the barrel of the pistol, cocked the striker, and pointed aimlessly into the darkness, the weapon bucking in my hand. Before I could reload, I was caught unawares and attacked from behind. The attacker's blow sent me flying to the ground, falling flat on my face, the pistol skittering from my hand. Instinctively, I turned to defend myself, distancing the assailant by using my legs, placing my feet flat on his chest. The attacker began thrashing, attempting to land a fist on my face.

While his arm was stretched out, I took hold of it and struck his elbow with all my strength, causing the attacker to flinch in pain. This gave me the opportunity to roll him onto his back. I climbed onto his torso and pummeled his face, knocking him out. I remained still for a moment, panting, trying to regain a steady breath. I reached for the pistol just a few feet away, only to be met by the sharp edge of a sword. "On your feet, *gris*. Move, pig!"

I examined the sharp edge of the sword, then peered at the man's face, his features obscured by the dim light. I had only two choices: abide by his order or attempt to reach for the pistol. I looked over to where the pistol had fallen and turned my gaze back to the sword, calculating the distance between the two. There was a fifty-fifty chance I could either grab hold of it or be pierced by the steel. I took my chance and reached for the pistol, only to feel the penetrating sting of the blade piercing through my chest, just below the clavicle. I let out a cry as the man withdrew the blade, falling back onto the ground. Instinctively, I placed my hand over the wound to decrease the flow of the blood, which appeared to stream endlessly.

I was unsure whether the pain of the stabbing or the sheer shock of the act had anything to do with it, but it seemed odd that the man who just seconds ago gored me with his sword was now lying dead beside me. Then I heard a faint but familiar voice continuously shouting my name, "Myles, Myles," becoming

349

louder as it grew closer. A man knelt beside me, looking down at me. I could not discern the person, as my vision became impaired due to the rapid loss of blood. I blinked repeatedly but hopelessly could not focus. I then heard several other voices, vaguely familiar to me, and the muffled sounds of people approaching. It was the last sound I heard.

***

Luis began setting up for the sand race at the beach. He positioned a line of beach chairs several yards apart, then placed a wager with his brothers on who would get from one chair to the other in the shortest amount of time. Luis looked at his mom. "Mami, are you going to call the race?" he asked, bouncing excitedly.

"*Sí, papito*. Get yourself prepared."

He yelled to his brothers, "Miguel, Johnny, come on! Let's get the race started."

The boys lined up alongside one chair, marking it as their starting point. *Titi* walked over to the makeshift finish line and yelled out to her boys, "On your mark, get set," then stopped to pick up a funnel-shaped seashell that had caught her attention. The boys looked at each other, confused, then turned to their mom. "Um... Hello!"

"Oh, sorry, *mis amores*." She began the intro again. "On your mark, get ready, GO!"

They ran as fast as they could, mustering as much speed as their small feet would allow, though the shifting sand hindered their traction. Luis trailed ahead as Johnny paced behind him, holding the middle position. Miguel grew angry as he fell behind both of my cousins. Luis looked back at them, sticking out his tongue in a triumphant taunt. Karma must have been racing alongside him, because he failed to see a beverage cooler sitting in front of him. He tripped over it, yelling, "Oww," as he hit the ground, falling flat on his face. Miguel managed to pass Johnny, so to be vengeful, Luis stuck out his foot and tripped Miguel when he circled around, dropping him out of the race. Johnny became distracted by the misfortunes of his brothers, giggling as he whizzed by, not realizing that he had veered off course and fallen into a shallow hole someone had dug up earlier. I watched the race from my floating raft, laughing at my cousins' chaotic antics.

I snickered. "You guys suck. You can't even race correctly." I then turned over on the inflatable raft, resting on my back. Unbeknownst to me, my cousins, in retaliation for my poking fun at them, sought the help of my brothers, Dennis and Randy. They hauled the raft, with me still on it, and pushed me out as far as they could onto the water. I considered jumping off but remained still, finding it amusing. I then yelled out at them once again, "You still suck."

My happy place has always been any body of water I could plunge into. I took in the present moment, floating on my back, allowing my body to conform to the movements of the waves as I faced the clear blue sky. I wasn't far from the shore, so I relaxed without panicking. Though I loved the element of water, fear would sometimes seize my mind with random thoughts of finding myself floating in the middle of the ocean with no one to save me. I forced my eyelids open, testing myself on how long I could stare at the sun without having to shut them too quickly—a silly pastime I enjoyed—to distract myself from that thought.

The movement of the waves intensified, causing me to take a firm hold of the side of the raft, which resulted in a cramp around my chest and shoulder. With the sun a blinding white glare above me, I could hardly open my eyes; just a narrow line of vision was all I could muster. I suddenly felt nauseous, wanting very much to vomit, but held it in as long as I could.

The ferocity of the waves subsided, but the cramping lingered, worsening with each undulation. Unable to resist the urge to vomit, I leaned over the raft, spewing the remnants of the meal I had eaten earlier. I watched as chunks of meat floated in a mix of other indistinguishable bits. The bile left a bitter and acidic taste in my mouth.

I leaned back on the raft, finally able to force my eyes open. I blinked rapidly as the sun beamed down, though not as brightly as before. It then disappeared, and I found myself surrounded by shade, which darkened slightly as my eyes fluttered continuously. The slower my eyelids moved, the clearer it became to perceive where I was. Splintered wood on the ceiling became evident, and by the subtle movement of the room, I knew I was on a ship again. I turned my head slightly just as a door opened, pinpointing the familiar cadence of the person I last heard after the attempt on my life. "William?"

"Myles, you are finally awake," William said, his hand, cool and firm, settling on my forehead. "And your fever has broken. We thought we would have to bury you at sea from this ship," he added, his eyebrows raised with compassionate concern.

"William?" I said with confusion still clouding my mind. "Is that really you?" My voice was raspy, and I felt a sudden, overwhelming rush of emotion.

"Yes. Rumor had it you were in distress, so I had to act on behalf of my brother!"

"But how... when...?" The questions tumbled out, disjointed and desperate.

William patted me lightly on my chest. "Do not fret over such matters, Myles. Just know that you are safe and amongst friends."

I forced a smile, feeling the corners of my lips split with the effort. My throat was dry, and I could feel the flakes of dried saliva crumble around my cheeks and beard. "Can I get some water, William?"

"Absolutely, at once. I shall return with haste." He opened the door and turned back to tell me, "I will inform the others of your awakening."

He left the room, leaving me to wonder, *What others?*

I tried resting my head but felt a throbbing pain pulsing from the wound I had suffered. I closed my eyes, still reeling from the fragments of the flashback I had during the fevered dream, hoping the dizzy spell I was currently experiencing would dissipate.

Swallowing became a challenge, so in a desperate move, I struggled to raise myself from the bed, placing my feet on the floor. I slumped over, breathing deeply with a moan, biting my lower lip to keep from screaming. The pain intensified—a sharp, searing fire that shot across my chest, causing me to cry out. My preoccupation with the pain was so intense that I failed to realize my feet were in a puddle of my own vomit.

I looked down at the bile, which sickened me anew. The sudden gag reflex caused me to dry heave with such intensity that it magnified the pain. Just as I cried out in agony, the door flung open, and my heart sank. Eilis, Rey, and Adam all barged in, their faces stamped with worry, bringing a look of utter shock to my face and tears to my eyes.

"Eilis?" I exclaimed, my eyes widening in disbelief. "I get Adam and Rey being here, but you... how... how did you get to be here?"

"Dinnae worrit over that, Myles," Eilis said, her sound soft and familiar as she raised a cup to my mouth. I swallowed with a grimace of discomfort. She placed her hand under my chin and muttered, "Slowly. Sip steadily."

"Myles, you have no idea how sick with worry we were," Adam exclaimed, taking hold of my hand, his grip warm and reassuring. "How dare you disappear and leave me in the company of this knucklehead!"

I winced, followed by a moan. "Now you know what I've endured most of my life."

"Screw both of you," Rey chimed in, a sarcastic edge to his tone. "If it weren't for me, you would still be lost," he declared with a smile.

"Don't blow so much wind up your ass," Adam expressed bluntly.

"Ye both settle down," Eilis demanded firmly, "let Myles finish drinking his water." She then turned to Rey. "Mr. Tirad, fetch a deckhand and have him come and clean this vomit off the floor."

I looked at Rey with a smirk. "You heard the lady."

Eilis sat next to me, aiding me with the cup. Adam kept a hold of my hand, his presence a comfort. "You gave me—*us*—quite a scare, Myles. Stop pissing people off."

"I will try, young man!"

Rey returned with the deckhand, and someone else towering behind him in the doorway. I focused on the face, smiling broadly despite my split lips, and rumbled, "General Brindley!"

"Aye, lad. I leave ye alone in the world and ye find yerself at daggers drawn, eh?"

"Mr. Brindley, seeing you brings delight into my heart."

"Lad, I canna tell ye how worrit I was when I received word of yer disappearance," Brindley exclaimed with a face-full of concern.

"Did Adam tell you?" I asked.

"Aye, lad. I happened to arrive at the Port of Dunmore East just as Mr. Towell and Mr. Tirad were about to board the *Spirited Sail*," Brindley said, his eyes hinting at a smile.

"What are the chances?" I commented, my mind reeling at the unbelievable timing.

"Aye. I was meeting with Lorcán O'Quinn to aid in a matter that ye are familiar with."

"So that is how Eilis came to be here," I sighed with a sudden, powerful sense of relief.

"'Tis correct, Myles," Eilis responded in a soothing murmur. "I have blessed news."

Brindley, not one to be left out of a dramatic moment, butted in. "Lad, with some persuasion, I managed to dissolve the one-sided agreement." He placed a firm, reassuring hand on my shoulder and uttered, "The lass is nae longer betrothed to the swine."

Eilis turned to look at me, a sincere smile on her face. A delicate blush colored her cheeks, and she then kissed me softly on the cheek. "'Tis true, Myles. I am nae longer tethered to the crackbrained."

I placed the back of my hand on her face, caressing it slowly, a moment of unspoken gratitude passing between us. "Now I know I will be well." She reciprocated my caress, then leaned in and whispered into my ear, "I also know the truth!"

***

Later that evening, I was able to consume food without regurgitating it, a welcome sign of healing that brought some color back to my face and a slight sense of rejuvenation. I felt an insistent need for fresh air, asking Eilis to accompany me up to the deck to take in the sea air and allow the cool wind to breeze across my face.

"Are you cold, Myles? I thought I saw ye shiver slightly," she asked, her concern a warm blanket around me.

"No, I'm quite comfortable," I replied, wrapping the blanket over my shoulders. "The covering is doing its job. Shouldn't I be the one asking you that question, Eilis?"

She grinned, with a soft, luminous smile that reached her eyes. "So, how *did* you come to know my secret?" I asked curiously.

"I recall the mention ye made of the fast-sailing ship, *El Galeón*. Ye made a comment about the nonexistent ship that has '*not been invented yet.*' I dinnae think too much about it at the time, but thereafter, I overheard ye and Mr. Tirad conversing about a... musical concert, 'The Crys,' I believe was the name ye said."

"Oh," I began, finding it strange to hear that name spill from her mouth. "In the year 2018, at Cen—"

"—Central Park was the place," she said, interrupting, her eyebrows raised with amusement. "I questioned Mr. Tirad, and he confessed."

"He was never good at keeping secrets," I said, unsurprised. "So, you know about Adam as well?"

"Aye. I had to pry it out of 'im. Stubborn bugger, that one."

"Know that I am open to questions you may ever have, Eilis." I took her into an embrace, enthralled by the way her eyes shimmered in the bright glow of the moon. We kissed passionately, a kiss that made me feel whole once more. I placed both my hands on her face, peering into her eyes, then smiled. Suddenly distracted by a movement in the water, I looked over her shoulder, pushing her softly to the side, shocked by what I was witnessing.

"What is it, Myles?" she asked with unease.

"I see the flags of the English Interregnum; Oliver Cromwell!"

Chapter 30 – Lord Protector

The name of Oliver Cromwell, though it had only been a part of my curriculum a few months ago, now carried a weight that was terrifyingly real. I found myself thinking of him often, piecing together the details of his life from my knowledge of the future, trying to understand the man whose shadow loomed over this century.

Growing up in Huntingdonshire, Oliver enjoyed the usual interactions with children his age and the occasional meddling with things he had no business with—the actions of every young boy, even in this century. He was quite reserved when it was called for, but more often had the tendency to act out rebelliously. He was born into a family of wealth, earned essentially by his grandfather, Sir Henry Cromwell, whose knighthood for Huntingdonshire had been bestowed upon him by Queen Elizabeth I.

Even having the means of such wealth, he was raised in a modest home. His family were referred to as landed gentry, having ownership of lands that they rented, earning a substantial income that gave them distinction, yet kept them below the highest social status. Religion played a major role in his everyday life. His strong religious faith stemmed from his upbringing as a Puritan. It was instilled in him from the moment he began to speak and understand words.

As a young boy, he attended Huntingdon Grammar School. His early education included language arts, Greek and Latin, mathematics, history, and, finally, education in religion and morals. Following his formal education, he attended Sidney Sussex College in Cambridge, where he majored in the Puritan ethos.

In 1617, Oliver's father suddenly passed away, so after having spent only one year at the university, he dropped out without ever obtaining a degree. With his mother, now a widow, and seven sisters who were yet to be married and still living at home, he knew he would have to become head of the household, as he was the only surviving son. He returned to Huntingdon to oversee his father's lands, taking on the farming to maintain the upkeep. It was rumored that during this time he paused his responsibilities at home to attend Lincoln's Inn of Court in London, but no concrete proof was ever produced to suggest that he did. Though no records were ever found to substantiate this, some argued that meeting his wife Elizabeth while in London suggests he did. Elizabeth was the daughter of a knighted leather merchant who owned lands in Essex and held influence within the Puritan gentry families, which would favor Cromwell's political and military career later in his life.

He added to his income by renting out the lands left to him by his father, becoming a minor East Anglian landowner. In 1636, Cromwell received a substantial inheritance from his maternal uncle, Thomas Stewart. He gained rents and properties in Ely, but he also acquired a house within proximity of a cathedral. He found this to be a blessing, being a devout Puritan, sometimes referred to as a radical Puritan, as the church was the primary focus of his life. He later relocated to Ely permanently with his family.

Oliver was able to provide for his expanding family, having had nine children of his own with his wife, Elizabeth, all but three of whom survived into adulthood. He achieved status within his county, which he obtained solely through inheritance and his faithfulness to Puritanism.

After becoming a member of Parliament in 1628, Cromwell made only a minor mark during his one-year tenure. In 1629, King Charles I dissolved Parliament, ruling without it for eleven years. As MP for Cambridge, Oliver returned to Parliament in 1640 after it was recalled by the king following the Bishops' Wars. In the same year, the Long Parliament was created.

***

Throughout history, the English monarchy had ruled defiantly. Their word was law, and no one ever dared challenge it. It had always been so, up to the reign of King Charles I, who proclaimed the king's divinity. Climbing his way up the ladder in Parliament, Oliver Cromwell became an influential and integral part of the legislative body. He grew frustrated with King Charles's tyrannical rule, becoming a public enemy to the state, thought of as a murderer, traitor, and tyrant.

Having gained influence with the support of the Long Parliament, Oliver Cromwell carried out something that could not have even been imagined. He had a sitting king put on trial for abuse of power. King Charles claimed it was the divine right of a king to rule, believing that God chose him to be king and that only God could judge and overrule him. With the king's beliefs going against Oliver's own, compounded by the ongoing war between the Royalists and the Parliamentarians, this was enough to put the king on trial.

On January 20, 1649, the trial of King Charles I began. The back-and-forth debates continued, with King Charles refusing to recognize the authority presented before him and declining to enter any sort of plea. The quarrel went on between Parliament and the king for several days. He conducted his own defense, at times making a good argument for himself, but was eventually found guilty on the morning of January 27, 1649. He was sentenced to death by beheading, to be carried out on January 30, 1649.

Before and after the trial and death of King Charles I, Oliver Cromwell was victorious in his campaigns, namely the battles at Naseby and Marston Moor. His victories made him appear somewhat superior in the eyes of his constituents. As a lieutenant general, he led his armies alongside Sir Thomas Fairfax, 3rd Lord Fairfax of Cameron. Fairfax led many triumphant crusades of his own, but was soon obscured by his second in command, Cromwell.

England's intent on creating a one-religion country was the irrevocable step that brought Cromwell and his armies to invade Ireland, not to mention his greed and hatred of the Irish Catholics. They wanted to end the Catholic religion and convert everyone within the land to Protestantism. Oliver Cromwell convinced his armies that Catholicism was the catalyst for tyranny and believed them to be heretics, using that sort of racist tactic to embolden them. He led them to believe that all Irish Catholics were dangerous and morally reprehensible. That empowered his men, who brought with them that mindset to Dublin on August 13, 1649.

***

Brindley's ship, the *Maritime Biest*, arrived at the dock of Dunmore East in the early morning of August 14, 1649. I was filled with anxiety after having witnessed the flotilla of ships a few nights before. My foreknowledge of what would be written in history books, and now seeing it with my own eyes, were as different to me as apples and a *Rubik's Cube*.

It weighed heavily on my heart, difficult to grasp that in just a matter of days, thousands of Irish men, women and children would be annihilated simply because of their religious beliefs. I needed to prepare myself—mentally, spiritually, and, as burdensome as the thought was, emotionally.

As we disembarked, I became a recluse, keeping silent, lost in my thoughts. The contemplation of what I needed to do to alter the present time was an unending battle within myself. If I succeeded in changing this pivotal moment in time, would Eilis be able to travel back with me to my time? That was the major question I wrestled with. I wanted to keep her safe from the anarchy that was to come, but on the other hand, if she could travel back with me, Lisa would be there as well. I felt stuck between a rock and a hard place.

We remained stationed at the port for several hours as Mr. Brindley arranged for our transport back to Springmount and the Killamery Church. I would need my beloved Moonlight, and a horse would need to be provisioned for Eilis, as Rey and Adam had left their trusty steeds nearby with the husbands of the wagging tongues.

I sat atop a crate that had been carried down from the ship, filled with artillery Grace O'Malley had gifted to Brindley. Eilis noticed that ever since the sighting of the flotilla, I had grown distant. She was conscious of the reason for my conduct, growing concerned that I would completely shut myself down. She stood before me, taking hold of my hand. "They feel cold," she murmured, her thumb stroking my knuckles.

I lifted my head, my lips forming a small grin. "I'm just a little nervous."

"What has ye alarmed so?" she asked, her brow furrowing slightly.

"Remember when we spoke of a woman that I once held feelings for?"

"Aye, I do," she replied softly.

"And I told you when the moment presented itself, I would explain?"

"Aye, Myles, I recall."

"The woman was you, just in my time."

Eilis gazed at me disconcertedly, her eyes wide. "I dinnae understand."

"I met her the night before I traveled to Ireland. She had your fiery red hair, your beautiful rust-colored freckles, milky white skin," I said, passing a finger gently on her cheek, "and the exact crescent-shaped birthmark, but on her neck."

"So, what ye are trying to convey is that this… person… is in fact… me, as if a *cúpla*? A twin?"

"Yes, identical."

She remained silent, processing the information, her gaze fixed on the distant horizon. I stood and guided her to the crate, allowing her to sit, as she seemed a bit taken aback. "Are you okay, Eilis?"

"Aye, Myles, aye. It just took me by surprise, 'tis all."

"Well, there is more," I continued. "In order for me to return to my time, I must change a crucial part of this period, this century. Something of great meaning and significance has to take place, and once I accomplish the task, there is the possibility that I can return home."

"Does it mean that I am to remain alone here wi'out ye?" she asked, a tear streaming down her cheek, descending over her birthmark.

I wiped the tear gently with my thumb. "No, no, no. I want to take you with me. I'm just not sure how it works, or if you can travel through."

"Myles, stop," she snapped, her hand pressing against my chest. "We will deal with the matter when the time arises. We needn't fret over it just now, especially with the impending doom before us." I placed both hands on her cheeks, blinking as I smiled, then leaned over and kissed her with adoration. She rose, continuously kissing me, not giving a care to the audience of men whistling and cheering around us. I looked at them and laughed, then turned back to Eilis, becoming distracted by a plume of dust.

A mass of troops emerging on the path leading out of the port grew visible from a distance. I froze for a moment, at first thinking it was the men of the New Model Army, then saw they were flying the Green Harp Flag. It was Major General Brindley's men, reporting themselves as commanded. Having knowledge not only of the Cromwellian invasion and its outcome, but knowing as well that the incursion was underway, Mr. Brindley had sent word to his troops stationed nearby to assemble at the port and prepare for defenses.

Adam and Rey returned, trotting behind the troops, having fetched their horses. William appeared behind them just a few minutes later, walking his horse. It seemed as if he was reading a letter, but quickly tucked it away in his *léine* pocket once he caught sight of me eyeing him. Adam rode up beside me, dismounting first. "Are we ready to go?" he asked excitedly.

I faced him, my eyebrows raised. "Not as of yet," I said, then pointed to the troops. "I assume they will transport us back to Springmount?"

"*Coño*! Can't we just double up on our horses?" Rey asked with a frustrated tone. William, his face impassive, cut in. "That would not be ideal, specifically for the horses."

"They can handle the weight," Rey responded, his posture tense.

"Precisely, were we to travel a short distance. It is over a half-day's ride north. The horses would lag in their pace considerably."

Brindley approached, a soldier by his side. "This is Private Flynn. He will accompany ye to Springmount, then to Drogheda thereafter."

Adam and Rey looked at each other, a shared look of confusion in their eyes. They knew well what was about to happen at Drogheda in just a matter of days.

"Are you mad, General?" Adam shouted with indignation.

Brindley glared at him, displeased. "Sir, best ye know to whom yer voice is being raised!" Adam matched his posture, both alphas taking a stance.

I cut in between them, acting as a referee. "Stand down, gentlemen," I said, turning to Adam. "The General and I both agreed that if we are to have any chance of making it back to our individual times, Cromwell will be the catalyst that takes us there."

Adam turned his gaze from Brindley to me, then back to Brindley. "You might be right. My apologies to you, General."

Brindley, his anger giving way to an indication of compassion, placed a hand on Adam's shoulder. "I know ye have been here all yer life, Mr. Towell. It is time ye went home to yer time." Adam nodded, then walked away and headed to his horse to prepare it for the journey.

William kept a distance from what he presumed would have been a dogfight, sharpening his dirk as he often did, remaining one step ahead should he find himself in a desperate situation once more. He appeared detached, more so after arriving at Dunmore East. I approached him, a melancholy expression on my face. "What are you to do, William?"

"I will remain here under the command of the Major. He has assigned me to take up arms with this gentleman."

"Good day to you, Mr. Roberts," a crisp English voice said.

I turned to look at the face behind the familiar voice. "Lieutenant Olson!" I exclaimed with a cheer, then hugged him as if he were a friend I hadn't seen in a lifetime. "So, with my added brothers, we are sure to win this fight."

"Absolutely, Mr. Roberts," Olson replied, his face gleaming with a smile.

We all reunited at a nearby tavern—Eilis, Rey, Adam, Brindley, William, the Lieutenant, and I—sharing what might be our last meal together. We indulged in roasted chicken, stuffed cabbage, carrots and radishes, baked bread with butter, ale, wine, and whiskey. I watched as they ate and conversed, laughed, and toasted, even made jokes, but I knew deep inside that they were all just as afraid as I was. With the knowledge shared with those of the present time, they had every right to be. I breathed deep, exhaled, and then emotionally embraced my seventeenth-century family.

***

September 4, 1649.

If I recall correctly, the siege should have begun yesterday. It is being felt as far down as Enniskerry, a town just a few miles south of the Dublin border. Though it might come back to bite me in the ass, I have chosen to become a prophet of sorts and spread rumors of the coming famine and disease resulting from that famine, hoping the residents would hear of it and stock up on essentials. Adam warned me not to interfere with the inevitable, that eliminating Cromwell would surely be the culmination of what we sought to transpire, but of course, I didn't listen. Tonight, we begin the fourteen-hour ride north to Drogheda, and to what I hope will be the demise of the Lord Protector.

***

"Myles, I have packed the provisions. Moonlight and the other horses have been tended to as well." Eilis reached over my shoulders and cuddled me from behind. "We are to take our leave in an hour's time."

367

I took a firm grip of her hands, stood and turned to face her, then took a bend of the knee. "Eilis."

She jerked her head slightly, expressing the brightest of smiles. "Aye, Myles?" she asked, with an eager, quivering sound in her voice.

"In the short time we have known each other, I have fallen in love with you." I dug into my pocket and pulled out a white silk kerchief folded into a square. "You are the woman that I love, have loved, and will forever love." I then unfolded the kerchief, presenting her with a white gold braided ring fashioned from my bracelet. I took hold of her hand. "You have pierced my body with your spirit and touched my heart with your soul. It beats solely for your essence, Eilis. With that said, may I be blessed to call you my wife?" I placed the ring on her finger, sliding it into a perfect fit.

She teared up with joy, nodding her head continuously. "Aye, Myles, aye. A million times, aye!"

The door swung open unexpectedly, and the first to appear was the last person I ever expected to see, cheering loudly in that all too familiar, soft-heavy voice. "*Huzzah*!"

"Mrs. Omi?" I bellowed, my voice heavy with surprise and overwhelming joy. She cheered continuously and took me into the strongest of embraces. She began weeping tears of joy, her body shaking with emotion, giving me the sense that the emotions emanating from her were, in fact, those of my own mother, Aida Luz. "My handsome lad. Love and *benison* to ye."

"Can I congratulate the lad as well, Omibheann? Dinnae hog him fer yerself!" Mr. Willis's familiar voice cut through the air. I wept joyfully, not only at the sight of the woman who took me in as a son, but also at seeing the man who had become my first seventeenth-century father.

"What are you two doing here?" I asked, collecting myself, wiping a tear from my eye.

"We were forewarned by our soon-to-be-*marrit* lad of the forthcoming invasion, which is now upon us, so *Mórghinearál* Brindley secured safe passage for us back to Scotland. We are to board the *Saint Maria* come the morrow."

I hugged Mr. Willis, a fierce, tight embrace that gave off the love of a son for his father. I stepped back to eye them both, still somewhat in shock to have them in my presence. "It brings me joy that you both will be safe. Just be mindful. On September 3 of next year, Cromwell will invade Scotland and annihilate yet another five thousand or so Scottish soldiers and citizens."

"Aye, lad. Dinnae worry. All will be well wi' us," Mr. Willis assured me, his hand clapping me on the shoulder.

"Have you met my bride-to-be?" I asked brightly, turning to Eilis, who stood beside me with a radiant smile on her face.

"If ye dinnae present her to us, then the answer is no!" Mr. Willis teased.

"I miss your bubbly personality, sir!" I said, a genuine laugh escaping me. Mr. Willis grinned and winked, then turned to Eilis and kissed her hand. "Yer eternal servant, lass."

She bowed gracefully, her cheeks flushed. "A pleasure to make yer acquaintance, Mr. MacKinney," she said, then faced Mrs. Omi. "Madame MacKinney."

Mr. Willis looked at me, his eyes dancing with amusement. "Ye havenae taught her our proper names yet, have ye, lad? She will learn soon enough."

I laughed, then pondered for a moment. I looked at them, then excused myself and walked out unexpectedly, a sudden plan forming in my mind. I found Adam conversing with Mr. Brindley. Stepping in between them, I interrupted. "Can a minister be summoned before we leave?"

Adam and Brindley looked at each other, then at me, their expressions a mixture of confusion and surprise. "Whatever for, lad?" Brindley asked.

"I would like for Eilis and me to be married before we leave this evening and would like for Mr. and Mrs. MacKinney to be present."

Adam replied with a shrug and a sigh. "Fine, kid, I will handle it."

I returned to the inn and pulled Mrs. Omi aside, informing her of my intent. She clapped her hands with excitement, took hold of Eilis's hand, and whisked her away to get prepared. Mr. Willis informed Rey, and everyone pitched in to prepare for the occasion. Mr. Brindley, with a generous gesture, paid the innkeeper to have a grand meal prepared for the occasion.

With such short notice to arrange the event, Mr. Willis, with surprising speed and skill, fashioned a suit for me using clothing from his trunk. The wife of the innkeeper, a kind woman with a ready smile, lent Eilis her own wedding dress. Adam, leveraging Brindley's influence, secured the church and a priest. The tavern at the inn was adorned with candles and hanging bells, their soft glow illuminating the room, and the keeper brought out two wooden casks of ale, one cask of whiskey, and another of wine, which he kept stored in the cellar. With the help of the neighboring wives, a flurry of activity and cheerful chatter, they created a menu comprising venison stew, roasted potatoes, turnips seasoned with garlic, cabbage soup, baked breads and bannocks with marmalade, and thick, savory gravy.

The immediate party met first at the church, accompanying Eilis and me as we made confession and received a proper blessing from the priest. The small church then quickly filled, everyone feeling relieved that we would not feel at risk by attending a Catholic wedding between an Irish native and a *Gall*, which was prohibited by the seventeenth-century Penal Laws. We knew we were safe simply by having the men of Brindley's regiment there for protection.

Once the church was prepared, Eilis and I took our places by the altar at the head of the church. We faced each other, then bowed as the father recited a prayer, followed by a short sermon. Being pressed for time, Mr. Brindley raised a brow with a subtle side nod of the head, implying for the father to hasten the ceremony. In acknowledgment, the father quickly turned the page of his Bible. He instructed Eilis and me to hold hands and wrapped a white rope with tassels on each end around our hands. "Do ye both come into this house of Christ and appear before him of your own free will?"

"Yes, Father," we replied together, our voices clear and steady.

"Lord God, Heavenly Father, bring abundant blessings upon Myles Roberts and Eilis Ceara Hileen O'Quinn. With your holy power and loving spirit, bring light upon them to live together in the bond of matrimony, embellish their family with children, and enrich their hearts with the deep-seated love of your word. By your will and blessing, I proclaim them bonded in this union. Amen."

The church erupted with joyous shouts, "Amen!"

Eilis and I kissed passionately; our love exuded as if like a cloud of light, spreading throughout every part of the church, being absorbed by the flock. Everyone was filled with the Holy Spirit. Though most of them were not acquainted with the bride nor me, they shared in our enjoyment and our glorious union.

The attendees dispersed and made their way to the tavern to partake of the awaiting buffet. Eilis and I remained at the request of Brindley.

"We cannae detain ourselves any longer," Brindley declared adamantly, the urgency of our mission returning. "Sundown approaches, and we will have to make camp, further impeding us."

"We understand, sir," I acknowledged. "We will eat, give our thanks, and be on our way."

Rey chimed in, his eyes gleaming with a wayward flash. "Can they at least consummate their marriage?"

Brindley looked at Rey sharply, his eyebrows furrowed, then curled his lips and burst out in laughter. "Aye, that they can!"

We made our way to the tavern, the sounds of merriment already spilling from its open doors, and took our place at the table provided for us. The wife of the innkeeper appeared at once and served us our meal and placed it on the table alongside a glass of wine for Eilis and two separate cups for me—one filled with whiskey and the other with ale. As we feasted on the rich flavors of venison stew and roasted potatoes, several of the guests approached, introducing themselves and congratulating us. Some presented us with small trinkets, and others with coins, their well wishes absolute.

A group of men gathered at the far corner of the tavern, close to our table. They brought out flutes, violins, and fiddles and played, their lively jigs and reels filling the air. Wishing I could bring out my phone to snap photos, I was pleasantly surprised to find an artist seated in front of us painting a portrait. I stood and led my new bride to the middle of the tavern, and we danced, our steps a playful, if somewhat clumsy, intertwining. Eilis was very much surprised that I knew how. Many of the guests joined in, and within a brief period, the entire room was twirling and bouncing contentedly. Just a few sets in, I found it to be the perfect opportunity to slip away and seal my bond.

Just as we were about to enter our room at the inn, Lieutenant Olson approached us like a man possessed. "Mr. Roberts," he said, panting as he caught his breath. "The Major has commanded that we leave now. Rumors of blockades are being reported by our scouts, some of which may be within our route, and if we are to make it safely to Drogheda, we must make haste."

I clenched my teeth, a nervous tic, then turned and looked at Eilis apologetically. "To be continued!"

***

We fell behind by just a few hours due to the delay of the unexpected wedding and festivities. We rode hard to recoup any lost time. Some time was gained, but just before midnight, the Major ordered us to stop at Swords, a town twenty-one miles south of Drogheda, and take a rest in Swords Castle, where part of his infantry were stationed.

I escorted Eilis to our sleeping quarters, hoping to be given the chance to consummate our marriage, only to be interrupted yet again by a shrill knock on the door from a soldier. "Me apologies, sir. The General has requested yer presence at his quarters presently."

I frowned in frustration. "Does he mean *now*?"

"Aye, sir. I will wait just here to escort ye."

I looked at Eilis, my eyes rolling. She giggled, pulling the blanket over her. "I shall wait fer ye return, me husband!"

"Aye, yai, yai!" I expressed, a frustrated grin forming itself. I followed the private into Brindley's quarters, where I was met by Adam, Rey, William, and Lieutenant Olson. "What's with the late-night discussion?" I interrogated, taking a seat in the only remaining chair.

"I have been informed by me scouts that Cromwell has an armada of ships blocking the harbor of the town and has positioned himself on the south side of the River Boyne alongside St. Mary's Parish."

Lieutenant Olson chimed in. "There is a church,"—he pointed at the map spread across the table—"named Gerrards. We can station there just before dawn, and camp out until nightfall."

Adam and I stood for a closer look at the map, surprised to find that the two churches were so close to one another. Adam circled his finger over the map, searching for an alternate route that would lead us straight into Cromwell's camp. "We can make camp here by St. John's Well. There is a trail that leads straight into the parish. Myles, Rey, and I can stroll along incognito, sneak our way into the camp, and rrrr"—he made a gurgling sound while making a cut-throat gesture—"slit his throat." With raised eyebrows, I looked at Adam, silently objecting. "You, sir, will remain here in safety. Rey, William, the Lieutenant, and I, along with a small group of soldiers, can make our way to the camp stealthily."

Ironically, Adam gave me the "not-today-kiddo" look. The familiar expression amused me. He then took a minute to think, considering that with his age and limited stamina, it would be best if he stayed behind.

Brindley agreed and ordered a handful of his most experienced men to gather in two hours' time, allowing themselves a catnap before marching into Cromwell's encampment. As much as I wanted to lie with my wife, doing so would cause me to become unfocused and lag in my duties, so I came, accompanied by Rey and William, to inform Eilis of the plans.

I entered the room, finding my new bride fast asleep, looking like an angel resting on a cloud of red cotton. Her fiery hair, a vibrant halo, was spread in a semicircle, almost mirroring the shape of her crescent moon birthmark. She stirred a bit but remained deep in slumber, so, as not to disturb her, I leaned down, kissed her gently on the forehead, and whispered, "I love you," before quietly leaving the room. The weight of the coming hours settled heavily upon me, but the image of her peaceful face was a small, steadying anchor.

***

It was pitch black along the road we followed, the darkness absolute, at times conjuring shadows that were not there as we trekked without torchlights. I felt

374

as if I were in the middle of an old espionage movie, sporting a black cloak with a hood. Occasionally, I had to dodge patrols, melting into the deeper shadows behind trees or whenever a moving figure was spotted. I secured my *sgian-dubh* in a hidden pocket of the cloak and kept a small pouch containing a few metal balls and some gunpowder close at hand. I carried a dirk and a pistol on the two left-side loops of the belt gifted to me by Mr. Willis, and a new *claidheamh* Lieutenant Olson had forged specifically for me.

Rey walked alongside me, keeping a few paces behind the soldiers and several feet ahead of William and the Lieutenant. We spoke in hushed tones, as requested by Olson, our whispers barely audible over the crunch of our boots on the damp earth. "Shitting bricks yet?" Rey jested in a low murmur.

"I had a bowel movement or two a few yards back," I confessed jokingly.

Rey laughed, a soft, muffled sound, followed by an abrupt "shh" from behind, sounded off by the Lieutenant. "You got me in trouble, man."

I laughed in a whispered "hmm," then elbowed Rey lightly, a comforting gesture in the tense silence. "Do you think we will kill Cromwell?"

Rey took a deep breath through his nose, exhaling slowly from his mouth. "It's the only way, or rather, the only thing, I can imagine being the pivotal event." He elbowed me in return. "I'll make the kill. You have enough blood on your hands."

We walked for another mile, keeping "radio silence" as we grew closer to the encampment. I considered the various scenarios that could play out should Cromwell be assassinated. I knew England would not be the same country it was before I left my time. The campaigns led by Cromwell gained England the respect it lacked for many years, perhaps centuries. Not killing Oliver, leaving history as is, oddly enough, might also be the pinnacle that might take us home.

It was an ongoing thought that eventually led me to believe wholeheartedly that Oliver Cromwell must live.

***

Reaching Cromwell's base camp, one of Brindley's spies approached us, flashing a *Claddagh* to reveal himself to Olson. He led us to the southern part of Cromwell's tent, where he informed the Lieutenant, "Cromwell had awoken early, claiming to have had an oneiric vision of God giving him commands on how to end the siege victoriously, so he headed into the church to pray upon it."

"Is he still in reflection?" Olson asked keenly.

"Aye, sir, and he remains alone."

My heart sank, a strange dread seizing me. I knew what was to come next, though this time, it was not foretold in history books. I pulled Rey aside and explained my theory, protesting solicitously that we should not go through with the killing. Rey shook his head. "No!" he exclaimed, his face in a frown. "He needs to die, Myles, simple as that. Let me just kill the bastard and get it over with."

I grew concerned about my best friend, my brother, and the stubbornness he possessed. In all the years we had known each other, never once was I able to convince Rey to reconsider when he set himself up to do something that I felt convinced was the wrong thing to do. This time, it was dire. I took to begging him, pleading my case as to the reasons he could not go forward with the assassination, explaining, "The carnage will be exponentially greater if Thomas Fairfax, William Lockhart, George Monck, or even John Lambert retaliated against the country, making everyone pay for the murder of their commander." Rey cocked his head, his eyes narrowed in thought. I placed my hand on his shoulder. "You understand, don't you?"

Rey raised his eyebrows, lips pursed, saying in an exhaling whisper, "Yeah, yeah, yeah."

We reached the entrance to the church. The spy peeked inside through a side window, finding Cromwell kneeling at the altar, head bowed, his hands folded in prayer. He turned to Olson to confirm that Cromwell was still there and remained alone. The lieutenant gave the command for the soldiers to circle around to the back and for William, Rey, and me to remain at a distance.

William set himself a few paces away from Rey and me, leaning against the corner of the building, fidgeting with his dirk. He then turned to look behind him, eyeing the soldiers and their positions. He appeared angsty, which was out of his character. I thought little of his demeanor and turned to walk toward the back of the church as Rey stood next to the front door in wait.

William stepped up to Rey, peering into his eyes. "I cannot allow you to execute my commander," he said, then placed his hand on Rey's shoulder and forcibly drove his dirk into his chest. Rey's eyes opened wide, mouth agape, and he let out a gasp, falling back with a loud thud as his head crashed on a rock.

I heard the noise and turned to find Rey on the ground, then looked at William, who was still holding the bloodied dirk in his hand. "What did you do?!" I yelled out in shocked disbelief. William stepped over Rey's body and positioned his arm to make me his next target. I was frozen in place, shocked not only by the sight of Rey's lifeless body lying on the ground, but by the action of the man before me whom I had allowed into my heart as a friend and a brother. I raised my hand instinctively in a defensive stance as William lunged forward, cutting between my thumb and forefinger. William retracted his hand, then gripped my arm, and just as he was about to impale the dirk into my chest, Lieutenant Olson came up from behind and thrust his sword through William's back, puncturing his lungs.

William fell back beside Rey, gasping for air. Olson stooped to face him. "Mr. Wexton, why?"

"You... heretics do not... deserve... to be in this... place. M... my... my commander... w... will... usher you all t... to hell." Blood trickled from his mouth as he let out a final gasp, then he was gone.

I was in disbelief, my thoughts becoming an empty space, not understanding what just happened. I fell to my knees, hovering over my best friend's lifeless body, suddenly pouncing on his chest, trying to resuscitate him, but he was truly gone.

Lieutenant Olson took hold of me and forced me back to my feet, appearing disconcerted. "William was a spy!"

I glanced at him, my eyes filled with tears, but in silence, shaking my head, then whispered, "He fooled us all."

The soldiers joined us, appearing just as shocked as we were. Olson ordered them to fashion a gurney using their cloaks to carry Rey and to leave William's body there as a warning. Olson led me from the church as we trailed our way out of the camp, changing the route by following the southeastern part of the encampment. The soldiers trudged behind, finding difficulty in keeping a firm grip on the gurney due to dampened hands brought on by the mist of rain, which also saturated the grounds. Soon, they got to a grassy area, giving them better traction.

The walk felt infinite, as the scene replayed continuously in my memory, an ongoing slow-motion loop. As much as I tried, I could not let go of the image. My eyes welled up once more, tears gushing down my face. I stood there with my head bowed down, becoming inconsolable, feeling embattled and brokenhearted. Getting a brief moment of clarity, I thought, *What if I made a mistake by allowing Cromwell to live?*

Lieutenant Olson consoled me, his hand rubbing comforting circles on my back, speaking to me in a soothing tone. "Myles, this is difficult to fathom. I understand. We may never know." He pointed at the rising sun, its shining honey-colored glow radiating over the horizon. "We must keep moving to avoid detection. We cannot rely on the cover of darkness from this point forward."

I took control of my emotions for a moment. "I don't care, Lieutenant. Being captured and tortured or killed would certainly feel better than having to live with the pain of losing my friend."

"Do you desire me to be captured and killed alongside you, Myles? I would gladly do so if you so wish it."

Brows crumpled; I glared at him. "Of course not. My soul would die if I were to lose another brother."

"Then let us continue forward. Your wife awaits you, and so does the beginning of your journey back to your time."

***

A few days had passed since Rey's funeral. It was held at a small church near the Maiden Tower, two hours east of the center of the siege. His body was placed on a pyre bed and cremated, his ashes placed in a leather pouch, tightly stitched. I did not want to leave his body buried in the past, so I knew the only viable way to bring Rey home was through cremation.

We traveled west, just a couple of miles south of the center of the siege, beginning our journey back to County Donegal; back to the watersfall. It was the 11th of September, marking the final and bloodiest day of the siege, and the sounds of cannon fire, pistols, and muskets, along with the echoing sounds of swords clanking and men screaming, reverberated far to the south of our location. It was just Eilis, Adam, and me traveling on our own, as Brindley and his troops set out to defend their country and their people. My heart weighed heavily, knowing that even though the General and Lieutenant Olson had knowledge of the outcome, the pride they had for Ireland could see them nowhere else but in a battle charge in its defense, conscious of the fact that they would never be seen alive again.

It gave me a glimmer of joy when I opened the metal waterproof case and found the "wee" book Mr. Brindley had authored and the *Claddagh* bestowed upon me by my hero, Lieutenant James Olson.

As the sounds of the massacre dissipated—the further along we rode—the more at ease we became. I paced alongside Eilis. "You're silent, *mi amor*," I expressed to her attentively.

"Nil a need fer concern. I am conversing with our Lord, praying for the souls of the masses being slaughtered by that wretched bastard who declares himself a servant of God."

She wiped a falling tear. "Fer anyone to bring upon such destruction and claim it was commanded by the voice of Christ is most certainly being guided by Satan himself," she expressed emphatically.

"I thought once about visiting Huntingdon a few years after I arrived," Adam added. "As absurd as it may sound, I once was served a stew that contained many olives. It made me think of the name Oliver Cromwell, presumably because of the name of the fruit. It brought on a memory of a production I was a part of in elementary school,"—he paused in a lighthearted laugh—"we had to dress up as prominent historical figures and one of my classmates was being mocked, choosing to dress as the 'Lord Protector' with the wig and lobster pot helmet and all. One student wrote 'Olives Crumbwell' on a piece of paper and taped it on his back." He frowned in thought. "If only I had taken the time to travel to Huntingdon, I probably could have ridden us of that tyrannical bastard," Adam said with renewed interest. "Possibly, this obliteration could have been averted."

"Must appear like rapture in the eyes of our Lord. All those innocent souls rising together and those yet to rise come the year next in Scotland, as ye history books say."

I sighed. The only response I could give was a solemn, "God rest their souls."

***

It was a four-day journey from Drogheda to Donegal. Adam led us to the home of a former soldier, Kevin, whom he had been acquainted with for several years. He kept a home on Fintra Beach, overlooking the ocean, finding it to be the ideal place for me to seek solace and recover from the ordeal. Eilis and I were accommodated in a room that looked out at the ocean, offering us a bit of serenity. To my amusement, I was able to use the skeleton key I had been given by—ironically enough—the concierge, Kevin, at the Caisleán Dhún na nGall Cottages Resort, to lock the door of our room.

Aside from consummating my marriage, her purity becoming mine, and mine alone, grooming and bonding with Moonlight, and chatting with my jovial companion, Adam, I would visit the beach and read for hours. Kevin held a vast collection of books, giving me an array of options. I came across a book titled *"Phases of the Sky."* It was a telling of the phases of the moon, eclipses, and astrology, exactly the information we needed to figure out the timing to best visit the cave and journey back.

I ran inside and shared the information with Adam. We studied the book for days, sharing it as if it were the only book in the house.

Kevin approached Adam and said in jest, "Plenty of books in me library, lad. Dinnae know why ye all keep reading the same book."

Adam expressed his pleasant, frivolous eyes, naturally, at a frown. "I'll keep that in mind," he said, then continued flipping through the pages. "What is today's date?" Adam asked abruptly.

"Now ye want answers, eh?" Kevin responded.

"Not today, champ," Adam replied.

"'Tis the third of November," Kevin replied.

"Myles, look," Adam said eagerly, "it shows here that tomorrow, there will be a partial eclipse of the moon."

I snatched the book from his hands, cautiously reading the page. "Shit, you're right. Maybe that is…" I paused for a moment and stared at Eilis openmouthed.

She reached her arm out and placed it on my shoulder. "We knew this time would come. We have made peace wi'it, me love. Dinnae be worrit. I will be fine."

***

Adam accompanied Eilis and me to the waterfall. He spent hours preparing himself to go back to a world where his parents would no longer be alive, and his siblings might be complete strangers to him. It had been a little over fifty years since he arrived in the sixteenth century, and he had completely given up hope of ever making it back. With me alongside him, he recaptured the pipe dream.

As we reached the entrance of the cave, Adam turned to look back at the place that had been his home, mentally bidding farewell. I tapped him on the shoulder. "Are you ready, young man?"

Adam smiled, nodding his head. "You go on; give me a minute."

I knew Adam had a sentimental attachment to this century, with all the memories he had made, good *and* bad, and the people with whom he had crossed paths.

I continued ahead with Eilis, hand-in-hand. We stopped at the threshold of the cave. "I love ye, Myles," she said, tears welling in her eyes. "Have faith in me when I say that I will be well."

I felt my throat begin to close. Not wanting her to see me cry, I bit my lip. "I don't want to go without you."

Eilis took me into a tight embrace. "Ye will go back to a world that 'tis ní mine. I belong here just as ye belong there. 'Tis the order of things." She then whispered, "Promise me that ye'll go."

I peered into her eyes apprehensively, then whispered back, "I promise you!"

As the partial eclipse became visible, the sky transformed, taking on a strange, dusky hue. I gestured to Adam that it was time.

He stood beside Eilis and stared at me, his eyes fluttering with a smile. "Have a safe flight, kiddo."

I leaned my head, seemingly confused. "I don't understand."

"I am where I'm supposed to be, Myles," he said, a peaceful note in his voice. "Plus, someone must escort Mrs. Roberts back to Kilkenny."

I shut my eyes tight with a grateful expression, then reached out to him and embraced him. "Thank you, Adam. I love you, old man!" I turned to embrace Eilis for one last time, then walked away, and entered the cave. As much as I wanted to turn around to gaze upon them for a final moment, I knew that if I did, it might deter me from moving forward. I stayed focused on the sight and sound of the waterfall.

The cascading wall appeared as majestic and serene as it did when I first visited. I felt cemented, anticipating the whirl of wind and the spray of the mist, which was always ever-present in my mind, to begin its cycle.

It remained eerily quiet, save for the sound of the water crashing against the stones. As much as I protested having left Eilis behind, I knew that if I didn't go through with it, she would never forgive me, as I had promised her wholeheartedly.

I turned to look at the entrance of the cave, debating whether to stay inside and wait, or face the consequences of Eilis' wrath by breaking the promise. With careful thought, I took one step forward, deciding to remain in this century and live out my life as it had been handed to me. In that instant, I felt the familiar pull of the wind draw me in. I turned again to stare at the waterfall, bracing myself for the impact. The anomaly that had taken hold of me over a year ago was once again invading me, absorbing my cells, one by one, tight in its grip. I then heard Eilis' voice over the noise of the rushing water, yelling out to me, "Myles, wait!"

I tried with every ounce of strength I could muster to reach for her, but it was too late. She became a distant blur, disappearing into the vortex.

Mere seconds later, or so I thought, I found myself lying on my back on the ground, struggling to open my eyes. I blinked rapidly, feeling as if my cells were still falling back into place. Although my vision was blurred, I discerned a small-framed figure moving towards me. "Eilis?!"

"By the gods, he is alive!"

The Waters Fall

Spirit of the Berserkr

Rob Mylo Vazquez

The Waters Fall-A Journeyer – Rob Mylo Vazquez

Prologue

Emotions have always been at the forefront of wars. They overtake the rational mind, allowing the worst to transpire.

There has always been a force within us all that, if invoked, could bring about the decimation of all that exists.

Some unexplained power influences the actions of humans; whether it be a whispered voice or simply some inexplicable force that cements one in place, compelling them to act against their will.

The wielding of a sword or the firing of a pistol can often lead to the demise of one's soul, but if faith usurps that fear with a genuine belief in God, or the gods, a calling will arise unlike any you have ever experienced in the past or present, or ever encounter in the future.

I have taken my place in this land; cleansed the physical and embraced the emotional. I now claim the spiritual and accept the inevitable!

Introduction

A wrong turn on Peachtree put me face-to-face with a massive, flashing digital sign: NORWDAN WINTER FESTIVAL. It was back. The biennial event was my second indulgence, the colder, more serious cousin to the Renaissance fairs I'd been going to since high school. I'd been furious with myself for missing the last one, but this felt like a sign from the universe. A bump of pure excitement went through me.

I tapped the dashboard screen. "Call Rey."

The phone rang a few times before clicking over to his impeccably professional voicemail. "You have reached Agent Reymond Tirad…"

"Hey, Inspector Gadget," I said after the beep. "Listen, I just saw an ad for the Norwdan festival. It starts next Saturday. Let me know if you're in, and I'll grab your ticket. I'm heading over there now to buy them. Call me."

My mind was already racing. This wasn't just a casual interest; it was a deep-seated passion for the mythology, the artifacts, the whole brutal, complicated Norse world. It was a fascination that had solidified in a college theology course, where I'd first seen the connections between belief systems. I'd noticed the parallels between the powerful Orishas of the Yoruba faith and the gods of the Norse pantheon. It was a revelation to learn the many names for a supreme being—Jehovah, Óðinn, Olodumare, Allah—and to realize that so much blood had been spilled over what often amounted to a difference in titles.

That's what this festival was really about for me: the story behind the artifacts. And this year's centerpiece was the stuff of legend: the longsword of Harald Sigurdsson, the man who would become Harald Hardrada, the last great Viking king.

I could picture the history as I drove. A fifteen-year-old Harald, fighting alongside his half-brother, King Olaf, at the Battle of Stiklestad. Olaf, the Christian king, trying to reclaim his throne and dying for it. Harald, grievously wounded, escaping into exile with the help of Rögnvald Brusason, that legendary sword supposedly at his side.

For centuries, it was just a story. Then, during a restoration of Grace O'Malley's tower in Ireland, construction workers found it, buried in the root cellar, wrapped in a burlap sack. The thought of it—of holding that direct, physical link to the sagas—made the traffic on Lenox Road seem insignificant.

My phone buzzed. A text from Rey: "In a debriefing. Will call tonight. Buy my ticket. Can't wait."

I sent back a thumbs-up emoji and pulled into the museum parking lot, my anticipation building. The line to the ticket counter wasn't too bad, maybe twenty people snaking out from the museum entrance. As I took my place, a large freight truck rumbled up the street and began backing into the loading dock. A museum coordinator waved for our line to step back.

The truck's swing doors opened, and workers began to unload a series of large wooden crates. Through the plastic windows on their sides, I could see the markings—a valknut with a white bear at its center. I recognized some of the pieces from the festival's catalog, artifacts I had only ever seen in books. It was like getting a private preview.

An hour bled by, the line barely moving, but I didn't care. I was captivated. My attention was fixed on the steady stream of history being wheeled into the building. Finally, the museum doors opened, and the line inched forward. Just as I was about to round the corner to the entrance, I saw them bringing out the last, most important piece. It was a large glass case on a dolly, covered by a tarp, but its shape was unmistakable. I let the couple behind me go ahead, needing to see it. They paused too, their own interest piqued by my obvious fascination.

It was Hardrada's sword.

The person at the back of the dolly, guiding it with a steady hand, was a tall woman in a ball cap. Strands of vibrant red hair escaped from underneath. As she passed, her eyes scanned the small crowd of onlookers and then settled on me. A slow, coquettish grin spread across her face. She stopped for a moment, removed her cap, and wiped a sheen of sweat from her forehead with the back of her wrist. With a fluid motion, she twisted her hair into a bun, secured it with a scrunchie she produced from her pocket, and put the cap back on. Her gaze found mine again. She gave me a playful, deliberate smirk, followed by a slow wink, and then continued on her way, leaving me standing there, speechless.

Author's Notes

Thank you for reading The Waters Fall - A Journeyer. I hope you enjoyed the story as much as I enjoyed writing it.

Myles Roberts's story was a labor of love, inspired by the loss of my older brother, Randy. We had planned to visit England to meet his newborn granddaughter, but he passed away a month after undergoing quadruple-bypass surgery. This loss fueled my desire to travel to the U.K., a place I had never been. After I began writing, I spent most of my time in Liverpool and Southport, England, with family and also visited Scotland. Also, visiting Ireland gave me the opportunity to visit some locations featured in the book.

The TV show Outlander also sparked my imagination. During the hiatus between seasons, or *"Droughtlander"* as the fans call it, I rewatched the series and found myself captivated by the concept of time travel. This inspired me to write my own story, and The Waters Fall series was born.

Initially, I was unsure how to begin, as I had never written, or even attempted to write, a book. I shared my idea with friends, and their encouragement motivated me to read and listen to books, studying storytelling techniques and character development.

My love of history and science fiction guided my writing. I wove these two passions together, and using my mother's birthday, 6-14-1941, led me to the historical figure of Oliver Cromwell. His actions during the 1649 Siege of Drogheda in Ireland intrigued me, and I decided to make him the antagonist of my story.

As a Puerto Rican of Spanish descent and a history enthusiast, I created a protagonist who embodied my interests. Myles Roberts, a college graduate and history teacher, became the central figure of the narrative.

While developing the story, I envisioned a mystical and majestic setting for the time travel portal. The song "Don't Go Chasing Waterfalls" by TLC sparked an idea: a hidden waterfall in a cave. My online search led me to the Secret Waterfall in Donegal, Ireland, which became the perfect location.

With the basic framework in place, I began writing, incorporating random thoughts and ideas that emerged organically. Some of these details might seem out of place, but they contribute to Myles's character development.

Chapter 24, "Absent," explores the impact of Myles's disappearance on those closest to him, maintaining a connection to the present-day timeline.

To enhance the story's authenticity, I incorporated 17th-century Irish Gaelic into the dialogue and narration. This experience ignited a passion for language learning, inspiring me to set the second book of the series, Spirit of the Berserkr, in 9th-century Norway.

Reference

The spelling of "**Watersfall**" throughout the story is intentional.

Eas Gorm i Bhfolach - Blue Hidden Waterfall. (In Irish dialogue)

Caisleán Dhún na nGall - Donegal Castle (In Irish dialogue)

Yer - Your (In Irish dialogue)

Ye - You (In Irish dialogue)

Fer - For (In Irish dialogue)

Yerself - Yourself (In Irish dialogue)

Gi' - Get (In Irish dialogue)

Dia dhuit - God be with you (In Irish dialogue)

'Tis - It is (In Irish dialogue)

Ken - Know (In Scottish dialogue)

Dinnae - Do not (In Irish/Scottish dialogue)

Nae - Not/No (In Irish/Scottish dialogue)

Aye - Yes (In Irish/Scottish dialogue)

Worrit - Worry (In Irish/Scottish dialogue)

Marrit - Marry (In Irish/Scottish dialogue)

Hangit - Hanged (In Irish/Scottish dialogue)

Wi' - With (In Irish/Scottish dialogue)

Níl - No (In Irish dialogue)

Ní - Not (In Irish dialogue)

An - The (In Irish dialogue / Singular)

Na - The (In Irish dialogue / Plural)

Mebbe - Maybe (In Irish/Scottish dialogue)

Wee - Little/Tiny/Small (In Irish/Scottish dialogue)

Mo leanabh - My child (In Irish dialogue)

Mac - Son (In Irish dialogue)

Stobhach Gaelach - Irish Stew (In Irish dialogue)

Meself - Myself (In Irish/Scottish dialogue)

Me - My (In Irish dialogue)

Mórghinearál - Major General (In Irish dialogue)

Seanathair - Grandfather (In Irish dialogue)

Oíche mhaith - Goodnight (In Irish dialogue)

Ná bí buartha - Don't worry (In Irish dialogue)

Oigheann – Oven (In Irish dialogue)

'Twill - It will (In Irish/Scottish dialogue)

'Twas - It was (In Irish/Scottish dialogue)

Eejit - Idiot (In Irish/Scottish dialogue)

Slàinte Mhaith - Good health / Cheers (In Irish/Scottish dialogue)

Slán agat, dia leat - Goodbye, God be with you (In Irish dialogue)

Cathbharr - Helmet (In Irish/Scottish dialogue)

Scéal - Story (In Irish dialogue)

Maiden - Virgin (In Irish dialogue)

Justificatio, by sola fide - Justification by faith alone. (Latin)

Canna - Can not (In Irish/Scottish dialogue)

Maidin - Morning (In Irish dialogue)

Captaen - Captain (In Irish dialogue)

Sgian-dubh - Hidden knife (In Irish/Scottish dialogue)

Gaol - Jail (In Irish/Scottish dialogue)

Cuirass - Torso armor (In Irish/Scottish dialogue)

As the crow flies - Travel in a straight line (In Irish/Scottish dialogue)

Sciob - Basket (In Irish dialogue)

Nollag - Christmas (In Irish/Scottish dialogue)

Nigh - Nearly/Near (In Irish/Scottish dialogue)

Ní gá a bheith buartha - No need to worry (In Irish dialogue)

Sean gabhar Gaelach - Old Irish Goat (In Irish dialogue)

Cén sort Éireannach a bheadh ionam mura mbeinn líofa ann? - What kind of Irish would I be if I weren't fluent in it? (In Irish dialogue)

Uisce Beatha - Water of life (In Irish dialogue)

Nó - or (In Irish dialogue)

Morrow - Tomorrow (In Irish/Scottish dialogue)

Babhla - Bowl (In Irish dialogue)

Leite - Porridge (In Irish dialogue)

Arán agus im - Bread and butter (In Irish dialogue)

Léine - Shirt (In Irish dialogue)

Bhean - Woman (In Irish dialogue)

A chara - My friend (n Irish/Scottish dialogue)

Calma sibh féin - Calm yourselves (In Irish dialogue)

Cailin - Girl (In Irish dialogue)

Cad - What (In Irish dialogue)

Ag ól mo fhíona - Drinking my wine (In Irish dialogue)

Nil aon duine chun cur isteach orm - No one is to disturb me (In Irish dialogue)

Babóg's - Babies (In Irish dialogue)

Buachaillí - Boys (In Irish dialogue)

Iníon - Daughter (In Irish dialogue)

Currachs - Traditional Irish Boats (In Irish dialogue)

Tréan - Strong (In Irish dialogue)

Aye, cad is féidir liom a dhéanamh ar do shon? - Yes, what can I do for you? (In Irish dialogue)

Já - Yes (Icelandic/Norwegian/Old Norse)

Din - Your (Norwegian)

Skynde deg - Hurry up (Norwegian)

Gris - Pig (Norwegian)

Cúpla - Twin (In Irish dialogue)

Claidheamh - A sword (In Irish dialogue)

www.ingramcontent.com/pod-product-compliance
Lightning Source LLC
Chambersburg PA
CBHW020254030726
47499CB00001B/199